EXECUTIVE ACTION

Richard Doyle lives with his wife and son on Dartmoor. His previous novels include *Deluge* and *Imperial 109*.

EXECUTIVE ACTION

Richard Doyle

ARROW

Published by Arrow Books in 1999

1 3 5 7 9 10 8 6 4 2

First published in the United Kingdom in 1998 by Century

Arrow Books Limited
20 Vauxhall Bridge Road, London, SW1V 2SA

Random House Australia (Pty) Limited
20 Alfred Street, Milsons Point, Sydney,
New South Wales 2061, Australia

Random House New Zealand Limited
18 Poland Road, Glenfield
Auckland 10, New Zealand

Random House South Africa (Pty) Limited
Endulini, 5a Jubilee Road, Parktown 2193, South Africa

Random House UK Limited Reg. No. 954009

A CIP catalogue record for this book
is available from the British Library

Papers used by Random House UK Limited
are natural, recyclable products made from wood grown
in sustainable forests. The manufacturing processes conform to
the environmental regulations of the country of origin

ISBN 0 09 926994 5

Typeset by Deltatype Ltd, Birkenhead, Merseyside
Printed and bound in Germany by
Elsnerdruck, Berlin

For my son CASPAR

ACKNOWLEDGEMENTS

A special thanks to Steve Ferris, who sparked the idea over Wild Turkeys in a bar in Vidouze. Thanks also to Corinne Clarke for her advice on altering appearances and to Doctors Mandy Roberts and Vivien St Joseph. At Red Rock Media, Alastair Gregory and Mark Anderson were generous with their time. Finally I owe a big debt to Gillon Aitken for all his encouragement and to Oliver Johnson at Century for his commitment and enthusiasm.

I

'The purpose of this group is to begin planning to win the nomination . . . It is not the purpose of the group to help me on issues.'

That Thursday eight men met in New York, in a suite of the Waldorf Towers that had once been Truman's. The same suite Nixon's people had used in '67. There was Tilson, the money man, a Wall Street banker who had been a fundraiser for Clinton in '96. There was Daniel I. Webster, Speaker of the House and keeper of the party conscience, labor leader Lee Jones from Detroit. Sag Walker, the Lieutenant Governor of New York, was present with his cigar. Dave Lewis, leader of the California Democrats, sat with Hunter, the Chief of Staff designate, and next him, Leon Perry, the Candidate's classmate, his best buddy, who went with him everywhere. And across from them all, the Candidate, Jack Meade, the man they were here to see, in a chair by himself where the light fell on him. He always picked the seat with the light.

The seven studied him and liked what they saw. 'Wherever he goes,' one reporter had commented, 'Jack Meade draws crowds like the TV star he used to be.' He had the stamina too. For six months he had been stumping the country, campaigning in thirty-five states, a bareheaded, coatless man with a boy's spring in his step and a face untouched by deceit or guile.

They knew all his history. On paper he was good, ideal even. Television soap star turned character actor. Runner-up for an Academy Award. Contested and won a Senate seat against a strong Republican incumbent to

1

become the youngest serving senator bar none. Championed 'Medicare 2', the Health Reform Bill subsequently vetoed by President Ivory.

To the Republican right he might be anathema but he had the blue-collar vote, women trusted him and the young hailed him as their spokesman. They came to hear him speak in halls and shopping malls, to Rotary clubs and Ladies' circles. The same speech, the same words often, but always delivered with conviction, always with apparent spontaneity.

The question was, did he have the will to go the distance, the sheer guts and determination to wrest the Presidency from Ivory? That was what these men were here to decide. To back this man or not. A presidential challenger needed guts and determination but above all money. Money for staff, for advance men, researchers, speechwriters, press aides, secretaries. Money for airplanes, telephones and pollsters, money for TV spots. Did Jack Meade possess the magic dollar pulling power to become President of the United States?

As always he was meeting their challenge head-on.

Issues, he told them, speaking quickly, forcefully, snapping his fingers to emphasize points, issues didn't matter. His strategy was simple. Attack! Attack! Whatever Ivory was for, he was against. Ivory was a soldier, an old man with an old man's rigid thinking. He himself stood for the independent voter, the young voter. Twenty percent of the electorate was under twenty-five. 'Ivory blew all his assets in the first two years. The country hates his guts for welshing on the tax promise and come this summer, Trott will challenge him for the Republican endorsement.' Ivory would win, he predicted, but be left crippled. When it came to the TV debates he would wipe the floor with Ivory and Ivory would look yellow if he refused to take part. 'Either way he's fucked.'

Sag Walker puffed on his cigar. 'He has $38 million in his war chest. And that's just gate money,' he growled.

'Plus the votes of two million vets and twenty state governors.'

Jack disagreed. It was a fact that no incumbent who faced a challenge in the New Hampshire primary had ever won re-election. Ivory's goose was cooked, he repeated.

Jack had national recognition, Leon Perry stressed forcefully. He had voter appeal. His visual factor was the highest in the field. He had beaten LeMay in the Senate race. He was a winner.

They knew that. It was why they were here.

Still speaking fast and fluently, Jack turned next to his own deficiencies. 'Let's be frank. I have youth against me, sure, but Jack Kennedy was younger. And I'm divorced.' That was a problem, he conceded. 'But half the country is divorced now.' The separation had been amicable. No third party involved either side and no children. He and his wife remained on friendly terms. 'She married an actor and found politics taking up too much of my life. End of story.'

The vital thing was the nomination, he said. About the election he had no fears. The nomination was a different story. The nomination process meant sucking up to the activists; the election entailed going for the center. To win the election he had first to capture the party assets via the primaries and that meant taking on the mighty Leyland Jordan.

Lee Jones interrupted. Don't underestimate Jordan, he warned. Jordan was older, wiser and cunning as hell. He knew all the tricks. He had a lock on the Senate Democrats. Jordan wanted the Presidency as badly as he had ever wanted anything and would fight dirty to get it. 'He'll kill for it if he has to.'

The Senator said Leyland's trouble was he wasn't ready yet. The challenge had come too early. He had allowed events to overrun him and he wasn't positioned. 'He has the Senate tied up and he thinks he has the party machine too. None of that counts for much any more, though. The electorate's too volatile.' Jordan's mistake was he was still too much of a background figure, too used to wheeling and dealing in the smoke-filled rooms.

On the settee, Dan Webster shifted his awesome bulk. 'He doesn't have national recognition. That's his weakness and he knows it. He needs to build himself up and there isn't time. My reading is he'll run out of steam early. You'll wipe the floor with him, Jack.'

Tilson, the money man, had a suggestion. 'A period as VP could give him national stature. Have you thought of that? I'll bet he has. He'd be perfectly positioned in '08.'

'Leyland as running mate? He'd never stoop so low. Besides, what is he now, sixty-four? He'd be too old.'

'He's a snake, remember, and snakes have no backbone. You can see his devious mind working, figuring the angles. Look at Kennedy, he'll tell himself. He was a young man too but LBJ had the last laugh on him.' His colleagues became thoughtful. Lewis was a lawyer. He specialized in legal advice on bond issues to state and local governments. Moving bonds is the heart-blood of local politics.

Jack eyed him. 'You're suggesting we neutralize Jordan? Offer him a place on the ticket? You think he'd go for it?'

The lawyer shrugged. 'Not right now maybe but later, possibly. It's a question of timing. Jordan's a realist. He'll figure the score. And don't forget he brings Texas with him.'

Jack brought the debate back to the present. Were there any questions? he asked. Anything at all they didn't feel happy with? They had a right to ask.

Hunter spoke up. Hunter the professional. Hunter the Chief of Staff designate. 'There are rumors,' he said, looking straight at the candidate as if he were on the stand. 'Rumors of a relationship. Is that going to lead anywhere? Because,' he went on bluntly, 'in this game it has to be all or nothing. You can get away with bachelor status. It may even attract the female vote. Fine, we can swing that but the public will not buy a philanderer. If there's going to be a First Lady they'd kind of like to look her over first, if you get what I mean, before they buy the package.'

The Senator frowned tightly, then met Hunter's gaze honestly, unflinching. 'You are correct. There is a relationship. It is entirely above board and frankly, a private matter. The lady concerned is unmarried, as am I.'

Hunter waited as if hoping for more. 'Sir, if this is not resolved one way or another, I cannot come on board,' he said eventually. 'I can't afford to see two years of my life washed down the tube because the candidate's private life is not under control.'

There was an audible hiss of breath from some of the others but no one spoke. The Senator frowned again. He breathed in and out rapidly, filling his chest, and blinked his famously brilliant eyes, 'filled with shattered light' someone or other had once described them. There was a moment of tension, then he smiled.

'I read you, Hunter. A tough one, but that's what you're here for. So be it,' he nodded. 'The matter will be resolved forthwith. Either by abstinence or, in the unlikely event, by marriage.' He held out a hand. 'You have my word.'

Hunter was not done. 'Marriage would be better,' he said.

The Senator's expression hardened. A shadow of anger surfacing through the tan. The temperature in the room seemed to rise suddenly. Everyone stiffened.

'That is for me to decide,' he said.

Hunter sensed he had gone too far. He held up his hands in apology. Jack relaxed. 'Okay,' he flashed a grin. 'Find me a wife if you must.' He shook a finger in mock

5

reproof, 'But a Jackie not a Hillary, right?' There was laughter.

Jack stood up. They all stood, then Jack hugged them all beginning with Hunter. He was surprised; he had been expecting a handshake. But that was Jack Meade all over, he was a hugger, one of the few men who could do it without awkwardness. It came naturally to him. It looked honest because he performed it so quickly, briskly. A manly gesture: spontaneous, youthful. And yet a kind of solemn moment too, like a ritual. Masonic, almost. A sense of being inducted.

'We'll make a good team. You'll see,' his smile embraced them all.

The debate began after he left the room.

'He lacks maturity. He has no wife, no family, no policies,' Walker ticked off the objections on his fingers. 'Zero administrative experience and no serving senator since Kennedy has won the Presidency.'

'He's a star,' Lee countered. 'Kennedy and Reagan rolled in one. We'd be crazy to turn him down. What d'you say, Dave?'

The lawyer studied his fingernails. He lifted his pale eyes and surveyed them all. 'He's a risk,' he agreed. 'An unknown quantity.'

He had the gift though, Leon Perry emphasized. Jack could reach out and touch people. He was intuitive, a communicator.

'Another Reagan, God save us,' grunted Walker.

'Does he have fire in his belly, I want to know?' Tilson asked. 'He has looks, he has charm but what drives him?'

Webster supplied the answer. 'You want to know? I'll tell you. Six years he's been in the Senate and not once in that time did he get to meet a president. Ivory calls him Little Boy Blue. Jack Meade hates Ivory's guts, it's that simple. He's running to spit in the General's eye.'

They watched one another carefully, unwilling to

commit totally yet. It was a big decision. The biggest. Careers and reputations hung in the balance. The right choice would mean power, cabinet posts, glittering futures. A wrong call would condemn all of them to obscurity.

Webster gave the lead. He was the oldest, his career drawing to its close. Age lent maturity to his judgement. 'Sure, he's a risk,' he said heavily. 'If we run with this guy we take the chance he may blow up in our faces. Turn out another Gary Hart.' Perry tried to interrupt but he waved him down. 'Okay, that's the downside. But the alternative is we choose someone safe, more of a name. Somebody we know and the party knows. Someone we can all trust. And if we do that Ivory will go down on his knees and thank God every night from here till November.' He rolled an eye round the room a moment, gauging the effect of his words, then continued. 'A heavyweight Democratic candidate would unite the Republicans behind Ivory. Jack Meade will prompt the young Turks on the other side to challenge the President's re-nomination and split the vote. If that happens Jack will whip him.'

The vote went six to one. Walker was odd man out. He would go along with the majority decision with one proviso. The Candidate must keep to his word. Not a breath of scandal must attach to his name.

They would not regret this, Leon Perry told the committee. Jack would deliver, he promised. Nine months from now, he forecast, they would be celebrating a Democratic victory.

After the election was over, one of a group of journalists who had followed Jack Meade's campaign from the beginning asked each of his colleagues to write down a single word which in their view best captured the new President-elect's appeal. By common consent the quality that summed up Jack Meade was vitality. He was seldom, if ever, still. Even at rest he gave an impression of motion forcibly constrained.

The journalist who recorded these impressions also noted something else. Jack was a chameleon, he wrote. He took his color from the people around him. It was the actor in him. Whoever he was with, after a while he became like them. Shared their emotions, their dreams, articulated their feelings. Their hopes for the future became his hopes, their fears his fears. In his company people felt an instinctive rapport. With a single glance he could somehow establish eye contact with an entire audience. He was your friend. He was speaking to you. He understood. That was his trick. It left unanswered the question what sort of a person really was Jack Meade?

January 14th, less than a week to go till the Inauguration and down in Florida's Jacksonville Naval Station hospital, Nurse Rita Phillips stopped by Room B3 to check on a bed.

The patient was a white male, medium height and build. His skin was still shriveled and bleached from long immersion in water and the face was so blistered by exposure to the sun that his age was hard to judge. The doctors estimated forty-two. He had been hauled from the ocean off St John's Point suffering from concussion, acute dehydration and hypothermia. He was lucky to be alive, they said. He had been naked practically, no way of telling his identity. And no one answering the description reported missing. A lone yachtsman knocked over the side by his own boom while relieving himself at night, was the theory. But then where was the boat?

Nurse Phillips checked the patient's vital signs and entered the data on the chart. For the first twenty-four hours they had treated him like a burns patient, wrapping him in space blankets, administering intravenous saline solution and morphine against the pain. Now he was off the drip but still sedated, the bloated body glistened beneath coatings of rehydration gel.

For the first time she thought she detected a response to her presence; a faint return of pressure when she squeezed his hand. The cracked lips twitched but there was no further response. The patient appeared to have lapsed into unconsciousness again. Phillips waited a while, switching on the wall TV and turning the sound low for diversion. Then she left the room.

Four hours later when she returned again however, the patient was awake and staring at the ceiling from under puffed and crusted eyelids. He turned his head to look at her and the ravaged mouth framed a question.

'Hi,' she greeted him gently, 'how are you feeling?'

There was a long pause. She wondered if he had understood her. Then finally he spoke.

'Wh . . . where is this?' His voice was a hoarse croak. 'What happened to me?'

'This is the Naval Hospital, Jacksonville. You fell into the ocean. You have some concussion.' She stood by the bed. 'Do you remember your name?'

He blinked a minute, concentrating. Slowly his gaze cleared. 'My name . . . is . . .' he squeezed up his face with effort: 'Meade. I'm Jack Meade . . . of course,' and he looked up at her questioningly.

'Oh sure,' she flashed him a humoring smile as she leaned over to straighten the sheet. Sometimes these things took time. She placed a hand gently on his forehead. 'Better you stay quiet now, huh?'

'I know my own name, that's something, right?' he asked.

'It's something,' she agreed. She moved to the door. 'Do you want me to turn down the TV?'

'No.' He twisted his head painfully on the pillow to see. 'No, leave it on, please. I kind of like the sound for company.'

He closed his eyes again.

When Phillips came on duty again the next day she found the patient awake and sitting up. His head no longer hurt him, he said, and the blisters on his skin were starting to heal.

'Does he remember who he is yet?' Phillips asked the Chief Nurse.

'Nope,' said the Chief Nurse. 'Still crazy as a bug.'

Phillips went in to see him. 'You know who he reminds me of, just a little?' she said when she returned.

'No, who?'

'Bruce Delahaye in *Winchester County*. Something about the chin.'

'Bruce Delahaye?' said the Sister. 'Wasn't that the character . . .'

'Played by Jack MacKenzie Meade? That's the one. Funny, huh?'

Weird, agreed the Chief Nurse.

During the evening the patient's mental condition deteriorated again alarmingly. When the night duty nurse came by, she found him crouched on the bed staring intently at the television, 'like it was the first time he ever saw one', as she put it later. In response to her greeting he pointed to the screen. 'Look!' he said excitedly.

It was a news item, reported the nurse afterwards, to do with the Inauguration. Clips of the election, shots of the President-elect, stuff like that. Because the patient seemed interested she turned up the sound, thinking it might help jog his memory.

Later it proved possible to isolate the section of the program concerned. It was of some significance. Against a backdrop of scenes from the past political year a voice-over continued, '. . . *most bitterly contested election of recent memory as well as one of the closest. So confident had the incumbent Republican administration under President Ivory been of victory against a demoralized Democratic party that they allowed their campaign to get off to a lack-luster start from which it struggled in vain to* recover. At first the Democrats seemed equally handicapped when a young upstart Jack Meade, the Senator from Indiana, snatched the nomination. "Senator Who from Where?" as the cartoonists unkindly dubbed him. But despite chronic lack of funding and the questionable disadvantage of being divorced and single, Meade proved himself a tireless campaigner whose youthful looks and vitality won him a wide following especially among the female electorate. The Republicans appeared to stage a late comeback when a series of televised debates exposed holes in his political agenda allowing the President to make the most of his age and experience while painting his rival as "all things to all men", an image without substance. At one point they pushed some eleven points in the lead. However the tables were turned again when Meade surprised the world with the announcement of his engagement to Caro Charteris, socialite and member of the powerful Kennedy clan. In the best-kept secret of the campaign the couple had been courting for several weeks. Aided by a series of gaffes from his opponents and finally by a late breaking financial scandal involving the Secretary to the Treasury, Meade clawed back his lead and coasted to victory, the final stages of the campaign marred for him only by his bride-to-be's ill health and subsequent hospitalization . . .'

In the background the commentary was continuing, ' . . . with the Inauguration only five days away, Meade is currently resting up aboard a friend's yacht off Florida following a long-planned bout of cosmetic surgery. During the vacation with party chieftains more appointments for his administration are expected to be announced. Likely to be included among these is Leon Perry, architect of his initial campaign and long-time friend, who has been strongly tipped for a cabinet post despite having shouldered criticism for charges of lack of substance in the President-elect's program.

'Meanwhile Caro Meade, bride of six weeks and soon-

11

to-be First Lady, shown here recuperating at Walter Reed Hospital after an operation to remove her gall bladder, will next week call at the White House at the invitation of Mrs Ivory to tour her new living quarters. At thirty-three she will be the youngest First Lady since the late Jackie Kennedy . . .'

'That's her! My wife!' the patient shrieked, clawing the nurse's arm, his features distorted with manic emotion. Frightened, with difficulty she managed to reach across with her other hand to press the bleep alarm clipped to her belt. Instantly a response bell sounded at the nurses' station up the passage and there was a noise of running feet as four nurses, two of them male, hurried to her assistance. The patient was raving dementedly. He made frantic efforts to escape the room and despite his weakened state it took their combined strength to subdue him. Finally the TV was removed and with difficulty he was coaxed back into bed. We'll listen to you, they told him. We'll hear what you want to tell us but only on condition you lie quietly.

Gasping and drained from his struggles, the patient lay back against the pillows. 'That was my wife they were talking about,' he said, and then he told them why the broadcast had triggered his memory, and who he was. They listened gravely as he explained how he came to be in the water and he read the disbelief in their faces though they tried hard to conceal it. Yes, they understood that it was a matter of urgency. Certainly the authorities must be informed at once. His wife too, she would be worried, naturally. Yes, they understood about the Inauguration. In the meantime surely he had a duty to conserve his strength? No, no, he said, they didn't understand! Someone had usurped his place! His wife was in danger! He was beginning to grow frantic again, struggling against the nurses' holds. 'For Christssakes,' someone shouted, 'hurry up with that needle! We can't hold him much longer!' He felt the prick in his arm and

12

fought wildly for a moment but there were too many hands.

'There, that'll keep him under for a while,' said the doctor. A great tiredness rolled over him and a blackness of despair. Someone drew the shades across the window. Rest now, they said, and everything will be sorted out, you'll see.

The spin doctors and media advisers had been against the yacht trip. It projected the wrong image. The press would label him a playboy, a rich man's president. Jack Meade said he didn't see why. It was not his boat. He needed a place to rest up and let the scars on his face heal. It was his last chance before his Inauguration and to blazes with them all anyway.

The Secret Service was divided over the plan. The Chief of the President-elect's detail approved it, but grudgingly. Restricted access was a definite plus, likewise the small portholes in the cabins. In the event of trouble the boat could be quickly moved, a definite bonus. On the minus side, the banks of the St John's estuary were perfect cover for a gunman with a hunting scope. The Chief would have preferred the boat should stand further offshore, only the ocean was liable to be choppy this early in the year even off Florida. An inshore berth within the limits of Jacksonville's Mayport Navy Air Station was the compromise agreed. The Navy to provide perimeter security, transport and patrol the shore. The Secret Service was to be responsible for on-board security and the President-elect's cabin was to face out to sea. Extra staff and the press could be accommodated ashore at the base. Phone lines laid on as required.

At a quarter after midnight the riding lights of the Navy picket boats dutifully maintaining their watch were intermittently visible. Aboard the yacht, which was rocking gently under her engines on the slight swell, the upper cabin lamps still burned but the future Chief

13

Executive had retired below. Steward Gary Lugg carried a tray of hot milk aft from the galley. With practiced ease he moved down the narrow passage. President-elect Jack Meade occupied the owner's suite consisting of stateroom, bath and private sitting room. As Lugg approached the guest cabin section his way was barred by a Secret Service man with a five-pointed red pin in his lapel. The agent lifted the lids of the jugs and ran a hand-held metal detector over the waiter, then nodded at him to proceed.

A few steps further on at the door to the suite a second agent studied Lugg and his tray silently and gave him a small yellow pin to wear in the lapel of his jacket. Lugg carried the tray inside the sitting room. Senator Meade was slouched on the small settee under the stern windows, wearing a toweling robe over shirt and pants and studying a paper. Taped gauze dressings masked the sutures beneath his ears and chin. The swelling from the scars elsewhere on his face was still apparent. With him was Leon Perry, a young, balding man with gnome-like features, talking animatedly. A fund of jokes and stories, Perry was 'the man who makes the Candidate laugh'. On the grueling campaign trail, he had slept in the same motel rooms, fed him one-liners, boosted his spirits when energy flagged. At the Meade wedding Perry had been best man. Now he saw himself in line for a top post with the new administration.

Lugg set the tray down on the table between them and poured out two glasses of the milk.

'Will there be anything else, Senator?' he asked, straightening up.

'No, thank you,' the Senator answered, glancing up briefly. That would be all, he said.

Lugg wished the two men good night and let himself out, nodding to the agent outside. Retracing his steps up the passage, he noticed the door of the cabin next the Senator's suite was slightly ajar. Inside, a middle-aged

14

woman sat at a paper-strewn desk. Her eyes met his briefly and dismissively.

The woman was Elaine Manken, for the past six years Senator Meade's personal secretary. It was Elaine's function to keep a track of the flow of paper across the Senator's desk, placing the sheaves of letters and documents in front of him between appointments, passing outgoing mail to her battalion of stenographers. Elaine it was who decided which replies were stamped with the Senator's signature and which received his personal scribble. Elaine noted when a senator was hospitalized or a congressman's wife gave birth, composed a suitable note or sent flowers.

Elaine kept the door of her office ajar so that she could hear if the Senator called her, only closing it if ordered to do so. All personal calls went through her desk. Elaine decided which he should take and which could wait. She was the liaison with his senior staffers, making time for them to see the Chief, passing on messages, pleas, complaints. Savvy assistants learned that the best place to catch Jack was to loiter in Elaine's office and ambush him as he stuck his head round the door.

Elaine, too, had her own agenda. She maintained her own secret log of every appointment with notes of what was discussed, promised and refused. She could be vindictive, as campaign staff had learned to their cost. Aides who crossed Elaine found themselves cut out from the loop, their calls unanswered, their names dropped from circulation lists, reports and submissions log-jammed at her desk.

No sooner had the steward departed than a second visitor came aft to the suite. General Carl Vorspuy had been designated as the new President's Adviser on National Security. Minutes earlier a military courier, ferried out to the yacht by launch, had delivered a pouch from CIA headquarters. The pouch contained an international intelligence summary similar to that submitted daily to the President. For the past two months such material had been made available to his successor in order that the future President might be properly briefed on assuming office. Owing to confusion in Washington as to Jack Meade's schedule, today's briefing had arrived late. General Vorspuy signed a receipt for it and made his way below.

The Secret Service agent on duty outside the suite recognized the General and let him into the suite. A perfectionist in every detail, Vorspuy duly recorded in his personal log the precise minute he had taken charge of the pouch and the moment it was handed over.

The President-elect placed the pouch in the safe installed for the purpose in a corner of the cabin and secured the combination lock. The time was then 12.32. Time to turn in, he told Perry. Decisions on a post for him would keep till another day. Perry left reluctantly. He was anxious to nail the Senator down to a specific job offer. On the way out he stopped by Elaine Manken's office for a nightcap. In the back-stabbing scramble for office that possessed the Meade camp, the two were current allies. Perry confided his ambitions to Elaine, hoping she might intervene on his behalf with her boss. Elaine promised to do what she could. Privately she did not give much for his chances. Perry had a reputation as a raconteur and gossip and the President-elect, she believed, held him responsible for a number of insider leaks over recent months.

Elaine had worries of her own. The President-elect, staffers joked, had three wives: Leon Perry, Elaine Manken and Caro Meade. The jibe struck a raw nerve. Though the first two had come to an understanding early on in Jack Meade's career, between the secretary and the soon-to-be First Lady there was friction.

Alone in his suite, the President-elect summoned one of his speechwriters on the ship's phone, instructing him to bring down the latest version of his inaugural address. He liked to read through the text of speeches in bed before sleeping. While he waited he went into the bathroom. Carefully he removed the gauze dressings and studied his reflection in the mirror. With the tips of his fingers he touched the skin under his chin where the tuck had been taken. The same surgeon had tightened the skin beneath the eyes a fraction and liposucked a layer of subcutaneous fat from along the jawbone, restoring his features to their former tautness. The swelling and irritation were annoying, but transitory. A few more days would see the scars fade and by the time of the Inauguration any lingering traces could be easily concealed with make-up. Already, he decided, he looked younger, more alert. Of course there had been the inevitable criticism and snide comments from the press, cracks about facelifts and young wives. Pure jealousy. That would blow over. Amazing how quickly people adjusted to the new image.

Caro would be pleased by the transformation, he was certain. It was good in a way that she wouldn't see him till the healing was complete.

There was a knock from the communicating door to Elaine's office. The speechwriter had arrived . . .

The President-elect finally climbed into bed 1.02 a.m. His last action before turning out the light was to press the bell to summon the guard from the passage. Agent Klein, the night man, responded promptly, entering the suite with his right hand inside his coat ready to draw his fifteen-shot Glock automatic while the second agent in the passage moved up ready to provide back-up if needed.

The President-elect asked Agent Klein to please unlock the scuttle and open the window. He disliked sleeping with the air conditioning on and the cabin was stuffy otherwise. It had been agreed that this could be done once the boat was underway and the cabin light out.

Agent Klein complied, turning off the alarm and unfastening the scuttle plate covering the porthole. He switched off the light and bade the President-elect good-night. The two agents then resumed their stations outside the door to the suite.

Jay Leeder, the deputy to the Chief of Staff designate, opened the file his secretary had placed before him and began to read through the personal résumés inside. Each was brief, no more than two pages long. With the volume of work passing across his desk there was only time for essentials. Also the applicants were young, they had to be to have the stamina the job entailed, and the young generally have clean lives without complications. Another reason for selecting them. As he finished scanning each, he placed a tick or cross against the subject's name on the list clipped to the inside cover of the file. When he was done there were four crosses and only one tick. He frowned and studied the résumé on the career of Karen Lipscombe again.

On the face of it she was ideal. Twenty-eight years old and single, a tireless worker in two presidential campaigns. Secretary of the Meade San Francisco office. During the candidate's tour of the West Coast she had prepared daily press briefings for him, something her master's degree in media studies from UCLA had well fitted her for. She was disadvantaged but had more than compensated. Her memory for facts was legendary. She had applied for a post with the Transition Team but had fallen through the net and was currently attached to a political think tank in LA. She was bright, loyal, attractive and hardworking. She kept her head under pressure. She was discreet. But she was also a girl, and no women were being considered for the job. Her résumé had been included to avoid charges of discrimination.

The trouble was, all the male applicants were less suitable. Undeniably so. And there was no time to run checks on another batch. The post had to be filled. It was one of these or nobody. It was Lipscombe or nobody.

18

The deputy Chief of Staff designate frowned. The presence of an attractive young woman so close to the Candidate had been deemed unsuitable during the campaign for obvious reasons. But the campaign was over. The criteria had changed, perhaps. And with a newly married president surely? Besides, this one was a double-header. Her appointment would satisfy the minorities all across the board.

He closed up the folder. Worth having the woman in anyway. He pressed a button on his intercom and issued instructions to his staff.

The dossier was sent up to the President-elect with the deputy's finding indicated. Three hours later the list was returned from the private office with a line through Lipscombe's name. *'No way!'* the future President's secretary had scrawled.

Well, they would just have to see about that.

The people-mover, so called, was American built, Japanese badged and borderline acceptable for anyone on the staff of the President-elect. Jack Meade's position on US jobs was a stated fact but the Honda was the only vehicle available for hire that would take them all. It was the Honda or nothing. The Honda was their best and only chance of making it on time.

There were seven on board, counting the valet, who was doing the driving because this was all his fault. He had brought down the word that none of them would be needed this side of Monday. A four day lay-over, he called it. Direct from the mouth of the Man himself. The President-elect. Jack Meade. The Man was on vacation down Florida way on a yacht belonging to some rich white honky who needed to kiss ass with the new boys on the block, was how the valet put it. So the team could stand down. Till Tuesday. Their first proper break in months. And Frankie, the number one cosmetician, 'the girl who makes the Candidate glow' as a journo once called her, Frankie had the idea of borrowing her parents' cabin in the Catskills. Log fires and mulled wine and long walks in the snow. So they had gone down Friday night. And this was Monday. Monday 5 a.m., exactly five hours since the switchboard tracked them down with a furious tirade from the Chief of Staff designate himself no less. Where in hell's name was the make-up team? The head-honcho due on coast-to-coast and where were his hairdressers, his valet, his cosmetician, his masseur?

The only flight available had dropped them in Orlando sixty-five minutes ago and now they were racing north on Interstate 95 breaking every limit in the book and arguing fiercely as they had done ever since the phone call about whose fault it was and what would happen if they didn't make Jacksonville in time? The valet, Humph, was cursing everyone, the van included, which drove like a three-wheel dumpster, swearing he had only passed on what the Man had told him, honest to God. You couldn't trust a politician, even the best, liars every one. It came on to rain, not heavy but enough to make the road surface slick as an ice-rink. Each time Humph eased off on the throttle they screamed at him to keep going, Goddammit! Just get us there!

Maybe there was oil on the road. Maybe it was the tires: they said afterwards the rubber was worn down on the front off-side. One of them later thought it was the wash from a truck they pulled out to overtake. The driver lost control, the van skidded sideways into the central barrier, bounced back across the inner lanes, smacked the fender of a Cougar, spun round backwards, and crashed down the embankment, pieces flying off, a muffler, a grille. And scraping and slithering down and on across a storm drain till it came to rest in the scrub on the far side, wheels spinning slowly, nothing else moving but no fire. No fire. That much at least to be thankful for. A shock, a scare, the occupants shaken up, bruised but nothing worse.

2

Across the country in California the sun was just getting warm. Karen Lipscombe was setting out for the beach when her friend called down that she was wanted on the phone. A few weeks ago when there had still been chances of a slot for her in the new administration she would have grabbed it by the second ring. Now disillusion had set in. She tried not to be bitter, but it was hard. No, impossible. When you knew you were as good as the ones that got the jobs. And better.

Trying to forget those nights in summer when the polls were bad and the Candidate down. A cheap hotel room with the would-be President in the hot and humid dusk. A man in her bed and the world to live for. Now he was married and the dream over.

It crossed her mind not to bother answering the phone but the hope still burned in her too strongly to be ignored and she went back inside.

'What, now?' she said incredulously. 'Right away?'

Immediately please, the voice on the line replied. Time was of the essence. A seat would be held for her on the 11 a.m. flight to Atlanta with onward connection to Jacksonville, Florida where transport would be waiting.

Eleven o'clock was twenty-five minutes away! With a gulp, Karen said that, yes, she would make it somehow. She slammed the phone down and dialed a cab, shucking off her beach kit as she spoke to the dispatcher. Thank goodness the suit she had worn for the Candidate's luncheon was back from the cleaners. She snatched it off the hanger, flung a few other things and her washing kit

21

into a bag and ran for the cab as it pulled into the driveway.

They made the airport with minutes to spare. 'You'll make it if you hurry,' the check-in clerk told her as if she wasn't doing just that. A flight attendant ran her through the gate and down the ramp and the door clamped shut after her like a trap.

All the way to Atlanta she wondered what she was doing and what it was they wanted. If a job, what kind of a job? The President-elect was in Florida all this week, that much was common knowledge, which suggested something on the inside, possibly within the White House itself. Her heart thumped pleasurably. In Atlanta there was a one-hour wait for the connection. The other passengers on the Florida flight were overweight families in Day-Glo polyester bound for Orlando and the Magic Kingdom. Twenty minutes before they were due into Jacksonville she took the suit into the toilet and changed awkwardly, brushing out her hair, hoping she didn't look a fright.

The next surprise arrived on landing. A stewardess came up to her seat. 'Are you Ms Lipscombe? Could you please come forward to the front exit directly the plane stops. There is transport meeting you.'

And transport there was. A Navy helicopter, its blades still turning, squatting on the apron close by. Karen tried to behave as though this kind of treatment was a regular occurrence as she climbed aboard under the awed gaze of the other passengers. She had never flown in a helicopter before.

'Where are we going?' she shouted to the pilot.

'Mayport. Senator Meade is taking a vacation down on a yacht on the estuary.'

The flight took minutes only. They clattered away over the city and the sun dazzle flashed on the canopy as the helicopter spun in above the river mouth. She smelt the sea at once when they landed. The wind clutched at her skirt as she was handed down into a Navy launch. In another moment they were powering off across the waves, spray flying. Exhilaration gripped her. This was power, this was living. Helicopters, boats and phone calls that picked people up and set them down again at the other side of the continent.

Cuter than her photo, the Deputy Chief of Staff designate observed, watching her mount the ladder. He liked the taut stance and crisp blonde hair under her white cap. A nice little hardbody. He went forward to meet her.

'Miss Lipscombe?'

'Mr Leeder?' She turned toward him. Encasing her upper face was a heavy white headset that hid the eyes, something like a virtual reality unit. Twin electronic ports stared outwards with a disconcertingly robotic effect. She moved her head and a central lens whirred, zooming in upon him. Momentarily at a loss, he stood gaping.

'Hi, there.' She held out a hand, smiling.

Karen Lipscombe was not completely blind. Technically she had 5–10 percent residual sight, sufficient to free her from the totally blind's random eye movement which the sighted find so disconcerting. Sufficient to let her walk without a cane in daylight. She hated canes. Sufficient to distinguish a person's outline but not enough to recognize faces. Not enough to read text, watch TV or drive a car unaided.

None of which she permitted to hinder her. At school and college, without sight to rely on she had trained herself to listen and to remember. She had learned to recognize people by their voices. She spoke six languages, four of them fluently. Her memory amazed people who wouldn't take the trouble to train their own. Karen could hear a telephone number once and never forget it. Ever. She played bridge to high amateur standard. At any point in the game she could call off the exact order in which every card had been played. Finally, to prove to herself that she was not afraid she had become an enthusiastic mountaineer.

In the last five years the advent of the Visionics Elvis Low Vision Enhancement System had changed the lives of Karen and thousands of other partially sighted people like her. Using technology developed by the Defense Department for spacecraft cockpit displays, the system formed a single image from triple video cameras located on the headset which it projected onto a screen before her eyes.

When she had tried out the system Karen had broken down in tears. For the first time in ten years she was able to see her mother smile. She could pick out street signs, even read people's expressions. Lead a near normal life.

'Personal aide to the President.'

The Deputy Chief of Staff designate was interviewing on the sun deck. Karen had met him only once before. She remembered he had a stutter and was sensitive on the subject, a twangy mountain accent. He asked if she would like refreshment. Karen opted for iced tea with lemon.

'How was your trip?'

'The helicopter ride was wonderful. It was most thoughtful. Thank you.'

'I'm glad. We certainly appreciate your dropping everything to come down here like this.'

He explained about the job they had in mind. There had been a switching of roles. Karen's predecessor in the post that was being offered had been promoted to a role in the West Wing.

Would she take his place? He apologized for the short notice. A sudden presidential decision. 'Our master's whims must be appeased.'

Would she accept? Presidential aides were a dime a

dozen in every administration. Dogsbodies. Personal aides, as the title implied, worked directly with the President, smoothing his daily schedule, accompanying him on trips, running errands. Menial work but right at the center. A springboard to greater things. And for an aspirant politician an unparalleled chance to observe the mechanics of government from the inside. Yes, of course she would accept.

'Great, then let's get you to meet with the Senator.'

That, it transpired, was another matter. The yacht was vast and luxurious. It seemed full of people. Launches tied up alongside, ferrying new arrivals, departures, every few minutes. The President-elect, someone told Karen eventually, would not have time for her today. Tomorrow, maybe. A bed had been reserved for her ashore at the base.

She spent the evening in the Bachelor Officers' Quarters mess wing along with two score more hopeful appointees like herself awaiting confirmation and a hundred-strong contingent from the media. Some faces she had encountered during the campaign but no one she knew well. Her room-mate was a soft-drawling girl from Alabama, a personal assistant to a special assistant designate. 'Don't bet on your luck yet, honey,' she warned Karen. 'All appointments to the Personal Office have to be cleared with Elaine.' The President-elect's secretary, it seemed, had red-lined every unmarried female candidate to a job carrying proximity to her boss. 'Elaine figures she preserved his reputation squeaky clean all through the campaign and she intends to see it stays that way.'

The President-elect was in an irritable mood. The staff endured him. It was understandable. His scars were itching today. He blamed the heat and was using creams with the dressings. The surgeon was offering to fly down

25

but he had told him no. He'd had enough of doctors. Also he was missing his wife. They had hardly been married any time. Caro had been taken ill on the honeymoon and now after surgery faced a lengthy convalescence. It was an inauspicious start to a life together. So Jack Meade sat in his rocker on the fantail, venting his anger at those around him. The appointments list was way off schedule. Liberal and conservative wings of the party were sniping at one another. Time was slipping by. Candidates for position were being selected in three-minute interviews conducted in the passage outside the suite. 'I had Chesney Goss tell me he won't serve at Commerce with an under-secretary from the South. Dammit, who does he think he is, setting conditions?' he snapped at his Chief of Staff.

The Chief of Staff said he believed Goss was raising objections because Leon Perry had reputedly been appointed to head the President's Economic Task Force. A report to this effect had appeared in yesterday's *Washington Post*.

The President-elect exploded. Perry was a gossip and a schemer, always plotting behind his back. When Elaine Manken came in, he demanded to be told the source of the *Post* leak. Elaine denied all knowledge. She attempted to pacify her boss. Perry, she said, felt that he was owed a reward for his loyalty. He was anxious to serve. If he had let his mouth run away with him, it was regrettable but understandable even so.

'Get on that phone,' Meade ordered his press secretary, pointing, 'and issue a denial of the story right away. And you, Elaine, tell Perry I want to see him.' He did not intend, he said, to preside over an administration of favorites and cronies.

Elaine went out tight-lipped to call Perry from her office. When she had left, the President-elect told the others that he had 'had it up to here with those two and their clique of buddies, manipulating people'. Elaine was a trooper during the campaign, he added, but the responsibilities of the new position had gotten to her head. She and Leon were thick together and now she was pushing Leon's case. He believed she was keeping a personal diary full of inside detail which she intended to publish one day, 'embarrassing the hell out of us all'.

Gary Lugg, the steward working the evening shift aboard the yacht, was busy again that evening. He waited dinner in the main saloon at 7.30. It was followed by an entertainment at which the principal act was a comedian who brought the house down with an impression of General Ivory learning he had lost the election. Afterwards Lugg and the other stewards were kept busy answering calls to the cabins.

Shortly before eleven, another steward returned to the galley from a trip to the stern to report that 'the top brass' was 'in a fight, shoutin' and carryin' on'. Lugg and his colleagues observed tense expressions among the staffers in the saloon bar and elsewhere, some pacing the decks, others talking in low tones. An hour later, though, the crisis, if crisis it was, seemed to have subsided. The parties in the saloon broke up, boats ferried a number of guests back ashore and calm descended on the vessel.

'Dammit,' the President-elect was saying, 'this is my fault. I shut my eyes to the problem. Elaine needed help but now it's too late. She has to go. She's a lush and she has to go,' he repeated.

'It'll look bad in the press,' the Chief of Staff replied. Media image was always the staff's first concern. 'Maybe there's some way we can finesse it.'

'There isn't.' The President-elect was tired of the topic. 'Play it how you like. She can blame family, medical reasons, whatever, but I want her out of here tonight.'

*

27

Ashore in the BOQ canteen, there was a whiff of drama in the air. Rumors spread of a falling out in the Meade inner circle. Elaine Manken was said to have resigned or been offered a cabinet post depending on whom you spoke to. The talk was all speculation and Karen felt left out. The idea of the newly elected President abruptly dismissing his secretary of many years was hard to credit. She joined the throng around the bulletin board where the Press Office posted lists of the latest appointments. She listened to the names for new positions called out. Hers was not among them. She phoned her mother to say she was thinking of coming back.

'Don't,' her mother told her. 'Don't give up yet. I have a sense this is a good time for you, a strong time.' Mom hated to have her children give up on anything. Life took grit, she always said. 'You hang on in there. You are in a trough for the present but that could all change real soon. By tomorrow or the next day, who knows, events may be swinging in your favor, working for you, not against.'

Karen said she would think about it. Do that, her mother urged. Remember, toughness had paid off for her in the past. Karen remained unconvinced and returned despondent to her room for the night.

It was nearing 1 a.m. when Lugg answered his last summons of the night. Not to the owners' suite but to one of the cabins amidship where Leon Perry and Elaine Manken were ready to depart with suitcases packed. Lugg carried the bags up to the waist and passed them down to seamen in a waiting launch. No one else was on deck and not a word was spoken as the two descended the gangway. The launch cast off at once, the couple seated in the stern. As it swung out toward the shore, the President-elect's secretary lifted her head for a last glance back at the boat in the moonlight. It seemed to Lugg that he caught the glint of tears in her eyes.

*

Karen awoke from sleep in the darkened BOQ. It felt late and from the absence of breathing from the other bed she guessed the girl from Alabama had paired off and was spending the night elsewhere. It was like the campaign all over. Sex and politics went hand in hand.

She reached out for the button on her speaker-clock. One forty-four. All the turmoil of her thoughts had returned. Should she stay? Should she go? Why had she been summoned if not to be offered a post? But one person's say-so counted for nothing; a candidate had to be acceptable across the board. To the formidable Elaine, for instance. Or anyone else with a favorite protégé to push. It could go either way.

Worrying wouldn't do any good, that was for sure. Maybe a stroll would help her loosen up and get back to sleep. She pulled on pants and a sweater against the night air, fitted the Elvis over her head and switched on the low-light lens for night vision. Outside, the base was still and silent, the moon casting long shadows between buildings with here and there a yellow pool of light from a lamp over a doorway. Somewhere in the distance a generator hummed. The sea smell was strong and she bent her path in the direction of the dock.

A prick of light was moving out over the water. At first she took it for the yacht but then she realized it was too small. A launch or similar and traveling fast. It was drawing nearer, closing with the shore. The Elvis night lens picked out the shapes of people in the stern. She could hear the engine now, changing its beat as it slowed to turn in, lining up with the dock. Over to her right, car headlamps came sliding swiftly down the road from the base, like a scene from *The Long Goodbye*. Curious to see who it was leaving this time of night, she quickened her pace.

An armed sentry stepped out from the shadows to challenge her at the ramp to the dock. Fortunately she had remembered her purse and ID. He stared at the Elvis and motioned her on. She climbed down onto the

29

dockside and saw that the launch had come alongside and was disgorging its passengers. They were two, a man and a woman walking briskly toward her. Both carried luggage and the woman was talking shrilly. Karen couldn't make out the words but there was no mistaking the anger and bitterness in her voice. As she came into the light by the sentry post, Karen had her first clear sight of the woman's face and caught her breath. Elaine Manken. And the man with her was Leon Perry.

If they noticed Karen standing on the dock neither gave indication of it. Elaine marched on by up to the waiting car, venting her fury in savage, staccato sentences. Karen caught only fragments: ' . . . eight years of my life and for what? . . . first chance he gets . . . ', but it was enough. This was dreadful. The rumors in the canteen had been right after all. Elaine was out. She had overreached herself. The President-elect's executive secretary, before whose wrath even chiefs of staff quailed, had finally been dismissed. But why? What could have caused such a catastrophic breach?

For a minute Karen stood at a loss, half-embarrassed at what she was witnessing. Terrible to go this way, skulking out in the middle of the night like criminals and with the Inauguration only days away. The two got into the car and the doors closed on Elaine's shrill voice. Out on the dock the launch gunned its engine throatily preparatory to moving off.

Karen came to life. If Elaine had been sacked, who was going to take her place? There would be a vacancy at the President's side. That post would have to be filled and quickly. None of the entourage ashore would know about this yet. Now was her chance.

'Hey!' she cried, darting forward toward the boat. 'Hey, wait!' A crewman in the act of casting off the mooring rope glanced back. Probably it was surprise at the sight of the Elvis headset that made him pause long enough for her to reach the side.

30

'Hold on,' she gasped. 'You're going back out to the yacht? You have to take me with you.'

The seamen glanced at one another. 'We got no orders,' said one in the stern suspiciously.

Karen could think fast in an emergency. 'But you must have. Lipscombe, Karen R.' She proffered her ID. 'I'm the replacement for the lady you just brought in. Deputy Chief of Staff Jay Leeder just sent for me to come out.' She detected the doubt still in the way they faced her. 'Dammit, I'm the President-elect's new secretary. Are you going to leave me here stranded on the dock?'

There was a moment's hesitation, then the crewman in charge shrugged. 'If you say so, lady. Nobody told us anything, is all.' He reached out a hand to help her aboard.

The short journey over the water gave her a little time to prepare her plan of action. She felt bad profiting from Elaine's misfortune, but the sacking had not been her doing. Chance had happened to put her in the right place at the right time. Even so, she was taking a big risk doing this, she knew. All the odds were she would be refused entry and sent back ashore ignominiously. In which event she could kiss goodbye to her last chance of a post.

They rounded a bend in the river and there was the yacht ahead, sparkling under her lights. The helmsman spun the wheel and the launch heeled over as they circled in under the stern.

'I was ordered to report on board by Jay Leeder, deputy Chief of Staff,' she said firmly to the guards at the entry port. 'Call him. He'll vouch for me.' She prayed he wasn't asleep yet.

There was a short hiatus, then Jay appeared on deck. He was still dressed, at least then she hadn't gotten him out of bed. He looked worried and *distrait*. He was not pleased to see her. 'I don't know what you think you're doing . . . ' he began crossly.

Karen stepped up close to him. 'It's about Elaine.' She spoke with quiet firmness. 'I am here to fill her shoes.'

For a moment the silence was awesome. Jay was staring at her, outraged. Karen could hear the blood thumping in her ears. She forced her lips into some kind of a smile, trying to look confident, not triumphant. Finally Jay spoke. 'You'd better come below,' he said. 'Follow me.' He spun on his heel. From the set of his shoulders she could tell he was very angry indeed. But at least he hadn't sent her back.

There seemed to be no one about on board apart from the ubiquitous Secret Service men. Jay led her down to his cabin. A poster of Jack Meade was tacked to the bulkhead, dead faxes overflowed the wastepaper basket, an open suitcase on the bunk and a laptop perched on a stack of colored files. Kicking a box of blue campaign buttons aside, Jay shut the door. 'Now, see here,' he began.

Karen cut him short. 'You need me,' she said forcefully. His jaw dropped and she followed up her advantage. 'You need me. You've just fired Elaine Manken. The President-elect is short an executive secretary. He desperately needs someone he can trust and he needs them fast. Well, he can trust me. Jack knows me; he's experienced the way I work in California during the election. I'll run his private office like a machine. I'm efficient, I'm discreet and I'm loyal and I don't play power games like Elaine. Above all I'm here on the spot, ready to take over.'

She stopped, conscious she had said enough. Jay Leeder wiped a hand over his face. He seemed temporarily at a loss. He sat down on the bunk and motioned her to the only chair. Someone had scrawled a phone message on the vanity unit mirror in green felt-tip but the number underneath was smeared and unreadable. 'Everything has happened so damn fast,' Jay said. 'Nobody knows what Jack's thinking on this is at all.'

She was correct that Elaine had gone, he said. He

didn't ask how she knew. There had been a power struggle and Elaine had lost. Leon Perry was gone too. He was vague about details. She had the impression he was still in shock. The President-elect had displayed a side to his character nobody had suspected him of possessing.

'You need me,' Karen repeated. 'I come clean, with no baggage. I don't owe anybody. And I can do the job, believe me.'

He was looking at her curiously as if seeing her properly for the first time. Perhaps he was revising his estimate of her. Or maybe just figuring his chances of hitting on her tonight. Karen let herself relax just a little. At least it looked as if she hadn't completely blown her hopes.

'You took a chance coming out here,' he said.

She shrugged, 'Nothing ventured, nothing gained. I saw an opening and took it.'

He nodded as if that were reasonable. 'Do you know what the President's executive secretary does?'

Yes, she did.

'Handling paperwork would not be a problem? Forgive me, but you are . . . differently abled.'

Karen controlled her anger. 'I used to be classified as blind. No longer.' She reached up to touch the Elvis. 'Right now in the dark with this, my vision is probably better than yours. I can hook up directly to a computer, a TV or a video. I can handle paperwork as well as you can, I just use different methods.'

'Please . . . ' he tried to say.

'My visual capacity is only one tenth of yours so I have to make it work harder, but that's all.'

She stopped. He was holding up his hands against the light in surrender. 'Sorry,' he apologized, 'that was clumsy of me.'

'That's okay. I get over-sensitive sometimes.' She managed a smile. It was forgotten.

'Do you have experience with the various office software systems?'

Aspirants to a job at the White House were required to be up to speed on Lotus Notes as well as Microsoft Office. Karen was familiar with both from her days on the campaign staff.

'Do you feel able to take on control of an office department? Managing personnel, keeping track of confidential records, dealing with the press?'

'Currently I run my section of the news team at the station. There are twelve people under me. I demand and give a lot. I like to think we get on. It's high-pressure work and I thrive on it.'

'Yes, it's in your dossier,' he confirmed. 'Your present employers are willing to release you, I take it?'

'No problem. That was a condition of my joining them and they are very understanding.'

She sensed his resistance wavering. 'And you would keep details of any offer to yourself, whether or not you accept?'

'Of course. I told you I'm discreet.'

Again he apologized. The point had to be made. He was sure she was a trustworthy person. He was evidently trying to come to a decision. She had some chutzpah, he said again, forcing her way on board ship in the middle of the night. He liked that, though. Sometimes you had to back your own judgement. Very well, he would take her to see the President-elect. A word of warning though: Jack was in a strange mood. Tread warily, was his advice.

'Karen, good to see you at last.'

The stern cabin was a blaze of lights. Jack Meade stood to greet her. He smelt of antiseptic and bourbon and the gauze patches were white against his skin. His welcome to her was cordial, just a fraction cautious, which was only to be expected in company after all that had happened. Great to see her again, he said. Really great. Hoped she had not forgotten him. They both laughed politely when she answered no, not yet anyway.

'I'd like you to meet my Chief of Staff, Irwin Hunter.'

'Irwin.'

'Karen.' They shook hands firmly.

He showed her to a seat and she reached out with her fingertips to find the arms.

'How d'you like our boat?'

'Swell, and a great place to do business too, I guess.'

'For us, yes. The press hate it because they can't eavesdrop on us.'

His voice sounded hoarse and strained. She recalled the tales of Jack Kennedy, his throat so weakened by weeks of campaigning he was reduced to passing handwritten notes. Otherwise Meade seemed just as she remembered, full of energy, wryly humorous, candid about himself and dispassionate in his judgement of others. They chatted. Of the task facing him, he was realistic. 'There's a story of a reporter asking General Ivory if he was looking forward to retirement. Ivory answers, "It'll be a cinch compared with the mess I've left for Meade."'

They switched tack to the business in hand. 'As you have heard I have a problem, Karen. My secretary, Mrs Manken, has left me. Regrettable, but these things happen and have to be faced. Jay tells me you came out here tonight offering to serve in her place. I want you to know how much I appreciate that.'

She tried to speak but he waved her down. He appreciated it but, he said, he wanted to satisfy himself she was sure what she was doing. This had all come about very suddenly. It wasn't the post she had been led to expect originally. Or possibly deserved. Now, some people might think executive secretary was a menial job, compared with an aide or a special assistant. As a matter of fact they would be wrong. Personally he would compare it to the post of Vice-President. The position of

VP was all show and no substance. Well, the secretary to the President was just the opposite, all substance and little show.

He opened his fist and clenched it again, still keeping his gaze on her.

'I'll make a deal with you, Karen. I want you to take this job for me. I remember the work you did for us in California. It's my judgement you're the very best person I could pick. With you running things I'll be free to concentrate on the issues. Free to devote all my energies to turning round our country. Above all, secure in the knowledge you're not setting out to build your own power base behind my back. So I'll make you a promise: I'll be a different kind of president and you can be a different kind of secretary. How's that?'

Karen clasped her hands tightly together in her lap to try and stop them shaking. A dozen thoughts clamored in her head. From presidential aide to personal secretary was a giant, an unimaginable leap. Upwards or downwards, she didn't feel able to judge at present. All that mattered was that she would be near him again. He had given her no signal, true, but he still cared. She was sure of it. Why else had he called her back? She felt hot now with excitement, her heart beating fast, her cheeks burning. She sensed the others were waiting for her to speak and took a hold of herself. 'Sir,' she said, her voice trembling in her throat, 'I'll be proud to serve wherever you . . . wherever you think I can be most use.' There, it was said, she was committed.

The atmosphere relaxed. All three shook her by the hand again. She was aware of a perceptible easing of tension. And within herself a sense of exhilaration overcoming her, almost of intoxication. This was a moment of transition. She was one of them now. The inner circle. At a stroke she had just become arguably the second most influential woman in the land.

The President-elect thanked her. Said he appreciated

her loyalty. Her willingness to put country before her career. Unlike others he could mention. This was something he would remember when the time came.

His silhouette shifted against the light as he cocked his head, a characteristic pose. 'Karen, you worked for us on the campaign. Then you were on the outside a while, now you're back where you belong. I'm interested because you have a better perspective than the rest of us. Different, anyway. How would you rate our achievements to date?'

Karen hesitated. 'There's a feeling the appointments procedure hasn't gone as smoothly as it might.'

Fair comment, he said. There had been problems, he acknowledged. Procedures had been slack at first. 'We were getting 3,000 résumé applications a day and we weren't prepared. People tried to dicker and bargain. We were adrift.' That had changed, he added.

'The American people don't like cliques,' Karen ventured.

Neither did he, said the President-elect. 'But that's all done with. Elaine and her cronies are gone.'

His tone was steely as he pronounced the name. Karen got the message. Stay away. Elaine's departure was taboo. She had been warned.

By morning the news was all around the base. Elaine the Mighty had fallen. Replaced by a slip of a girl, a nobody. Leon Perry was gone, others too. People were speaking of a palace coup, a night of the long knives with wholesale dismissals among the upper echelons. Press comment was divided. An administration in disarray, wrote one. Others read it as a healthy sign, a new leader flexing his muscles, distancing himself from the party hierarchy.

Karen cared nothing for the gossip. She was too busy. With Elaine gone the office was all to pieces, the workload frantic. She moved into Elaine's cabin aboard the yacht for the final two days of the trip. 'Jack needs us,' she told the stenographers and pleaded with them to stay on. Most agreed. If some of the old guard Meade loyalists carped behind her back, well let them. She was happy. Jack Meade had brought her back in from the cold. He had kept his promise.

Karen Lipscombe made friends, but warily. Being a woman and blind made her doubly vulnerable. In Karen's book pity was damnable – the sin for which there was no forgiveness. At least not from her. She was aware that a deep vein of cripple's anger flowed within her and she refused to let it poison her life. Instead she used it as a spur to independence. Besides, she reminded herself constantly, she was having it easy. She could see – a little. Plus she had the Elvis.

And certain things she could do better than other people. Now she had a chance to prove it. Not just to herself but to Jack.

At least once a day he told her to get his wife on the phone. Karen tried to push away feelings of jealousy but it was hard. Especially when he spoke in front of her. Or when she answered the phone to hear that breathy voice, at once soft and demanding. Caro Meade wanted her husband to come back to Washington but the appointments schedules were way behind and the work was piling up. Caro pleaded to be allowed to quit the hospital, fly down to join him, but Jack was adamant. She mustn't take risks with her health. Karen suspected he didn't want her to see him till the scars were properly healed.

3

'You may find this intimidating at first.'

The President-elect faced the apparatus nervously and took a deep breath. 'I'll do my best,' he said. 'Just hope I don't press the wrong button.'

It doesn't matter, they reassured him. Everyone makes a few mistakes. You can always start over.

It was a solemn occasion at the Pentagon. The President-elect had flown in from Florida for his induction. His bandages were off at last, leaving no trace of scarring, just as the surgeons had promised. An Air Force jet had brought him to Andrews AFB and the Joint Chiefs had been on hand to welcome the helicopter that ferried him into the capital. They had met before naturally but today was official. In less than a week he would be their commander-in-chief. The old order was changing and there were formalities to be gone through.

He had been welcomed with salutes and ceremony. He had had the tour, seen the war room, the tank where secret conferences were held, the egg-shaped table round which the Joint Chiefs conferred, the computers and the map displays. He had met the technicians and the commanders who controlled the most powerful war machine on earth. But what he had really come for were the codes.

There was a time back in the Eisenhower era, before the beginning of the missile age, when all this could have taken place after the Inauguration as was proper. Under the Constitution the President was commander-in-chief. On him alone rested the awesome responsibility of launch authority for thermonuclear war. Not until his successor took the oath of office could the burden pass. But in the modern world any delay was unacceptable, so nowadays the induction took place in advance of the ceremony so that the new President might step smoothly into his predecessor's shoes with no hiatus for an enemy to exploit.

The inducting officer was an Air Force colonel with a boyish enthusiasm for his toys. 'The procedure we follow here, sir, involves ascending grades of security. It starts out with basic information about yourself, your family and background, then builds up through voice recognition, finger and palm prints, to biometrics including retinal pattern analysis, facial thermogram and finally blood and DNA typing.'

The President-elect suppressed a shudder. 'It certainly is comprehensive,' he said.

'The intention,' the officer continued, 'is to build up a cumulative effect. So while it might be possible, say, for someone to steal a code or counterfeit your voice, an impostor would also have to be familiar with your personal details and in addition pass a palm or eyeprint check.'

'It's possible to fake my fingerprints?'

'It's not easy to imagine, sir, but there might be circumstances involving perhaps physical violence where it could conceivably happen. That's why you'll find top-level access always requires triple verification.'

'I just hope I'll be able to remember it all when the time comes.'

'For the most part, sir, we don't rely too much on memory. There is a code procedure for the missile targeting systems which will be explained to you later. What we are concerned with now is verification, and the procedures are pretty well automated.'

The President-elect said he was glad to hear it.

'If you will please follow me now, sir, we can

commence the induction program by entering your personal data.'

Behind the heavy doors of the National Military Command Center in the restricted JCS area, they showed him into a small windowless room decorated in soothing pastel tones. Two chairs faced a pair of video monitors side by side with a single keyboard.

'If you care to sit here, sir –' the colonel indicated the left-hand seat. He took the other and tapped a key. Instantly the left-hand screen came alive with a colored image of the presidential seal.

'Welcome to the National Military Command Authority Verification Program,' a woman's voice filled the room, melodious and neutral. 'My name is Lieutenant Fellows, and I will be guiding you through the program. You will now be asked to give certain details from your personal background. This is primarily so that the computer can have a chance to learn your speech rhythms. If requested to repeat an answer please comply in the same tone as before.'

There was a short pause, then the voice said, 'Please give your full name.'

'John MacKenzie Meade,' he answered and saw the names appear at the bottom of the screen.

'Is that the correct spelling, Senator Meade?' asked the voice.

'How does she know I'm a senator?' he whispered to the colonel.

The officer grinned, 'We cheat a little.'

'Yes, that spelling is correct.'

'Thank you,' the voice continued in the same unhurried mellifluous accent. 'Would you please state your date and place of birth.'

'January 10th, 1956, Boston, Massachusetts.'

There was a pause. 'Please be more specific.'

'Oh . . . ' he stumbled. 'Boston Memorial Hospital. Will that do?'

'Thank you. Please state the full names of both parents . . .'

At the White House, a dark green Chrysler Cherokee cruised smoothly into the circular driveway and drew to a halt at the South Diplomatic entrance. As the Secret Service driver held open the rear door for the single woman passenger, a dark-haired man of medium height stepped forward. 'I'm Brad Sewall, Chief Usher,' he introduced himself.

'Caro Meade.' Her reply was so low as to be almost a whisper.

'Welcome to the White House, Mrs Meade.'

How young she looked, he thought. Dressed in a coat of dark red, wearing gloves, she might have been the nervous wife of a new congressman paying her obligatory call. She was taller than he had expected, as tall as him even in low heels. Very thin, she seemed, and pale despite the dark allure that so many women strove to copy along with the artfully careless coiffure, the street clothes, the big, soft mouth. Tradition decreed an incoming First Lady be shown over the executive mansion alone by her predecessor prior to the Inauguration. An aide had phoned from the hospital to say Mrs Meade would require a wheelchair for her tour. The still First Lady Mrs Ivory had bridled at the news. 'Who does she think she is? Demanding this and that. She's not living here yet!'

Delicately Sewall had pointed out that Mrs Meade was still recovering from a serious operation.

Mrs Ivory looked down her nose contemptuously. 'Very well, we'll get her a chair,' she paused, 'but keep it out of sight, in a closet somewhere. She can have it *if* she asks for it.'

Caro Meade was a political enemy and woe betide anyone who forgot it.

Wordlessly, she accompanied him inside into the oval Diplomatic Reception Room, gazing round her at the furniture and paintings, the scenic wallpaper depicting an early American landscape and, still without speaking, through the hallway towards the elevator. Her wide, uncertain eyes, filled with wonder, seemed to look for ways of escape.

'Mrs Ivory is waiting for you upstairs in the private apartment.'

They stepped together into the elevator.

At the second floor the door opened. At the far end of the long central hall Mrs Ivory stood waiting, wearing an expression of lofty disdain. Caro Meade took a deep breath.

'Mrs Meade,' Sewall announced formally. The First Lady made no move toward them but allowed the Chief Usher to escort her guest down the length of the hall to where she stood.

'How d'you do, Mrs Meade.' She extended a hand imperiously toward the younger woman, her lips drawn together in a tight line. 'I trust you are feeling up to this visit?'

Caro Meade's response was barely audible in the long room. 'Good morning, Mrs Ivory, it's very kind of you to receive me.'

'Not at all. Not at all! Just part of the ritual. If you'll come along with me I'll show you where the President and I have made our home these past four years.' The First Lady did not trouble to suppress the bitterness in her voice as she spoke. She had enjoyed her time on Pennsylvania Avenue and had hoped to be staying on. Now she felt a deep antagonism toward the upstart young couple who had inflicted the humiliation of defeat on her husband.

Dismissing Sewall with a curt nod, she led off: 'Now, this is my sitting room. What we call the Yellow Oval Room . . .'

*

43

The Chief Usher of the White House is the general manager of the executive mansion. As such he is responsible for the smooth administration of a 132-room building that is both a museum housing priceless works of art and a national monument visited by three million tourists a year, a hotel for entertaining heads of state and an impregnable fortress for protecting the life of the Commander-in-Chief. Finally it also serves as a temporary home to the First Family. The Chief Usher controls the 200 staff permanently employed catering to the needs of the President and his guests, private and official, as well as supervising all official entertainments. He supervises the maintenance of the building and grounds and prepares the annual budget for Congress. Last but not least is his ceremonial role as receptionist responsible for receiving and caring for guests calling on the President and First Lady.

Brad Sewall had held the post since the start of the current administration, having previously served five years as assistant. Prior to that he had been with the Secret Service.

In the Chief Usher's twelve-by-twelve office located behind the first door to the right off the marble-floored main lobby, he waited for the First Lady to ring down for the wheelchair for her guest. The call never came. Instead, at precisely 12.30 a buzzer sounded on the video monitor indicating that Mrs Ivory and Caro Meade were descending. He left his chair and walked to the elevator to meet them.

The two women entered the hall and walked out through the south entrance in silence to where their vehicles were waiting. Without a word of farewell the First Lady climbed into her limousine and was sped regally away. Caro Meade walked slowly over to her Chrysler. As Sewall caught up with her, he saw a shadow of pain pass across her face.

'Are you all right? Would you like to rest a minute?'

'No, thank you,' she responded in her quiet voice. Then she turned on him, her eyes luminous and accusatory. 'They phoned from the hospital to ask if I could have a wheelchair. You know I've not been well. Why didn't you let me have one?'

Sewall felt his face redden. 'We had a chair all ready for you. In a closet by the elevator. I'm sorry, you should have been told.'

Caro Meade continued to stare at him searchingly. 'I see,' she said softly. 'She wanted me to ask.' She compressed her lips tightly. 'It wasn't your fault,' she said.

And clutching his arm for support, she stepped into the car.

Down in Jacksonville, the patient drifted in and out of consciousness. Vaguely at intervals he was aware of faces bending over him; of hands turning his body, taking his pulse or changing a dressing. His few waking moments were filled with a sense of frantic anxiety so that he thrashed feverishly in the bed to escape the black trough of despair which rose up to envelop him again. On one such occasion during the afternoon of the fifth day as he lay semi-torpid from the drugs, he heard the door click open and clutched at the sound with his brain in a desperate effort to hold himself awake. Through the fog inside his head he heard footsteps approach the bed. More than one person, it seemed. There was a murmured exchange and sounds of a container or case being unlatched. An item was set down on the table by his head. He half tensed, expecting the prick of a hypodermic again.

'Both hands?' asked a male voice.

'Best if you can,' came the reply. 'Try not to wake him. We don't want any trouble if we can help it.'

'No chance of that,' said a woman's voice. 'The shot we gave him will keep him down for couple more hours yet easily.'

More suggestions of equipment being arranged on the bedside table. 'Okay, well here goes,' said the first man. The patient felt his right hand taken in another's, the thumb separated out and pressed against a damp surface in a hard rolling motion that was somehow familiar. Then whatever it was was removed and the action repeated on a different surface this time, one that felt dry and shiny to the touch. His thumb was released and the whole procedure was begun again using his forefinger. He had a curious sense of detachment as if observing an operation performed on somebody else. For no reason that he could fathom, relief washed over him.

When the right hand was finished they swabbed the ink off carefully with alcohol; the smell made his nostrils wrinkle. They moved round to the other side of the bed to start on the left.

'You reckon you'll be able to tell us who he is now?' inquired the nurse.

'Depends,' answered the man holding his fingers, 'if he's on file with federal or state governments or the law enforcement agencies. If not then we have to think of something else.'

'Even if his prints are listed could be a while before they come up with a match,' added his colleague. 'C'mon, that's done it. Let's wrap up.'

Tales of a mystery man pulled out from the river spread around the hospital by word of mouth and outward like ripples in a pond through the Navy base, then out into the wider world of Jacksonville. The *Meteor* ran the story on its front page, quoting 'an authoritative Navy source' as stating that the man was suffering from traumatic amnesia and inquiries were continuing to establish his identity.

The report had been compiled by Troy Reece who worked the *Meteor*'s police desk. Troy had been ten years on the paper, waiting for the big break, the one that would make him professionally. He hadn't given up hope yet. In a slack week the story looked like it might fill out to run one more day and he stopped by the Duval County Sheriff's Department to see what more he could dig up. He spoke with Deputy Sheriff Harry Marks, an old acquaintance who was happy to brief him on the facts such as they were.

'Okay, this is a summary of the County Sheriff's report, right? Just before 1 p.m. on the 13th the office in Mayport received a call from a Fitzroy Grape. Grape retired this year from the Bureau of Census and is some kind of fitness nut. Runs four miles every day, nothing else to do with his time probably. Anyway down along the shore he finds a body washed up by the tide. First off he thinks it's a corpse but then he looks closer and the guy is still breathing. Alive, but only just. So Grape dials 911 on his cellular phone.'

'He recognize the man at all?' Troy had his pad out and was jotting down shorthand.

'Uh-uh, I spoke with him and no way was that possible. He says the fellow's face was so puffed up from immersion in water you could hardly see his eyes. Skin all shriveled an' flaking from exposure to the sun. All he could do to tell he was a white male, and that was guessing some. Luckily Grape did a course with American Red Cross, knows the basics of resuscitation. He pumps out the man's lungs and wraps him round with the top of his jogging suit. Seems the guy was wearing nothing but short pants, maybe swim trunks, he thinks. Anyway he keeps him warm till the paramedics arrive and take over.'

'The guy say anything all this time? The corpse, victim that is?'

'Grape says he was groaning a lot, seemed anxious, distressed about something. He asked him his name but all he got sounded like Jake or Jack, he's not sure. Says the guy was half drowned and spewing up water, couldn't hardly breathe much of the time, wonder he could talk at all.'

'No ID, nothing on him?'

Harry unwrapped a stick of gum. He proffered one to Troy who shook his head silently. 'All three paramedics who attended the call swear no. The guy was bare, they are sure, except for the pants, not even a wrist-watch. And no pockets in the pants either.'

'Fingerprints?' Troy asked.

Harry sighed. 'You gotta remember this was not anything big. Mayport Sheriff's office reckoned either a drunk or a suicide, maybe both if you know what I mean. Description don't match any reported missing persons. No suggestion of criminal intent or foul play. Navy are acting on the presumption he may be one of theirs on account of the proximity to the base. So file and forget far as Sheriff's Department are concerned.'

The victim had been taken to the Navy Hospital in Jacksonville, Harry continued, where he was diagnosed as suffering from shock and exposure. 'They ran tests for alcohol and the standard range of drugs. The doctors there are not being very informative but according to a nurse who was on the ward there were traces of phenobarbitone.'

'Puncture marks?'

'I asked but she says hard to tell because his skin is in poor condition. Also he was bruised about and scratched where he banged on the rocks etcetera. Anything could've happened. Most probably he was in the water some twelve to fifteen hours. Must've found a buoy or piece of timber to cling to, keep him afloat.'

Troy spoke. 'Did the nurse say if the patient gave a name?'

Harry switched the gum across to the other side of his jaw. 'She said he claimed he was the President-elect of the United States,' he answered calmly.

*

Troy took the ferry across the river and drove down to the end of the lane. It followed the shore round and ended at the point where half a dozen white-painted houses clustered facing up the sound. Faer-sith was the furthest along. Troy parked by a picket fence and got out. There was a salt tang in the air and the breeze whipped his coat. Yachts and small craft dotted the water. A haze shrouded the woods on the far shore. A sprinkling of roofs marked what would be St John's Point. He felt suddenly envious.

The door opened.

'Mr Grape?'

'Call me Fitz. You're from the *Meteor*, right?' They shook hands. 'Come on in.'

Inside the house was wood-floored and airy. Cotton ticking furnishings and photographs of boats. Mr Grape had the look of a man who would have been happier living on a boat. He was lean and deeply suntanned. His hair was sparse and his beard neatly trimmed. He wore a blue Guernsey sweater and white shorts. From the general air of comfortable mess Troy deduced he lived alone.

'Want some coffee? Fresh made.'

'Thanks, I could use it. Certainly is fresh out today.'

'You get used to it. We retired here six years ago. My wife died in '96, cancer. A woman comes in three times a week to clean up. Luckily the boat keeps me occupied. That's her.' He indicated a picture of a modest-sized cruiser.

'You like to keep fit too, I understand.'

'Try to. Oh, you mean the running?' He poured coffee in two earthenware mugs and pushed a bottle towards Troy. 'I generally take a shot of something in it this time of day in cool weather. Privilege of age,' he winked.

Troy added a generous slug of rum to his mug and was rewarded with a gleam of approval. 'We'll go through

49

into the sun lounge. You can see pretty much where it all happened from there.'

The sun lounge had an air of bachelor shabbiness which suggested this was where Grape spent the majority of his time ashore. Windows on three sides gave a view right along the point. A pair of massive binoculars was handily placed by a well-used armchair.

'Right there down by those rocks at the head of the point was where I found him. Lucky for him I did.'

'He was pretty near gone then?'

'He certainly would have been in another few minutes.' Troy glanced at him inquiringly. 'The tide, you see, was turning,' said Grape. He frowned. 'Guess maybe I had better tell you from the beginning.'

They sat down. Troy took out his pocket recorder. 'Any objections?' he asked, placing it on the table between them.

'No, no, go ahead. Normal procedure, isn't it.' People nowadays were so used to the idea of being recorded they tended to resent it if their remarks were not taken down, Troy found.

'I generally try to get out for a run in the morning. Wakes me up and gets the circulation going. Doc says a walk is less hard on the joints but the way I see it they're my joints and if they're not giving me any trouble, why shouldn't I run if I feel like it? You run?'

Troy, who neither walked nor ran if he could help it, shook his head.

'This time of year I usually start out around ten. Saturdays I like to sleep in a little longer. Also my daughter called up so it was nearer twelve when I started out. Well anyway, so off I go. I have two routes, A and B as Martha used to call them. Martha was the wife. A is northward toward the point. B takes me back inland. I generally take that when the wind is blowing. It's more sheltered. Last Saturday was windy but for some reason I decided I wanted to see the waves hitting on the rocks off the point so I took A. The guy's first lucky break you could say.

'I spotted him the instant I came over the sand dunes. Only I didn't realize it was a body then, just something in the surf at the water's edge. Looked like a block of timber washed up. I was interested because I like to collect driftwood. This porch was made from drift.'

Troy mumbled a compliment on his handiwork and they continued.

'When I get close I see at once it's a man lying in the water. He's wearing these flesh-colored shorts or whatever and lying wedged up against a kelp shelf so he shows up, light against dark, which was the reason I picked him out from up on the dunes. At first I thought God he's a dead one but then he made a movement with his arms and I realize he is alive still.'

The tape recorder emitted a click and a bleep. Troy took the tape out and inserted a fresh one. 'Okay,' he said.

Grape had taken a course in first aid. 'Way back when we had the kids. Then when we moved here we went for a refresher. Never know when you may need it, right? So anyway, there he is and I'm trying to remember what it is I'm supposed to do.'

Grape chuckled as he described how he dragged the man out of the water, turned him over and started trying to pump the water out from his lungs. 'I'm heaving away at his back when all of a sudden I remember I'm carrying my phone. I only bought the damn thing in case I have an accident or a coronary or something when I'm out on my own and the first time I need it I almost forget all about it.'

Which was the man's second stroke of good fortune, he added, because though he had managed to keep him breathing, the guy was still in poor shape and it was a relief when the paramedics arrived to take charge. 'If I had had to run all the way back to the house to call them,

51

he would've been gone by the time I got back to him. That's what the paramedics said.'

'You mentioned something earlier,' said Troy, 'about him having a piece of luck coming ashore where he did?'

Grape nodded. Simple, he answered. The tide was running out, had been for some fifteen minutes. The flow was pulling the man away from the beach. 'I figure he fell off a boat somewhere off of the Navy Air Test Center. If the current had carried him a touch further on he'd have missed the beach altogether and been washed out into the bay and the tide would've carried him clear out to sea.'

Troy nodded. 'So like you say he was a lucky man, a three-time winner in fact.'

Troy Reece drummed his fingers on the wheel of his Toyota. The police scanner was alive, crackling with voices cutting through the static. There was a big wreck out by the airport on Route 95. After ten years on the job he had developed the capacity to listen to the messages while driving the vehicle and concentrating on his other problems at the same time. The item on the man in the river was shaping up into a useful story. It would play well just as it was but Troy had a hunch there was more to be had. He unhooked the phone and dialed up the office. 'Hi, it's Troy. Is Cal there? She did? Okay, listen, have her bring her kit and meet me at the lay-over on Roosevelt this side of the base.'

Forty minutes later Troy's Toyota cruised in at the gates of the Navy base and parked in a bay in front of the hospital building. 'Name's Murray, Hank Murray,' he lied breezily at the desk. 'This is my wife, Cal –' he indicated the fair-haired young woman with the shoulder bag at his side. 'We called up earlier. County Sheriff's Department sent us over. Seems like the mystery man your people pulled out of the St John just happens to be her brother, Jack, we think. Show the man your driver's license, hon,' he told his companion.

'That's okay, Mrs Murray.' The Clerk waved the ID aside. He pressed a buzzer. 'I'll have someone take you down to the ward.'

'That's great,' Troy beamed. He glanced behind the clerk's shoulder to where patients' names were listed on a board. UWM – Unknown White Male, that would be the one, Room 31C. 'We'll walk along to meet them. Down there on the right? Thanks, appreciate your help.'

Nurse Phillips was in the dispensary with the chief nurse, making up the evening medications, when the buzzer sounded outside. 'Damn,' said the chief. Whoever it was would have to wait while they finished measuring this dose. Quick footsteps came down the corridor, probably a couple of the doctors by the sound.

By the time Phillips had gotten to the phone there was no sign of the visitors. She hurried down to find them. A man and a woman were standing over the bed, peering down at the unconscious form of the man who called himself Jack Meade. The woman was fumbling with her bulky shoulder bag.

'Who let you in here? This patient is under sedation,' she said crossly.

'Hi!' The man turned to her, grinning brightly, too brightly, Phillips thought. 'The front desk sent us down. County Sheriff said as how you had a guy pulled out of the river last week with no ID giving the name Meade, could be a misread for Murray. Chance he might be the wife's brother, Jack, gone missing since Tuesday last.'

'Still no joy, I'm afraid,' added the girl, heaving a sigh.

'Yeah, too bad,' Troy agreed. He shook his head at the comatose patient. 'Jack Meade, eh? Funny, he does kind of bear a resemblance to the President at that.'

'Doesn't he though?' the nurse whispered. 'We've all noticed it on the ward. Must be related to the family at the very least, we figure. Kind of mystery man, huh? They took his fingerprints while he was under sedation so I guess we'll find out soon.'

'Have the shrinks seen him?'

Yes, the nurse nodded. And the neurologist, she said. He had been diagnosed as suffering from concussion, which probably explained the delusions and temporary amnesia. Also he had recently undergone cosmetic surgery procedures.

'A facelift, huh? He looks pretty sick. How long has he been in here?'

'He was brought in six days ago suffering from exposure, dehydration and hypothermia. We treated him for that but we had to sedate him when he became frantic and now he's developed an infection on the lung which has brought on a fever. We're treating him with antibiotics and he's responding, but slowly.'

'What's going on here?' demanded an angry voice.

Everyone jumped. Behind them stood a female officer in naval uniform. Her dark hair was tied back in a tight coil and her stare was as bleak as a winter night. The name tag on her left breast read Shapiro and she wore the sleeve rings of a commander. 'What are you people doing in here?' she repeated.

Troy was the first to react. He stepped forward, hand outstretched, beaming genially. 'Afternoon, Doctor, sorry to be barging in like this. As I was explaining to your colleague here we're searching for the brother-in-law and Sheriff's office told us it was a possibility you people might have him up here so naturally we came straight on down.'

Commander Shapiro ignored his hand contemptuously. 'Who in the Sheriff's office gave you this information?'

'Deputy Warner, I believe his name is, ma'am. If you like to call him I'm sure he'll be glad to straighten the matter out.' Troy mentally crossed his fingers hoping that Warner was out or off duty. 'We don't want to cause you people any bother, ma'am. Fellow we're searching for is

54

the same age an' build as your patient there . . .' he let his voice trail off despondently.

The Commander's eyes glittered like hailstones. 'Let's get one thing straight. I am in charge of this section of the hospital. Patients here are under my authority and in future you will clear any visits with me beforehand. Is that clear?'

Troy decided to drop the family member pose. If the woman wanted to play it tough that was fine by him. He held her gaze for a count of three. 'You're in charge of this ward?'

'I just said so.'

'Then you were responsible for having that guy in there fingerprinted?' They had moved out of the room now and were standing in the corridor.

Commander Shapiro's mouth tightened. 'What of it?' she snapped.

'Did you obtain his consent first?'

The question seemed to throw the officer, 'Well, no, I mean . . . that is, it wasn't practicable. The patient had not yet recovered consciousness. We were trying to establish his identity.'

Troy nodded as if that sounded reasonable. 'But he had been conscious earlier?'

The Commander nodded warily. Yes, that was so, she admitted.

'And was subsequently sedated. So you first rendered him unconscious and then had him fingerprinted when he was in no condition to consent. You violated his legal rights, Doctor.'

Commander Shapiro's fists clenched and unclenched spasmodically and he knew he had scored a hit.

'We, uh, had no choice. The patient was suffering from temporary amnesia. His fingerprints were taken to assist in establishing his identity . . .'

Troy moved past her and toward the exit, propelling

Cal in front of him. 'Sure, sure, tell it to the guy's lawyers,' he called back over his shoulder.

Nurse Phillips watched them depart and shook her head. Some people, she thought.

A green canopy at 1651 Pennsylvania Avenue, diagonally across from the presidential mansion, marks the entrance to Blair House. Actually four houses joined as one – Blair–Lee House, it was here in April 1861 that Montgomery Blair, a close adviser to President Lincoln, offered command of the Union Army to Robert E. Lee. Here too in December that same year the decision was taken to give Union command of the attack on New Orleans to David Farragut, born and raised in the South, while Confederate forces defending the port were commanded by General Mansfield Lovell whose father was the house's builder.

Acquired by the government during World War II, the mansion's primary role is as the nation's official guest house for visiting heads of state. President Truman stayed here following President Roosevelt's death and again during the 1948–52 renovation of the White House. On November 1st, 1950, two Puerto Rican nationalists attempted to assassinate him as he left the house. A plaque on the iron railing at the front entrance commemorates Leslie Coffert, a Secret Service guard killed resisting the attack. At a changeover of the Presidency Blair House also serves as the residence for the President-elect during the run-up to Inauguration Day.

The President-elect was at work. He paced the library of Blair House, gnawed by impatience. He walked with quick, short steps, consulting the sheaf of notes in his hand, occasionally flexing his shoulders or swinging his arms to relieve the tension inside him. He had come to a conference direct from the Pentagon induction without even a breathing space to greet his wife, who had taken to her bed upstairs exhausted by her White House tour.

On couches by the fire, members of the transition team nursed liquor or coffee, according to taste. Papers littered the tables, spilling onto the carpet. Policy documents, discussion papers, position statements, schedules, appointment lists graded A, B, C. Who was to have what. Who to be cajoled, persuaded, pushed, placated into this slot or that.

His advisers wore a defensive air. Their chief was flexing his muscles, feeling his strength. Consensus was out of the window suddenly. Positions that had seemingly been agreed a week or more ago were all at once being called in and reassessed. The administration's program toughened with a new less liberal slant. No opposition brooked.

Even cabinet appointments were not immune. Too many names on the A list, supposedly persons of superior merit, were in reality little more than time-servers, Meade had declared. 'I want to bring youth into government, people with ideas, vision!'

His Chief of Staff designate tapped a pen against his teeth. He was angry. The President had come up with his new proposals out of the blue while they were down on the yacht and he had been fighting against them all week. 'The names on the A list are going to be very disappointed. Many of them are heavy contributors.'

'And many are party hacks who bring nothing to the job beyond a thirst for their own prestige,' the President-elect countered. 'I am not going to allocate the most vital posts in government to people whose sole merit is that they voted early for me. I want all these remaining lists redrawn and you had better be prepared to defend every name submitted. There's no room for dead wood in my government.'

'You're going to make a lot of enemies.'

'If it's a choice between enemies and good government, I'll take the latter,' answered the President-elect grimly.

He dismissed them but later called back his Chief of

Staff. 'Trust me, Hunt,' he said. 'Believe me, I know what I'm doing. Being seen to start clean will appeal to the American people. No one's done it before.'

The Chief of Staff looked unconvinced. 'For good reasons; painful reasons,' he said.

'I'm prepared to absorb some pain,' the President said. 'If it means not being surrounded by yes-men.'

'Does that include me?'

'It includes everyone, Hunt. You've never feared me. It's what I value most in you. Try to realize that things will be different from Inauguration Day. It won't be easy for you to stand up to me when I'm in the Oval Office. Compromise will be forced on us. That's why it's important for us to start right. Above all with the right people.'

The Chief of Staff gave a rueful laugh. 'You've certainly changed, Jack.'

'I have?' The President shot him a searching look. 'In what way?'

'You've matured, grown in stature. These last weeks especially. You've become a statesman, a leader. It's a privilege for all of us to work with you. I mean that sincerely, Jack.'

'The privilege is mine, Hunt,' said the President, clapping him on the shoulder.

He went upstairs to see his wife. She had moved into a bedroom next his own. He opened the door softly. A lamp by the bed provided the only illumination. He stood for several moments watching the sleeping figure.

Caro Meade woke with a start. She saw the tall figure motionless in the shadows by the door and felt a momentary fear. 'Is that you, Jack? You nearly scared me.' She strained to make him out in the gloom. 'Why don't you come closer?'

He took a pace toward her, still staying on the edge of the circle of light. 'You were sleeping.' He kept his voice low. 'I didn't want to wake you. How are you feeling?'

'Oh, I just dozed off a minute. The tour wore me out but I'm fine now.'

'I'm sorry, it took longer than expected. Those damn schedules.'

'You sound hoarse. Is your throat playing up again?'

'Nothing serious. I talked too much at the Pentagon and now I've been arguing with Hunter.'

She was holding out her arms to him. 'Aren't you going to kiss me?'

'Of course.' He stooped over the bed, then hesitated. 'What's the matter?'

'Nothing, I had forgotten how lovely you are, that's all,' he said. 'We've been so long apart I feel like a stranger almost.' He touched his mouth gently to hers.

'Oh, it's so good to be together again,' she whispered, holding him close. He made no answer and she drew back. 'Your mouth feels different.' She pulled herself up against the pillows and turned up the lamp. He sat down on the edge of the bed. The light fell on his face and he reached out to twist the shade down.

'Now I can't see your face properly.'

'The light was in my eyes.' He leaned forward. 'Is that better?'

She stared at him for a minute. A line furrowed her brow. She put up a hand to stroke his face.

'You do approve?' he said warily.

'It's funny, you look quite different and yet the same. I can't quite make it out. But yes, I like you, I think.' She caught a swift shadow pass over his expression and added teasingly, 'Of course I do really. It takes a little getting used to is all.'

He relaxed slowly. 'The lifting of the skin stretches the corners of the mouth. I should have warned you about that. Also the scars are still tender even though you can't see them. My lips may feel unresponsive for a while. Don't worry, it'll pass off.'

She was instantly contrite. 'Did I hurt you? I am sorry. You should have stopped me.'

He permitted himself a grin, pleased with the way he was handling the encounter. 'It was worth it,' he told her, perching on the end of the bed to talk. 'So tell me, how did things go this morning?'

'At the Big House? Pretty much as we guessed it would. Mrs I. doesn't want to quit. She believes we're turning her out and she was determined to make me pay.'

'Bitch,' said the President.

'Oh, I don't mind. There's nothing she can do to us any more. I just lowered my head and let it roll right over me and that made her madder than ever.'

She began to tell him about the ideas she had for making the apartment more homely. He let her rattle on for a while then with feigned reluctance got up. He needed to work some more on his address, he said. He had been practicing for days but there were passages that he was still not completely satisfied with. He used the phone by the bed to have Hunter summon the speechwriters back to the library.

'It's a pity Callaghan left the team. You always said no one understood what you wanted to say like he did.'

'Maybe so, but he's gone and we have to make do.' He changed the subject. He was worried about her and the upcoming round of ceremonies. 'Hunt says the forecast is continuing very cold with a possibility of snow Inauguration Day. Maybe you should consider at least passing up on the parade?'

She wouldn't hear of it. 'Of course I'm going to be there. Miss my husband's first Inaugural? I'll be fine. I've a warm coat and they're putting up screens round the viewing stand against the wind.'

He planted a farewell kiss on the dark hair. She smiled back, then frowned worriedly. 'I haven't been much of a wife to you so far, have I? It's been hard; first the election and now this damn operation. And the thought of living in that great place frightens me. Do you think we'll ever be able to make a home over there?'

He shrugged. 'We'll manage somehow. Every other First Family has.'

'And it will be okay to have children in the White House, won't it?' she asked anxiously, leaning forward after him for reassurance as he moved away. 'Jackie Kennedy did, didn't she?'

Karen Lipscombe had asked Elaine Manken's staff to stay on under her. All had agreed save one, whom she had replaced with a girl of her own age, Jodi DuCharme, a Californian like herself but who lived in Washington. Jodi would be her guide, her eyes. In the final days before the Inauguration, they drove together in at the south gate of the White House.

A guard located Karen Lipscombe's name on his clipboard. 'To see Ms Rabinowicz, right? Okay, ladies, you park over there where it says Visitors. Then you go to the main desk inside the entrance and identify yourselves. They'll phone through to the secretary's office to let them know you're here.'

There were four phones on Magda Rabinowicz's desk. 'Red is a direct line to the Oval Office, blue goes into the switchboard, green is another direct line to the second-floor private apartment and grey is an outside line bypassing the switchboard.'

Magda Rabinowicz was General Ivory's personal executive secretary. It was she who had suggested this meeting, a familiarization tour. Karen appreciated the gesture but was daunted by the prospect, anticipating a steely-haired shrew, fiercely protective of her boss. Instead Magda proved to be a young forty, trim and friendly. The office she ran had a busy, informal atmosphere. Karen determined to keep it that way.

61

Magda nominated one of her subordinates to familiarize Jodi with the West Wing while she and Karen got acquainted.

'You pick up a receiver, ask for a name, a number, the switchboard connects you. Simple as that. Any person, anywhere. There is a whole floor of the basement filled with Army signalers. They can't locate who you want, they go on trying till they find them, even if the person is on the other side of the world.'

Karen nodded. Everyone had heard of the legendary White House switchboard. 'My chief likes to place his own calls.'

'No problem, they can give him a dial tone if he prefers. My president was the same to begin with. In the end though it's just easier to pick up and say, "Get me so-and-so".'

First Family members were allocated code names. 'So, for instance, the First Lady can pick up a phone and say "Singer to Saber" and straight away she's connected to her daughter, Clarice, in Dayton, Ohio. Could be she is in her bedroom on the second floor or in a limousine somewhere or on Air Force One out in mid-Pacific. Doesn't matter.'

Karen listened, trying to take everything in. She was grateful for the way Magda made no reference to her sight. She seemed to take it for granted that Karen would be up to the job.

'Would you like to eat?' Magda suggested. She led off along the corridor and down a short staircase to the White House mess. The 1 p.m. second sitting, restricted by pass to senior staff only, was the most exclusive luncheon club in Washington, she explained. Especially when the President graced it with his presence. Otherwise there was an early sitting at twelve, open to all who worked in the executive mansion or, for those in a hurry, a quick-service canteen across in the Old Executive Office Building.

A dignified chief steward in a white coat greeted Magda by name and asked how was the President today? Magda thanked him and introduced Karen as her successor. He welcomed her and said he looked forward to seeing her frequently in the future. Several senior figures in the administration acknowledged Magda casually as they were shown to their table. Some others stared openly at the Elvis headset. Karen was used to that. A Filipino steward brought the menus. She chose smoked salmon and pasta.

'And to drink? A glass of wine or a spritzer?'

'Water for me. I'm not much of a drinker.'

The menus were heavily subsidized and invariably delicious, Magda explained. Mess privileges, especially second sitting privileges, were highly prized. 'It's the badge of authority round here, proof positive you belong to the inner circle.'

The Mess was filling up fast. Magda pointed out a few faces. 'The guy over there at the round table is Rex Coffey, Chief of the Military Office. You'll find the military run just about everything here. Including this mess, incidentally.'

As well as the obvious assets like Air Force One and Marine One, the presidential helicopter, she said, the military also owned the White House communications, the computer systems, the medical unit, the White House garage together with the cars and drivers, the TV unit and Teleprompters and Camp David. Rex could help out in a lot of ways and it paid to stay in with him.

The rest of the clientele Magda dismissed with a sniff. 'Staffers, advance men, media manipulators, personal aides, special assistants: in other words, mice.' Mice, not her term but a good one, and there were upward of 3,000 of the little pests, who were the bane of the White House. 'They're hired by the Chief of Staff or his deputy and suffer badly from Potomac fever. You know, "the President wants this . . ." or "the First Lady says . . ."

And they use the imperial "we" a lot. Even cabinet officers get intimidated. Don't take any flak from them. Me, I look them in the eye and say, "Really, I must remember to check that with the President when I see him ten minutes from now. And for the record what was your name again?"' She laughed, 'Never fails. Or you can call up Rex and have him strike the guy's name off the Air Force One list. That brings the toughest to heel.'

Unfortunately it was a fact that the White House brought out the worst in people. Luckily the President's secretary was pretty well untouchable.

Karen thought of Elaine and was not so sure.

The meal indeed tasted delicious. Neither wanted dessert. Magda signed the tab and suggested they return to her office for coffee. The Chief Steward was on hand to bid farewell as they left. He trusted he would be seeing more of Miss Lipscombe in days to come.

Magda apologized for not being able to let Karen have a peek in the Oval Office itself. 'Most days my president likes to work in his study in back of the office but today there's a meeting for the Mid East peace process in progress.' Visitors always insisted on photographs of themselves in the Oval Office. 'Often it's the only tangible evidence they have of a meeting with the US President and vitally important to them domestically. All their entourages want to get in on the act, it can take forever sometimes and the protocol officers go frantic.'

'Your chief prefers the study?'

'Often they do. More private, for one thing. They can leave papers out, have clutter on the desk, generally act more like normal people. The Oval Office is more for formal occasions. It can be nice in summer though with the patio. And presidents differ. Ronald Reagan used the Oval Office exclusively and installed his chief of staff in the study.'

She explained about mail. Mail was the biggest item on the secretary's workload. It arrived at the White House by the ton. Literally. Most went out to Anacostia for screening, then was brought in to the mailroom in the basement where it was screened again and sorted.

'Personal mail from relatives and friends of the First Family is distinguished by a five-digit numeric code on the envelope. The sorters will pass them through unopened. My president likes to slit any from his son and daughter himself. Sort of like a ritual for him. You get to recognize the handwriting in time. The rest I deal with. The First Lady's mail is handled by her own staff. The mailroom also sends up a selection from the unsolicited mail.'

One tip, Magda said: avoid replies going out over the President's signature wherever possible. 'That way if there's a boob, and there always will be, it doesn't look so bad.' There was a story that Jackie Kennedy had signed a letter written by one of her secretaries congratulating a Roman Catholic archbishop on the birth of a baby.

The President's daily schedule was the responsibility of the appointments office. The social secretary dealt with private entertaining. Invitations to official banquets and receptions were handled by the protocol office, including eight calligraphers to hand-letter invitation cards. Karen's eyes widened in disbelief. Eight calligraphers? For invitation cards?

Other topics were covered in rapid-fire succession. 'Security. One of the biggest headaches is obtaining passes for First Family visitors. Try to cultivate good relations with the Secret Service. They can smooth your path or make life hell by the way they apply the regulations. Nothing maddens a president or a first lady like having an old friend held at the gates. The ultimate decider on clearances is the Attorney-General, so a call to his office or a quiet word when he's passing through to speak with the President can work miracles. You don't do that too often though. It's a question of judgement.'

Full security clearances, including mandatory FBI field investigation, took six weeks on average to come through, she added, but if there was any kind of glitch the procedure could drag out for months. Temporary passes were liable to be withdrawn inside that time, so Karen would have to keep pushing for clearance on any staff she hired.

A presidential aide tapped at the door. He had come to collect some documents. Magda made him sign for them. He lingered a minute, obviously angling for an introduction to Magda's guest. Magda did not oblige and he departed.

'You must keep a track of documents passing through. If a copy goes astray the easiest way out for a staffer is to blame the secretary's office. Keep logs and get signatures for every last item. It's time-wasting and you'll draw a lot of flak but it can save your life. It has mine.'

Karen asked about facilities for storing classified material. Magda opened a closet behind her desk to reveal the massive gray steel door of a walk-in safe. There was also a strong-room on the basement level reached by an elevator. She offered to have a member of her staff show Karen over. Maybe some other time but thanks anyway, Karen said. 'And thank you for all your help. I truly appreciate it.'

It was nothing, Magda assured her. She was happy to help. 'By the way, I almost forgot, these arrived for you.' She produced a packet of letters.

'Already?'

''Fraid so. First of many.' She held out her hand. 'Well, I guess this is where we part. I wish you luck. It can be tough, I know. The White House is wonderful and it's been a privilege to work here. But in a way although I shall be sad to leave this place, I won't be sorry, if that makes any sense.'

Karen said she understood. Magda walked her down to the end of the passage.

'I have to leave you here.' She pressed her hand. 'But listen, if you ever need help or advice, or simply want to talk, strictly between ourselves and off the record, I'll let you have my number before I go.'

'I'd like to think I can take you up on that.'

'Please do, I mean it.'

Back in her own office at Blair House, Karen found another letter waiting on her desk, hand-addressed with her name. She slit it open and flicked the focus on the Elvis to close-up.

Dear Karen, it read in a loopy scrawl, *I'm so glad you have come to work for my husband. I do want us both to be friends. Jack tells me you are having problems finding a place to live. Why don't you stop with us at the White House till you find your feet? The rooms on the third floor have a terrific view and you can be as private as you like. Think it over and let me know. Do say yes!*

It was signed, *Sincerely yours, Caro Meade.*

Well, that was certainly a kind thought. And it would solve her most pressing problem. Karen hated to be beholden, though. She was conscious of a qualm at accepting hospitality from Jack Meade's wife. She wondered about her motive too.

She set Caro Meade's offer aside for the moment and turned her attention to the first of the letters Magda had given her. It contained a single sheet of paper and the message was distinctly unfriendly. Gummed letters cut from a magazine spelled out: *Cyborg Bitch! Elaine was worth ten of you!*

Her first hate mail.

They were calling it 'The People's Presidency' and already it was billed as the biggest Inaugural ever. Certainly the most expensive. Fifty million dollars, five days of celebrations, 1,500 stars and acts. Half Hollywood was in the line-up on stage. Fireworks and parades, free food, solemn commemorations and speeches, partying, balls, festivals and entertainments. Above all it was to be a popular event, something for everybody, as the President-elect had stated. The theme was Renewal. A Fresh Beginning. 'America Awake!' was the slogan he had chosen.

'I have a vision . . . !' the President-elect declared from the steps of the Lincoln Memorial. Flanked by cohorts of celebrities beneath the stony gaze of his mighty predecessor, he had opened the People's Inaugural, as he named it, with a homage to Martin Luther King's great speech from this same spot some forty years earlier.

The Democrats were back in office.

Today's Democrats were different from their predecessors; more glamorous, more radical. More sophisticated. The President-elect was forty-five. His wife thirty-three. Together they would make the youngest couple to inhabit the White House since the Kennedys. The media spoke of a second New Frontier and other catch-phrases evocative of Camelot.

But Jack Kennedy had been murdered and Camelot ended forever when this President was still a child and his wife as yet unborn.

4

Four a.m. on Inauguration Day, and the Secret Service began passing the first of an estimated 400,000 spectators through metal detectors in the Pentagon car parks. Throughout the night police and federal agents had been sealing manhole covers, checking roofs and windows along the parade route. Snipers donned electrically heated survival suits preparatory to taking up their freezing vigil on the rooftops. All told, 20,000 police, military, federal and Secret Service would be on duty. Today was the biggest event in their calendar and they had been working toward it for weeks. In the words of one senior agent, 'Two presidents, twice as many nuts.'

To date, 1,800 specific death threats had been made to federal agencies or via the media. The White House mailroom also reported an extra-heavy crop of hate mail. At Secret Service headquarters on G Street across from the World Bank, the computers of the Protective Research Section were continuously at work chewing out updates on the latest security position surrounding the incumbent President and his successor: 200,000 names were held on file, of whom 22,000 had at some time uttered a threat against either man. Nineteen hundred of these were graded 'potentially dangerous', of whom 200 were currently listed Category A – 'known to harbor a grudge – believed capable of violent action'. Their names had been circulated to every law enforcement agency in the country and all bar eighteen had so far been traced, interviewed and, if judged necessary, either detained on some legal pretext or placed under surveillance. Details and photographs of those that remained had been issued to every officer on duty today

69

and intensive efforts were being made to track them down. Elsewhere two white males had already been arrested carrying concealed weapons within the cordoned-off zone around the Capitol but it transpired this was a routine criminal matter with no political connections.

Meanwhile a biting wind was dashing intermittent snowflakes against the capital's windows. The weather was the one ally they had. The cold would keep windows sealed and the wind would throw off any rifleman's aim. The cold and Caro Meade's health had also put paid to any dreams of a Jimmy Carter type stroll down Pennsylvania Avenue. Presidential exposure would be kept to an absolute minimum. They were even angling to have the snow close down the swearing-in ceremony completely, forcing it to be held inside the Capitol but thus far the President-elect had vetoed the proposal.

Already at this hour, the sidewalks outside Blair House and along Lafayette Square were filling up with sightseers braving the freezing temperature in the hope of an early glimpse of the Meades. The police had closed off the street to non-essential traffic and new arrivals were spilling out into the roadway between the numerous TV outside broadcast trucks parked out front, their big dish transmitters aimed skyward in anticipation. Behind the police line outside the front entrance, parka-clad news correspondents thrust microphones at early callers and jockeyed for position for 'stand-ups'.

Inside, on the topmost floor, Rear Admiral Creighton Thomas, the President-elect's Pentagon appointed doctor, was preparing to shave when Chief of Staff Irwin Hunter and Press Secretary Barney Nikolis, the two advisers closest to the future President, came in. 'What's the view like out front?' they asked. 'We can't see anything from the rear.' Nikolis parted the curtains and studied the crowd waiting in the cold. 'Must be a coupla thousand,' he murmured with satisfaction.

The Admiral asked was the President-elect awake? Hunter told him yes, and in great shape. 'He's working on his speech.' The two then thanked the Admiral and left.

Two floors below, the future President paced up and down the Blair House library in his bathrobe with the big embroidered A of his college football team, a sheaf of notes in his fist. From time to time he flexed his shoulders to relieve some stiffness. Today would be another back-breaker. Especially with the Secret Service insisting he wear a bulletproof overcoat lined with thirty pounds of protective kevlar.

He was rehearsing his address: '. . . *the gift of citizenship carries great responsibility . . . the time has come when delay can no longer be tolerated . . . therefore let there no longer be doubt, either at home or abroad . . . whatever the cost, whatever the sacrifice, whatever the hardship, whatever the struggle . . . we will rebuild . . .*'

He paused and drank some black coffee. These were the words he would be remembered by. These were the words which would set the tone for the Presidency.

Last night he had attended a pre-Inaugural gala at the Mayflower Hotel for 200 invited guests. From there he had gone on to a private celebration with the cabinet and their wives, then back to Blair House with a few of the inner circle for a final round of champagne. Strangely enough he felt no tiredness, only a sense of steadily rising excitement.

He halted in front of the mirror. His hair was smoothed and damp from the shower. The barber was due in half an hour to give him a final trim. He had been careful not to drink too much last night and his face betrayed no hint of puffiness. A light daily session under the ultraviolet lamp had brought on a look of health and vigor without too blatantly tanning.

With a discreet tap at the door Karen Lipscombe entered.

71

'Good morning, Senator. You sent for me?'

She stood just inside the room facing him, back straight, head up, the light gleaming from her devotedly brushed hair. The low-vision goggles trained on him like gunsights. He found the combination of the impersonal, almost menacing, helmet and fragile femininity oddly arousing. Of course one never knew exactly how much she was seeing.

'Is Mrs Meade awake yet?'

'I believe so, yes, sir.'

'Will you check, please, she has everything she needs. We have a tight schedule. And that maid of hers, May . . . Mary . . . ?'

'Maxine, sir. Maxine Ryan.'

'Yeah, well whoever, for Christsakes keep her on the ball today.' Maxine Ryan was another campaign worker, who had volunteered as Caro Meade's dresser for the Inauguration. 'Seems she was all over the place last night except where she was wanted and my wife couldn't get a hold of her.'

Karen promised to see to it.

He resumed his pacing. The transition was concerning him, he said. He had heard that when the Clinton people took over from the Republicans they were disorganized. They had not done their homework and the pre-planning was sloppy. He was determined his administration would set a better example right from the start.

They had been over the ground before but he wanted to re-emphasize certain points. The phone directory was to be gotten out promptly. That was a priority. And he wanted it right. Nothing looked so dumb as not being able to locate people. The office plan likewise. Division heads were responsible for ensuring staff had parking passes assigned. Proper coordination with the GSA was another vital area. Too often incoming appointees put the backs up civil servants with their arrogance. He would come down hard on that. Cooperation not confrontation.

He paused. He was not done yet. She could sense him groping for the right words. Strange how high office changed a man, made him wary of committing himself in different ways.

It was about the van smash, he told her, coming to the point. The cosmetician, Frankie and the others, Humphrey the valet. An awkward business to handle because they were still on sick leave. Not really hurt though, thank God.

He had decided to let them go. Hell, he didn't need a valet anyway. The White House was crawling with housemen. Its own barber too, come to that. The daily massage was an indulgence he didn't need now there was an indoor pool again.

'I've asked Jay Leeder to take care of them. Find them jobs in the civil service, whatever's appropriate. They've served me loyally. I'd like you to compose a personal letter to each for me to sign and select a suitable gift to accompany it. I leave the details to you.'

'I'll see to it.'

He nodded. That still left Elaine Manken. Elaine could pose problems if she became vindictive. 'It would be politic for you to call her on my behalf, let her know I'm thinking of her today.'

Karen swallowed, 'If that's what you want, sir.'

He took a last glance at the pages of his speech. 'I made a few changes again.' He handed it to her. 'Nothing big but it flows easier now. Have it retyped and bring me a fair copy as soon you can.'

'Right away, sir.'

'My address to Congress at the inaugural luncheon, you have that to hand?'

'Right here, sir.' She held out a red folder.

'Okay, I don't need it now. Just make sure it's there when I do.'

'Barney Nikolis will carry copies of both your speeches today, sir, and ensure that the autocues are working. And

73

Captain Bong, your military aide, will have back-ups as well.'

'You'll liaise with Barney over changes to the texts for release to the press?'

'Yes, sir, just as soon as you okay the final versions.'

'Those are the last edits. Tell Barney he can go ahead with them.' 'So that's it then. The words are set in stone.' He mused for a spell, still looking at her. 'This may be the last time we meet as ordinary citizens together, for a few years at least.'

'Yes, sir.' The zoom camera clicked, changing focus fractionally as he moved closer. 'I want you to know, sir, what a privilege it is to be working with you. We all of us feel the same way. You're going to be a truly great president, sir. I believe that.'

He sighed and reached out to touch the fringe of her hair where it escaped under the edge of the helmet. 'You feel very humble in my presence, don't you?' he asked.

Her mouth trembled. She nodded dumbly.

'Then try to imagine,' he said gently, 'how very much more humble I feel in yours.'

She would have died for him then.

Across town in a small apartment with only the television for company, Elaine Manken sat in bed nursing a box of Kleenex. Tears trickled intermittently down her cheeks. On the screen the image of the future President tracked back and forth in a pre-run of the day's ceremonies. Shots of the campaign trail in different states, of a younger, leaner Jack Meade addressing crowds in featureless meeting halls. Speeches that were harsher then, more strident, without the polish that was to come later. Images too of the followers from that period, younger themselves with a weary embattled look that she recognized all too well. The tears were flowing again even before she saw her own face appear among them.

It was some moments before she heard the warble of the phone at the bedside.

'Elaine?'

The voice was distantly familiar.

'Elaine, this is Karen. Karen Lipscombe from California. Remember me?'

'Oh,' she swallowed. Voices from the past. They made it harder to bear. 'Yes, of course I remember. You were . . .' she choked back the word she had been about to say: 'blind'. 'You went home to LA,' she managed.

'Yes, and now I'm back again.' The clipped way Karen said it suggested she knew too well how she was tagged by people. 'Listen though, how about you? How are you doing?'

Elaine stared out the window without answering.

'Elaine? Elaine, are you there?'

'I hear you're working with Jack now. Isn't that right?' She was amazed at the calmness of her voice. 'You've got my job.'

'Yes, they called me in last week. Originally for an aide posting. Ben Kotz was transferred across to State and—'

'Ben Kotz was fired.' The words came out with brutal contempt. 'There never was a State posting. They tricked him into resigning from the President's staff. Ben had worked for the campaign from the beginning without a break. He would have done anything for Jack Meade. Now it's as if he never existed. Loyalty means nothing any more.'

'But that's terrible. I had no idea. Surely there must have been some reason?'

'The same as there should have been for me? Or Stewart Joll? Or Marilyn Kubitschek? Jay Leeder told Leon Perry when he was let go that the President didn't want a cabal around him.'

'A cabal?'

'A kitchen cabinet. Jay said the President wanted a fresh start, no cliques or favorites. Everyone to get the same treatment. Didn't all our years' work count for anything? We believed in Jack Meade before most of you people round him ever heard his name. Leon was best man at the President's wedding. Now he can't even get through on the phone.' In spite of herself Elaine began to sob loudly.

'Elaine, Elaine, it's not like that, really. The President does care. I know he would like to do something for you. For all of you who have not yet been found places. It's just that these things take time.'

'Is that what you were told to say?' There was a silence at the other end of the line. 'If it's true, why doesn't Jack Meade call me himself? Answer me that if you can.'

Over at Blair House, Karen Lipscombe replaced the receiver. That was cheap of Jack Meade, and unlike him, to duck out of making the call himself, today of all days. Still, it was done and she had enough other business to occupy her.

For how long the patient had lain drifting into and out of sleep he had no means of telling. When finally he awoke his brain was clear and the fever gone. It was early morning and a kind of stillness had descended on the ward. He lifted his head and listened but could detect no sounds of anyone in the vicinity. The sense of anxiety returned, sharper than before. If he stayed here they would come to give him another shot. And then another and another till his mind rotted and all memories of who and what he was were lost for good. Taking a deep breath, he slid from the bed and stood up. His head felt muzzy, his limbs still leaden, the extremities tingling numbly. Clutching the furniture for support, he shuffled across the floor and opened the door a crack. The only signs of life were at the distant end of the corridor.

The door opposite was partially open. Without conscious intention, he lurched across and peered inside. It was a single room, the light on, the bed tumbled but empty. From sounds within he guessed the occupant was in the bathroom. At that moment the door to the next room down opened and a man in medical whites came backing out with a gurney. Another nurse followed the first, maneuvering the trolley out carefully. Under the sheet was a dark-haired man, apparently semi-conscious. A third nurse held up a bottle attached to a drip. They passed the door where he was cowering without noticing him and disappeared down the corridor.

He waited till they had turned the corner and then, still moving like an automaton, stumbled to the room that had just been vacated. The layout inside was the same as the first, another single bedroom. Nausea twisted in his belly. Shutting the door, he slumped on the bed, exhausted. After a minute or two, he began to feel stronger. Anxiety to escape urged him on. He checked the closet. An officer's uniform hung inside. Winter blues. Lieutenant-commander's stripes, a part of his brain registered through the drug haze. Shirt and tie on a hanger alongside. Shoes beneath. Clean underwear. Even a gold-braided cap on the shelf. He stood for a moment absorbing the find. From somewhere outside came the distant scream of a plane engine running up to take-off power. An idea slowly took shape in his mind. He dragged the coat and pants off the hanger and pulled them roughly on. The fit was tight; their owner was similar in height but lighter built. They would do. On a hanger behind was a navy pattern raincoat. His heart thudding, he scooped it up with the rest and made for the bathroom.

Safe inside he locked the door. He blinked at himself in the mirror. The face that stared back at him was puffy from inactivity and gray with stubble, the eyes sunken with anxiety and fear. Small wonder no one believed him. He scarcely recognized himself.

The room occupant's shaving tackle was conveniently to hand by the basin. He set to work. His fingers seemed to have forgotten how to use a razor. He grimaced as several days' growth sliced away under his fumbling hand. It seemed to take forever. He prayed no one would come in to straighten the room before he had finished. When finally it was done, he washed himself and brushed his hair. He looked in the mirror again. A little more human at least, he decided. The scars from the surgery had healed over completely, he was glad to see. Hard to tell if it made a difference in his present state. If only he weren't so weak.

In a pocket of the coat he found a key which fitted the locker beside the bed. Inside was a wallet containing a military ID. Apparently he was now Ferris J. Casey, aged forty-one, currently attached to the Naval Dental Center, Bethesda Naval Hospital, Maryland. So a dental surgeon. The Washington posting accounted for the winter uniform. The photo showed a heavy-jawed man in spectacles; a poor likeness to himself but it would have to suffice. Also in the wallet were $140 odd plus half a dozen credit cards. He stuffed cash and cards into his pocket. With luck it would be some while before the theft was detected.

He went back out into the corridor.

Next door to the ward where he had been put was a service recess with containers of used linen. Before leaving he stripped the sheets and coverings off his own bed and dumped them in one of the bins. Anyone who came looking would assume he had been discharged or transferred. That might buy him time before pursuit got underway. Then he tottered toward the elevators. It took all his concentration to reach the doors at the far end. Instructions from his brain seemed to take a long time to reach his limbs and he felt terribly frail but he could manage. It was a question of keeping going.

At this hour there were few people about and the dental officer's uniform made it natural that he should be on the premises. No one gave him a second glance. He took the elevator to the ground floor and followed the signs to the main exit. He was still rocky from the drugs they had pumped him with. It was an effort to push his lethargic brain into figuring out some kind of a plan. All his energies had been bent on escaping from upstairs without a thought to what came next. He was not even certain what day it was.

The duty clerk was absent from the desk. The patient was approaching the main doors when to his alarm he saw the pretty nurse from his first wakening heading toward him from the outside. He turned aside to a bulletin board, supporting himself against the wall till she had gone.

He was sweating as he pushed through the doors, the nausea hitting him again, but the fresh air revived him. He had made it this far. His mind was beginning to clear too. For the first time a sense of purpose came to him. Washington. He must make it to the capital.

Getting into town proved simple. A Navy bus ran a regular shuttle. His main worry was bumping into someone else who might have seen him on the ward but the bus when it came was full of kids. Downtown, he hailed a cab to take him out to the airport.

'Washington? I'll check on the computer, sir,' said the clerk on the ticket counter. Again he was in luck. 'I have United to Atlanta departing in fifteen minutes with onward connection to Washington, arriving 10 a.m.'

'I'll take that.'

'Certainly, sir. Single or round-trip?'

'Single.'

He proffered the dentist's MasterCharge. There was another anxious moment as he signed the slip.

'That's fine. Thank you, sir. Window or aisle seat?'

'Window.' His tongue felt thick in his mouth but the clerk seemed to notice nothing.

'I'm sorry, sir. It appears only aisle seats are available.

The flight is almost full up. The Inauguration, you see,' she apologized.

He stared at her stupidly. 'The Inauguration?'

Still watching the screen, she missed the dismay in his face. 'Wish I could get up there to see the parade someday. Maybe next time.'

His heart hammered against his chest. The Inauguration was today? How long had he lain in the hospital? His eyes flicked to the clock above the woman's head. If the flight reached Washington at ten that gave him – Mother of God, two hours, no more. Panic surged inside him.

'Here's your ticket, sir. Atlanta–Washington National, boarding now, Gate 3. My pleasure, sir. Have a good flight. I hope you catch the parade.'

He reeled away, dazed.

The announcer was already calling the flight. With shaking hands he stopped at the newsagent and bought copies of the *New York Times* and *Washington Post*. Frantically he scanned the headlines. They were devoted to the Inauguration and the new Presidency. The *Post* carried an article by Leon Perry accusing his former mentor of abandoning his populist roots and allowing his policies to be dictated by a group of elitist intellectuals, lawyers and economists. Nothing else. What was happening to him?

Nurse Phillips was late on duty. The Chief Nurse gave her a scowl and sent her to check on the patient without a name. She found the bed stripped and empty but something in the way it had been left made her suspicious. She looked in the laundry and saw the sheets dumped in the bin. Then she glanced in the other side rooms. There was no sign of the man anywhere. She hurried back up to the desk.

'I think we've got a runner,' she informed them.

When security arrived they were unimpressed. 'You

sure he hasn't just been moved somewhere else?' suggested a tall sergeant. 'I mean why does a guy strip his bunk before he takes off? Doesn't make sense.'

To fool dumb cops, Nurse Phillips felt like saying but she held her tongue.

'You positive he couldn't have transferred out?' asked the second man. 'Did you check?'

'We checked,' confirmed the Chief Nurse laconically.

'Yeah, well, hell this place,' sighed the Sergeant. 'Who knows where anybody is, I mean?' The others agreed he had a point. 'You two ladies just came on shift, right?'

'When they transfer a patient out, they mark it up on the chart,' objected Phillips. 'Right there –' she pointed to the wall behind. 'And they haven't,' she added.

The Chief Nurse backed her up. 'We keep good records.'

'Okey-dokey,' said the Sergeant wearily, 'we do it by the book.' He took out a pen. 'Patient's name?'

Phillips and the Chief Nurse exchanged looks. 'He had no ID,' answered the Chief Nurse. 'He said his name was Meade, Jack Meade.'

'Meade, Jack. NMI,' the Sergeant repeated. 'Description?'

'Medium height, five-eleven, six?' Phillips glanced across at her colleague for confirmation. 'Hundred sixty pounds, light hair,' she continued. 'Age forty-two, maybe a little more. Oh, and he was white.'

'White Caucasian male,' the Sergeant grunted as he wrote. 'What was he in for?' he asked curiously.

Both women snorted with laughter. 'He thinks he's going to be the next President of the US!' It was a good joke and the Sergeant was still chuckling when he passed his report in to control a few minutes later. They thought it funny too and there were more laughs all round but someone higher up the chain of command didn't see the joke at all and the details were put on the teleprinter to the Secret Service. That was also about the time someone else remembered that the missing man's fingerprints had been taken the previous day.

By then it was soon after 9 a.m. January 20th: barely three hours to go till the Inauguration.

United were on time. The wait for the next leg was twenty-five minutes. The man now calling himself Commander Casey was still in a state of shock. How was it possible for his disappearance to have been missed? Whose were the photographs in the papers? Had they found a double to stand in for him? He had searched the newspapers in vain for answers. Bewilderment and doubt combined with despair in his heart.

He found a bank of televisions on the concourse. '. . . *the President-elect and Caro Meade appearing at last night's pre-Inaugural gala thrown by friends and supporters from the world of film . . .* ' The cameras lingered on the new leader's features. The patient gave another strangled cry. It was himself. His own face, eyes, mouth. his walk, his gestures. Himself on stage hand in hand with his wife, kissing her on the lips, being kissed . . . Himself to the life.

No! It couldn't be. It wasn't possible. He tore his horrified gaze from the screens. And yet . . . and yet there it was happening before his very eyes.

His heart began to race again, his breath coming in short, panting gasps as the panic struck. His vision seemed to be pulsing in and out and the tingling sensation returned to his hands and arms. He leaned his head against a pillar and took long, deep breaths, willing himself to relax.

A passing attendant stopped and asked, 'Are you feeling okay, sir?'

He nodded. 'Motion sickness. Be fine in a minute,' he said thickly.

The thing had to be faced. Ducking the obvious was no escape. Acknowledgement of a problem was the first step to beating it. The impossible had happened. How was not so important right now as what to do next.

Someone must believe him.

Partly because of the urgency his brain was working better now. Some of the fog seemed to have lifted from his thought processes. He found a bank of telephones in a secluded corner and dialed from memory: 202–224–3121.

'United States Capitol.'

'Put me through to Speaker Webster, will you.'

A click, then a young woman's voice, 'Speaker's Office. How may I help you?'

'Yes, this is Senator Meade. Is the Speaker there?'

'Oh, why I'm not sure, Senator, please hold a moment, while I find out.'

There was a wait of several seconds before she came back on. 'I'm sorry, Senator, but the Speaker just stepped out for a moment. Can I have him call you back, sir?'

'Look, please can you page him for me? It's urgent that I contact him.'

She would try, the woman said. Again there was a wait. 'Hello, hello!' he called impatiently.

'Senator, I'm sorry, I've tried raising the Speaker on his mobile but I'm getting no response. I think he may have gone over to the Senate side.'

'You don't understand, it's vital that I speak with him!' His voice began to crack. 'There's been a switch. The one who says he's the President isn't me!'

'What was that again?'

'They've pulled a switch! I've been replaced by a double! The Speaker has to be warned. He must stop the swearing-in . . . !'   He heard the girl choke and then the line went dead.

'Wow,' said the Speaker's aide up in Washington, blowing out her cheeks, 'there certainly are some crazies out there.'

'Who was it?' one of the men in the office asked.

'Some clown claiming the President-elect has been replaced by a man from Mars or something. Wanted to have Dan call off the Inauguration, can you believe?' She shook her head in disbelief. 'He had Jack Meade's voice off pat. Almost fooled me for a minute.'

Standing instructions required that all hoax calls be reported. The Capitol police traced the call number and, because it concerned the President-elect, passed the details to the Secret Service. An agent contacted the Atlanta Police Department.

'I'm sorry, Senator, Mr and Mrs Tilson already left for the Capitol. They drove in with friends. I don't have a phone number for the car.'

Trembling, the patient cut the connection. He replaced the receiver and moved away toward the other side of the concourse. The phone was no use. No one believed him. Only face to face would convince people. But how to get near anyone who counted? He came to a row of offices, one with the door half open, inside, a blonde in a blue uniform stooped over a desk. Alone. The sight of the uniform brought the glimmering of an idea into his head.

Pulling the cap down to hide his eyes, he tapped at the door. She glanced up inquiringly, 'Yes? May I help you?'

'Sorry to disturb you, ma'am. Commander Casey, USN,' he held out his identity. 'And yes, you can help me. I need to call Washington right away. I don't like to use a public phone . . .'

'Oh, that's fine, Commander, go right ahead. Use this one.'

'That's very kind of you.' He hesitated, 'It's . . .'

She caught on at once. 'Of course, I understand. I have to go out anyway. Please feel free. Just dial 9 for an outside line.' Smiling brightly, she stepped out, closing the door behind her.

He dialed.

'Directory. What name, please?'

'Blair House, Washington, DC. Most likely it'll be listed under US Government.'

A pause. 'Blair House, 1651 Pennsylvania Avenue NW?'

'That's the one.'

'The number you require is Area Code 202–395–7041,' the computer-generated tones informed him tinnily.

He tapped in the digits and waited.

Six hundred miles to the north, traffic on the guest mansion switchboard was hectic. Nola Mooney had just placed a person-to-person to the White House Chief of Staff for Mr Hunter. She cut her connection, saw the lamp blinking on the next incoming and, scarcely pausing for breath, flicked the switch to take the call.

'Blair House, how may I help you?' she said for the hundredth time that morning.

The display was showing up a dialing code she did not recognize but there was no mistaking the familiar, confident tones of the President-elect on the line. 'This is the Senator speaking. Is that Marjorie?'

'Oh no, Senator, this is Nola. Did you want to speak with her, sir?'

'I apologize, I mistook your voice. No, I wanted my wife.'

'Mrs Meade?' Nola could not keep the surprise out of her response. 'But we understood your wife was with you at the church, sir.'

His mouth went dry. How could he have been so stupid? The first item on the inaugural schedule called for the incoming President and his wife to attend morning service at St John's Episcopal, the President's church, on Lafayette Square. Right at this moment the future First Couple should be kneeling side by side in pew 54, traditionally set aside for the First Family's use.

Somehow he managed to force himself to utter a

chuckle. 'I'm sorry, I don't know what I'm saying this morning. I meant to ask for Captain Bong. Or is he still over at the Pentagon?'

The trick worked. Nola couldn't help chuckling back. 'I understand, sir. I'll just check for you.' She glanced over at the status board displaying the whereabouts of all senior officers in the entourage. Captain Bong was the President-elect's chief military aide. 'Hello, Senator? Captain Bong is in his office at the Pentagon right now. Shall I have him call you, sir?'

'No, don't bother. I'll do it myself. Just give me his number, will you.'

'Certainly, Senator. Captain Bong can be reached on 703–545–6700, extension 5901.'

'5901. Thank you, Nola.'

'It's a pleasure, sir, and our best wishes to you and Mrs Meade today from all of us here.'

'Appreciate that. Thank you for all your help during our stay. Goodbye.'

The lamp on the switchboard blinked off and Nola cut the connection automatically. She puzzled for a second because Senator Meade had come in on a non-government line. Maybe he had picked up a phone hooked to another network. There was no time to bother with that, though. More calls were coming in all the time.

The computers in the basement logged the call and the number away for future record and for the moment there the matter rested.

Down in Atlanta, the patient hung up, sweating. Damn, how could he have been so stupid as to forget about the church attendance? The switchboard must think he was mad but the mistake had given him another idea. He waited till his breathing had eased and dialed again.

'Presidential Attaché's office, Captain Richard Bong speaking.'

Pitching his voice low and modulating his accent to

suggest a Signal Corps telephonist, he said, 'Captain Bong? This is Blair House. Senator Meade wishes to speak with you.'

He paused and held the receiver away from his mouth a moment. 'No, not that one, the blue cover,' he snapped out in his own voice as if calling across a room. Then, 'That you, Bing?' he spoke into the phone.

'Good morning, Senator. What can I do for you, sir?'

Captain Richard 'Bing' Bong was the newly appointed Naval Aide to the incoming President. At midday he would be departing his Pentagon office to take up permanent station at the White House.

'Bing, I'm sending an officer over to you. A Commander Casey, a dental surgeon who's joining my medical team. I'd like you to fit him out with a pass from your office for the White House and for the parade. Mrs Meade's teeth have been giving pain and in this cold I want him on hand today.'

'I'm sorry to hear that, Senator. The pass will be no problem. I'll have the papers ready when Commander Casey gets here.'

'Fine. I'll have Hunter provide a letter of authorization for me to sign.'

'Understood, sir.'

'You're joining up with us at the White House when we go to meet with Ivory, am I right?'

'That's correct, sir. I'll be departing the Pentagon in forty minutes but this office will remain fully manned and my assistant, Lieutenant Macmillan, will attend to the Commander's requirements.'

'Good man.'

He hung up. The voice had passed, but then it would. That much they couldn't deprive him of.

This was only the easiest stage.

The blonde was chatting up a pilot across the way as he let himself out. She gave him a mock salute and he nodded his thanks. The strain of the last few minutes had left him drained. He rested on a vacant seat and checked his watch. Only a short while to go till the Washington flight departed. If there was anything he would need, now was the time to get it.

Downstairs in the retail mall he found a pharmacy and bought some Tylenol for his headache, a tube of hair gel and a comb. He also selected some sunglasses with light tinted reactolite lenses. Then he took himself off to the rest room and experimented in front of the mirror. His hair needed trimming but it would have to do. The gel smoothed it down, made it seem much darker. It was a technique they had taught him back in acting school. With the sunglasses on he looked neater, more military. At a pinch he might actually pass for the dentist in the photo. Satisfied, he washed his hands and went back out to wait for his Washington connection.

Patrolman Scott Krogh of the Atlanta PD detachment at Hartsfield Airport responded to the request to check out the public phone on the concourse. He located the booth within five minutes of the message reaching him. There was no person in the immediate vicinity, he radioed in to his dispatcher. Had any other calls been recorded on the phone since the hoax? Affirmative, the answer came back; within a minute and a half of the first, one further call, probably by the same person. Krogh roped off the site with a roll of police tape and ordered up a forensics officer. While he waited, he questioned staff at a nearby service counter. One of them remembered seeing a man in a uniform near the booth. But uniforms were a dime a dozen in an airport.

Patrolman Krogh's request for a forensics officer was answered by Detective Ruby Banner. Owing to the holiday shift workload Detective Banner did not reach the airport till 10.50. She registered approval at the young officer's prompt sealing off of the scene. Ducking under the tape, she set up her equipment case and carefully dusted receiver and dialing buttons with powder.

Twenty minutes later, she had lifted a good set of prints off the handle of the receiver. Four fingers, left hand. The caller had been quite careless.

At Jacksonville Naval Hospital, Nurse Phillips was still exercising her mind over the escape of the patient. 'He had no clothes. He was wearing nothing but a gown. How in heaven did he get through the main door? Was security asleep there or what?'

The Chief Nurse sniffed her opinion that the way the hospital was being run these days a man could walk out stark naked for all anyone would notice.

'He still had to get through the main gate in his gown. Either that or climb the fence. Don't tell me this guy walked out in what he was wearing. Either he's still here in the hospital or he stole a set of clothes.'

When the security patrol looked in again she voiced her doubts to them.

'You guys catch him yet?'

The two men shook their heads. Not yet they hadn't.

'This one,' the Chief Nurse indicated Phillips, 'reckons he's still around here somewhere, hiding up.'

'That a fact?' said the Sergeant mildly.

Phillips emptied a pack of dressings on the desk and commenced counting them.

'If you ask me,' said the Sergeant, 'someone screwed up. Happens all the time round here. Orderlies mix up numbers, stop on the wrong floor, pick up the wrong gurney. Right now your man is probably down in theater. In an hour or two they'll bring him back up minus a lung.'

'Only one gurney has been past here this morning,' Phillips answered with a pout. 'That was Number 21, the dental surgeon from Bethesda. Strangulated hernia.'

'That's true,' confirmed the Chief Nurse. 'They brought him up just before you came.'

'Sure it was him and not your missing mystery man?'

'Course we are.' The Chief Nurse glanced at Phillips for confirmation. 'He's dark. The other patient was fair haired.'

'Sandy, they call it,' supported Phillips.

The Sergeant hitched up his belt. 'No harm if we take a look, I guess.'

They went down the passage, the nurses' shoes squeaking on the rubber tiles alongside the patrolmen's heavy tread.

'He's still sedated,' the Chief Nurse said, as she opened the door.

'Yeah, well he doesn't fit the description, awake or asleep,' agreed the sergeant, studying the comatose figure in the bed. 'Guy couldn't be hiding up in here, I suppose?' He looked inside the bathroom. The two nurses watched. 'Nope, nothing in the closets either,' he said. 'Clean as a whistle.'

'Gives me goosebumps,' shivered the Chief Nurse, hugging herself, 'the idea he could still be around somewhere. I didn't mind when I thought he'd run off.'

'Want us to take another look around? Check out the whole wing again for you?' the Sergeant offered.

'Oh, that would be sweet of you, Sergeant.' The Chief Nurse laid a grateful hand on his arm. 'I feel safe when you're around.' Phillips snorted to herself and went back to the nurses' station to continue counting the dressings. She had finished the task and was putting the box back in the closet when a thought struck her.

She ran back down the corridor. The Sergeant and the Chief Nurse were giggling together in an empty bedroom. 'How come I'm the only one round here using her head?' she demanded, dragging them back to the sleeping naval officer's room. She flung open the closet door again. 'Are you going to tell me this patient came in naked as well?'

*

Up in Washington, the man who currently called himself Commander Ferris Casey shivered as he fed a five-dollar bill into a subway Farecard machine. Even down here the temperature was noticeably cooler. It had been too much to expect the Commander to have carried a topcoat down in Florida. He would have to make do with the waterproof. Also the shoes pinched. If the snow started in he was going to wish he had some rubbers before long.

The Farecard unit churned mechanically and spat the bill back at him. Stifling his impatience, the man smoothed it out and reinserted it. This time it proved acceptable. He tried not to keep looking at his watch but his nervousness increased with every minute that passed. There was a further wait for a train and when it came there was standing room only. He climbed aboard with relief and hung onto a strap as they lurched off. Excited talk about the Inauguration filled the compartment. Where the best points were to view the parade. Would the weather clear? Would they catch sight of the new First Lady?

He opened his paper again at the timetable of the day's events. By established custom, at 10.30 a.m. the President-elect and Mrs Meade left Blair House to take morning coffee with the outgoing president and Mrs Ivory at the White House. Then at 11.30 the President and his successor would drive together to the Capitol, their wives traveling behind in a second limousine. Following the swearing-in ceremony, the new President and his First Lady were to be the guests of the Joint Congressional Inaugural Committee for luncheon in the Capitol, after which they would return to the White House to watch the inaugural parade from the viewing stand.

His head was beginning to throb again from the effects of the drugs exacerbated by the stale air inside the car as he tried to recall the details of the President-elect's personal schedule. The version in the paper had been provisional but there wasn't a lot they could change, not on this day.

He left the subway at Metro Center. The freezing cold of the open air stung the recently healed skin on his face. Two blocks up found a print shop open with computer facilities. Here he began to put into effect the plan he had managed to work out on the flight up. There were no other customers present as he settled at a keyboard and, forcing himself to concentrate, tapped out a header. Then he dialed up a menu. From a choice of fonts he selected a Times Roman 12 point with the extra embossing option. For the message itself he switched to Helvetica-Narrow 14. Anxiety over time gnawed at him, but he made himself take care to get the spacing and placement looking just right. When he was finally satisfied he spent further minutes on the choice of paper. There was a wide variety on the shelves. He hesitated between a white bond and a heavyweight cream and eventually settled on the white. He pressed the print button. The sheet rolled smoothly off the printer and he examined it critically. The embossed address header was impressive. It was not facsimile perfect but it would have to do. He daren't wait any longer. He signed the letter in black ink, printed up an envelope to match, paid and hurried on his way.

Ironically, the most difficult part was reaching the Pentagon. Every platform on the subway was jammed with hordes of incoming sightseers. It was a quarter after eleven before he made the Mall entrance. Men and women from all four services were streaming in and out the doors. The uniform and ID took him past security without a second glance but that was only to be expected. The real test was still to come.

According to theory a person was supposed to be able to reach the furthest point on the seventeen-odd miles of corridors in six minutes – provided he or she was familiar with the building's layout. He was not, and in his haste he mistook a ring number for a floor and had to start over. Finally he reached the Presidential Attaché's section. Mentally he braced himself. This was the point at which his cover would be tested. He was relying on his darkened, slicked-back hair, so far removed from the always immaculate presidential candidate, plus his blotched, unhealthy appearance to protect him from premature recognition. If word of his escape had gotten out from the hospital, it would be a different story.

He put the thought from his mind and tapped at the door.

'And you sign here, Commander, and here. And once more here on the snapshot. Thank you, sir.'

'Thank you.'

He was hard put to keep the relief from his voice. It was all proving too ridiculously simple. Captain Bong had been true to his word. Temporary twenty-four-hour passes for the executive mansion and viewing stand were waiting for him ready drawn up and requiring only signatures and photographs. The brief confirmatory note he had printed up himself over the presidential signature had been accepted without question. Casey's ID was given cursory scrutiny. The supposed call from Blair House had done the rest. There was only one bad moment, when he had to remove the glasses to pose for the Polaroid camera.

'Gee, Commander.' The Lieutenant was young and impressionable. 'Did anyone ever tell you you look like the President? The President-elect, I should say?'

He swiveled, fixing the boy with a look to match the weather outside. 'No, nobody else has remarked on that before. Why?'

The Lieutenant blushed crimson. 'I'm sorry, sir, I didn't mean to cause offense. I guess it just seemed for a minute there was a resemblance. I mean from a certain angle, that is,' he stammered. 'Please forgive my impertinence, sir. Here are your passes, sir. And have a good day.'

5

In the end the snow held off. The West Front of the Capitol, brilliant with flags and red and white bunting, was already filling up with guests when the President-elect and his wife departed Blair House at 10.30 to meet with President Ivory and his wife for coffee at the White House prior to the ceremony. Afterwards Ivory and the President-elect rode together by limousine up Pennsylvania Avenue to the Capitol, escorted by Senator Strobel, chairman of the Inaugural Ceremonies Committee. It was an awkward journey; the campaign had been a bitter one and the two first executives had nothing in common. The Senator's efforts at small talk had little success. President Ivory spoke in monosyllables; his companion seemed nervous.

The media were already labeling the new President 'a second Kennedy', underscoring the age gap between them as much as the difference in policies. The parallels were in any case striking: James Ivory was one year shy of his seventieth birthday, a former Chief of Staff of the Army, the first military man elected since Eisenhower and a dyed-in-the-wool Republican. His successor was just forty-five, one year older than Kennedy in 1961. Like Kennedy he quoted from Lincoln, his hero. He was not a Catholic but he had served in the Navy and possessed a charming and beautiful wife, Caro, short for Caroline, a Kennedy name. 'He brings with him,' wrote the *Washington Post*, 'the same aura of glamour that Jack Kennedy carried. Perhaps because he is so newly married, the first candidate actually to do so during a campaign, he and his wife seem younger even than the Kennedys.*

Most of all he comes to Washington free of much of the political baggage that has so bedeviled incoming chief executives. The new President will have a substantial fund of goodwill to draw upon as he begins his term of office. May he use it well.'

'Steady, Bobo. Steady, boy.'

The poodle's claws skittered impatiently on the marble floors of the Supreme Court building. Its fur was a bluish gray, cut to resemble an Airedale.

'Not long now, Bobo.' Justice Aaron Phelps gripped the dog leash tightly as he was dragged along the hall toward the elevators. His two law clerks, husky young men, flanked him on either side, half a pace behind. Some justices chose their clerks for their brains, others for their legs or tits, depending. Aaron Phelps demanded broad shoulders. Bringing up the rear was an armed officer of the Supreme Court Police, his leather gunbelt emitting a reassuring squeak at every stride. A second guard held open the door to the elevator, eyeing Bobo with distaste as the little dog scrabbled inside the car. All the guards detested Bobo, though they knew better than to show it.

When they reached the limo downstairs, the guard held the door and Bobo entered first again, hopping up onto the rear seat. Aaron settled himself in afterwards. A wool rug was tucked around him. He placed Bobo on his lap. Courtney, the chauffeur, glanced in the mirror. 'To the Capitol, Justice?'

'The West Front,' Aaron told him. 'Justice': he enjoyed the title. Just as he enjoyed the limo, the pay, the prestige. The reserved seat on the podium at today's ceremony. A Supreme Court justice ranked above a senator or a cabinet officer. A justice received $350,000 in salary, higher than any other federal official except the President, Vice-President and the House Speaker. Sure, the politicians got the publicity but what were they? Here today, gone tomorrow. The Supreme Court was an appointment for life. None of this could be taken away from him. Politicians always had to kiss ass to someone. A justice had respect. Even retirement was optional on guaranteed full pay. Short of impeachment, and no justice had ever been impeached in the whole history of the nation, he was untouchable.

The limousine purred out into the daylight, its nose pointing toward the Capitol. There were crowds in the Plaza. Bobo put his nose against the window and yapped.

To the sound of the Marine Corps band playing 'Battle Hymn of the Republic', the official guests filed to their seats: the senators, led by Minority Leader Lamar Swinton; the justices of the Supreme Court, President Ivory and his wife. Of the 103 men and women on the platform the great majority owed their presence to rank: three former presidents and their wives, the Vice-President and Mrs Jordan, Chief Justice Roscoe who would administer the oath, cabinet members, leaders of House and Senate. The next most numerous were members of the extensive Charteris clan, the wealthy and politically prominent family of the new First Lady. A mere handful only could claim kinship with the incoming President, all of them by marriage rather than descent.

Immediately behind the podium, in Reserved Section 1–A were 700 places set aside for the friends of the new couple, political and personal. Few of those present knew each other well, a fact indicative of the character of the man they followed, who had many acquaintances but few intimates and discouraged the formation of cliques about him. In his six years spent as a senator he had formed few close relationships, an explanation perhaps for the break-up of his first marriage. In consequence the seats were filled not with cronies but with labor leaders, financial big hitters, media moguls and Hollywood luminaries who had lent their names to his campaign, congressmen whose support he would need in the days to come.

The minutes ticked by. Late-coming guests slipped into their places. In the ornate Presidential Reception Room inside the Capitol where in former times American presidents sat at a green baize table signing bills into law late in the closing minutes of their administrations, Jack Meade waited with only Senator Strobel for company and a Secret Service guard. Neither spoke much. It was hard to think of anything to say which did not seem trite on such an occasion. The President-elect read and re-read the notes for his address as twelve noon approached.

A discreet knock came at the door. Both men rose at once, anticipating the summons but it was only a uniformed page. The bus bringing members of Mrs Meade's family from Dulles airport had been delayed in traffic and was only now approaching the Capitol.

The two men resumed their seats under the gorgeous Brumidi ceiling. Senator Strobel remarked jokingly that this was the very last time that Jack would have to wait for anybody. The President-elect smiled mechanically and fidgeted with his wrist-watch. He was wearing a dark club coat, striped pants.

A silence seemed to fall upon the great building. In a room near at hand an unattended telephone shrilled impotently. Another minute passed. The gilded dial of the French clock on the mantelpiece showed 12.12.

'Sorry, Commander. If your name's not on my list, I can't let you through.'

Perdue G. Lawrence of the 300-strong Capitol Police was polite but adamant as he had been with all the other attempts to gatecrash the Inauguration through his checkpoint. A fresh-faced young man with very short hair, he had his orders. No amount of special pleading was going to overturn them.

Security around Capitol Hill was tight. Triple cordons manned by police and military controlled all access. The naval officer with the raincoat was affecting not to understand why his newly minted pass had carried him successfully through the first two barriers only for him to be brought up short at the steps to the Capitol itself.

'Sure, Commander,' Lawrence agreed patiently, 'but that's a pass to the White House and the parade stand this afternoon. This here is the Capitol and you need a seat number allocation for the swearing-in ceremony. No seat, no admission, no argument. With respect, Commander.'

The officer trembled with agitation. From an inner pocket of his jacket he produced a letter. 'Read this,' he told Lawrence. His hands, the policeman noticed, were white with cold at the knuckles and shaking. He wondered why the man wasn't wearing a thicker coat. Not that it was any of his business.

Lawrence read the letter. He noted that it was signed by Senator Meade with the added title 'President-elect' and that the officer named was requested to attend on the First Lady 'for the duration of the Inauguration and for such period afterwards as the President may direct . . .' Which had to be reason enough, Lawrence decided. He told the Commander he could pass through the barrier but warned him that he still did not possess a seat ticket and might therefore be turned away from the stands on the West Front.

He took the main steps three at a time, every minute vital now. He must stop the ceremony somehow before it was too late. Pain lanced his chest but he ignored it and ran on. A few late-coming congressmen and their families went hurriedly past below, making for the ground floor entrance to cut through to the West Front. At the Columbus Doors there was more security; immediately following the ceremony Congress would entertain the new President and his wife to lunch in Statuary Hall. The great bronze doors swung to behind him and immediately the immense emptiness of the place struck him. Always when he had been here before the Capitol had been humming with life: politicians, researchers, lobbyists, secretaries, journalists, TV crews, gaggles of staring visitors, senators and congressmen hurrying between appointments, being briefed or giving interviews on the move. Now the soaring rotunda stood vacant and abandoned, sealed off by guards, the only sound the rapid echo of his own feet on the marble floor as he fled left in the direction of the House Chamber and the offices of the Speaker.

A guard was on duty at the roped-off corridor to the House Reception Room but a sight of the White House pass was all it took to let him through. The Speaker's administrative offices overlooked the East Front from the 1962 extension to the façade. He tried the first door he came to. Locked. And the next and the next. Rattling at the handles and banging drew no response from inside. Alerted by the noise another guard appeared, overweight and indolent. Everybody was out watching the ceremony, he said indifferently.

Meade gritted his teeth, hanging onto the remnants of his self-control. The panic was real inside him now. He clenched his fist and waved the White House pass under the guard's nose. 'Find the Speaker for me!' he yelled hoarsely. 'If not him, someone else in authority. I'm on a mission of utmost urgency!'

The guard shrugged. It was not his business and he couldn't leave his post even if he wanted to. The offices were locked. Speaker Webster and his staff all out on the West Front with the rest of the big shots, he repeated.

'There has to be somebody left in the building?'

Already the guard was waddling back to his post. 'Could try the Speaker's Chamber office. Might be people in there still.'

Frantically Jack Meade raced down the empty corridors, past the pillared reception hall and into the House Wing. The Ways and Means Committee rooms were next the stairs and elevators across from the House Chamber. Beyond was a room used by the Speaker on formal occasions when the House was sitting. There was still a chance he might find help there. Still a faint hope of averting the catastrophe.

Down in the stands on the West Front, Leon Perry's wife blinked back tears. She and her husband had been allocated seats on the Capitol podium for the swearing-in. It was the proudest day of her life. Then three hours ago, just as they were about to leave for the ceremony, came a phone call to their hotel. Owing to a miscalculation of numbers, they would not in fact be sitting on the podium after all. Instead they were being allocated seats in the stands immediately below. Apologies.

Leon had clenched his jaw and said nothing. It only underscored what he had known ever since his own dismissal and the departure of Elaine: he was outside the circle now. Frozen out by the new people round Jack Meade, the experts, the lawyers and economics gurus. Goodbye, they were telling him. So long, pal.

Well, if the President didn't want him, others did. He still had useful connections. The Koreans had been after him for weeks with consultancy offers. The money would be some consolation. He would call them up after the ceremony, maybe even fly out tomorrow. Anything to get away from Washington for a while.

When they reached the Capitol precincts there was a further disappointment in waiting. Their seats, their new seats, were not as they had been promised in the front section of the stands but in the second to last row from the rear. Their view of the proceedings was almost non-existent. Mrs Perry could not control her tears. How could the President treat his former best man so shabbily?

Up in the Capitol, the man in naval uniform raised his fists to heaven and pounded vainly on the doors to the

Speaker's Chamber Office. For all the response he drew he might as well be hammering on a coffin lid. The entire building might as well be deserted for all anyone cared. Any moment now across in the Senate side, the Sergeant at Arms would be knocking on the door of the President's room to summon its occupant to the podium.

The Senate side. Of course, why hadn't he thought of that before? There might still just be time.

The President-elect was growing impatient. What in hell was causing the hold-up now? he demanded. Senator Strobel spoke on the phone to one of his aides. Two minutes, he was told. Just two more minutes and everything would be in place.

The Senator apologized to his companion for the delay. The President-elect grunted edgily. It was a poor way to open the show, he said.

Down the stairs to the ground floor, Jack Meade sprinted like a madman. It was the quickest way. Across the Hall of Capitols and through the tobacco-leafed pillars of the Hall of Columns into the Small House Rotunda. Lincoln's head loomed ominously at him in the low-ceilinged crypt. Astonished guards jumped aside to let him pass. On the Senate side, even the appointments desk was closed. He was underneath the Senate Chamber now. He swerved right down the Brumidi Corridor, past the famous murals, found the stairway he was looking for and sprang up it.

By virtue of the Constitution, the Vice-President of the United States was ex-officio President of the Senate, fulfilling the referee role of the Speaker and casting a decider vote in the event of a tied count. In practice day-to-day business in the Senate was conducted under a president *pro tempore*, elected from the majority party as substitute chairman when the Vice-President was absent.

Nevertheless, a suite of offices for the Vice-President's use was provided close to the chamber.

As with other offices in the Capitol that morning, those vice-presidential staff who had come in to work on the holiday had taken time out to witness the ceremony. This year Audrey Schaffhauser had chosen to stay behind. She had seen it all before. It was a freezing day and she had a cold. She would stay at the front desk and watch the ceremony on TV.

The Inauguration proper had still not begun when the man in Navy uniform burst in. His face was flushed and he was gasping for breath as if he had been running. Audrey glanced at him severely.

'Are you lost, young man?' she said acerbically.

'Please . . .' he struggled to get the words out. 'Please . . .'

He wore the rings of a surgeon lieutenant-commander, she noted, on a creased and ill-fitting uniform, and he had tinted glasses. Had the circumstances been different the resemblance to Jack Meade might have struck her. As it was she thought at first there must have been an accident, then she worried he might be ill, he seemed so agitated. 'How can I help you, Commander?'

'Yes . . . have to help me . . . appalling mistake . . . wrong man . . .' he gasped spasmodically.

Audrey experienced rising alarm. She wished one of the others was here. 'Are you sure you have the correct place? These are the Senate offices of the Vice-President.'

The officer snatched off his glasses, clutching convulsively at the desk for support. 'My name . . . is . . . Jack . . . Meade!' he gasped out.

The President-elect paced the room with rising choler. He felt caged, he said, like a prisoner. The delay was intolerable, it was undignified. It was just how he did not want to start his Presidency. Finally he could contain himself no longer. 'Get on the phone again,' he snapped

102

his fingers at the Senator, 'and say to them I'm coming out right now, ready or not.'

Before Strobel could comply there came the sound of footsteps outside in the passage. The door was thrown open to reveal the Sergeant-at-Arms resplendent in full dress uniform, come to summon the President-elect. It was time.

The President-elect breathed a sigh of relief. 'About time,' he said. 'Okay, lead off.'

'For God's sake, woman, you're not listening! I'm telling you I am Senator Meade, the real Jack Meade! That man out there is a fake, an impostor!'

Audrey Schaffhauser was frankly scared now. The officer was clearly disturbed. She tried to speak soothingly but he only became more and more agitated. He began shouting incoherently and waving his arms. She fumbled for the panic button under the edge of her desk. He lunged forward, grabbing her wrist before she could press the button. She screamed and there was a brief scuffle across the desk. Her chair fell sideways with a crash.

Fury erupted corrosively in the man's belly. Silly bitch, what had she started screaming for? He hadn't wanted to hurt her. Now she would bring the whole building about his ears.

He ran out into the passage, panting wildly, looking about for a way of escape. He heard voices, people moving. Up at the west end of the corridor a little procession emerged from another door. A uniformed usher leading another figure attended by a posse of guards. For the space of a heartbeat he had a profile glimpse of his rival. Less than a hundred feet separated them: the President-elect on his way to the podium to take the oath of office. Then the guards closed round, cutting off the sight. The man staggered forward after them. He tried to cry out that it was all a terrible mistake.

They had the wrong man. But the words strangled in his throat as his strength ebbed. Before he could recover they were gone, descending the stairs to the ground floor.

Dazed and exhausted, he reeled against the wall. The blood roared in his ears. He sank to his knees, too weak to go on. Dimly from outside came a sound of trumpets. His moment had passed. He had been too late to halt the ceremony. He had failed. Failed his country. Failed himself.

It was time. A buzz of anticipation ran though the onlookers. To the accompaniment of 'Jubilant' from the trumpets of the band of the Marine Corps, from out under the arched door of the west terrace proceeded a bejeweled sergeant-at-arms escorting the President-to-be. Bareheaded and youthful in the cold midday sun, he greeted friends and supporters on the podium, waved briefly to the crowds below.

As prescribed by tradition, Leyland T. Jordan took first turn on the podium, repeating the oath administered by Justice Toffler to become Vice-President, reflecting perhaps that no fewer than seven past presidents had died or been murdered before their time to be succeeded by their deputies.

It was time. Slipping off his topcoat, echoing perhaps unconsciously the actions of Kennedy once more, Jack MacKenzie Meade placed his left hand upon his mother's family bible, raised his right hand and solemnly repeated after Chief Justice Roscoe the thirty-five-word oath of office – the only event of the whole five days' celebrations that was demanded by the Constitution – '*I do solemnly swear that I will faithfully execute the office of President of the United States* . . . ' His voice was pitched up and seemed to shake a little at first as might be expected, but it gathered strength: ' . . . *and will to the best of my ability preserve, protect and defend the Constitution of the United States.*'

The assembled guests broke into applause. The only two members of the executive branch to be elected by popular vote embraced their wives and families and returned the waves and greetings of the crowd. The first boom of the twenty-one-gun salute to the new Head of State rolled out across the nation's capital and Jack MacKenzie Meade duly entered into office as President of his country, Chief Executive and Commander-in-Chief of the Armed Forces.

On East Capitol Street between the Library of Congress and the Supreme Court Building, a naval officer in glasses and a dark coat was seen to stumble as the echoes of the cannonade pealed out. A tourist and his wife from Manitoba, Canada, who went to his aid, assisted him to a nearby bench. Shocked by his ill and exhausted appearance, they tried to persuade him to let them call for an ambulance but he would not hear of it. He had been recently hospitalized, he said, and was prone to fits of weakness. It would pass. He drank a cup of water they brought him and thanked them for their concern. The last they saw of him, he was setting off northward in the direction of Union Station.

Over at the White House, staff from the General Services Agency began furling the flags flanking the presidential desk in the Oval Office and replacing photographs of General Ivory with those of Jack Meade. As the sound of the cannonade died away, a marine helicopter clattered into the air above the Capitol, bearing the Ivorys away from the Capitol to Andrews airbase where Air Force One, redesignated for the trip 'Special Air Mission 28000', was standing by to fly them home to Kansas and retirement.

On cue, a stampede of staffers from the new administration rushed the East and West Wing offices, impatient to stake claim to the best space. The pecking order was never-changing: the closer to the President, the greater the prestige; so West Wing rated over East and a closet in the White House carried more weight than a suite in the Old Executive Office Building. All through the mansion, desks and drawers were emptied, name plates removed, furnishings and equipment fought over. Decorators began touching up walls and woodwork while builders knocked out partitions and put up fresh ones. FBI locksmiths moved from room to room, changing safe combinations. Phones clicked and shrilled as new aides tried out their lines and argued with the Parks Service over allocation of parking spaces on West Executive Avenue. It was a time too for triumph. Champagne corks popped, toasts were drunk from paper cups and across a thousand video screens flashed a graphic image of a Democratic donkey screwing a furiously trumpeting elephant. It was captioned *Tomorrow Belongs to Us!*

The new President stepped back to the podium. Tall and erect, he lifted his head, a glow on his face as he gazed out for a moment across the heads of the crowd, across the Mall with its breathtaking view of the Washington Monument and the Lincoln Memorial, across the Potomac and west toward the heart of the nation he had just sworn to govern. There was a brief pause, then his voice rang out in the cold, clear air: '*Friends and fellow Americans* . . . '

In Jacksonville, the hunt for the missing patient was gathering momentum. A fresh description was issued. Local and state police were warned to be on the lookout for a man in a stolen uniform. At the same time a more detailed search of Lieutenant-Commander Casey's room was instituted. The locker drawer was opened and its contents checked. Navy security was alerted to the missing identity documents and the theft of the credit cards reported.

'... my predecessor, whose half-century of service to his country deserves our gratitude, our admiration, our heartfelt thanks ... now takes his rightful place in the pantheon of the nation's leaders.'

The warmth of the new President's tribute to General Ivory came as a surprise to his audience, who were aware of the bitterness of the election struggle. 'His generous words setting the tone of reconciliation and healing of divisions in keeping with the One Nation theme of his address,' commented a correspondent approvingly.

At MasterCharge security division an operator tapped in Casey's name on the central computer. The screen flashed up a list detailing the most recent card usage.

'Some of those are secondary cards issued to family members,' observed the supervisor leaning over her shoulder. 'Screen them out and concentrate on the principal holder.'

The operator complied. The list shortened considerably. 'Looks like only one recent transaction. That was today. United Airlines – $96 plus taxes. Before that there's a gap of almost four days.'

'Highlight that transaction and bring up the detail.' The supervisor was already reaching for the phone.

A single call to United was sufficient to establish the ticket destination. Since the inquiry was a military matter the supervisor reported the findings to the Provost-Marshal's office in Jacksonville. At around the same time first reports of the intruder at the Vice-President's office at the Capitol reached the Secret Service. The result was an urgent upgrading of the threat level. A copy of the patient's medical record was faxed to the Secret Service, a naval courier summoned, and within the hour the original was on its way to Washington by air.

'... the Presidency is an act of faith, an act of faith in our nation. I have that faith ... I ask you to share in that

107

faith with me . . . Faith in the land we love. Faith . . . in . . . America!'

The applause was strong and sustained. The band played 'Hail to the Chief'. Buoyed up on the wings of the cheering, the new President left the platform. His young wife joined him inside the Capitol, whispered, 'Oh, Jack, what a day,' and softly touched his face.

The new Presidentiad had begun.

Karen Lipscombe had not been a part of the ceremony at the Capitol. A seat close to the podium had been offered her and she had declined. Her task was to ensure that the President's personal office was up and running without delay. Before the salute had ended the MPV transporting her team was rolling down the ramp to the West Wing entrance.

A line was already forming at the turnstiles where the uniformed Secret Service guards were checking identities. More gawping at the Elvis. 'Excuse us, please. The President's secretary.' At Jodi's clipped request the press of staffers divided as if by magic, with those slow to move elbowed hastily aside by colleagues quicker on the uptake. No one but a fool was about to kick off their White House career antagonizing the woman with the President's ear.

Doug Blacker, Commander of the White House Secret Service detail, waited immediately inside the barrier. He watched Miss Lipscombe remove her Elvis set to pass the thermogram security check. Without it, she looked suddenly vulnerable, fragile boned, delicately pretty. He liked the way she carried herself though, straight-backed, head up to confront the world. Fine but durable, he decided. A survivor.

He waited for her to put the headset on again, then stepped forward

'Miss Lipscombe. Doug Blacker, Commander of the White House detail,' he introduced himself. Karen and

Jodi shook hands and allowed him to lead the way down toward the Oval Office corridor. Agents stationed at intervals scrutinized their security badges as they passed.

Three officials from the GSA were waiting at the entrance to the secretary's suite. More handshakes, wide smiles. Yes, this was a great day. The doors were unlocked. Karen entered the lobby. Fresh paint smells, flowers on the desks, a nice touch. Behind her, the assistant who had been detailed in charge of phones, settled herself at the mini-switchboard, slung her coat over the back of the chair and began flipping switches. 'Switchboard? Hi, this is Gemini Kelly in the Personal Office, we're on line as of now. Okay? That's affirmative, will do, thank you.'

Karen stepped through into the secretary's office. Her room. The paint smell was strongest in here.

'The secretary's room was redecorated for your convenience last night,' the manager of the GSA team was explaining. 'We chose magnolia like before. It's a light, neutral shade but if it isn't to your liking, just say and we'll redo it how you'd prefer.'

Karen thanked him. 'This is fine, great. Everything is wonderful. The flowers are a most thoughtful touch. I really appreciate it.'

'I understand you're having special equipment installed?'

'Our own computer terminals and fileserver, yes. We plan to use Lotus Notes where possible.'

'If you need assistance, let us know. We have experts to help you set up and link into the main systems.'

Out in the lobby more of the secretarial staff were arriving, squeezing through into the inner office, dumping briefcases and boxes of files on desks. Excited chatter filled the cramped rooms.

Karen touched her speaker watch: 12.58. 'I have FBI secure transport scheduled to show at 1 p.m. with classified presidential papers.'

Blacker spoke briefly into his lapel mike. After a minute he turned to her. 'The truck is in sight of the gates. There's some congestion at the moment but it should be cleared and able to start offloading in around twenty minutes. We'll open up one of the side doors so the barrows can have direct access.'

'That will be a big help, thank you.'

'No problem.'

His tone was friendly. She was trying to concentrate on the voices, isolating accents and speech rhythms, linking them to names. Blacker was from the Midwest, a faint elision on r's and l's.

She reached out and brushed a hand along the wall till she felt the edge of a doorway. 'This connects through to the President, right?'

'That's correct.'

'Is it locked? I have some items for the President's desk.'

Blacker stepped past her and rapped twice on the door with his knuckle. The lock clicked and the door swung open noiselessly on oiled hinges to reveal a uniformed guard, who stepped aside.

Blacker held the door back for Karen to pass. 'This is armored,' he warned. 'Remember to watch your fingers.'

'We'll be sure to.' Karen drew a deep breath and stepped purposefully over the threshold. The oval room was smaller than she'd expected. Magda had warned her of that. The deep blue rug with its ring of gold stars and golden eagle in the middle was amazingly soft underfoot. The light from the tall windows of the bay threw the big desk into sharp relief, the flags behind it still and solemn. The thick bullet-resistant polycarbonate panes dimmed the view of the gardens outside. The significance of the moment overwhelmed her suddenly: she felt her eyes prick, her heart beat quick and shallow.

Swallowing hard, she opened the plain cardboard box she had brought in with her and took out the gold pen

110

and pencil set presented to Jack Meade by the Indiana legislature, a Navy emblem on a bronze paperweight, a glass seahorse that was a childhood memento, a silver-framed portrait of his mother, and arranged them on the desk. Into the top left-hand drawer she placed a new Sony dictation machine and a box of fresh tapes.

Jodi gazed down at the fireplace with the twin high-back chairs. 'It's all just like the photographs and yet totally different somehow,' she whispered, awestruck. 'And to think this is where we'll be working now. Right at the nation's heart.'

'At the nation's heart,' Karen echoed. Yes, if there was such a place it was here.

6

Down in Jacksonville the pictures of the patient had turned out well. Brilliantly, in fact. Cal had used her head. She was one smart girl, no doubt about it. She had brought two cameras along, one pre-loaded with Kodak Color Negative 400 ASA. She had managed two shots crouching down at an oblique side angle with the light from the window over her shoulder. The result was a near-natural look as if the patient were standing up against some kind of a cloth background instead of lying flat on a pillow. She had set to work in the darkroom, lightening the face, airbrushing out the stubble and shadowed hollows under the cheeks. She called Troy in and proudly showed off the final results.

When Troy saw the pictures he whistled. 'Will you look at these?'

The resemblance to Jack Meade was unmistakable.

Cal was equally excited. 'He just has to be some kind of close relation. Like, you know, a brother or a cousin or something. No way else they could look so alike.'

Troy sucked in his cheeks and stared at the photographs. There was a story here, a big one. What the key was he didn't know, yet. He intended to find out though. One thing he was certain of, this was too good to blow prematurely. They would sit on the discovery a while till they had found out what was behind it all.

One hundred miles above the Pacific, a swiftly moving speck of metal trailed a plume of vapor as it plunged through earth's atmosphere, west of Hawaii. Tracked anxiously by the global network of dedicated radar and electro-optical stations of the Deep Space Surveillance System, the craft maneuvered into a descent path configured to a touch down in Southern California. As its speed began to fall away, a computer-generated voice at Mission Control began to intone: *seven minutes . . . six . . .*

Across the country at the Capitol, an Air Force major wearing the braids of a presidential aide snapped shut his cell-phone and slipped unobtrusively back into Statuary Hall. The new President was coming to the end of his luncheon speech. '. . . As Speaker Webster remarked to me on the way in here, "If you thought getting elected was difficult, just wait till you start on the job."' In the pause for laughter that filled the hall, the Major whispered discreetly in the ear of Captain Bong, the President's senior military aide. Bong felt in an inside pocket for a notepad, scribbled a brief message, tore off the page and beckoned to a Secret Service agent. The note was passed to the President, who glanced at the contents and flashed a thumbs-up sign of congratulations back at Bong.

'Happily,' he continued as the applause subsided, 'I have been given the perfect tag line to finish up. I've just learned that the Space Shuttle, the *Enterprise*, has landed safely at Vandenberg. And that is the best present I've had all day.'

The hall rose cheering and clapping. Shaking hands and waving to friends and supporters, the President and his wife were escorted from the hall. As they moved towards the Rotunda, still surrounded by a dense throng, a man in a dark suit with a purposeful air and bearing a blue leather folder, pushed through the crowd.

'Excuse me, Mr President, Dunster Woodrow, executive clerk. How d'you do, sir? If you have a minute, sir, we have some business to transact.'

'We do?' The President was momentarily taken aback. The Executive Clerk was the oldest career post in the

113

White House, originating under George Washington. From his office in the OEOB, Dunster Woodrow kept a track of the proclamations, executive orders and statutory instruments requiring the President's attention.

'Executive Order 7162, Mr President, Medical Records Disclosure Requirements for Cabinet Rank Nominees. It requires your signature.'

Someone suggested an ante-room off the hall. Woodrow placed the folder open on a desk and produced a pen.

The President looked put out. 'Mrs Meade has a Parker 51 that belonged to Jack Kennedy. I was going to use that for all official documents and now it's gone to the White House.'

'The business of government goes on, sir,' Woodrow apologized.

The President took the proffered pen. He hesitated. 'I suppose it's all the same. It's the signature that counts.' He stooped and wrote in the characteristic sloping hand, *Jack MacKenzie Meade*. Cameras flashed, capturing the moment. 'There,' he said, stepping back. 'That's done.'

The First Lady had eaten nothing at the luncheon in the Capitol's Statuary Hall.

'How are you feeling?' her husband asked as they rode off down Pennsylvania Avenue towards the White House in the presidential limousine.

'Cold,' she said, clutching herself.

Through the windows they could see the crowds lining the Avenue, waving at them, mouths open cheering, but so thick was the armored glass that no noise penetrated the interior. It was an eerie, unreal sensation, like traveling in a fish tank or watching a movie with the sound turned down. The First Lady felt trapped and at the mercy of the grinning, gesticulating figures. Automatically and without thinking, she opened her purse and reached inside for her Ray-Bans.

'Take those glasses off,' the President told her out of the side of his mouth, still smiling back at the lines of well-wishers. Sunglasses, he believed, masked the wearer's personality, presenting a hostile, unfriendly appearance. Caro Meade looked surprised for a moment but she complied.

'Stagecoach now approaching grandstand,' the earpiece of Agent Nelson Davis' radio squawked and went momentarily silent again. Translated, the message warned that the presidential motorcade was drawing abreast of the FBI Hoover building, a block east of where Davis was stationed. He stamped his feet to restore their circulation. Today was his birthday. He was thirty years old and standing on Pennsylvania Avenue with his back to the parade and the wind-chill cutting through his thermal underwear, two sweaters, goosedown parka and insulated moon boots right to his bones as if he were jaywalking naked.

The swelling roar of the crowds at his back indicated that the President's car was coming into view. Davis lifted the rubber armored Zeiss field-glasses in his gloved hands and trained them on the building facing him, scanning for an open window. By law all windows along the parade route were required to remain closed for the duration of the parade. Nelson Davis was there to see the law was observed.

The sound of cheering grew louder. 'Caro! Caro!' they were screaming. The new First Lady was proving as big a crowd-puller as her husband. Bigger. Davis switched his gaze to the buildings fronting onto 10th Street. In the event an unfastened window was detected, a search team would immediately be ordered in. Davis and his fellow agents carried on them master keys to every building along the route.

The patient took the subway uptown, got off at Metro Center and walked slowly south on 11th Street, crushed by despair. Nausea was hitting him again. It was all he could do to stay on his feet. He passed a fast-food stand and the smell brought home to him suddenly how hungry he was. It was days since he had eaten properly. He wolfed two hot dogs, washed down with milky coffee, and felt a little strength return.

He picked out the Hoover Building against the skyline and headed toward it. The side streets onto Pennsylvania Avenue were all blocked off with concrete barriers and the growing security in evidence made him nervous. Every intersection seemed to be policed.

Nelson Davis raked his glasses across the last row of windows. Check, negative. The excitement of the people around him was reaching fever pitch. The presidential vehicle was in sight, drawing almost level. Davis murmured to himself the law officers' prayer – *Please God, not on my watch*. He switched his attention down in the direction of the Hoover Building. And as he did so he stiffened. A few yards back up 10th Street a man was standing. He wore a dark coat and sunglasses and the crowd pressing down against the barriers to see the motorcade had left a momentary clear space around him. Davis might have taken him for another agent had it not been for the field-glasses. He focused and under the ten-power magnification the figure's profile leapt into sharp relief. At that moment the figure reached up to remove the sunglasses in order to see better. Maybe it was the effect of the tight focus cutting off the uniform cap, isolating the subject's face from the background, or possibly it was because as a Secret Service agent he was trained to memorize features. Davis' pulse gave a jump. He blinked. Shit, there had to be something wrong. What he was seeing wasn't possible. There had to be some mistake – and yet there couldn't be. Not at this range. Davis jammed his eyes against the rubber cups of the field-glasses.

But the doppelgänger had vanished.

The afternoon sun was sinking lower in the western sky and outside the parade Washington was beginning to take on a bleak, forbidding aspect. On the White House reviewing stand Leyland T. Jordan hunched his shoulders beneath his thick topcoat and waved mechanically at a contingent of Irish bagpipers marching past below. It was three hours since he had sworn the vice-presidential oath of office making him the second most important man in the country. A few feet away the President had shed his coat once again, impervious to the biting cold, applauding each band of marchers, receiving wild cheers from the crowds in return.

Leyland Jordan watched and his stomach knotted. As of this moment there was no single individual on the face of the earth whom he would ever hate as intensely as he hated Jack Meade.

This should have been his day. His, Leyland T. Jordan's. The culmination of a political career that had spanned a quarter of a century. Twenty-five years of scheming, dealing, trading favors, clawing his way up the party ladder. And finally it had all fallen into place. He had cut his deals with the party managers. Swamped the early primaries with cash from the richest war chest ever raised for a nomination race. He had bought the unions, the networks, he had bought everything and everyone in sight and what couldn't be bought he had neutralized by threats or cunning.

Leyland Jordan had wanted the Presidency, wanted it badly. The other contenders had wanted it too but Leyland Jordan, the son of a Texas storekeeper, was prepared to compete for the Presidency with the same desperation that a man would fight for air to breathe. There was simply no other contender to stand up to him. The nomination had been practically in his pocket.

And then out of nowhere had come Jack Meade. The

117

Hero from Zero. The Forgotten Senator. Jack Meade, ex-soap star, a nobody with one overriding advantage that Leyland Jordan could never match. Youth.

His reflections were interrupted by a touch on his arm. A horse-faced woman stood grinning up at him with the cynical enthusiasm of the seasoned political spouse. With the efficiency of long practice he summoned up her name from memory, forcing his features into a semblance of cheerfulness. Yes, it was a wonderful day, the start of a new era. The President's speech had been wonderful, yes, inspirational. Finally to his relief the woman patted his arm again in farewell. 'Your turn in eight years, Leyland, we'll all be looking forward to that.'

Jordan's expression froze into a grimace. The woman saw the taunt strike home and turned away with a jaunty chuckle. The Vice-President stared after her venomously. Early on in the campaign for nomination he had rejected her husband for some minor office on his team. The slight had rankled and now she was getting her own back, reminding him of the arithmetic of failure.

Jordan's breath hissed between his teeth. Jack Meade was forty-five, Leyland Jordan sixty-four. Assuming the President won his second term, Jordan would be seventy-two before his chance came to run and eighty when it came to a second term. Against younger challengers his age would count fatally against him. In all probability he would not make it beyond the primaries. This had been his best, his only, shot at the Oval Office and Jack Meade with his good looks, his pretty wife and above all his youth had ruined it.

The main stand was a mass of uniforms and braid on the generals and flag officers clustered in the retinue of the Commander-in-Chief. The Secret Service was in full force, at least a dozen agents in close attendance with a second cordon further back and teams guarding every entrance and exit. Immediately behind the presidential podium were the seats of the principal dignitaries.

Speaker of the House, Daniel I. Webster, Chief Justice Roscoe, former Democratic President Bill Clinton and his wife Hillary, cabinet members and Senate leaders. Across the Avenue, perched among the mounds of plowed snow, a forest of cameras from the world's press and TV swept the viewing stands continually, focusing on the new First Couple and their entourages.

He picked out the First Lady in a red coat buttoned up high to the neck with a pillbox hat of dark fur. The fur would be fake, unlike his own wife's mink because Caro Meade's position on animal rights was a matter of public record. Jordan watched a guest approach her, hand out to shake hers. A Secret Service agent stepped promptly between them, grasping the man's arm. 'But I'm family!' the guest protested, outraged. He fumbled in a pocket for identification and was released with apologies but the incident left Caro Meade clearly distressed. The bars of the cage were already closing round her. Leyland Jordan smiled inwardly. Serve the bitch right. She had chosen what she wanted, now let her learn to want what she had chosen.

A flurry of snowflakes battered the glass screens of the podium. Underneath the stands the Catering Corps were serving hot coffee. Despite the intense cold there was an almost carnival atmosphere to the celebrations. Media reports were speaking of a political renaissance, a rediscovery of the American soul. Jerks, the Vice-President thought savagely, what the hell did they know? It all boiled down to the one factor – youth. A young man at the helm. It was Camelot and the Kennedys over again.

What made the position more galling still was the certain knowledge that it was only his presence on the ticket that had enabled the Democrats to squeak in. The margin of votes had been tiny; fewer than 200,000, one tenth of 1 percent of the electorate. Meade had lost California but squeaked home in Texas. Texas was Jordan's home state. Without Leyland T. Jordan, Meade would not have taken Texas; without Texas he would have failed to win the Presidency.

Small wonder Leyland Jordan was feeling bitter today.

He must not give up, not yet. There was still his wife. At all costs she had to be warned. Butting into the teeth of the wind with lowered head, the man in Lieutenant-Commander Casey's clothes made his way doggedly south on 14th Street. In spite of the cold and his exertions he was feeling less weak, the result of the food he had consumed. The crowds grew thicker as he neared the White House. A vendor on one street corner was offering for sale Jack Meade masks. The crude copies of his own features bobbed in the breeze, sharpening his bitterness. Further on, the monolithic Ionic colonnade of the east façade of the stately Treasury building came in view. He followed the moving throng of sightseers right on E Street. Here he had his first glimpse of the mansion rising from its green lawns, luminous and beautiful, smaller than he'd expected against the massed granite of the surrounding buildings.

He halted to study the instructions that came with his pass. Commander Casey was required on first entering the White House to register with the East Wing Military Office. Picking his way among the vehicles parked along Old Executive Avenue, he strode briskly in the direction of the south-east gate.

There was a line of other people waiting to pass through. Uniformed guards examining papers. Some kind of a special check in progress. Probably routine on changeover day. He felt a twinge of unease and moved into the lee of a delivery truck to wait developments. A pair of guards were pulling people out of the line apparently at whim. At first he took it for a random check. None of those asked for papers were turned away. As he watched, an admiral was thanked politely and his ID returned to him. The guards saluted and moved on unhurriedly towards the rear of the line. They paused again. Another officer looked surprised and fumbled inside his coat. It struck him that only men in uniform were being stopped. The officer handed over his documents, a captain's rings showing bright against a dark sleeve. And with a shock he realized that they were singling out naval officers.

Commander Casey's cover had been blown.

Down on the parade stands, the crush around the President began shifting to let a couple out. Two women. One was the First Lady in her red coat and dark hat, the other younger, fair haired, her left hand resting on Caro Meade's arm.

Karen Lipscombe was playing truant from her new duties for an hour to enjoy the parade. She had wanted to wear her thick navy duffel but Trish Beale, the new deputy press officer, had decreed that all presidential staff were to sport fawn because that would show better on the cameras. So she had splashed out on a brand new English camel-hair which felt wonderful but let the chill in more. Determinedly she hung on, clutching the hand warmers concealed in her pockets, bobbing up and down to restore the circulation to her toes as each fresh contingent paraded past the stand.

It was wonderful to be back, in the thick of things once more. Amongst the crowds on the podium were all kinds of people she knew from the campaign. Every few minutes someone or other came up to hug and congratulate her, grasp her hand or kiss her cheek. She was bruised and squeezed half to death, physically battered but wonderfully, breathtakingly alive. So when Caro Meade indicated they should return to the White House in one another's company, it was hard to keep the resentment out of her face. It had not struck her till then that her new job put her at the beck and call of the President's wife. Possibly Caro Meade was only trying to be kind, but when the First Lady grasped her arm Karen had to suppress an instinctive desire to free herself.

At the moment when Jack Meade placed his hand on his mother's family bible in front of the Capitol, two sets of removal vans began rolling down the ramp to the service entrance beneath the White House North Portico: the first to take away the personal effects of the Ivorys; the second lot to bring in the Meades' furniture and possessions. According to tradition not a single item of the incoming president's is permitted into the White House until he has been duly sworn in. During the two hours of the oath-taking ceremonies at the Capitol and the luncheon following, all the departing chief executive's belongings must be moved out of the mansion and his successor's moved in. For the ushers it was a point of honor that when the new master returned from the parade he would find himself moved in, unpacked and put away just as if he and his wife had lived in the house for always.

This Inauguration Day had been a tighter squeeze than ever. The Ivorys had managed to amass a great deal of stuff during their four-year occupation and Mrs Ivory had set her face against departure, refusing to contemplate removal until the very end. Every member of the White House staff had had to be pressed into service, from doormen to bandsmen, butlers, maids, carpenters and electricians. Even as the inaugural parade rolled past the viewing stand, marine helicopters were snatching away the last of Mrs Ivory's treasures from the South Lawn. Sewall was supervising the disposal of the final items when word came through from the Secret Service that Caro Meade was leaving the parade. He hurried down to the south entrance to meet her.

She squeezed his hand wordlessly as he greeted her. Underneath her gloves her touch was icy, her lips bloodless from the cold. He led her inside and through to the elevator. They had lit a fire for her in the Oval sitting room, he told her as they ascended.

'Oh, that's kind of you,' she thanked him in her whisper, 'but I really think I should like to lie down a while.'

They stepped out into the apartment and the maid, Gina, was there to help her off with her coat and hat. 'And these boots too,' she said softly, sitting down on a chair to pull them off. 'The damn things are too tight. You shouldn't have sent me out in them,' she added petulantly.

Gina said nothing. She helped her mistress off with the boots and accompanied her through to her bedroom. Sewall watched after them and shook his head with a sigh.

By mid-afternoon the continued failure to detain the patient posing as Commander Casey was causing concern to those in charge of the security situation around the President.

At 4 p.m. Blacker ordered his assistant, Dick Porter, to try FBI Headquarters again. 'Say I must speak to Judge Watson personally, that the matter is urgent and concerns the presidential safety.'

Porter used the secure direct link bypassing both switchboards to ring straight through to the Director's office. 'Sir, Judge Watson is absent at the parade. I have Deputy-Director Harvey on the line for you.'

Blacker took the phone. In fact he preferred to deal with Harvey, a long standing colleague and a professional law officer who had worked his way up through the ranks of the Bureau, whereas the Judge was a political appointee and a fervent Republican into the bargain. With Harvey he could speak the same language untroubled by political repercussions.

In a few curt sentences he outlined the urgency of the situation. 'We're working in the dark here, Bill. Our records have turned up nothing. Ditto the Pentagon. What I need is those prints expedited to find out if the guy is listed nationally. I'd appreciate any help you can give us.'

Harvey rang back inside ten minutes. Bureau finger-print files, including those of the Counter-Intelligence Division, had been searched with negative results and the national computer register which compared prints held by all law enforcement agencies in the country had come up with nothing.

Harvey suggested they try Langley.

A few blocks away, Commander Casey was on the move again. He sought out a luxury hotel and cut swiftly through the lobby into the shopping arcade, his cap peak pulled down low to shade his face. As he expected, many of the boutiques were open through the holiday. A pretty girl in a florist's flashed him a smile and inquired what she could do for him.

Gardenias, he told her. White gardenias. All that she could manage. 'Like those will do.' He pointed.

She shook her head, sorry to disappoint. Unfortunately the blooms in question were already spoken for.

This was a special order, he explained. He was on the staff of the Military Office. The aides wanted to send a tribute to the new First Lady, Mrs Meade. White gardenias were her favorites.

The girl's forehead furrowed, 'I'm not sure ...' she began uncertainly.

From his inside pocket he took the White House pass. Her eyes widened. 'Oh, gee, I'm sure in your case we can make an exception,' she stammered. 'Do you want for them to be delivered tonight, sir?'

'As soon as possible.'

'The boy just left with another bunch of orders. I can rush them across myself personally if you like,' she offered hopefully.

'Mrs Meade would surely appreciate that kindness.'

She produced a card. He wrote swiftly the message he had worked out, trying to keep it brief and lucid; above all, convincing.

The girl studied the envelope awed. 'This is all I need?

'That number code I've put indicates a personal family gift. You go to the East Wing security building. The Secret Service will take the order from you and deliver it to the White House Flower Room, okay?'

'The Secret Service, wow,' she nodded, still dazed. 'And how do you like to pay, Commander?'

Send the bill to the Military Office, he instructed. He wrote it down for her.

It was a long shot but it might work.

He returned through the arcade the way he had come. Exhaustion was hitting him now. He needed to find help, somewhere to rest up. At the hotel entrance there was a line waiting for taxis. He joined it, tugging his cap down over his face again. When his turn arrived he gave the driver an address in Kalorama Heights.

The journey seemed endless. He fought the urge to sleep. At last they arrived. He paid off the driver and staggered to the doorway of the building. There was no sign of the doorman. 'Come on, come on,' he prayed under his breath as he pressed the bell for her apartment. He had almost given up when the intercom grille crackled. 'Who's that?' a woman's voice slurred.

'Elaine? Elaine, open up for God's sake,' he croaked. 'It's Jack.'

It was almost five before the President finally abandoned the viewing stand. The other guests had long since gone home or, in the case of those favored family friends and relatives, sought the warmth of the White House where a reception had been laid on for them in the State Dining Room. Only the Secret Service and the military and civilian aides remained shivering in the gathering gloom.

Finally to everyone's relief, the new Commander-in-Chief signaled that he had had enough. The Chief of the White House Secret Service detail summoned up the cars, stood by while the President climbed aboard and checked the door was shut. He then took a seat in the front with the driver. Other agents and aides scrambled aboard the back-up vehicles and the convoy moved off.

Three minutes later they drew up under the portico. Sewall was on hand in the entrance hall. The President shook hands and exchanged a few words. He tossed his coat to a doorman, asked after his wife and said he would like to freshen up, then join the party.

'You can say to the First Lady it's okay for her to come down now,' he added.

A fresh team of agents formed up about him as he moved off towards the State Dining Room. They threw open the double doors, forming a protective arc before him as he entered, followed by his aides. The crowd of guests which had fallen quiet in anticipation of his arrival, broke into wild commotion, friends and relatives pressing in round him, wringing his hands, flinging their arms round his neck even, congratulating him emotionally on every side. The glow from the cold air was still in his face, he looked fresh, vigorous, bursting with energy and confidence as he accepted their welcome, laughing, shaking hands, kissing the women and children.

Abruptly he swung back on Sewall. 'Where's my wife?' he hissed urgently. 'These are her family. She should be here to greet them. Get upstairs and ask her to please hurry along down.'

The President's private family apartment occupies the entire second floor of the White House. A long central hall, divided into three sections with an arched window either end, runs east to west the length of the mansion with rooms leading off either side. From the middle section, the yellow Oval sitting room faces south with its balcony built for President Truman over the portico. Beyond are the formal guest suites for visiting heads of state, the Queen's Room and Lincoln's bedroom. The First Family live and sleep at the west end nearest the elevators. The President and First Lady occupy adjoining suites on the south front overlooking the gardens to the Washington Monument. On the floor above are more guest suites and a solarium for relaxation.

Tonight, the long halls were a mêlée of cosmeticians, hairdressers, dress designers and their assistants, maids and secretaries, darting from room to room, wringing their hands and calling querulously to one another. Silk gowns lay out in rows on beds and settees ready for the First Lady to try on. Sewall found an agitated Gina waiting in the central hall. The First Lady was still in bed. She was refusing to dress and go down to join the party. She was weeping. It was impossible. Sewall said he would see what he could do.

They tapped at the door to the First Lady's bedroom. There were sounds of sobbing inside but no response. He signed to Gina to open the door. A scent of gardenias enveloped them in a sickly embrace. At first glance it was as if a blizzard had struck the room. Every surface lay blanketed with heavy white petals. They covered the carpet in snowy drifts of smashed blooms. Sewall had never in his life seen so many flowers in one room before. The heady sweetness of the perfume was so thick it was difficult to breathe. Upturned pots and broken stalks were mute survivors of what had clearly once been a staggering display. Why on earth? he wondered. Did Caro Meade have some bizarre dread of gardenias? Was she allergic to the pollen or something? The First Lady was sitting on the bed in a wrap. Her hair was loose, there was sulkiness in her eyes and at the corners of her mouth, and something else, something Sewall couldn't place.

'Ma'am,' he said gently, 'the President's compliments and he asks would you like to join the party downstairs?'

'Oh,' the First Lady's voice shook, 'are they all there?'

'Your guests? Yes, indeed, ma'am.'

'All my family?'

'I believe so, ma'am.'

'Uncle Bill and Aunt Sarah and the rest? Oh my God!' she cried.

'The President particularly requested that you come down, ma'am,' Sewall persisted.

The First Lady shivered. There was silence between them for a while. She was staring at her hands. The nails, Sewall noticed, were gnawed down to the quick.

'I can't!' Caro Meade wailed suddenly. 'I just can't! I can't face them all. I have to get ready for the balls tonight and I just can't see any more people!'

Sewall took a deep breath. 'Your guests will be very disappointed.'

'I don't care! I can't help it!' Caro Meade broke into sobs. 'I just can't see anybody else now, not yet. You'll tell them for me, please, won't you?' she begged. 'You understand, don't you? I must have some rest, some time to get prepared.'

On a clear patch of carpet by the door lay a crumpled scrap of card, flotsam from the storm. Without thinking, Sewall scooped it up. '. . . *impostor! Stay away from him at all costs! Will try . . .*' he read. Whatever else the message had contained had been torn away in fury.

He glanced at Caro Meade. 'Charming, isn't it? A nice surprise to welcome me to the White House,' she said bitterly.

'This was with the flowers? I don't understand. I was told they were a gift from your husband's campaign office.'

She gave a weary shrug. 'The "Meade for President" people. They all hate me. The election was good as lost when I came on the scene. I saved Jack's career and they know it. I made them look small. Maybe this is somebody's way of getting even.'

No, she said, she didn't want him sending for the Secret Service. It was just a piece of petty spite from someone with a sick mind. Ordinarily it wouldn't have bothered her except that it had come on top of everything else, the Inauguration, the lunch and the parade that had left her drained, utterly exhausted . . . The combination had been too much for a moment. It had tipped her over the edge. But she was okay again. She was breathing normally, her eyes back in focus, the hysteria gone out of them. She was better now, she said. Not to worry. Truly, she said.

Sewall looked again at the scrap of paper in his hand. 'Would you want me to tell the President about this, ma'am?'

No, she said at once. No, she didn't want her husband worried. This was the kind of thing she was having to learn to live with. There had been incidents before, unpleasantnesses. That was what the Secret Service were for, to protect her. She had confidence in them. 'The President has enough on his plate,' she repeated. 'I can cope.'

Sewall folded the slip away inside his breast pocket. Maybe he would show it to the Secret Service later.

Across the river in Alexandria, Frankie Davis, one-time cosmetician to the President-elect, picked up the telephone. 'Yes?' she said.

'Frankie, this is Elaine. No, don't interrupt. I have someone here wants to speak with you.'

There was a pause, then a man's voice came on. 'Frankie, is that you?'

Her heart gave a leap at the well-remembered tones and began to beat fast. 'Senator? . . .' she hesitated. 'Senator, is that really you, sir? I mean, Mr President, sir?'

'Yes, this is Jack Meade. Listen, Frankie, I need your help. Now, this minute. Elaine will tell you what has to be done. Please do exactly as she says and believe me when I say this is the most vital task I shall ever ask of you. Do you understand?'

She gulped. 'Yes, Senator, but what . . . ?'

He cut her short. 'There isn't time to explain over the phone. I'm passing you back to Elaine. Don't fail us, Frankie. I'm counting on you.'

Elaine came back on. She spoke rapidly and succinctly. Frankie was a level-headed person. When Elaine was done she responded that she would gather her kit together, her cosmetics and brushes, and come right over. She also added that she had Humphrey, Jack Meade's former valet, staying with her. Should she bring him along?

Do that, Elaine told her, and hurry.

7

The protection of the President of the United States is the responsibility of the Secret Service. In the 200 years of the nation's existence, no fewer than four presidents, almost one in ten, have been murdered in office and two others seriously injured by assassins. The Service is a division of the Treasury Department, a legacy of the time when its primary role was the combating of counterfeiters. In recent years, the Service's remit has expanded to include members of the First and Second Families as well as former presidents, cabinet members and senior presidential staff when threats warrant protection. The Secret Service also provides security for visiting heads of state and, since the murder of Senator Robert Kennedy, at election time for presidential candidates.

Nevertheless the primary role of the Secret Service remains the security of the executive mansion and the person of the President. By direction of Congress, bodyguards must be in the immediate vicinity of the President at all times. The ultimate duty expected of agents is exactly what the term implies – to interpose their bodies between the President and the bullet intended for him.

Douglas E. Blacker was head of the White House Secret Service detail and for the past five years the man charged with responsibility for the protection of the person of the President. In an era when threats against his masters had increased exponentially it seemed with every passing year, Blacker had fought off maniacs who crash-dived aircraft into the executive mansion, bomb plots by fundamentalist fanatics, lone wolf snipers, even drive-by shootings by passing motorists. During those five years not once had an assassin come close to endangering the President, the First Family or any of the heads of state and other important guests passing through the White House.

The liberal press might chaff at the ever-tighter cordons drawn around the person of the President, the ever-greater distances photographers were made to stand at public events. Civil liberties groups might rail at the restrictions he imposed on access to the White House or the closing off of side streets within rifle shot of the executive mansion; foreign ambassadors might protest at being shouldered aside at public functions by cohorts of Secret Service storm-troopers; Blacker bore all such criticism with chilly indifference. A man given to laconic understatement, his only recorded public statement to a journalist had been, 'Keep your distance.' Douglas Blacker's universe was centered on 1600 Pennsylvania Avenue and behind those gates he was the keeper of the flame.

Captain 'Bing' Bong and his junior assistant, Lieutenant Macmillan, were unhappy men. For the past forty minutes in a windowless cubicle in the Secret Service East Wing command post they had been grilled mercilessly by Blacker and two grim-faced investigators from US Navy Intelligence. Over and over the same question: how in the hell could they have been dumb enough to issue a White House pass to a man posing as a Navy dentist with stolen ID?

Because of the phone call from Blair House, from the President-elect in person, the Captain repeated desperately. He would swear it was his voice. No, he hadn't thought to verify the call. The Senator had referred to him by his nickname, specifically stated that he was sending the Lieutenant Commander over and requested he be given a pass. Yes, he agreed wearily, he had heard of security checks. Yes, he knew the procedures, but this was a naval officer with a letter of authorization notepaper signed by the President-elect. Yes, he understood now the letter was a forgery but at the time . . .

And what of the identity check? The interrogators turned on Macmillan. Hadn't it occurred to his tiny brain to compare the ID photo against the man in front of him? But he had, the wretched officer protested in vain. He had, he had. Sure, the guy had seemed different a little, so did they all. Those snapshots never looked like anyone human. He had been told to issue a pass to a man called Casey and he had done so . . . he had checked the ID, he even recalled remarking on the officer's resemblance to Senator, sorry, President Meade . . .

How was that again? Blacker interrupted. You're saying he looked like the President? How alike?

The Lieutenant repeated what he had said.

'You asked him that to his face?'

The Lieutenant nodded. Yes, he had.

'And how did he respond?'

He had seemed put out, the Lieutenant answered.

'You didn't make anything of that?'

'I figured he was pissed off with people asking all the time, sir.'

Blacker and the Navy interrogators exchanged glances. 'Describe the man again for us,' Blacker said.

Medium height, the Lieutenant said. About the same as Jack Meade but lighter built. Hair darker than the President's and wet looking. 'Like he used a gel. And long, long for the Navy that is. Pale face, sunken eyes, skin scraped as if he had shaved in a hurry. It crossed my mind he looked kind of sick but I figured with the cold weather and all . . .'

Blacker cut in, 'And this likeness to the President, was it just an impression he gave or was there something more positive, a definite resemblance?'

The Lieutenant looked across at Bong. Both their faces were ashen and sweating. He moistened his lips with his tongue. 'When he took off his cap it was like he had to be family, I thought,' he said fearfully.

The door opened and Rex Coffey, head of the Military Office entered with Rusty Castoro, deputy chief of the White House detail. Blacker looked up questioningly. Rusty shook his head.

'Nothing? Nothing at all?'

'Not a smell. No pass in the name of Casey has been presented at any of the entrances. We've used the computers to cross-reference every naval officer below flag rank entering the mansion between now and midday and not a tickle. Currently we're running through the videotapes from the gate cameras in case he showed up then got cold feet, but we're back to 2 p.m. so far and no luck.'

Coffey had more to report. The Pentagon had checked its logs and the call to the aide's office had been traced back to Atlanta. Blair House had also logged a call from Atlanta around the same time and so too had the Speaker's office at the Capitol. The call to the Speaker and the subsequent incident at the Capitol were the subject of a separate investigation. There was no doubt the same person was involved. The call to Captain Bong had been made from an airline office and Atlanta PD were trying to trace personnel on duty at the time.

'It looks like our man rang Blair to obtain the number for the Captain. The operator was fooled by the voice too. According to the Blair operator the caller first asked for Mrs Meade.'

'Why wasn't he put through to her?'

'Mrs Meade was in church. With her husband. The caller claimed to have asked for her in error; said he really wanted Captain Bong.'

There was silence in the room. The men exchanged glances.

'A crazy,' said Coffey. 'Definitely a crazy.'

Blacker checked his watch and stood up. 'Get their statements,' he told Rusty in his curt way. To the interrogators he said, 'You can keep your boys' mouths buttoned till we pick up this voice artist.' It was not a question.

The two scowled. The Navy was embarrassed. Which was almost worse than a security breach. For Captain Bong and Lieutenant Macmillan it was worse. 'Oh, we can keep them quiet for you,' the senior of the two snapped. 'They're not going to be seeing or talking to anyone for quite a while.'

'Good,' said Blacker and left.

At Elaine's there could be no doubts about the rightful president. Elaine had been worried how Frankie and Humphrey would react. Suppose the pair were not convinced? Suppose the impostor had fooled them just as he had apparently fooled the rest of the presidential entourage? But if anyone in the world outside his wife knew the real Jack Meade, she reminded herself, it had to be these two. But then again they hadn't seen him since the surgery.

In the event she needn't have worried. Frankie actually broke down and cried when she saw Jack. The President hugged her and wrung Humphrey's hand. It was an emotional moment. 'I knew all the time something was wrong,' Humphrey said, speaking for both. 'I said Jack Meade doesn't ditch his friends like that.'

After relief came astonishment and outrage. How could this thing have happened? they demanded. How was it possible for the President of the United States to be replaced by a double? Why had no one else realized? And most of all, who was the impostor who had taken his place?

'I've been asking myself that same question,' Jack told them.

There was no time to spare for speculation. Elaine sent Jack off to shower and rest. They had worked out a plan; she would explain it to the others.

Frankie confided to Elaine that she was worried. The President was in poor shape, she whispered. He wasn't well. 'His color is bad, gray looking and his skin tone is just dreadful. It's lost all elasticity and he's developing a stress rash. I'm going to have to work on him before he can appear in public.'

He had been through a lot, Elaine agreed, but he was strong, he would pull through. 'A few hours' sleep will put him back on his feet. Remember how it was on the campaign trail? He can catnap any time, any place. He'll wake up refreshed and you can get to work on him.' Elaine was more concerned about the state of Jack's hair. It badly needed trimming but Frankie said she could handle that. She had started her training in a salon and always carried scissors in her kit.

Elaine herself looked pretty beat, Frankie thought. Her face was puffy, her hands shook and there were liquor bottles among the garbage. Her mind was sharp as ever, though. She had made coffee, swigging cups as she rapped out instructions. Humphrey's job was to round up a set of fresh clothes. No problem, the valet promised. He still had contacts among several of the big stores and boutiques that would open up their shops to him even at this hour if asked. 'Jack is a tailor's dream. He can wear suits straight off the rail.'

7.55 p.m. the evening of the Inauguration, the new President, his First Lady and their guests assembled in the North Entrance Hall prior to setting out for the Kennedy Center at eight to attend the first of the inaugural balls. Outside, the great lantern burned under the North Portico and the cold night crackled with radio static as staff and security men milled about in an atmosphere of controlled panic, marshaling vehicles into line and assigning seats, their breath hanging like gunsmoke in the bitter air.

As on every occasion when the President enters or departs the White House, a Secret Service SWAT team armed with machine-guns took station on the roof of the executive mansion. A second counter-assault team would travel with the twenty vehicle convoy.

Each of tonight's venues had been previously sealed, searched and maintained secure by FBI bomb teams with sniffer dogs. Anyone entering, guests or staff, had to pass through metal detectors, and video surveillance cameras were in place to monitor ballrooms and halls. The backgrounds of cooks, waiters, maids, doormen and other employees had been checked against the computers of the Secret Service Protective Research Section, known agitators were excluded and the remainder issued with color-coded badges.

Leading the convoy was a pilot car with two police motorcycle escorts. Their instructions were to maintain a lead of at least 200 yards on the rest of the procession. If there was going to be trouble of any kind they were the ones to raise the alarm.

No trouble was anticipated tonight. If trouble did come it would most likely be in the form of the crowd breaking through the police lines at the approach to one of the venues. So the agents in the lead car would remain in constant radio contact with the rest of the convoy all the way.

Stagecoach, the presidential Lincoln Continental limousine, drew up to the portico and the Chief Usher escorted the President and First Lady to the entrance. Douglas Blacker again checked that both rear doors were closed before taking his seat beside the Secret Service driver. By his knees within instant reach was a compartment containing a loaded assault rifle. O'Gara-Hess & Eisenhardt Armoring Company of Cincinnati, whose vehicles had protected every American president since Harry Truman, had installed the limousine's armor. Their conversion added more than 3,000 pounds to the Lincoln's original curb weight. The vehicle had been disassembled and rebuilt from the floor-pan up. New armored pillars were installed; an armored rear partition and windshield integrated into the bodyshell; complete new armored door assemblies manufactured and installed and an armored roof fabricated. The titanium-ceramic armor would withstand a 155mm shell air-bursting five meters overhead or a twelve-pound mine detonating under the chassis. The two-inch-thick bullet-proof windows had been tested against .50 caliber armor piercing ammunition. The passenger compartment was provided with its own oxygen supply and fire suppression system, a global position indicator accurate to within one meter and a Milstar secure, jam-resistant satellite communications terminal. Even in the event of its tires being shot out the limousine would still be able to maintain a speed of 50 m.p.h. on the steel rims of its wheels.

No other civilian wheeled vehicle in the world delivered a comparable level of ballistic and blast protection. Inside, the President was as near invulnerable as it was possible for any person to be, short of traveling by tank.

Preceding Stagecoach was a decoy vehicle with four agents up. The President's close escort consisting of fifty agents traveled in eight GM Suburbans, also armor plated, three out in front, the other five trailing the limousine. One vehicle in each section was equipped with the 'Beady Eye-Viper' counter-sniper system, its acoustic and infrared sensors capable of instantly pinpointing the firing position of an urban assassin. Following them came the presidential party in four more black sedans bearing personal friends, among them Vice-President Jordan and his wife, the Chief of Staff and Mrs Hunter, and personal and military aides to the President and First Lady. Eight additional vehicles completed the motorcade. These contained more agents, bringing the total in the party to over one hundred, the headquarters communications car, code-named Halfback, with its own Milstar terminal, a fully equipped and staffed ambulance and the standby armored limousine in the event the first suffered a breakdown. Also included was the NSA technical vehicle, the sweeper van, packed with top-secret electronics, fielded and manned by the National Security Agency which constantly scanned the airwaves for the electronic signatures of bomb radio-detonators and missile homing radars, automatically jamming their frequencies.

Bringing up the tail were the official White House photographers to record the evening's celebrations and the White House press pool, ghoulishly known as the 'Death Watch' and present in case anything dramatic should occur – such as the President being shot. Police outriders escorted the rear of the convoy and flanked the presidential vehicle. Additional security vans patrolled neighboring streets ready to provide instant on the spot back-up. A helicopter circled overhead monitoring traffic and alert to potential threats. All vehicles were in constant radio contact with one another, with the Secret Service, military, police and White House staff additionally each maintaining their own separate frequencies.

The lead motorcycles gunned their engines and at a signal over the radio, moved slowly off down the driveway and out through the gates. Sirens wailing, the procession swept up Pennsylvania Avenue, picking up speed. Along the route police barriers blocked off every intersection. At Washington Circle the traffic was held back to give priority as the police motorcyclists leaned their big Harley-Davidsons into the turn.

In the back of the fourth car behind the President's, Karen Lipscombe clung to the seat arm as they heeled over and headed down New Hampshire, over Juarez Circle and swung parallel to the river. Her three-year-old ball gown, a twenty-fifth birthday gift from her parents, was a perfect fit still and she wore her grandmother's pearl choker. At her side, Major Bruce Schaller, resplendent in dress uniform and her escort for the evening, gave her hand a friendly squeeze. Perhaps a little more than friendly. The atmosphere and excitement were getting to everybody. He was from Texas and a fellow Westerner so she returned the pressure, but just a little.

Lights blazed outside the windows. The wail of the sirens up ahead died away as the convoy slowed. They were arriving.

'And now, ladies and gentlemen, your applause please for the President of the U-nited States . . . Jaaack Meade!'

The roar of 500 invited guests at the inaugural gala being thrown by two of the President's chief Hollywood supporters drowned out the loudspeakers in the ballroom. The band was already striking up 'Hail to the Chief' as Jack Meade strode into the spotlights.

'My friends . . . !' He seized the microphone. 'My friends and fellow Americans . . . we stand this night upon the threshold of a great adventure!'

The passionate rhetoric rang through the lofty room and even though they had most of them heard similar messages before, not a man or woman in the place remained unmoved. He saw the shining faces upturned toward him and felt a warm glow of satisfaction. The speech might seem impromptu, but few knew that such an appearance of spontaneity was only achieved by practice and training. Every gesture, every phrase had been mirror-rehearsed till it was perfect, till he knew every cadence, every shift in emphasis by heart. The sensation of holding an audience in his power, of calling forth their emotions, be it anger, fear, hope or laughter, brought him a sense of almost physical release.

'. . . Jack Nicholson once said that every American boy had to decide whether he wanted to be President when he grew up or to have fun. Tonight, ladies and gentlemen, I tell you I intend to achieve both!'

The main body of the ballroom was so packed that dancing was impossible. People stood shoulder to shoulder staring up at the presidential party and celebrities on the stage. More agents, some in tuxedos and black ties and all sporting discreet color-coded pins bearing the five-pointed Secret Service star in their left lapels, were mingling with the guests, the ring drawn tight to prevent anyone getting in close enough for a shot. Every one alert for the tell-tale signs of an assassin keying himself up; the quick eye movements, the tensing of the limbs, flexing of the fingers. 'Watch for sullen faces,' their training warned them. 'When the President is out in public it's a happy occasion normally, so if there's someone in the crowd who doesn't look cheerful, that's an alarm signal.'

'*Hollywood ready to join Hero.*' The flesh-colored receiver in Douglas Blacker's ear squawked abruptly. *Hero* was the President, *Hollywood* his wife. First Family code names shared the same initial letter. The First Lady and her escort were in back of the stage and about to come forward. Blacker made his way round to the edge, passing through the cordon with a nod to the men on duty. He swiveled to check the crowd, his gaze raking the ranks of faces, automatically comparing features with those of the hundred individuals listed Category 3 threats and whose details were imprinted on his memory. Over by one of the doors a tall man with a blond mane, so thick it might be a wig, had his right hand tucked inside the breast of his dinner suit. Blacker flicked his radio transmit button but already an agent was cutting through the revelers to intercept him while another positioned himself to block any possible line of fire to the target. 'Okay, he's clean,' came a message over the air. Most likely the man had merely been reaching for his wallet. Such incidents could be expected throughout the evening.

Not one in a thousand represented an actual threat but all had to be treated the same.

For more than a century every American president elected or re-elected in a year ending in a zero had died in office. The so-called twenty-year death cycle. President William Harrison, elected 1840, had died in office. Lincoln, elected 1860, had been killed, as had Garfield, elected in 1880, and McKinley, elected in 1900. Harding, 1920, and Franklin Roosevelt, 1940, had both died in office, followed by Kennedy, elected 1960 and murdered. Ronald Reagan, elected in 1980, barely escaped death when an explosive bullet fired by a deranged youth bounced off the limousine door, puncturing a lung and lodging an inch from his heart. While the Secret Service rushed him to George Washington University Hospital inside four minutes, the seventy-year-old President had lost so much blood doctors could no longer find a pulse.

Twenty years later would the pattern be repeated again? Blacker was fully aware there were people out there sufficiently mad to try to make it so.

To a fanfare of music the First Lady stepped forward into the lights. Her ball gown was a dark red silk, voluptuous and shoulderless. She lifted her white arms in salute to the gathering, ablaze with triumphant radiance.

'*Caro! Caro! . . .*' Applause thundered through the hall. '*Caro! Caro! . . .*'

At Elaine's Jack was woken again at 9 p.m. They would have let him sleep longer if they could but there was too much to do with little time and limited resources. He took another shower and the team was relieved to note that the gray fatigue had washed out of his face. His whole attitude was more positive. Finding himself among friends again with the knowledge that he was no longer on his own had given his morale a boost. Frankie trimmed his hair and insisted on shaving him herself to avoid nicks or scrapes. Elaine had a sun lamp and Jack was put under it for a brief spell to add a touch of health. Then Frankie set to with moisturizers and foundations to repair the damage of the past ten days.

Elaine looked in before he dressed. She handed him a set of gold sleeve links embossed with the presidential seal, a gift to her father from Carter. The final touch to make his attire complete. She brushed aside his thanks and went to make another call. Using a business directory it took her only a few moments to locate what she needed. When she dialed the number there was a courteous response despite the lateness of the hour.

'We are used to emergencies. Does your friend have access to a cassette recorder? Many of our challenged citizens find them a convenient way to receive messages.'

'Unfortunately my friend is doubly challenged. She suffers a hearing impediment.'

'Oh dear, I am sorry. Such a burden. In that case I am sure we could be of assistance. If you care to come over I will see the requisite equipment is on hand.'

After the presidential couple had left the mansion, Brad Sewall remained on the second floor to supervise the clearing up. Everyone but the maids was permitted to go. Unworn gowns were put into their bags and dispatched back to the couture houses, which had generously loaned them. The sheets on the First Lady's bed were changed and fresh towels placed in the bathrooms. Rugs were vacuumed, cushions plumped up. Only when he was satisfied all was correct and in its place did Sewall take the elevator to his office on the state floor.

He dialed the White House Flower Room and spoke to Ange, the woman in charge. Ange had a powerful personality. Yes, of course she remembered the gardenias for the First Lady's bedroom. They had come in from one of the big hotel florists. Who had sent them? That was no secret; the flowers were a tribute from the Military Office.

'Can you be positive? I thought Mrs Meade said they were from the campaign staff.'

'I can check in the book if you want,' said Ange huffily.

'If it's not too much trouble. We seem to have lost the card.'

Ange ran a tight ship. In less than a minute she was back on the line confirming that she had been right, naturally. The flowers had come from the East Wing.

Sewall apologized for doubting her. All the displays had looked fabulous, he said.

'Of course,' Ange snapped and rang off.

Sewall dialed the Military Office. 'Rex? I was afraid you might be at the balls. Okay if I stop by?'

His shoes rang on the marble North Entrance Hall as he cut between the pillars of the Cross Hall and took the staircase down to the ground floor. Turning left, he entered an elegantly vaulted marble corridor. To his right lay the Vermeil Room, named after its collection of French and English gilded silver, opening to the left was the Library. Directly ahead a glassed colonnade overlooking the Jacqueline Kennedy Garden led to the East Wing.

'So what I wondered, Rex, was could you ask whoever it was ordered these flowers sent to the First Lady what the message was?'

Presidents might come and go but some things did not change. Within the precincts of the White House, three people counted: the Chief Usher, the Chief of the Secret Service detail and the head of the Military Office. Brad Sewall and Rex Coffey got along in the way that men who cannot afford to quarrel have to.

Rex studied the torn-off portion of the card. 'I didn't know we bunched the First Lady flowers,' he said. He flipped his intercom and tried to raise the aides' extension but there was no reply. 'All out at the balls.' He frowned. 'I guess we could find out from the florist's. Ange will have the name.'

There was no answer from the shop. Rex hesitated not a moment. He rang the switchboard and told them to track down the salesperson on duty. Using the authority of the White House, the switchboard extracted from the hotel the name and number of the concession owner. A call to the individual at his home produced a number in Queens for the girl behind the counter. She was out but her mother knew where she could be reached. Inside fifteen minutes they had her on the line, astonished and not a little nervous.

She had no trouble in recalling the order. She had delivered it herself, she explained. The account had been charged to the Military Office as instructed.

Who had instructed her? Coffey asked, still puzzled.

The officer of course who had come by. From the Navy, he was. He had made a particular request to have them delivered tonight so she had—

His name, Coffey interrupted. She must have taken his name for her records.

'Yes, sir, I have it here somewhere. I wrote it down in case someone at the White House asked but they didn't, they just signed the receipt and said it was okay. I guess they had so many . . . Yes, sir, I'm trying to find it. Just one moment, sir . . . oh, here it is, Lieutenant-Commander Casey, USN . . .'

Doug Blacker had cut short his inspection of the inaugurals and was back in the command post eating supper off a tray in his office. He heard out Rex and the Chief Usher, then spoke by radio to the agent in charge of the President's close protection ordering extra vigilance. Then he pressed a red button on his intercom. 'Institute Measure Five,' he instructed tersely.

Rex's eyes bulged. 'Measure Five? Aren't you over-reacting?' Five was the code for an immediate search of the entire White House area. 'There's no call for panic.

We're talking about a flower delivery here. We know the guy hasn't obtained access to the building.'

Blacker's mouth tightened. 'You may. I don't.'

'We checked every gate. The pass hasn't been used once. We both know that,' Rex said, exasperated. 'It's not the security risk factor I worry about,' he continued. 'We've circulated his name to every government agency and building in the country. He uses it to try and gain entry anywhere official and he'll be in jail before his feet touch the ground. But this kind of mean trick getting to the First Lady really makes me mad.'

Sewall chipped in, 'She was pretty upset, Doug. We have to nail this creep before he tries again.'

'A weirdo,' Rex added. 'A creep but not a threat. A weirdo.'

'Sort of like John Hinckley?' suggested Blacker and Rex scowled.

Rex was rattled, Blacker noted wryly. This business of the escaped patient and the ease with which he had obtained a pass reflected badly on the military and therefore on Rex. Rex was a man with ambitions beyond the Military Office. He cultivated contacts outside the mansion. On leaving the military he was toying with entering politics. A scandal could dent his hopes.

Which was all too bad for Rex. Blacker's sole concern was for the safety of the presidential couple. Within fifteen minutes a small army of uniformed and plain-clothes agents were combing the 132-room mansion from basement to chimney stacks including both wings and the private apartments, opening closets, peering under beds, checking identities. Meanwhile outside in the biting wind, dog handlers with flashlights and infrared glasses poked among the bushes, cursing their commander as they went.

Neither search, internal or of the grounds, turned up anything. The grumbling agents were stood down. An uneasy peace returned to the mansion.

*

Elaine had tickets for the inaugural ball being held at the Mayflower. The President and First Lady were due to look in around 11 p.m. The plan was for Jack to be smuggled inside and somehow reach Caro. He and Elaine worried how he was to get past the door without alerting the guards. Humphrey solved the problem. From a street vendor he bought one of the joke Jack Meade face masks that had proved so popular during the parade. Disguised in a caricature of himself, Jack would go to the ball.

The dinner suit that Humphrey had found was a near enough likeness to the outfit previously selected for the President to wear tonight. To be doubly sure they had watched the impostor's arrival at the Hilton on Elaine's TV before leaving. In the car Frankie gave Jack's hair a last brush. The transformation she had worked on his appearance was astonishing. The shadows under the eyes had been banished, the cheeks were smooth and unlined. His face had the bronzed sheen of a man just back from Florida. In his fresh new clothes he looked every inch a president.

Elaine offered to accompany him. He would be less conspicuous with a companion, she said. Jack shook his head. Once inside he preferred to be on his own. Elaine should stay home where he could reach her if there was trouble.

They dropped him off a block short of the hotel. 'Goodbye,' they whispered. 'And good luck.' Humphrey would wait around the block with the car in case he needed to make a getaway. Under the entrance canopy there was a noisy mêlée of people waiting to pass inside. With the presidential party due soon revelers were crowding into the venue. The Secret Service at the barrier were under pressure. The metal detectors were playing up. Guests kept trying to go through with cameras and other objects, setting off the sirens. The line was backing up and growing impatient, people complaining at the delay. Also they were under orders to check for naval officers, of which there were many. The Jack Meade mask drew a few chuckles but his was not the only one and he slid easily into the crush moving down toward the scrum at the barrier. Elaine and Humphrey had stripped his pockets of anything likely to trip the alarms. No fears on that score. The only risk was of being recognized. As he came abreast of the guards he pushed the mask up onto his forehead so it still concealed his hair and held out his ticket with a cheerful grin. They had practiced this back at Elaine's. The guards would be concentrating on tickets, they theorized and with only half a face to go on would be hard put to make a match. The ticket was in the name of Frank Wilson, Elaine's brother-in-law, and he had Frank's driver's license to support the identity.

The agent glanced at the ticket. His gaze flicked up mechanically to Jack's face and his mouth twitched faintly at the sight of the mask. 'Thank you, sir,' he returned the ticket and waved him on through. 'Next . . .'

After spending a little over an hour at the Kennedy Center ball, the presidential party climbed back aboard their motorcade for the drive to the next of the night's celebrations at the Washington Hilton, and more ovations. By midnight they were on the move again, heading back downtown toward the Mayflower where more crowds and cameras waited to greet the President. The First Lady was showing signs of flagging. She had taken a duty turn on the dance floor with her husband then retired to rest in a suite upstairs. The President though was full of energy still. In the blaze of lights constantly trained on him he moved about the ballroom, greeting supporters, hugging and kissing old friends, clapping people on the back, waving and beaming with evident delight in his new role.

Behind the cover of his mask, Jack Meade stared in horrified amazement. Applause was thundering against the ceiling as only yards away the First Couple passed him, bathed in the glow of spotlights, waving to the audience. There could be no mistaking his wife, her ecstatically parted lips or radiant expression, as she posed hand in hand with the impostor that he had seen on the television and glimpsed momentarily back in the Capitol.

It could not be, it was not possible. A copy so perfect in its likeness that no one, not even a man's wife, could detect a difference. Yet there the creature was, surrounded by his, Jack's, own former friends: dupes or accomplices – which? His own wife clasping his stand-in's hand in careless familiarity. Was there no lingering doubt, no shadow of suspicion in her mind, in theirs?

Unable to tear himself from the scene, he gaped mesmerized at the facsimile of himself up there on the stage. There was a grotesque fascination in hearing an impostor mimic his voice, watching him ape his mannerisms. The spectacle seemed unreal. Like watching re-runs of himself on video. Who was this man and where had he sprung from? Some bit-part actor with a grudge against him or a wider conspiracy?

'Caro! Caro!' The cheering roared in his ears. He could stand to look no longer and, turning, slipped away into the throng. His wife. Somehow he must reach her. Somehow he had to get her alone.

Karen danced a turn with Major Schaller and another with Jay Leeder. She was still waiting and hoping for the President to invite her on to the floor but so far he seemed to have overlooked her presence. The noise and the heat were beginning to tell on her. Her Elvis set was out of place for dancing and anyway of limited use in such a close crowd so she had left it off. Her eyes were so light dazzled she knew she would be totally blind for the rest of tonight. When the music ended she asked Jay if he would mind finding someone who could see her to the ladies' rest room.

149

'No problem, Trish Beale is just over there. She'll be happy to go along with you.'

He led her by the hand to the other side of the room. 'I'm sorry to be such a nuisance,' she apologized, 'but with these glaring lights and hordes of people everywhere I'm just about helpless.'

It made her angry having to admit to her condition like this and be dependent especially on an air-headed social butterfly like Trish Beale but there was nothing else for it. Fortunately Trish seemed keen to leave: the noise in the ballroom was giving her a migraine, she said as she took Karen's arm, steering her like a zombie.

A suite of rooms close by had been set aside for the use of the President's party with a pair of Secret Service guards on the door. Several others were there before them also taking time out. Trish showed Karen into the bathroom and made sure she had everything she needed. 'I'll be here when you're through,' she promised. 'We can go back down or sit it out here for a while if you'd rather. I know I'm bushed.'

Karen felt stronger having splashed her face with water and run a comb through her hair. When she emerged, Trish was waiting as promised. Karen found herself being introduced to another couple, the Hinksons, both, to judge by their voices, in their eighties. He it seemed had been the husband of Jack Meade's aunt on his mother's side. She was now dead and he had remarried. 'But we've always stayed real close to Jack. Splendid boy, great guy. Always knew he'd make it to the top some day.' He seemed a little excitable.

They chatted for a moment, then Trish said she supposed they ought to be getting back to the ball and Mr Hinkson said, yes, it would be a shame to miss out simply on account of being weary. Karen picked up her clutch purse and laid her hand firmly on Trish's forearm before she could be seized by the biceps again. As she did so she heard the click of the door being opened, letting in the throb of music from the dance floor.

'Karen.'

She knew the voice instantly. Simultaneously she felt Trish's body at her side stiffen in recognition.

'Why, hi there nephew,' Hinkson cried out jovially. 'You come to join the party? Bridget here says I've had too much excitement for my own good as it is.'

'Now you hush, Tom,' his wife hissed. 'You're speaking to the President of the United States, remember.'

'Hi, Uncle T.,' came the President's voice and then, 'Karen, you're looking wonderful.'

It wasn't what he said so much as the tone which sent warm shivers up Karen's spine. It made the whole evening suddenly worthwhile. Keep a hold of yourself, she thought.

'Thank you, Mr President,' she managed somehow to respond, praying her voice sounded natural. 'It's . . . it's great to be here.'

The Secret Service men were attempting to interrupt. They seemed concerned about something. 'Sir, Mr President, what happened to your escort?' one of them was demanding.

'You know, Jack, I was just saying to Bridget here . . .'

'Charlie Bravo this is Foxtrot Three.' One of the agents was speaking urgently into his microphone, 'Hero has separated from escort. He is now at Station Eight. Foxtrot Three and Four have eyeball. Send back-up. Repeat: Hero is at Station Eight without escort. Over.'

'Nephew, you know I don't believe I've seen you look this smart since your high school prom,' Hinkson sounded faintly put out at being ignored.

'Oh, Mr President,' Trish was gushing, 'I've been wanting to tell you this is simply the greatest day of my—'

'Karen,' came the President's voice again. 'Karen, I have something for you.'

Someone was knocking on the door outside. 'Who is

151

it?' an agent shouted. The response was inaudible above the other voices. 'Don't come in!' More knocking. 'Stay outside please!'

'Goddammit,' the other agent was muttering close by Karen, 'I can't hear what they're telling me.'

'Karen, Karen . . .' the President's hand found hers. She clutched it hard and had to choke back a sob at the answering pressure.

'Sir, please . . . what can I do?' she whispered, straining to make out the shape of his face among the shifting shadows around her.

'Are they mad or what?' the second agent exclaimed suddenly. 'They're saying Hero is across in the ballroom. I repeat: We are eyeball with Hero up here on Eight. Over.'

'Karen,' the President was saying again. He seemed to keep repeating her name. She could feel the tension in his voice and the way he gripped her hand. All at once she began to feel frightened.

'They're sending over a team,' the agent exhaled with a sharp hiss of breath. He sounded relieved. 'They still claim they have eyeball on someone in there.'

'How can they be that dumb?'

'Beats me. They say the Tracker system is down. The laser show on the dance floor is knocking out the electronics. There's going to be hell an' all to pay, that much is for sure. Sorry about this, Mr President, sir, seems like there's been a glitch. We'll have it sorted in one minute. There's a fresh team on the way. Meantime you're safe here with us.'

'Karen.' Again her name but quieter this time, almost a whisper, the anxiety very apparent. Then unbelievably his lips against her cheek. 'Help me. You must help me.' She felt a hand fumble at her purse. 'Karen, this is for you,' he whispered in her ear.

Before she could make sense of his words he had released her again. 'It seems I should return downstairs,'

Karen heard him say in a more normal voice. 'You two had better escort me.' A chuckle. 'And try not to let me get away this time.'

'Sir, it's best you wait here. There are more men on the way.'

'Then we shall meet them on the stairs. So long Uncle T., Bridget. Are you coming along, Trish? You mind giving Karen your arm?'

'Sir, I have to insist ... You must wait here.'

The other agent chimed in. 'Please, sir, it's for your own security. There aren't enough of us to guarantee your safety.'

'Miss Lipscombe here is coming with me. Stand aside and let her pass, please.'

All at once confusion broke out. Karen was propelled vigorously forward, cannoning against a large body. For several moments she was jostled in the doorway. Someone trod heavily on her foot, making her cry out in pain and her purse flew from her grasp.

Then unaccountably she burst into tears.

At the end of the passage Jack snatched the mask from its hiding place behind the fire extinguisher and pulled it on. Damn those agents: without them he could have pulled it off. He should have guessed they would panic if he came upon them suddenly like that. Mentally he cursed himself the most. He could have tried to brazen it out, force a show-down there and then. Why had his nerve failed him? He knew the answer. It was the sight of that mirror image of himself in the ballroom, Caro's willing hand in his paw. The likeness was too perfect. Too many had been duped. As of this moment his double was the President with all the awesome powers of the state at his command. To challenge the doppelgänger openly at this moment would likely cost him his own life.

Caro was the key. People would have to believe her. Only first he must get her alone to break the spell of the impostor's hold. Unless she were a willing dupe. Doubt tore at him.

Right now his greatest danger was of being trapped inside the building. Walking swiftly he threaded his way back through the throng of guests toward the main entrance. The Secret Service at the barrier were trying to make sense of conflicting reports coming over the radio net. Already he could detect sounds of pursuit at his rear and quickened his pace. He pushed through the doors just as reinforcements hurried up to seal off the building. There were no cabs free and he daren't wait around to be picked up. Ducking his head, he made off up the street, shivering with the cold in his light clothes.

Somewhere close by a siren started up and instinctively he increased his pace. Then there were shouts and the sound of pounding feet up ahead. He ducked into a doorway as a uniformed squad doubled across a junction. The authorities were reacting fast, sealing off the streets at the intersections, throwing a cordon around the area. He took a left, still walking fast. To run would draw attention. Damn! Two blocks down he could see the flashing blue lights of another road block cutting him off from Humphrey and the car. There were few pedestrians around up here; he was growing conspicuous. Must get off the street. Too risky to try and reach Elaine's tonight. He had a fallback plan but it wasn't tested. He would just have to hope. Two streets west was a place to hide up. Maybe.

14th Street. 15th Street. It seemed like forever. Set into the wall of the 15th Street side of the Chrysler-Lincoln Hotel was an unmarked brass door. Sometimes it was unlocked. He prayed this was one of them. The handle was recessed into the metal. He gripped and twisted. A mechanism turned with a weighty clunk. The door swung open. Seized with relief, he ducked inside.

He paused a minute, adjusting his eyes to the moist darkness within. He was standing in a steam tunnel, part of the network running under the hotel. Feeling his way by touch, he descended an iron ladder. A wheeze of steam muted the traffic noise and laid a film of moisture on every surface. At the bottom a greasy refulgence from the street lamps filtered down through grilles in the roof, barely illuminating the huge pipes snaking away in front and behind down dripping tunnels into blackness. A man who knew the tunnels could travel clear through to Union Station it was said, without once coming up for air. The air was the worst part of it, a poisonous compound of fouled vapors that seared the lungs at every breath.

Gasping, he crept stooping beneath the pipes till he came to a vault-like hatch recessed in brickwork. He pounded on it with his fist.

'Roy!' his voice boomed in his ears. 'Roy, are you in there?'

'I'm telling you it was him! Hero! You think I don't know what the President looks like? I may be dumb but I'm not blind as well.'

It was after 2 a.m. The celebrations were over, the President long since safely escorted back to the security of the White House. In further emulation of Kennedy he had elected to spend his first night asleep in Lincoln's Room. Meantime the cordon around him had been tightened as never before and the city-wide search for the impostor intensified. All of which was being kept from the President.

When the agents arrived Blacker listened to their accounts of what had occurred. Occasionally he posed a curt question but for the most part he heard them out in silence. A twin-tape recorder on the desk automatically recorded every word said.

'Okay, once more, from the beginning.' If Blacker was tired no sign of it showed in either face or manner. His eyes like chips of gray slate bored into the unhappy agents who stood before his desk. Petrescu, their supervisor, leaned against the wall, listening.

'This man then, who you took for Hero, how was he dressed?'

Like most everyone else tonight, in black tie and tuxedo, was the answer. And if he wasn't the President then he was his twin brother. Both men affirmed that much with a sincerity bordering on desperation, Blacker thought, looking at them.

'Right, step by step. The two of you, Colton and Suter, are on duty in the rest room. The President's uncle, Mr Hinkson is there with his wife, no one else till Mrs Beale enters with Miss Lipscombe. Did you recognize either of these women?'

'I recognized Mrs Beale,' Colton, the older of the two, nodded. 'Seen her around the President-elect once or twice. The other one was the President's new secretary, Miss Lipscombe. I remember her because she don't see too well.'

'We checked their passes even so,' his partner added defensively.

'Then the President walks right into the rest room, or so you both assume. How about the others present? Did they take it for granted this was the President too?'

'Like I said, sir, everyone did,' Colton sighed resignedly. He had told the story so often even he was beginning to doubt himself. 'Mr Hinkson, the President's uncle, was talking to him about his school days, the President's that is, and Mrs Beale, she seemed to know him fine too.'

Also, he added, twice earlier in the evening at other events the President had slipped away from his escort to join parties in private rooms.

'Stick to the point.'

'I just mean it didn't seem so crazy at the time.'

'Enough,' Blacker growled.

He glanced down at the envelope which lay on the desk

before him in a transparent plastic pouch, the sole tangible evidence of what had occurred. 'You think this might have been dropped as the impostor, the man you took to be the President, forced his way out the door?' Both men nodded. 'So there was a jam in the doorway. The President, as you thought, trying to push his way out with Miss Lipscombe. Was she a part of this, you reckon?' He watched carefully for their reply.

The two glanced at one another and shook their heads. 'She was confused. She had no idea what was going on,' answered Colton, the senior one.

'So what happened next?'

'The rest room opens right off the foyer to the ballroom. There must have been 200 people coming and going. Tuxedos all. Hero plunges in among them and he's gone. We didn't know what to do. We still thought he was the President. Suter and I pushed into the crowd after him but he's vanished like he fell down a hole.'

'Looks like he simply walked out the exit with the crowd,' put in Petrescu, the supervisor. 'Guards had orders to check guests entering the building, not leaving. Only other way was back into the ballroom.'

Blacker shook his head. 'Two presidents in the same hall. Somebody would have noticed that much. No, he had to leave by the front. Kept his head down to avoid being recognized and escaped in the crush.'

Colton continued his account. 'So then I ran back along to the rest room. The guests were getting ready to go back to the dance. Mrs Beale wanted to know where the President had gotten to. I told her he had most likely gone to find his escort. When the others left I found the envelope just inside the doorway. I figured the thing might be important so I picked it up.'

'The first sensible thing you did all evening,' muttered Petrescu.

'Sir, none of this is our fault!'

157

'Enough,' Blacker scowled. 'The others, Miss Lipscombe, Mrs Beale and the Hinksons, what did they make of these goings on?'

Colton looked at his partner again and shook his head. 'Miss Lipscombe was upset but that was only because she got tramped on. I guess the rest of them thought like we did, that the President was acting kind of weird but it was, you know Inauguration night and all . . .'

'There was no alarm given,' Petrescu said dourly. 'At that stage we were still figuring in terms of a communications glitch. Either that or else a hoax. Had to be one or the other.'

'Jesus,' whispered one of the agents, 'I mean there can't be two presidents, can there? It just isn't possible.'

A heavy silence fell across the room. Blacker seemed lost in thought. With an effort he roused himself. 'Maybe this will tell us,' he grunted, picking up the envelope in its cover. 'You had better get it down to Technical.'

When Petrescu and the two agents had gone, Blacker sat a moment longer. He pressed the button on his desk which automatically locked the outer door. Opening his personal safe concealed behind a closet door, he took out a blue folder embossed with the presidential seal in gold. Within the covers was everything that was known about the personal and political life of the man calling himself Jack Meade and currently occupying the Lincoln bedroom. Returning to his chair, he slipped off his shoes, put his feet up on the desk, lit a cigarette and settled down to read.

He was still reading twenty minutes later when a phone call from the technical unit in the basement informed him that the envelope had been declared hazard-free and was ready for unsealing.

Blacker went down to watch.

The unit was located in a windowless underground complex burrowed beneath the South Lawn. The duty officer slipped on a pair of disposable gloves and, handling the envelope carefully by the edges, placed it flat on a glass-topped box. Smudges of red fingerprint powder dusted the surface. At the press of a switch a strong light illuminated the paper from underneath, revealing the contents of the envelope in dark relief.

The technician stared intently for a surprisingly long time. 'I'd say two sheets, 80 gram,' he said, frowning. 'Folded once over.' He cocked an eye questioningly in Blacker's direction.

'Get on with it,' Blacker snapped, irritated by the performance.

The officer fed the envelope through the electric opener. There was a brief whir as the hidden revolving blade skimmed a quarter-inch slice off the bottom edge. Using tweezers, the technician extracted the folded sheets from inside the envelope, separated them out and laid them parallel on a glass-topped desk for inspection.

'They haven't been dusted yet,' he warned.

Blacker waved him back and bent over the desk. His first reaction was surprise.

Both sheets were blank.

Blacker stared at the pages closely. The paper was a brilliant white, shiny smooth but the surface was marked by lines of embossed groups of dots in differing combinations of three as if in a kind of code. He chewed his lip, thinking. Then abruptly his expression cleared.

The clocks in the main house were just striking three as he and one of the technicians made their way through the colonnade to the West Wing. Outside the Oval Office the duty clerk met him with a set of master keys. At a curt nod from Blacker they unlocked the door to the secretary's suite.

Inside the inner office, two desks formed an angle, backed by tall filing cabinets. The further of the desks was almost entirely taken up with a huge VDU screen with a flat-bed scanner to one side, a fast laser printer the other. Blacker glanced at his assistant. The young man threw him a grin, 'No problem, Chief.' Pulling up the chair, he switched on the power. The screen hummed and flickered into life. 'Good morning,' intoned a cheerful metallic voice, 'and how are you today, Karen?'

Blacker scowled, 'Damn machines. Won't she have password security?'

'Doesn't matter. We only need to operate a program, not touch any files. This here is the Braille reader. All we have to do is scan each page. The computer will convert it to normal text and print off a hard copy.'

Blacker chewed his lip and waited. He badly wanted another cigarette. His patience had almost run out when the laser printer clicked into action. He snatched the first page off the bin.

'*My dear Karen*,' it began. '*I am addressing this to you for the single reason that I have no one else to turn to I can trust. Memory plays such tricks. The very last thing I can positively recall is hearing that you were joining my staff as a special assistant. The next is waking up in bed in Jacksonville Naval Hospital to learn that I had been rescued from the ocean two days ago, a man without a name. If that statement sounds hard to believe, I am going on to ask you to accept something even more difficult, monstrous in fact:*

The man calling himself the President of the United States is not who he claims to be!'

With growing incredulity Blacker read on.

'*. . . I am desperately worried for Caro's sake. Her life is in terrible danger. She must be warned. It is imperative she invent some excuse to stay away from the impostor. I tried to reach her this afternoon but the guards were everywhere. Show her this letter. Tell her I will try to arrange a meeting so she can see the proof with her own eyes . . .*'

'What you want me to do with this?' The technician indicated the text on the screen.

Blacker was still trying to adjust to the import of what

he had read. Wipe it, he told him finally, and any back-up along with it. He wanted no evidence left behind of their visit.

The young man's fingers rattled over the keys. 'All gone and I cleared the memory too. Nothing to show we've even been here.'

The technician however was sighted. Like most people he had no conception of the world from the standpoint of the blind. He could not conceive for instance of Karen's perpetual anxiety about losing documents. The computers were her lifeline. She protected them with UPS on-line batteries and surge protectors. A software developer working with the American Institute for the Blind had run up a neat little program which automatically backed up every document onto a tape streamer. Thanks to the Elvis headset Karen's reliance on the system was diminished but she maintained it as a last resort safety measure. The tape streamer copied the text of the letter within seconds of it flashing up on the screen. An LCD button light flickered for a moment as the drive spun but Blacker and the technician were too intent on what they were doing to notice. Since this was the first document on the tape and no file number had been assigned, the system allocated it the reference code 0001, added time and date, switched off and reset. The subsequent instructions to delete original and back-up affected only the main program; the tape archive retained its data intact as it was designed to.

Back in the privacy of his own office, Blacker locked the door. Using his personal copier, he made a single photocopy of each page. The originals he locked in his safe together with the debriefing tapes of the agents. A strict security blackout on the incident had already been decreed while outside a massive search was underway across the city to locate and arrest the former patient masquerading as Commander Casey who was believed to harbor a grudge against the President.

Then he settled down to personally type up his own report. He had still not finished when one of his officers brought him a videotape with a compilation of film shot by security cameras in the Capitol and the hotel. Blacker took time out to watch the clips. The images were grainy and indistinct but where the impostor's face was visible Blacker felt his stomach tighten. The resemblance to the President could not be doubted. And it was not just a facial similarity. The height, the build, the figure's gestures, even the way he carried himself were uncanny reminders of Jack Meade.

8

January 21st in the White House. A bright day dawning with no snow forecast and much less cold. A houseman bearing an armful of clothing tapped softly at the door to the President's bedroom. 'Seven o'clock, Mr President.'

The President awoke from sleep. His first impression was of immense stillness. The mansion was set in 90 acres of parkland. It was almost like being in the country. 'Okay,' he muttered. Outside in the second-floor passage, the Secret Service night man heard and lifted a phone. 'The President is awake.' The message would be transmitted immediately to the basement situation room and across the Potomac to the Pentagon, informing the military machine that the Commander-in-Chief was on the bridge again.

The houseman entered the bedroom. Silently crossing the carpet, he placed the clothing carefully on the back of a chair and deposited a bundle of newspapers on the four-poster bed. He wished the President good morning and drew back the drapes on the long windows. Returning, he collected up the clothes the President had shed last night and let himself out again.

The President shook himself and switched on the lamp by the bed. Next it lay the black leather wallet with the plastic code card for launching nuclear war. The ever-present reminder of the awesome responsibility of office. He glanced cursorily at the papers, rolled out of bed and snapped into an aerobic routine. Stretches, squats and sit-ups. Plus two minutes' jogging on the spot. Get the blood circulating. This was it, the first day in office. A fine day by the look of it too. Perhaps that was an omen.

163

He showered, shaved, flicked on the TV to catch the news headlines while he dressed. Protests at abortion clinics, blizzards in the Midwest, drug seizures, Russian hostage crisis, Israel. Now they were his problems. He brushed his hair and checked himself in the mirror. Cream shirt, silk tie with red lozenges on dove gray, gray-blue suit, freshly pressed, with half an inch of handkerchief showing. Important to look neat. Kennedy changed three times a day, or so they said. The wallet with the code card into an inside pocket. It felt heavy there next his heart. Symbolic. The houseman looked in again. The First Lady was still asleep. He told him to let her rest on.

Breakfast was waiting in the elegant little private dining room across the passage. Another houseman in a white coat poured coffee. More newspapers ready in a pile on the table. Bold spreads everywhere of the Inauguration. Himself with hand upraised, reciting the oath, speaking from the podium, embracing Caro. It seemed an age ago.

There was a tap at the door. Barney Nikolis and Sheldon Harris, his deputy in the Press Office, entered. Both were beaming. Coverage of yesterday's events was brilliant, Barney enthused. Terrific pictures, particularly of the First Lady. They had more shots with them for him to look at. Boxes of them. Reaction to the speech was extremely positive by all commentators. The 'One Nation' call had struck a definite resonance with the electorate. The speech pulse rating . . .

He broke off. In the doorway behind them stood the First Lady. Caro Meade wore an antique lace wrap and her hair was down loose about her shoulders. Her face was deadly pale, her mouth drawn tight. 'How dare you?' she hissed. Both men blenched. 'How dare you come up here uninvited?'

Barney Nikolis apologized hastily and profusely. They had not thought. They had simply wanted to give the President the good news. Please forgive their mistake . . .

'Get out!' Her slim figure was charged with fury. For an instant it seemed she was going to strike them. 'Get out! This is my home. A private place. Don't you ever, any of you, dare set foot on this floor without my permission again!'

'He's coming!'

On the electronic monitor in the West Wing corridor a green light had begun to flash. POTUS was on the move. The position indicator carried at all times by the President was heading out from the mansion.

Doors opened, hurrying feet sounded in the passages. Everybody wanted to be there to welcome their chief. In the secretaries' office excited chatter broke out. Karen stilled it with a sharp word. 'This is the President of our country, not a pop star. Have a little dignity, please.' An instant hush fell. Everyone stared at their desks or video screens. Those who had got out mirrors to check their appearance surreptitiously replaced them.

At the ground floor the car stopped. The doors hissed open. Four Secret Service agents stood waiting. 'Good morning, Mr President,' they greeted him in unison. Two in front, two behind, they escorted him out across the flagstone colonnade bordering the Rose Garden, past the emergency pistol in its disguised box which Ivory had once pointed out to him, to the armored door of the Oval Office. Admiral Thomas was outside to wish him good morning. Yes, he had slept well and was feeling fine. Never better. The stewards had the fire ready lit, the cushions plumped. Photograph of his wife on the desk. Fresh flowers. The Chief of Staff and his deputy were there to meet him with the first day's schedule, Karen with an armful of correspondence, General Vorspuy, stiff and erect, bringing the daily intelligence summary. Aides and staffers clustered in the doorway. The bagman clutching the nuclear football like an undertaker at a

165

wedding. Cameras flashed and clicked, recording the scene.

'Good morning, Mr President,' they chorused.

He smiled at them. 'Great,' he said. 'Well, here we are. We made it. A lot of people said we wouldn't but we did it. Now that we've proved them wrong, let's see we make every day count.'

Irwin Hunter, Chief of Staff to the 44th President of the United States, pressed the button to illuminate the NO ENTRY light outside his office door and drummed the tips of his fingers on his desk. The desk was made of mahogany from a former British man-of-war and had been presented to the White House by Queen Victoria. Successive presidents had used it in the Oval Office but President Meade had demanded a desk free from foreign taint. Whereupon Hunter had appropriated it. It gave him a kick to rest his heels on a 200-year-old ship. Especially a British one.

He read through the Lipscombe letter. Then he read Blacker's report. Finally he watched the videotape. A president of the United States claiming to have been replaced by a double so perfect none of those round him had guessed. It sounded on the face of it too incredible to be credited. Somewhere, someplace there was an exact double of the President. What was more, this man had used his resemblance to get dangerously close to the Head of State. If the story were once to get out he knew for certain it would take a hold on the belief of the American public that would be impossible to dislodge. Even the very fact that it had reached his attention meant that it was within striking distance of becoming one of those urban myths whose potency defies all rational denials. And if two members of the President's family could bring themselves to believe it, then how long before others found it possible too?

'A pity your men didn't catch him at the hotel when they had the chance.'

'Yes.' Blacker made no excuses.

Hunter moved on. The point had been made.

'How the devil, Doug, are we to fight this one?'

'I don't know. In fact it gets worse the more I think about it. Have you considered for a start whether we actually tell the President?'

'He'll hit the roof. It implies we're giving credence to the story. On the other hand if he isn't told and the rumor gets out he could be vulnerable. Offhand I'd say whoever is behind this planned to destabilize the administration at its outset.'

Blacker's eyes were stony. Political vulnerability was not his problem. Physical threats to the President were. They dominated his every waking moment and much of his sleep. 'I take it you want this investigated?'

The Chief of Staff frowned, 'No, not as such,' he said carefully. 'The allegation is clearly nothing more than a malicious falsehood. Nevertheless,' he continued, 'you might consider it within your remit to investigate the source – just in case it presages some wider threat to the President.'

Blacker grunted and flipped the pages of his copy of the report. 'This may be more complicated than we think.'

'How so?'

'Even disregarding the tape, it's clear there is a strong physical resemblance between the impostor and the President. Sufficient for at least two members of the President's close family to be fooled.'

The Chief of Staff propped his elbows on the desk, shooting his cuffs. Gold sleeve links, presidential seals. Fast work, Blacker thought. Such tokens of a president's esteem were highly prized. 'There must be plenty of ways to demonstrate this person is a phoney without –' the Chief of Staff emphasized the word – 'the President being involved. Fingerprints are just one instance.'

'The President's prints are on record,' Blacker agreed. 'Standard procedure for all incoming chief executives.'

'Then I fail to see any problem. You will find and arrest this impostor and that will be the end of the matter.' Hunter closed his copy of the report with a snap, terminating the interview.

Blacker did not stir. 'Unfortunately,' he said quietly, 'the President's fingerprints were filed on January 16th, four days before the Inauguration during the course of his induction visit to the Pentagon and approximately a week after the report claims that substitution took place.'

There was a brief silence as the implications of this sank in. It was not simply a question of fingerprints. A moment's recollection was sufficient to remind the Chief of Staff that the President's official medical examination had taken place at Walter Reed Hospital the day after the Pentagon visit. Theoretically at least any blood or DNA samples could be those of an impostor.

'He had a very thorough medical test under the supervision of his own physician, Dr Webber of Los Angeles, at the commencement of the campaign. Those records could be compared with the current ones. For blood type, for instance.'

Blacker nodded. 'That still doesn't let us out of the wood.' In order to gain access to the President's private records they would first have to secure his permission, he pointed out.

'If it were simply a question of the President's blood type I could probably finesse that,' Hunter meditated. 'Say we need it for back-up blood supplies, something similar.'

'Again, it may not be that simple. Many people share the same broad blood types. That's how the transfusion system works. We might have to get more specific. And there's another thing . . .'

'What?' the Chief of Staff said warily.

'If this impostor really does bear such a likeness to the

President, there are two possible explanations: either plastic surgery or that they are related in some way. Cousins or brothers even.'

'The President doesn't have a brother, dammit, or a sister. He was an only child.'

'So far as anyone knows. And even if it were true it might not rule out half-brothers, illegitimates or some kind of concealed connection he may have no idea of. All kinds of things are possible. His old man might have had a fling someplace, never told the family. May not even have known himself. But there could be a child that grew up to look like its half-brother.'

'That's pretty damn far-fetched.'

'So is what we're talking about. My point is that if a family connection does exist then the two could possess any number of similarities. Proving which was which might be difficult. I'm not saying it couldn't be done, dental records would be a clincher, I should think, but I am saying that if this impostor really is some type of a doppelgänger, then I don't see how we can avoid alerting the President.'

'How about little Miss Lipscombe? Do we think she's in on the plot?'

Blacker shook his head emphatically. 'The wording of the letter implies not. Also my agents were positive she seemed completely bewildered by what occurred in the hotel suite.'

'Perhaps.' Hunter sounded unconvinced. 'You're keeping her under surveillance, I take it?'

'She's living here in the White House, remember? Courtesy of the First Lady.'

'I'd forgotten that. We can hardly tap the President's private phone or steam open his letters. Damn, this gets more complicated.'

Not necessarily. The switchboard would automatically log all her calls, Blacker pointed out. 'And we know where she is and who she sees.'

'Talking of which, note that the letter is addressed to the one person on the staff who could not visually identify the impostor with any certainty.'

'Yes, I've been considering that,' Blacker agreed.

'Concluding what?' said Hunter impatiently.

The Secret Service Chief regarded him straight in the eye. 'That this is an attempt to plant a seed of doubt in the heart of the administration,' he replied unemotionally.

When the Secret Service Chief had gone, Hunter buzzed his intercom for his secretary.

'Sir?'

'Ask the President's Counsel if she can let me have two minutes, will you.'

The response came back within moments. The President's Legal Counsel was meeting with a Senate delegation in connection with cabinet confirmation hearings. She would not be free for the next hour at least.

The Chief of Staff rose and turned to stare out of the window. His private patio was larger even than the President's. Beyond the trees the winter sun gleamed palely on the Washington Monument. For two years he had dreamed of standing where he stood now. Ever since he had followed the man who yesterday had assumed the mantle of the Presidency. Two years of dedication, planning, plotting, fighting off opposition from the left and right of the Democratic Party, vicious hostility from the Republicans. In that time Hunter had earned a justified reputation as the candidate's chief centurion. While the presidential challenger rode loftily above the fray, it had been Hunter who had fought the secret, dirty battles to protect his master's back. The scars from that bitterly contested election were still fresh but under his president he had become one of the most powerful men in the land. For the next four years and with luck the four after that he and his kind would place their stamp upon the nation. Now all that was imperiled.

'"... *before he enter on the execution of his office, he shall take the following oath* ..." The wording of the Constitution is unambiguous.'

The President's Counsel ran her eyes round the table. The meeting was being held in the West Wing corner office of the President's National Security Adviser, its tall windows facing down on to the White House driveway and Pennsylvania Avenue. Of the six people present she was the sole woman. Facing her across the table were Hunter, his lean, ambitious deputy Jay Leeder and Blacker of the Secret Service. To her left sat the President's personal doctor and beyond him at the head of the table the National Security Adviser, General Carl Vorspuy.

In Washington political circles the new administration was known as the Troika. Within the broad confines of policy agreed by the cabinet, three people directed the flow of decisions emanating from the Executive. These three decided what papers reached the President's desk, what calls he should take and whom he should see. When appointments were made they drew up the short lists and indicated the favored choices. Since they commanded all access to the President they effectively controlled the country. They were also unelected. The three were Irwin Hunter, Chief of Staff, Carl Vorspuy, NSA and Miriam Sheen, Legal Counselor to the President.

These three alone shared walk-in privileges to the Oval Office. In a sense the government of the United States was in session within the confines of the room. There was one caveat: the three controlled the Presidency, not the government, and the limitations of their powers were now being put to the test.

Carl Vorspuy was fifty-two years old, a Methodist and workaholic. His strengths were his weaknesses. Sheen

171

had originally opposed his appointment, arguing that the NSA's principal role was to act as mediator between the rival monoliths of the Departments of State and Defense. As a military man, Vorspuy would therefore be compromised from the outset. However the President and Hunter, who valued the General's voter appeal to the Right, had overruled her. This decision was to have consequences for the crisis unfolding upon them.

Miriam Sheen, at thirty-seven the youngest of the Troika, had cut her teeth as a prosecuting attorney in the President's home state of Indiana. A string of successful convictions in high-profile cases had brought her to the Senator's attention and she had volunteered her services to his election committee at the outset of his campaign. Her petite frame and demure appearance belied a ferocious intellect. Campaign staff feared Hunter, respected the General and crossed the street to avoid the President's Counselor.

'In summary,' she resumed, 'we face a difficult decision. If the allegation is proven that the man who won the election is not the same person who took the oath of office then technically the nation does not have a valid president. In such circumstances the 25th Amendment dictates that the Presidency automatically devolves upon the Vice-President until such time as Congress decides whether to call another election.'

She paused again. Around the table her listeners regarded her soberly. Before each lay a copy of the report which Jay Leeder had taken the precaution of photocopying personally.

'The first question is, do we have a duty to investigate? And if we decide to do so is there an obligation on us to inform the constitutional authorities, in this case the Vice-President and the Speaker of the House?'

At the mention of the Vice-President, the Chief of Staff scowled inwardly. The presidential running mate was an ideological enemy who owed his position to the fact that he could deliver delegate votes from the Deep South.

'What then do you advise?' he said.

'That we decide right here whether we believe there to be any substance in these allegations. That we minute our decision formally together with our reasons for arrival thereat. That if we do conclude they are substantive we take appropriate action forthwith,' she responded crisply.

The Chief of Staff frowned. 'No tapes. Jay, you will take a brief note of what's said. You can make a fair copy afterwards which I will keep in my safe. Anyone who wishes may consult but not remove. Agreed?'

The table nodded. Jay Leeder pulled a legal pad towards him and uncapped a gold fountain pen.

General Vorspuy's fingers twitched. As a patriotic soldier, the dilemma cut him to the quick. 'I can't believe I'm hearing this. On account of a passing likeness some psycho gets it into his head he's the President of the United States and we, the nation's top advisers, take him seriously and start pleading the 25th Amendment or whatever.'

The Counselor did not suffer fools. Her eyes narrowed. 'You saw the tape. There is more than a passing likeness, as you call it, at issue here.'

'Some fuzzy tapes, an elderly couple up late at a party, what does any of it amount to? Does any one of us have any doubts at all that the President is who we know him to be? You, Miriam and Irwin, you've known him longest; say if either of you have noticed any change in him since becoming President?'

The Chief of Staff and the President's Counselor glanced hastily at one another. 'A touch more aloof than before, a little more formal,' said Miriam, 'but I guess that's only to be expected. So no, I've not noticed anything different.'

'Same goes for me,' Hunter agreed awkwardly.

The General turned his gaze on Blacker and the Chief

of Staff's deputy. The latter indicated assent. Blacker shook his head, 'The Secret Service watches the crowds not the candidate.'

'Admiral?'

Rear-Admiral Creighton Thomas, Chief of the White House medical unit, removed his gold-rimmed spectacles and pinched the bridge of his nose. Formerly assigned to Bethesda Naval Hospital, his specialty lay in the field of stress management. In this context and given the new President's comparative youth, Thomas had seemed an ideal choice to oversee the health of the First Family. As a career naval officer however the prospect of being sucked into a political crisis unnerved him. He marshaled his thoughts carefully before replying.

'If you are asking me whether the individual currently occupying the Oval Office is the same as the one whose physical examination I observed last week, then the answer is affirmative.' He stopped, frowned and then continued. 'On that occasion the medical team of which I was a part had the opportunity to study the patient's accompanying records, including service records, and to perform a range of tests including X-rays and body fluid samples. All records fully accorded with my own observations, as did the test results. I am therefore entirely satisfied that the person who presented himself for the test was who he claimed to be and for the matter of it, still is.'

When he had finished there was silence for a moment. Miriam was the first to break it. 'Then medically speaking you are completely satisfied this entire allegation is a hoax?' she said.

With every eye upon him, the Doctor shrank from committing himself.

'On the available evidence, certainly . . . it would be difficult to come to any other conclusion.' He hastily qualified himself further for the record. 'It being understood that I have been expressly prohibited from raising

174

the subject with my patient and that I was not his previous medical attendant.'

Miriam and Hunter exchanged glances. 'That I think settles it,' she said briskly.

'In which case, the rest of us being of one mind on the subject, this letter –' the General slapped the document with his hand – 'this letter is nothing but a hoax and a damned lie and the people behind it ought properly to be indicted for treason.'

There were murmured indications of approval around the table. A general air of relief settled over the meeting.

The Chief of Staff summed up: 'I think then we are all agreed that we firmly believe the allegations are utterly without basis in fact. That furthermore they constitute a threat to the person of the President and therefore the Secret Service should investigate to establish the originators of the lie with a view to bringing them to justice.'

'Deputy-Director,' Hunter addressed Blacker formally, 'would you bring the meeting up to date on the progress of your inquiries so far, please?'

The Secret Service chief opened a file. He cleared his throat. 'With the greatest respect to everyone present but I think we may all have gotten hold of this business by the wrong end. And it is a lot more serious than we think.'

The room went quiet again. Jay Leeder's pen poised itself to write.

'We are listening, Deputy-Director,' said Hunter.

'This case isn't about a substitution that has taken place, we all of us know that. It's about one that is due to happen.' Blacker saw the puzzled looks on their faces and began to explain. 'Just suppose for a moment that there actually does exist a man who is the exact double of the President. A man who believes that he not only looks like him but can carry off the speech, the mannerisms, the whole works. He still has one insuperable problem, right?'

'I thought we had just all agreed that such a thing was impossible,' Counselor Sheen interposed.

Hunter frowned. 'Aren't you forgetting about last night?'

'The evidence of a bunch of partygoers, all elderly or half drunk, is hardly conclusive. In the circumstances they'd probably have sworn Batman and Robin were present.'

'Two of those fooled last night were my agents,' Blacker replied in a voice of iron. 'Both are young and fit, they had not touched alcohol and were familiar with the President. I know what has happened flies in the face of known facts but for the moment let's just suppose it is true. I ask you what is the biggest difficulty the would-be impostor faces?'

When no one answered him he went on. 'It's access. Don't you see? His big obstacle is the screen around the President. It's impossible for him to pull the switch. There are guards and surveillance every way he looks. He can't get close enough. The President is never alone for a moment. So what does he do? He has a clever idea. He'll get the President's own people to do it for him. All he has to do is to persuade a few highly placed individuals that he is the rightful President and convince them to smuggle him into the White House and effect the switch. He banks on their fear of scandal to help him. "Think of the nation's reputation," he tells them. "Imagine if it got out that the wrong man was sworn in. Nobody must ever know."'

A second silence fell over the room. The others exchanged skeptical glances. The Chief of Staff cleared his throat. 'Aren't you letting your imagination run away with you a little? We have just heard from the Doctor here that there is no doubt in his mind as to the President's identity.'

'How can we be sure? From the records? Records can be altered, data substituted. In fact it would be a whole heap easier to transpose the President's medical records than it would be to impersonate him successfully. As it is I'm willing to bet that at least some parts of those records will have been tampered with. Sufficient at any rate to throw doubt on the rest.'

As the rest of the meeting still stared at him in slowly dawning dismay, he continued, 'We have to recognize that we face here a very clever plot. A very clever plot indeed and one that has been a long time in the preparation.' He shook his head. 'What worries me is the timing. He has got it so right. That's what makes me afraid he may be right about other things.'

'Explain,' ordered the Chief of Staff.

'Just now, in the first weeks of the administration, is a vulnerable time. People are new to their jobs, to each other very often. And the President under more pressure than anyone. A short while ago he was an ordinary citizen like the rest of us, then in a single day he is transformed into a head of state, one step short of a monarch. From living in hotel rooms and apartments he wakes up in a palace surrounded by guards. Whenever he appears in public he is mobbed. Naturally it affects him. He acts differently, with you, with his family, even with his own wife. That is why the impostor has chosen this moment. When everything is in flux. If he is as good as he thinks he is,' he shrugged, 'maybe he can pull it off, who knows?'

There was a sound of hammering from overhead. Workmen were busy making alterations to the office layouts to accommodate the new staff. The rest of the table were digesting his words. It was evident they made sense. Finally Miriam Sheen spoke.

'How about the First Lady? You're not trying to tell us that any impersonation is going to be good enough to fool the man's wife in the sack?' she said bluntly.

'Especially a wife of less than two months,' put in the General crudely.

'She only met Jack Meade during the campaign. She fell sick immediately after the marriage. How much time did she get to spend with him alone? Days, hours even? I'll bet many of you in this room probably know him better than she does.'

Admiral Thomas looked up at the ceiling thoughtfully. 'I am inclined to think so also. And consider, two people living in a strange house, seeing very little of one another. The start of an administration is an intensely stressful period. Almost the only time they are alone together is in the privacy of their own bedroom. Even there the President is liable to be called away at any hour. Imagine a wife, a wife of only a few weeks' standing, who is enduring these tremendous strains, suddenly catching a rumor that the man she believes is her husband may after all be an impostor. Mightn't she begin to have doubts? To question her own reason perhaps?'

'That's what the pretender is counting on. He hopes to make us reject his rival before it ever comes to a show-down between the two. He intends that by sitting here talking as we are doing, we will do his work for him. That's his plan.'

At Blacker's words everyone in the room was suddenly afraid for the President.

'In all my life,' said the General slowly, 'I never once met two people so alike that they couldn't be told apart. With the exception of identical twins, that is,' he added.

'So maybe the President has an identical twin,' said the Counselor. 'Anything's possible.'

'And in any case,' said Blacker, 'it is not absolutely necessary for the two to appear identical. The claim is not that they are the same but precisely the opposite – that they are different. Because an impostor has been substituted for the real office-holder. In such circumstances certain minor variations would be expected.' He paused, waiting for comment. There was none and he went on: 'Impersonating the President of the United

States has become a big money-spinner in showbusiness. Some are good. Worryingly so from our point of view. In the last administration a man called Novak cultivated such a good likeness of President Ivory that he even had the First Lady fooled briefly on one occasion. In another incident a Secret Service agent spotted Novak on Pennsylvania Avenue and called a security alert on the assumption that the President had somehow become separated from his detail. Novak was a one-time realtor who cut and colored his hair to resemble Ivory's and placed pads in his shoes to bring his height up. Put him alongside the real thing and you'd have laughed. But he'd hire a stretch limousine, deck it with flags, outfit a bunch of waiters with earpieces and dark glasses and there was almost no one who didn't fall for the act. At one time he was earning more than a million dollars a year. Among others he fooled was the Mayor of New York. The hardest part, he told us, was perfecting the President's accent.'

'An actor?' Hunter mused. 'It sounds plausible. Yes, I suppose a clever actor might pull it off. Like you say, it's been done.'

'Briefly, on occasion, sure. Or against strangers. This is different. No one could pull off a permanent switch. We're not in fantasy land. There has to be another angle to it,' said Miriam. 'I don't believe an actor, however good, could hoodwink a man's wife.'

'On the other hand,' Hunter said, 'even if the First Lady thought she could tell, the question is could we rely on her?'

There was no answer to this.

'The President recently underwent cosmetic surgery and according to the medical report the patient at Jacksonville carried the scars of a similar procedure. Could there be an explanation there?' suggested Leeder after a moment.

Again everyone looked to the Admiral. He shrugged. 'It's not my specialty,' he admitted, 'but I think it is safe to say that while modern surgical techniques can improve, they can't work miracles. There would have to be a strong pre-existing physical resemblance.'

'The President's procedures were all minor. Nips and tucks,' Hunter pointed out.

'Supposing though a foreign power discovered they had an agent with that resemblance,' suggested the General. 'It would be possible then for them to create a presidential double?'

'It would depend on the degree of similarity. And in any case facial matching alone would be insufficient. The double would need to be trained to mimic the President's speech and mannerisms. Only a handful of actors possess that degree of skill. The chances of one closely resembling the President are remote.'

'Nevertheless it seems clear that one at least exists,' remarked Miriam drily.

Jay Leeder paused a moment in his note-taking. 'There is another point,' he said hesitantly.

'Which is what?'

'If this imposture was a long time in the planning like you say, then when it began the President was not married. His engagement came as a big surprise to the general public. We managed to keep the courtship very private. God knows how we succeeded but we did. The press even claimed later that it had been timed and kept secret as a political move.'

'Yes, I remember that,' Blacker agreed.

'Well, surely that means any plans of the impostor would be seriously put out. I mean, whichever way you look at it an unmarried president is easier to pull this trick on than a married one, I should have thought.'

'And what does that suggest to you?'

Leeder blinked as if frightened by the logic of his own argument. 'That either he thinks his plan can cope with a wife or . . .'

'Precisely,' Blacker agreed heavily, 'or . . . ?'

'Or it won't work with her in the picture, in which case he plans to eliminate her.'

The dismay around the table was palpable.

The Military Records Command, a division of the Pentagon responsible for maintaining details of all current and former members of the US armed forces, had recently spent $350 million upgrading its fingerprint recording system. The new software was superior, they claimed, to the FBI's FINDER 2000 program, though the Bureau disputed this. Prints were now held in digital format on a constantly updated database which could be searched in its entirety in a matter of minutes. The new software was extremely efficient. It allocated any print twelve primary identification features. When an unknown print was presented for identification, it was first analysed and its primary features pinpointed. Once this was done, three such features were selected and the database searched for matches. This initial run would inevitably throw up a number of possible matches. The operator then selected a further three signal features and repeated the process. While apparently time-consuming, in practice this was a considerable advance on earlier methods. By the end of the fourth run the list of possibles was reduced to a handful which could then be checked by human eye for an exact match. The staff at Records Command prided themselves on being able to process any print and find a match, if one existed, within four hours.

In the case of the patient formerly held at Jacksonville, no such match was found to exist. The patient was not, and never had been, a serving member of the armed forces. A report to this effect was made to Jacksonville. Since the patient had anyway absconded, Jacksonville might have left it at that. Thanks to Nurse Phillips' detective work however, it transpired that he was now masquerading as a naval dental officer. The matter was therefore deemed sufficiently serious to warrant details being passed to state and local police.

In any event on this particular day Florida's fingerprint laboratory was grossly overloaded with search requests. The fact that it was the Inauguration weekend and therefore a national holiday into the bargain did not help. Additionally the onset of a new administration meant there was a countrywide backlog of security applications for government posts waiting to be processed with the Justice Department screaming for the clearances. The military's request was flagged low grade/non-urgent and set aside for checking at the start of the new week when more staff would be available.

9

'Oh, Karen,' the President called.

She left her desk and stepped through into the Oval Office.

'Yes, Mr President?'

Only their first day and so far they were working smoothly together. They had agreed to schedule two forty-five-minute periods, morning and afternoon, for administration time when he would work on papers and she alone would have access to him unless otherwise directed. During these sessions he had indicated he wanted the connecting door between them kept ajar. He preferred calling out to speaking to her down an interphone. Squawky mechanical voices irritated him and he missed the human contact. Letters: he liked to give an outline of what he wanted said and leave composition to her. Dictation was something he did better on a machine. It was hard to collect his thoughts with somebody sitting waiting, pencil poised, like a seal waiting for a fish, as he put it.

Much of the time he liked to work in the study off the main Oval Office. It was more private, less formal, somewhere to unwind with a bar and a bathroom, a full-length sofa and TV. He could leave his desk cluttered, nap on the sofa or relax over a Black Label with Speaker Webster or one of his staff. In the alcove between the two rooms they had set up a signing table, a French Empire desk imported into the mansion by Jackie Kennedy, on which the secretaries placed the presidential correspondence, the letters, memos, messages, photographs, endorsements, all the papers requiring Jack Meade's signature or initials, approval or rejection.

The rest of the President's schedule was handled by the Appointments Office with fifteen staff and a workload to keep them jumping. A typical day might include fifty separate interviews lasting from five to thirty minutes, plus cabinet and National Security Council sessions, a press conference and perhaps a state luncheon or formal reception. Internal meetings and unscheduled visits, principally involving members of the Troika, added to the President's workload.

During the night she had agonized over the incident at the ball and the President's behavior. The memory of that kiss still haunted her. For his part though the President appeared to be acting as if the incident had never happened. Which was galling, but understandable. Probably it was for the best, Karen thought sadly. After all, he was newly married. And even a president could be excused for losing his head momentarily on the night of his inauguration. It was lucky Trish Beale hadn't noticed. In fact nobody present seemed clear about what had taken place. Everything had been confused by the security scare as a result of the President giving his escort the slip.

But Jack had kissed her. That was one undeniable fact and the memory left a warm glow in her heart.

It is incredible to observe the public's fascination with the new First Couple. Men are wearing hats again, because Jack Meade does. Stores report they are running out of his wide-brimmed homburgs. You see them everywhere, sported at the same jaunty, devil-may-care angle as Jack wears his. Cigarette sales are up too, because Caro Meade uses them. Women strive to copy her casual, raffish style of smoking, just as they emulate her Italian suits and loose hair. The Lincoln Continental Coupé, modeled on the car Jack drove as Bruce Delahaye in Winchester County, is the vehicle of choice among the smart set, outclassing Mercedes and Jaguar.

Divorce is apparently acceptable for a president but so

too is romance. It's fun to be in love again. Re-marriage is chic. At least three senior administration officials are currently tying the knot a second time around. Expect a family in the White House before long.

Caro Meade might seem physically frail but she made up for it with an iron determination, Brad Sewall discovered. When he arrived at the residence to receive instructions, he found the new First Lady already in conference with Dorothy Fine, her personal secretary.

'We are working out a schedule for the decorators to come and view,' she said in her whispery tones after bidding him good morning. 'It is going to be necessary to make over all the rooms. This place has become positively dowdy.'

Parts of the apartment could certainly do with refurbishment, Sewall agreed. Under the Ivorys the budget had been restricted because of expenditure on the state floors.

'Perhaps I ought to start,' the First Lady said, 'by getting acquainted with all the staff. How many people do you have working here, Mr Sewall?'

Ninety-nine, Sewall answered, including the maintenance crews, the painters, electricians, carpenters and plumbers who kept the mansion functioning, but not the outdoor staff who came under the National Parks Service which administered the grounds.

Both women looked amazed. 'So many, I had no idea,' said Caro Meade.

'Actually we are short one butler at the moment.' Good butlers were hard to find, he added.

Well anyway, the First Lady continued, she would have to meet them all. The best plan would be for the Chief Usher to take her round and introduce her to them so she would have a chance to see them in their place of work. 'That way I can get an idea of their different duties.'

'It might be easier for you, ma'am, if I brought the staff

up in groups for you to meet with here. I'm thinking of your health. This is a large building.'

Miss Fine backed him up. 'He's quite right. You don't want to wear yourself out your first morning on the job. And we still have the decorators to see.'

'Oh very well,' Caro Meade agreed. 'Dot and I want to get some fresh air so we're going for a walk round the south driveway. Please start bringing them up in forty minutes.' She glanced at Dorothy Fine for confirmation and Dorothy nodded.

So starting with his three ushers and the four butlers, Sewall escorted the staff up in the elevator to the central hall, where the First Lady greeted them in slacks and a sweater, perched on the arm of a settee. As each person was led up and introduced, she shook them by the hand and repeated their names in her barely audible voice. The staff were awed as always on meeting the new First Lady. And Caro Meade seemed so young, so glamorous – 'so unexpected', as housekeeper May Beth Deans put it.

When the third-floor maids and the kitchen staff had been presented, she called a halt. 'Are there many more?' she asked Sewall.

'The maintenance section, the flower shop staff, four laundry workers, two from the storeroom, eight garden-ers . . .'

Caro Meade said she thought they could keep over for another day. She seemed fatigued. 'So many people, the house must cost a fortune to run.'

Around eight million dollars a year, he informed her. Mostly incurred on wages and housekeeping expenses such as heat and lighting.

And even that was only a fraction of the real cost of maintaining the White House establishment. Many of the costs were carried on the budgets of other departments. Nobody knew what the total bill was, certainly several billion dollars. The Secret Service budget allocation alone came to almost $500 million.

*

At midday when in Washington the revelers from last night's parties were just settling down to a light brunch, the fax machine at the Provost-Marshal's office down in Jacksonville sprang to life. Against all expectations the state files had come up with a match. The Navy's patient was a former employee and as such his fingerprints were on record. According to these the prints were those of a forty-five year old white male born 1–10–1956 in Boston, Massachusetts under the name of Jack MacKenzie Meade.

Blacker stood by the window of his office. Mavis, his secretary, entered and stopped before his desk. A grim-faced, taciturn woman, she spoke mainly in silences. She had been in the job twenty years, serving both his predecessors, and was a repository of the secrets of four presidencies. Without comment she handed him the fax from Jacksonville.

Blacker read it through once. He sat down at the desk and read it through a second time. 'Is this a hoax or what?' he demanded.

'Could be,' she nodded unmoved.

Blacker tightened his lips. He stared at the fax copy again, conscious of a mounting alarm. The affair was moving in six different directions at once and the Chief of Staff was going to have a coronary.

'Page Eddie Lomax,' he said crisply. 'Have him drop whatever he's doing and come back in right away. He's to inform his supervisor that he'll be working personally for me till further notice. Then tell Porter and Dell I want to see them right away.'

A buzzer interrupted briefly. He looked up. On a video monitor beside his desk a green light began to flash. The President was on the move again. The digital position indicator carried on his person at all times below the second floor displaying his precise whereabouts. Blacker watched the blinking light track from the West Wing on to the state floor into the Blue Room, the elegant oval reception area where in 1886 Frances Folsom had married Grover Cleveland under the jaundiced gaze of portraits of the first seven presidents to become at twenty-one the youngest ever First Lady. Here he would confer briefly with his aides before striding confidently down the red-carpeted hallway and through the tall double doors into the East Room to address his first White House press conference. Blacker hoped none of the hundred or so correspondents present had attended last night's inaugural balls and had noticed the ruckus at the Mayflower.

The sound of hammers thudding echoed through the West Wing to be joined by the shrill whine of a power tool. The first few weeks of a fresh administration were unendurable as offices were ripped out and torn apart to suit the new occupants and builders filled the wing with noise and dust. For the Secret Service it meant an added nightmare of screening hundreds of workers and deliverymen on top of their normal duties.

Dick Porter and Stephen Dell, his two deputies, arrived. Without explaining why, he told them he was shifting temporary responsibility for much of the day-to-day security of the executive mansion onto their shoulders, leaving himself free to concentrate on other duties. He spent half an hour with them running over the routines. When they were gone there was a knock at the door. It was Lomax.

'Mavis said you wanted to see me, Chief.'

'Yes, come in and shut the door. Take a seat.'

Eddie Lomax had narrow shoulders and a thin, sharp face. He looked more like a jockey than a Secret Service agent. Most of his career had been spent in the Banknote Division, hunting down counterfeiters, often overseas. Forgers of US currency do not take kindly to snoopers and Lomax still carried pieces of shrapnel in his legs from the time when a gang had fired an anti-tank grenade into his car in Beirut. He walked with a slight limp. Unusually, he had done a spell with the Bureau before moving across to join the Service. Blacker had chosen him for that very reason. The job they were faced with called for detective skill, not bullet-stopping.

Lomax dropped into the chair in front of the desk. Blacker pushed across the fax from Jacksonville. 'Read that.'

Lomax read it once and his jaw fell open. 'They can't be serious. Is this the guy from last night? I heard about that. Now they tell us he has the identical same prints as the President of the United States? Who are they trying to kid?'

Blacker hated to sit behind a desk. He rose now and walked over to the window. Outside it had begun to snow again. Fat white flakes like frozen cream.

'Whoever's responsible has put their head on the block. The state fingerprint records may have been tampered with. Question is whether it's deliberate or not. It's conceivable an impostor might have planted false prints as part of a ruse. Either way we have to run this one down quickly before it gets out and causes embarrassment. If it does a lot of people around here are going to be very angry. Starting with the President.

'From now on until the business is cleared up you and I will be working together on it. Get a pad and take notes. This is what I want you to do. First, get hold of another desk and set it up in the corner over there. From now on nothing goes outside this office. Tell Mavis to see you have a direct outside line bypassing the switchboard. I don't want anyone listening in. Mavis will act as our joint secretary. I'll brief her personally later. For leg work you can use Suter and Colton from last night. Set them to watching the Lipscombe girl. I want her followed anywhere outside the White House grounds.'

'You think he'll try to reach her again then?'

'I'm hoping so. It's about the only lead we've got. Your next task is to contact our field office in Miami. Speak to the agent in charge and have him get on to the administration down there and run this fingerprint mess-up to ground. Find out exactly how and when this shambles originated. I want an explanation in writing by tomorrow that I can show the Chief of Staff so that if necessary he can issue a statement to the press.'

'Understood, Chief,' Lomax hesitated a moment before going on. 'Where do we stand with the Pentagon on this? Do we come clean with them or what?'

Blacker thought a moment. 'No, that's a call above our level. The Chief of Staff will have to make that decision. What you can do though is get on to Naval Security and have them put a lid on their people in Jacksonville. Make 'em understand that if this story leaks out they'll answer for it with their heads.

'Thirdly, shake up the FBI, the DC police and the Provost-Marshal. I want the man using the alias of Commander Casey picked up before he makes another attempt to reach the President. Play it low key but make them understand that we are concerned. He must be holed up somewhere so it means checking the hotels, boarding houses, airlines and the rest. See they give it priority.

'Four. I'm concerned about how this person is able to pass himself off as Jack Meade so cleverly. Could be he's a professional, an actor of some kind. Get on to the theatrical agencies and obtain a list of political impersonators. We may get a lead there.

'And lastly, get your ear to the ground. Choose one of our best researchers. Choose someone you can rely on to keep his mouth shut and have him check around the studios. See if he can get a line on anyone bearing a close likeness to the President.'

Lomax was scribbling busily. He glanced up. 'You think this impostor may have a connection with Meade's acting career?'

Blacker shook his head. 'It's just a hunch. At this point until we can pick up a lead we're feeling in the dark.

You'd better get started on that list. Send Mavis in to me and I'll put her in the picture.'

As Lomax left the room, Blacker threw a glance at the video monitor. The winking green light was on the move again. The President had completed his first press conference and was returning to the Oval Office. And he still had no idea what was happening behind his back.

In a Virginia suburb a phone rang.

'Fenwick Backhouse here. Who is that?'

'Fenwick, it's Jack, Jack Meade.'

'Who?'

'Jack Meade, for God's sake.'

There was an indecipherable grunt. 'You don't mean . . . ?'

'Yes, that's right,' snapped the impatient voice. 'I mean exactly that. Class of '75 in case you've forgotten already.'

Fenwick Backhouse stared at the receiver. Instinctively he stood up straighter and his voice took on a more respectful tone. 'What can I do for you?' He hesitated and added, 'Sir.'

'I need your help, Fen. I want you to meet me downtown at your office in an hour from now.'

'One hour, yes, sir,' Fenwick repeated automatically. 'My office, are you . . . ? That is don't you mean at . . .' he swallowed '. . . at the White House?'

'Dammit, Fen, I haven't time to argue. I'm your president and I'm instructing you to meet with me.'

'Yes, sir, Mr President, I understand. If you could just give me some idea of what it is . . .'

'Just meet me in one hour's time down at your office. I'll be using the name Casey, Lieutenant-Commander Casey. Have you got that? Casey. And don't breathe a word of this to anyone else. The fate of our country depends on it.'

'You can rely on me, Mr President, Jack . . .' but he was speaking to a dead line.

He hung up, puzzled. Across the room his wife lounged on the settee, watching TV.

'Who was that?'

'It . . . he was the President.' He swallowed hard, 'Jack . . . Jack Meade. You know, I told you we were at law school together.'

'Oh yeah, call us up to invite us to drop round, did he?'

'No, he uh . . . he wants to see me downtown. On business. Real important, he said.' His face brightened. 'You think maybe he wants to offer me some kind of post? You know, in government?'

'He told you that? Just now over the phone?' She glared at him witheringly. In the background there came a sound of cheering from the television. 'Shit, there's a sucker born every minute.'

He looked blank. 'It was his voice, I'd swear. I'd know it anywhere.'

His wife gestured towards the screen where a familiar figure was stepping down from a podium. 'It was his voice,' she mimicked savagely. 'Then it must have been his double, you dumb ass, because that was your friend Jack Meade on the TV while you were speaking, giving his first press conference in the White House.' She saw the disappointment and fury dawning in her husband's florid features and broke into peals of raucous laughter. 'And you thought it was your old college buddy calling up to offer you a cabinet post. Oh boy, did someone ring your bell today! Wait till the girls at bridge hear this!'

Fenwick Backhouse shot her a look of pure and undiluted hatred. 'If you breathe a hint of this to a living soul, I'll leave every penny to my kids,' he swore, stumping out in a rage.

Two miles from the White House, a young woman in a Chevrolet Blazer that had seen better days pounded her horn at the driver of a Cadillac ahead that was refusing to pull out past a bus stalled in the right-hand lane. A fresh fall of snow had turned downtown Washington into traffic chaos. Plows and blowers churned along the roads, pushing the drifts into great piles or dumping it in trucks. 'Move your butt, dammit!' Jean-Alice Spellman shouted, winding down the window and leaning out into the cold. The Cadillac driver waved a fist as much as to say go to hell. 'Well, screw you too, buddy,' she muttered. Switching on her headlights, she wrenched the wheel over and kicked the throttle. An exhaust plume spouted in her rear and with a roar the Blazer shot out alongside to the amazement of a couple in an all-black Mercedes coupé approaching from the opposite direction who hastily squirmed out of the way.

This was more like it, she thought as the traffic divided miraculously before her lights. Ten minutes later she was negotiating the ramp down to the car park of Dorfinger, Backhouse and Stern. The guard waved her through and, hardly slackening speed, she shot down through the tunnel and dived into her space. One compensation for coming into work at the weekend, at least the place was empty. The Blazer was not the easiest of vehicles to maneuver in tight spaces, especially when those spaces were occupied by expensive imports belonging to the partners. Before Christmas she had managed to crack a Jaguar's rear light, a feat which had run her in at an unbudgeted $400. Subsequently there had been hints dropped about the unsuitability of the Blazer to an employee. The same comments had been directed at her interpretation of the firm's dress code, which in today's case involved sheepskin boots and an aviator's jacket with LAWYERS SUCK in studs on the back. Underneath she was wearing a Gianni Versace chiffon blouse with a stretch pencil skirt, also Versace, that fitted like an underskin and was either stolen or a counterfeit, she hadn't inquired which. The label inside was genuine enough and the pair had cost $295 off the back of a van.

'Only you and me on today,' the receptionist, Darleen, who was her friend and prettier than any girl had a right to be which was why she had the job out front, told her. 'Inauguration weekend too, that's tough.'

'Tough is right. This is the fifty-first straight week that I've worked through. I was even working so hard I never got to vote. Not that Jack Meade needed it in the end.'

Darleen chuckled, 'Shame on you, a Democrat in this den of Republicans. Anyway think of all the dough you're making. It's all right for some.'

'All right for you, you mean. Costed over a year, my salary equates to an hourly rate of sixteen bucks. That's less than you earn for sitting behind that desk and looking cute. Plus you get a lunch break. Also Backhouse smiles at you and when he sees me he spits.'

'Not when he sees you in that top he doesn't.'

They both laughed and Jean-Alice went through into her cubicle office. The pile of backed-up files seemed to have grown since last night. She inspected the titles and found sure enough that a late leaver had dumped a couple of extras. They were all heart in this profession. With a sigh she rolled up her sleeves and got down to business.

Two hours later her stomach lodged a formal protest at having skipped breakfast. The weather outside looked to be threatening more snow. She might have sent out for a donut but what the hell, she could use the fresh air. Besides, she needed a cigarette. She pulled on her coat.

As she came through, a visitor, a man, was pacing up and down the lobby in the distracted manner adopted by clients with certain kinds of legal problem. He had on a dark jacket which appeared to be part of a dinner suit. He wore a hat indoors and there was a dirty scarf wrapped around the lower part of his face. Evidently he was waiting for someone and she hoped it wasn't her.

'Excuse me, Miss!'

Suppressing her irritation, Jean-Alice composed her expression into one of greeting. 'Good morning, sir. May I help you?'

'Uh, yes, that is I hope so.' He was medium height with distinctive cheekbones. There was a yellowing about the eyes as if he had not been sleeping well recently. Jean-Alice sympathized. She put his age at around forty and she had the strong impression she had seen him before. The office handled a number of celebrity clients. It was hard to tell what lay under the hat and scarf. The discreetly dimmed lobby lighting didn't help. His eyes narrowed as he focused on her. 'Are you an attorney?'

'Yes, I am.' She took off the coat and slung it over her arm inside out.

'I'm looking for Fenwick Backhouse, he . . . he knows me,' the man stammered.

'I didn't know he was coming in to the office today, what with it being the weekend and the Inauguration. Did you have an appointment?'

The man nodded violently. 'I called him up. Two hours ago. He said he'd be here.' He spoke in gasps as if each utterance cost him a huge effort.

'Well, in that case I'm sure he will be,' she said soothingly. 'Would you like me to have them call his home and find out what time he left? What name was it?'

'Casey,' the man said. 'Lieutenant-Commander Casey. Mr Backhouse knows me,' he repeated. 'I'm a personal friend.'

Sure, Jean-Alice thought, and I'm his first wife. Even so she had better go through the motions. Detaching herself, she asked Darleen to call through.

'I already did,' Darleen whispered. 'Mr Backhouse said he doesn't know the guy. He has no appointments today and he ain't coming in. His wife thinks it's some kinda prank. He sounded real put out. You ask me,' she confided, leaning over the desk, 'this one is a weirdo.'

Jean-Alice went back to break the news to the visitor. They didn't teach you this in law school.

The man was still pacing the carpet agitatedly. He read the answer in her expression. 'He isn't coming, is he?' Seeing her hesitate, he tensed as if exerting all his willpower to maintain a semblance of self-control. Breathing deeply and rapidly, he took her by the arm. 'Please, I must speak to someone. You see,' he added earnestly, 'it's a matter of constitutional importance.'

Oh boy, thought Jean-Alice, we've a real screwball here. She glanced round the lobby but there was no sign of any security. There never was when you needed them.

She turned back to the client, trying to think of a polite way to tell him this was a law office not a therapy center. He had stopped pleading and was waiting for her to speak, his head cocked slightly to one side. The scarf had slipped down and he was standing directly underneath one of the low-wattage ceiling spots. For the first time she found herself taking a hard look at the man. Her stomach turned over suddenly. Maybe it was a gesture or that so often heard nasal twang or perhaps she had simply been half-attending before and was only now fully concentrating, but all at once, as if she were seeing him afresh, the features resolved themselves in the blink of an eye into the face so familiar from TV and newspapers. The lobby seemed to heave around her slowly. Her hand went to her mouth and she felt her knees trembling. 'Oh my God,' she said thickly, 'it can't be ...' The words sounded so foolish that afterwards the memory made her feel hot with embarrassment. 'How, sir? I meant ... are you alone?' And then, 'What are you doing here?'

A look of total relief came into the man's eyes. He let go of her arm. 'Thank you,' he said simply. He took another deep breath as if the emotion of the moment were almost too much for him also.

Jean-Alice cast about for the right words. Another situation where law school didn't help. 'Would you like to talk privately, sir? Our conference room is free,' she suggested hesitantly.

He shook his head at the offer. 'If it's all the same to you,' he said. 'I'd prefer to go out somewhere.'

Later in the morning Eddie Lomax reported back. When he did so the news was good.

'I spoke on the phone to the state records supervisor in Miami. Name of Panton. He's anxious to be helpful to us any way he can and has personally checked back through the files. What he's come up with is this: way back in 1980 Jack Meade, the real Jack Meade that is, applies for a position with the Miami District Attorney's Office. He was fresh out of law school with a good résumé and he gets the job. As a matter of course his prints were taken. It's a rule, same for all state employees.'

'Jack Meade worked for the Miami District Attorney? I don't recall that on his record anywhere.'

'That's just it. As it turns out, Jack decided not to take up the offer in the end. He opted to go to drama school instead. Or whatever. So he never was employed by Miami. That's why it's not listed on his record. Now according to normal procedure his prints should have been taken off-file. The way I figure it though some clerk was asleep at the button and they got left on the file. The impostor must have learned of this and somehow tampered with the system, substituting his own prints for the President's. The President's prints were deleted and the prints of the guy down in Jacksonville were retained on file under the name of Jack M. Meade. Those prints do not fit the President. I know because we've checked.'

Blacker rubbed his eyes. Thirty hours without sleep was beginning to tell on him. He reached for the phone and punched the number for the Chief of Staff. This was the first piece of success since the affair began. He only hoped it wasn't the last.

10

Jean-Alice and her new client had had to walk two blocks to find a place open. A lunchtime watering hole with high-backed booths that had stayed open to catch the tourists. In the event they were almost the only customers.

'I'm afraid I have to ask you to pay,' he apologized. 'I don't have a bean.'

Not to worry about it, she assured him. Her privilege, truly. Her head was spinning, she was in a daze. Here she was with her first client and he had turned out to be the President of the United States.

They ordered food and a cold beer for her with a bourbon on the rocks for him and took themselves off to a booth where they could not be overheard.

'I still don't understand,' she whispered after a moment.

'No more do I,' he said. 'That's why I need your help. Not just for me,' he hesitated, 'but for our country. But before that, before I tell you anything, I want you to swear, on your mother's grave, on everything you hold sacred, never to reveal one word of what I am about to say except by my permission.'

Jean-Alice was still finding it hard to form the words she wanted to say. She swiveled her head in the direction of the bar TV where the new Chief Executive was shaking hands with his political opponents. 'Then if you are the real President, who's that in the White House?'

'I don't know. That's what frightens me. A complete stranger has usurped my place. A double so exact that even my own wife cannot have detected the difference. He has lifted my identity and I have no idea who he is or how it happened!' For a moment he looked away. 'And for the record I am not the real President,' he paused. 'Neither is whoever is currently occupying the Oval Office. I am elected and not sworn; he is sworn but unelected.' He gave a lop-sided smile, 'It could almost be comical if it weren't so serious.'

Then he began to speak. And Jean-Alice listened.

What it amounted to, he said, what it came down to, put simply and so far as he had been able to work it out, was that despite all the guards, the Secret Service, the technical surveillance and God knew what, Friday, January 12th, he, the President-elect of the United States, had been dropped off a boat into the sea and a substitute put in his place.

He described waking up in the hospital not knowing who he was or where; then the dawning realization that a switch had been made, that an impostor was standing in for him. 'I looked at the TV and there I was. Like looking in a mirror. It was me and it wasn't me. I was him and he was me. I thought either I'm gone mad or else this is some kind of a nightmare. There couldn't be any other explanation. Only now I know there is.' He stared down at the table.

Jean-Alice leaned closer to catch the words. Their heads were almost touching. Anyone watching would take them for a couple of illicit lovers, she thought bizarrely. The story was incredible and yet in spite of that it had the ring of truth. As a lawyer she had dealt with liars and maniacs in her time; this man was neither.

He went on, 'Until nine days ago I was Jack Meade, President-elect. I was the people's choice. I was certain of who I was, or thought so. I can still recall everything about my life till then, my childhood, school, college, marriage, and divorce, the Senate. I could describe the campaign to you in every detail, the Convention, the nights on the trail, the speeches, the TV debates, election night. Did you know I was in the shower when Ivory called to concede? Hunt brought me the phone. I was so nervous I dropped the receiver in the water. I couldn't take in what he was saying at first. The margin was that close. They were still counting votes in Cook County.

'All that seems a long time ago now. The ten weeks following an election is a form of limbo. You try to relax, recover from the stress of campaign, only it's next to impossible, there's too much to get through. Meetings, briefings, trying to pick candidates for posts. There's never enough time. All the same it's an exhilarating period. You're on a high, everything seems possible suddenly.'

He sighed and a shadow passed across his face. 'At the same time, you're aware of changes. Walls going up, barriers between you and ordinary people. Close friends greet you like a stranger. Even my wife . . .' he broke off.

Jean-Alice looked down at her plate. It was empty. She had no recollection of eating yet she must have done so.

'The fortnight before the Inauguration I was scheduled to spend aboard the yacht of a friend and supporter, Bob Rappaport. I had had surgery to my face. The plan was for me to recuperate and with my close advisers seclude ourselves from distraction while we blitzed on a final round of administration appointments . . .'

'You don't recall the names of any appointees for instance?'

His brow furrowed with the effort of concentration. 'I can remember a few names. Is that important?'

'It could be if it would help us establish exactly when the switch-over was made. When we approach the authorities it is vital we present as clear a statement as possible of what happened.'

'Well, we had dinner on board, I can remember that much.'

'This was Friday, January 12th?'

'Yes, Friday. The chef served Baked Alaska and we were making jokes because it was so cold back up in Washington. Afterwards I worked some more on the lists of names with Hunt, my Chief of Staff and his deputy, oh, and Miriam Sheen, Counsel to the President. We kept at it till late.' He paused, frowning again. 'Then much later one of the speechwriters wanted to run through a new version of my inaugural address. I remember being sore at him because I wanted time to think about it more.'

'That would be around what time, would you think?'

He pursed his lips. 'My impression from memory is that it occurred just prior to my going to bed. Eleven to midnight, say.'

'Do you remember actually undressing and getting into bed?'

A shake of the head.

'And that's all till you woke up in the Navy hospital?'

He thought a minute, then shook his head again, exasperated. 'Yes.'

'And if what they told you there was correct, you were found washed up on the shore at around midday on the Saturday. So the substitution was made sometime between midnight, Friday and early the following morning. Do you think you could show me on a map where exactly the yacht was moored and where you were washed up?'

'I'm not sure. The yacht was kept moving at night. Security. I should be able to pinpoint where we anchored the day before because I remember there was a bridge just upstream. I should guess too there would have been a report on the rescue in the local press. In fact I'm sure there must have been because I overheard the nurses mention it.'

Jean-Alice made a mental note to order cuttings of the relevant editions of the Jacksonville papers.

Then she asked, 'Mr President, do you have any idea at all who might have pulled this on you? If it's a plot then who could be behind it?'

But he could give her no answer.

*

They went back together to Jean-Alice's apartment. Her new client rode in the rear of the Blazer. At traffic stops he lay down on the seat to avoid being seen. There was a heavy police presence on the streets. Every junction seemed to be staked out. All looking for the President's double. His appearance at the ball last night had alerted the authorites and they were combing the capital for him. Homes of relatives were under surveillance, former colleagues being watched. There was no one he dared turn to. He had taken a chance with Fenwick Backhouse only because he hadn't seen him in years.

Jean-Alice lived out behind the Cathedral on the attic floor of a huge old brownstone with a red tile roof and no elevator. It was called the Orthodox Bible House and mainly housed Eastern European students. Jean-Alice never understood a word anyone in the place said.

The bedroom was a double. Jean-Alice offered to move out for him and he nodded absently, taking it for granted that she should do so. She dug out a clean shirt that a live-in lover had abandoned and which she used for sleeping in and showed him where the razors were kept in the bathroom. While he showered and changed, she scoured the papers till she found a firm offering a complete video recording of the entire Inauguration ceremony and ordered a copy sent round by messenger. He seemed dazed somewhat and she put that down to fatigue. She found she kept glancing at him when she thought he wasn't looking, studying him covertly as it were. Noticing details like a silver thread in the chestnut hair, the laughter lines around mouth and eyes, the way the hairs ran on his wrists. And all the time she was asking herself the same unanswerable question: Can it be? Is it really him? Or am I being a fool? Am I putting myself in danger just listening to him?

She had a sense of giddy excitement, of standing poised on a knife edge between loyalty and high treason. If her instincts were right about this man then the course she was engaged on would be the single most important of her life. Her decisions, her actions, would be scrutinized in days to come by Congress, by the courts and most likely by the entire nation. It might literally be correct that the fate of the country depended on her. If she had got it wrong, if she had allowed herself to be deceived, then the consequences would undoubtedly be fearful. She must keep a clear head. Treat this just like any other case.

And there was another thought too, a frightening one. If he was telling the truth, if somebody had tried to have him killed and take over the Presidency, then when whoever was behind the plot learned he was still alive his life would not be worth a candle. And hers with it.

Most of all he worried about his wife.

'What would happen if you tried to call her up? Would the White House operators think it was the President on the line? I mean the impostor, that is?' God, this was getting complicated.

He nodded. 'Yes, yes they would.'

'You're positive of that?'

He gestured impatiently. 'Of course I am. It's the whole point, isn't it? His voice and mine are identical. Otherwise the thing wouldn't be working.' He began to pace the room again. 'The problem isn't as simple as you imagine. Especially now they're on to me. First, I would come through on an outside line. That might alert the operator right off. Any suspicion of a threat or a hoax even and they can lock the line open and trace the call back.'

'Unless we picked a time when the President was on the move. We can find out his schedule easily enough. Or perhaps it might be better to do it the other way around? Wait till your wife left the White House and try to make contact outside. It's worth a try surely? After all, you pulled the identical trick at Blair yesterday and almost got to reach the President . . . the impostor, I mean.'

'Which is exactly why it won't work a second time,' he said wearily. 'You have to understand how the system operates. Presidents and first ladies don't live in the same world as ordinary people. Their calls are placed for them by secretaries and aides, people who work together all day and are familiar with each other's voices. They have their own communications net manned by the military. Access is tightly controlled and designed to screen out just this kind of attempted contact. Blair was a fluke. I was lucky and they weren't on guard. They won't make a second slip-up.' The first thing they would have done, he added, would be to change all the codes. 'I wouldn't even know what number to dial now.'

'How about when they're alone together?' Jean-Alice said. 'I mean in an intimate situation surely your wife would detect a difference?'

He shot her a look. 'When he tries to make love to her? Is that what you're trying to say? D'you think I haven't been torturing myself wondering that?'

'I'm sorry, it has to be asked.'

He shut his eyes and spoke through clenched teeth. 'We hadn't known each other long. During the engagement there was the campaign and then Caro was sick. She went into hospital days after we were married for surgery. She was due to come out just before the Inauguration. If you must know, we were barely lovers at all. Sex was painful for her. On doctor's advice we had decided to wait until she was fully recovered.'

'So it would depend on her health.'

'Yes unless,' he gnawed at his knuckle, 'unless he were to . . . insist.'

Her heart went out to him. 'Suppose we try to pass word to her doctor?'

'As if he'd believe us!'

Jean-Alice sensed there was something else too. She said nothing and waited. The President continued to stalk the room, clenching and unclenching his fists. When he turned to her again the agony was visible in his expression. 'This other person, he has to be a perfect likeness, in every respect. An exact physical copy. How else could he fool her otherwise? I call her up on the phone, try and tell her the truth, no way is she going to believe me. She's going to think this is some freak mimicking the President's voice. It's him she's going to turn to, him she'll trust.'

He was looking at Jean-Alice for confirmation. She swallowed and nodded slowly. 'I guess you're right, sir. I hadn't thought of it that way.'

'The only way I can reach her is to confront her in person. Face to face. She has to believe the evidence of her eyes. It's the only way I can prove to her the reality of what's happening.' He halted, breathing deeply. 'The only way,' he repeated. 'You have to get me to see her.'

The video Jean-Alice had sent for arrived. She set him down to view it, noting down any detail which struck him as unusual or helpful. 'And anyone you can think of who might listen to you.'

She had a selection of books on constitutional law in her personal library. First she tried under the heading of Elections. Election fraud was governed by the Federal Election Commission, a bipartisan six-member body which concerned itself with such matters as PAC contributions and voter registration. The trouble was that so far as Jean-Alice could see there had not been any breach of the law here. The President had been duly elected. The switch had come afterwards.

Squatting down at her desk in the study corner of the living room, she began to scribble notes. First off she listed the line of succession from the President. In descending order these were: the Vice-President, the Speaker of the House of Representatives, the Senate Majority Leader. Should she start by contacting them?

Could they be trusted though or might one or more of them be part of some wider conspiracy?

According to Article 2 of the Constitution:

In case of the removal from office, or of his death, resignation, or inability to discharge the powers and duties of the said office, the same shall devolve on the Vice-President, and the Congress may by law provide for the case of removal, death, resignation or inability, both of the President and Vice-President, declaring what officer shall then act as President ... until the disability be removed, or a President shall be elected.

As far as she could see though, Jack Meade had not been removed from office. Neither had he died or resigned, nor was he suffering from an inability to perform his office. He had simply failed to swear the oath yet. It might be more accurate to describe him as remaining President-elect. In effect he was in limbo. The question then was, who in the meantime should properly be governing the country? Was it Vice-President Leyland T. Jordan? Or did the failure to swear in the new President mean that former President Ivory remained technically in office still? If so would a fresh election be necessary? But the last election had been almost too close to call. Suppose a new one yielded a different result, as well it might? Reversing the tide of history was not a road she wished to travel down. These were questions for the Supreme Court, not a newly qualified counselor.

Looking up, she saw that the strain of the day had proved too much for Jack Meade. He had slumped over on his side against the cushions, eyes closed in sleep. Looking down at the exhausted figure, Jean-Alice asked herself again why she believed him. And if she could, why did no one else? Because I'm a lawyer, she thought. We have to believe in our clients. But it went beyond that.

Tiptoeing from the room, Jean-Alice returned with a

blanket. Gently she tucked it round him. She turned off the TV and unplugged the telephone.

The team had a break finally. Lomax rang his chief sounding excited. A bellhop at the Staedtler-Hilton had reported seeing a man answering Casey's description using a phone booth in the lobby shortly after nine this morning. The Bureau were checking with the phone company to try and obtain the dial records.

Blacker told Lomax 'to make sure and get over there ahead of the Hoover people'. To Blacker the FBI were always 'the Hoover people'. So far as Blacker was concerned this remained a Secret Service case. If the call had been made out of state, then Lomax was to contact the nearest field office or go there himself.

'Right, Chief,' Lomax rang off. When he reported back he had further news. 'The call was made to a Georgetown number belonging to a Fenwick Backhouse. Mr Backhouse is an attorney. I spoke with him. According to him he received a hoax call this morning at home from somebody purporting to be the President requesting him to meet in his offices downtown. Claims the voice was a good likeness to the President's. He and Jack Meade were in college together for a period back in the seventies so he is familiar with the way he speaks. He showed me a class photograph with them both in. Seems it was a pretty close imitation and he was fooled at first.'

'At first?'

'It sounded like the request was so absurd it just had to be a phoney. Backhouse and his wife were actually watching the real President on TV at the moment the phone rang. Backhouse says he had the impression whoever it was was pressed for time and definitely unstable.'

'And he didn't call back at all?'

'Not to the house. Around lunchtime someone, probably the same guy, showed up at Backhouse's firm, Dorfinger, Backhouse and Stern, claiming he had an appointment but Backhouse had already warned them and the staff showed him the door. I went down and spoke with a young lady who was on the front desk at the time. She couldn't tell us much except that the guy seemed agitated. "A weirdo," in her words. From the description he's definitely our man. Apparently he was escorted off the premises by one of the junior lawyers, name of Jean-Alice Spellman. Spellman left the office early, possibly to return home. We haven't been able to establish if Casey was with her. We've tried reaching Spellman but no luck. She lives up beyond the Observatory. I'm sending a car out there to bring her in.'

'What would our man be wanting with a lawyer?'

'Maybe he wants to give himself up.'

Maybe. Somehow Blacker doubted it.

But at least they had confirmed the impostor was still in the capital.

It was going on four when Jean-Alice decided on a course of action. She put the phone back on the hook and dialed.

'Hi, this is Jean-Alice Spellman. May I speak with Judge Phelps please?' She spoke softly so as not to wake her sleeping client.

'What is it in connection with please?' the voice of the young man on the other end of the line demanded.

'I am an old friend of the Judge's. I used to clerk for him at one time.' This was true but Jean-Alice mentally crossed her fingers that Phelps would recollect. Supreme Court justices saw numerous clerks pass through their offices over the years. Phelps possessed a giant legal mind with an ego to match; she had learned a lot during her six-month stint. The time had come to cash in on the contact.

The voice thawed. Not much, but some. 'Please hold, Miss Spellman, I will see if the Justice is available.'

There was a pause of some moments, then her ears caught a faint scratching sound. That damn dog, she thought. Was it still the same one or had he gotten another of the mutts?

'Jeannie? Is that you? Where have you been all this time?'

'Good evening, Judge. How are you keeping?' There was a yelp in the background, high pitched, querulous. Yup, she thought, same stinking pooch. She would recognize that yap anywhere. 'Is that my little friend Bobo I can hear there?' she inquired, despising herself for sinking to such depths.

Aaron Phelps had been nominated to the Supreme Court by President Carter in 1980. The only objections coming, it was said, from dog-hating members of the American Bar Association unable to stick the former Yale Professor's emotional dependence on small elderly canines of the poodle variety. 'Work here, kiss Bobo's furry ass' had been the rule in his chambers during Jean-Alice's clerkship. Jean-Alice liked dogs but she had spent every day gritting her teeth to keep from stamping on Bobo's spoilt head.

Judging her former boss was sufficiently sweetened by inquiries after Bobo's health and welfare, Jean-Alice switched to business. 'Judge, do you recall telling me when I left that I could always call on you for advice? That's right and I truly appreciated it. Well, sir, a problem has come up that I need help with. How's that again, Judge? No, sir, strictly speaking it's not a legal question, more of a constitutional problem, I guess you'd say. No, sir, it doesn't concern a current case, uh, if you could just give me fifteen minutes of your time? Yes, sir, right now this evening if you can. Yes, sir, it is truly important. And urgent. No, sir, it won't keep, you'll understand when I tell you. Thank you, Judge. At your residence? I'll be right over.'

She replaced the receiver carefully and tiptoed over to the settee. Let him sleep, she decided, scribbling a note, 'Back at 7' and propping it up on the table beside him.

She switched on the answering machine and let herself quietly out.

Karen was feeling whacked. The President was entertaining a picked band of Democratic faithful to a private dinner. Caro Meade had asked to be excused, pleading exhaustion. Karen sent Jodi, who had remained behind with her, home and retired upstairs to catch up on her correspondence.

The window of her third-floor room faced out across to Layfayette Square and the housekeeper had warned her the roof was patrolled by the Secret Service. That was something she still had to come to terms with about the White House, the total lack of privacy. There were compensations, though. Like the maid and laundry services, the absolute security, the awe of living at the epicenter of world affairs. Another advantage was being able to order what you liked from the kitchens. She was about to pamper herself by ringing down for eggs Benedict when there came a tap at the door.

It was Caro Meade.

'Hello,' she said. 'I was afraid you might have gone to bed early.'

'No, I was just going to order some food. Is there something I can do for you?'

'Do you have a moment? I want to show you something.'

Karen was wearing slippers and a wrap. Closing the bedroom door behind her, she followed the First Lady down the passage. No staff were on duty this late; the third floor had a hushed, empty feeling like a house in the middle of nowhere. Caro Meade led the way along to the middle of the south side and up the ramp to the glass-sided solarium built out over the portico.

'Have you been up here before?'

No, she said. She hadn't even known it existed. 'It's lovely. So light and airy.' It was snowing again and the floodlights outside lit up the whirling flakes as they darted against the great windows while the glass shook with every buffet of the wind. 'It's like standing on the bridge of a ship in a storm.' She laughed. 'Not that I ever have. Been on a ship in a storm, I mean.'

Caro Meade was not listening. She had pulled up a cane chair and was climbing on it to reach a bronze plaque on the wall taken from the former presidential yacht *Honey Fitz*. 'Hand me up that screwdriver, will you,' she commanded, pointing to a small tool-box.

Karen obeyed. She watched puzzled while the First Lady set to work to unfasten the plaque from the wall. 'Jackie Kennedy told me she had this set up here good and high so no one would try to take it down again. She guessed Lyndon Johnson would want to eradicate all memories of Jack.' The first screw came undone and she paused to pass it down to Karen. 'Jacqueline Kennedy was my godmother, did you know?'

'I knew you were related. I wasn't certain how exactly.'

'We were also cousins of a kind. Second cousins. But most of all she was my godmother and I admired and loved her tremendously. Still do. Here,' she passed down the final screw and clambered down again, clutching the plaque and something else.

'Look,' she said, holding it up.

Karen twisted the Elvis focus control. 'A coin?'

'A silver dollar. Jack kept it for luck. So she claimed anyway. She hid it up there for a memento. A small revenge on Johnson and the others who came after. She also designed a memorial plaque to Jack to go in her bedroom but Nixon had it ripped out.'

Karen couldn't think of anything to say that seemed appropriate. Caro Meade continued, 'When we were young, Jackie used to tell us the secret of the lucky dollar. She said the first Kennedy to return to live in the White

House must recover it.' She gave a rueful smile. 'I don't think she ever thought it would be me.'

Karen touched her hand. 'I'm glad for you,' she said.

'Yes, poor Jackie, I don't know that her time here was very happy, even while Jack was alive, though she did find happiness later.' Her expression became serious again. She slipped the coin into her pants pocket and looked squarely into the cameras of the Elvis. 'I didn't just bring you here to watch me doing this, I wanted to talk to you about something.'

Karen looked blank. 'Yes?'

'You had an affair with my husband, didn't you?'

Lomax decided to drive out to the Cathedral to interview Spellman himself. He took along Bob Colton. At the Bible House there was still no response from the apartment. Colton went in search of the superintendent while Lomax took a stroll around the block. There was no Blazer in the immediate vicinity that he could see and the cold was biting. When he returned Colton was waiting in the lobby.

'I spoke with the super. He says Spellman went out around five. Thinks she was alone but won't swear to it. Showed him the photo of our man but it didn't jolt any memories. They have foreign students in the building so faces come and go.'

'You get the keys off him?'

'He's bringing them up now.'

Both agents had their hands on the butts of their guns beneath their coats as the super unlocked the door. They entered warily, watching one another's backs. The living room was unoccupied, spotlights glowing in the vaulted loft ceiling, a plaid blanket tossed on the strip pine flooring near the settee. Behind was a study corner with bookshelves and a desk with computer.

'Nice place, huh?' the super volunteered. Lomax ignored him.

Colton came out of the bedroom. He shook his head. 'Nothing. Bed's made up. It hasn't been slept in. Oh, and yeah, there's a man's razor on the washstand.'

'She have men friends?' Lomax was moving through to the kitchen, tossing the words over his shoulder. The super followed.

'She's a babe, you know.' He sketched a shape with his hands. 'Wouldn't mind a piece of it myself.'

The kitchen was low rent. An old-fashioned gas range and a museum-piece fridge. In the sink were a pair of unwashed earthenware mugs with coffee dregs in them.

'She friendly with other residents?' One of the mugs had a faint pinkish smudge of lipstick on the rim.

The super shook his head, 'Wouldn't know. She was out a lot, you know. Up early, come back late. Worked downtown one of 'em big law firms. Lotsa dough but they sweat 'em.'

Lomax moved about the kitchen, opening and shutting cupboards, looking in drawers. 'You got a list of the other tenants in the building?'

The super scratched his jaw. 'Like I said it's transient. Students stay a coupla months, then move on . . .'

'Yeah, well do the best you can. Give it to my pal.' Lomax sent him off. When the man was out of the kitchen, he opened an eye-level cupboard to the right of the sink. The lower shelf held several mugs, one of them a match for the two in the sink. He took it down and placed it in the sink. In a drawer he found a roll of plastic freezer bags. He tore one off and used it to lift out the used mug without the lipstick. He tipped the coffee dregs into the replacement, dribbled in some water from the tap and swirled it around to get the right effect. Then he stowed the used mug carefully away in the bag and put it in his coat pocket.

He went back into the living room. Colton was leafing through the papers on the desk in the study corner. The computer was running a screensaver featuring barerumped girls pursued by barking dogs. 'You turn up anything?' Lomax muttered.

'No way. There's a mound of junk here. Legal stuff. Take all night to go through.'

Lomax looked round for the telephone. Finally he located it, a combination unit with integrated fax and answering machine. The message indicator button was lit. He pressed the rewind and waited.

'Hi, J-A,' came a voice. 'This is Darleen. If you're listening please pick up. We have the FBI round at the office. That guy who was here when you went to lunch, the weirdo you spoke to, well, he's a real crazy. He escaped from a Navy hospital down in Florida, stole some officer's clothes and now he thinks he's the real President of the United States and the Secret Service are looking for him, would you believe? I told the agents you only spoke to him to tell him get lost but they need to take a statement from you anyway. They took mine down. I couldn't remember hardly anything. Listen, hon, you stay away from that guy, he's poison, you hear? And call me.'

Lomax frowned. He pressed the erase button and reset the tape.

'You reckon?' Blacker said.

Lomax was picking his teeth with a match. 'Gut feeling,' he acknowledged. 'The caretaker says she went out around four-thirty, five. Thinks she was alone but won't swear to it. Showed him a picture of our man but it didn't jolt any memories. They have foreign students in the building so faces come and go. I took a walk round the apartment. Bed is made up but not slept in. Looks like the owner is away for the weekend. Some cooking recently but no telling if our man was there short of sending a forensic team through.'

'One thing,' Lomax added. 'There were a load of

books spread out on her work desk. I made a note. Titles all relate to constitutional and electoral law.

'We won't know for definite till the prints off the mug come in but five gets you ten he was in there. He heard the phone message, figured we'd be round and took off.'

'Which puts Spellman in the frame. Question is, will he be back or did the call scare him off for good?'

The newly appointed Attorney-General for the United States was guest of honor at a reception being given by the American Bar Association when an aide drew him aside. A Justice Department official was outside needing to see him. 'What now?' he said, frowning. 'Can't it wait? Oh, very well then.'

He excused himself briefly to his hosts. The small lobby was empty except for a neatly dressed, iron-haired woman in a chair by the door. She rose at his approach. 'Mr Attorney-General, Helen Hilker, Department Counsel for Intelligence Policy.' She showed him her ID. 'I apologize for calling you out, sir, but we urgently require your approval to a wiretap request under the Foreign Intelligence Surveillance Act,' she said quietly.

The Attorney-General took the papers from her. He adjusted his spectacles. 'This suspect, Spellman, is an American citizen?'

'Correct, sir. The application originates from Secret Service. It concerns a threat to the life of the President.'

'I see.' The Attorney-General scrawled his signature at the bottom of the page. 'What happens now?'

'The surveillance can begin directly on your authority. Application for continuance must be made to the courts.'

'Keep me informed of the progress of the case.'

'I'll see to that, sir.' Hilker locked the forms away in her briefcase. 'Secret Service asks you to please keep this from the President till the suspect has been apprehended. They don't want to worry him or the First Lady.'

'I understand. Thank you, Counselor.'

'Thank you, sir. Good-night.'

The assistant building manageress was working late. She wrote the number of Agent Colton's badge on her note-pad alongside his name and crossed her legs beneath her desk. She pushed her glasses back on the ridge of her nose and sat up straight in her chair, pushing out her chest. 'Happy to do anything in our power to assist the Secret Service,' she said briskly.

'We have a number of apartments vacant just now,' she continued. 'The holiday season, you understand.' Her fingers toyed casually with a button of her blouse. The nails were lacquered brilliant red. 'If you could give me some idea of your requirements . . . ?'

'Like I said we're conducting a surveillance operation,' Colton explained.

'The Bible House?' the manageress inquired.

Colton indicated assent. The main essential was a view up the street to the north, he explained. That and absolutely lute privacy. 'We leave the choice to your judgement.'

The manageress rose and stepped over to the key safe on the wall behind. The scarlet nails hovered for an instant before swooping to their selection. With a deft movement she slipped off her suit jacket and dropped it on the chair. She picked up a clipboard and swiveled back to face him.

'Shall we go?' she smiled brightly.

Agent Colton's eyes almost bulged out of his head. The woman had on a white blouse so sheer it was almost completely transparent. And underneath she was wearing a bra that was . . . totally see-through. In the office lighting it was as if she were . . . he swallowed . . . naked from the neck down. Seemingly oblivious of the fact, she stepped past him to the door and held it open. In profile the effect was if anything even more dramatic. The woman's breasts were . . . outstanding was the only description.

In a daze he followed her out to the elevator.

'This is one of our choicest apartments. As you can see it is beautifully appointed.' Her voice dropped discreetly. 'It is very private.'

Colton tore his gaze away from her chest to the picture window.

'We like to think the view is special,' the woman said.

'Great,' he agreed. 'Superb. Of the Cathedral. I was hoping . . .'

A scarlet-nailed finger crooked, beckoning him. She led him across the lobby and opened a door. 'Would this be more what you were wanting?'

Colton gulped. This room did indeed have a clear view of the objective. It was also the master bedroom. The bed itself was a four-poster seduction piece complete with silk drapes. The woman was standing by helpfully, clipboard in hand, every inch the professional executive, except she was . . . pointing those things right at him again. Colton backed against the wall. His training had dwelt extensively on the problem of avoiding agent compromise. Hell, this woman compromised you just being there.

'Will you want to be starting tonight?'

He nodded violently. 'We'll be bringing in equipment. Probably a couple of us. At least. My supervisor may also want to stop by.'

'Sounds exciting.'

'We'll need keys.'

She dropped the bunch into his palm. 'Anything else?'

'No, this will do fine. It's great, just great. Exactly what we need. Thank you, thank you very much.' No, there was nothing else she could do right now. He would be sure to call her if there was. Just get the hell out of here, he wanted fervently to add.

But the apartment was ideal. From the window of the bedroom there was an unobstructed view of the entrance to the Bible House. No one could approach the place without being seen. And winking at him from the attic

217

floor were Spellman's living-room lights. He drew the drapes and settled down to wait.

'I know it sounds weird, Judge, but you have to believe me and it's true. So help me God as we are speaking here the President of the United States is lying asleep right on the settee in my apartment while some pretender out of nowheresville occupies the Oval Office.'

Jean-Alice was feeling elated with herself as she eased the Blazer into the nearside lane by the Cathedral. There was a congestion at the lights: a sixteen-wheeler with a heavy duty tractor unit had jack-knifed on the junction and was backing and filling with snorts of diesel smoke in its efforts to squirm clear. While she waited Jean-Alice ran a reprise of the interview in her head. What had surprised her were the things Phelps had not said. He had not, for instance, called her a madwoman and ordered her out of his house. Or threatened to call the FBI or the ABA. He had not even seemed very surprised. Instead he had heard her out calmly.

'How do you intend to proceed?' he had inquired in a detached voice for all the world like a Harvard professor discussing a class case. His eyes locked on her were beady, though.

'I was kind of hoping you would have a suggestion on that, Judge.'

'Hmm, what does the Constitution have to say on the subject?'

'Directly, not a lot, sir. I guess it wasn't a problem the Founding Fathers foresaw.'

'No? From memory the 22nd Amendment has some bearing, I should have thought.'

'Section 3,' she had nodded: '". . . if the President elect shall have failed to qualify then the Vice-President elect shall act as President . . ." There's also the 25th, Section 4: "if the Vice-President and principal departmental officers of government inform Congress in writing that the

President is unable to discharge the powers and duties of office, then the Vice-President shall assume the powers of Acting President.'"

'The problem there being that this is a question not of incapacity but of failure to qualify by reason of not having been legitimately elected. No, I think you would be advised to rely on the 22nd.'

'Go to the Vice-President, you mean?' Lay out this tale before Leyland Jordan, the Texas Strangler? She could see herself. Not that Jordan wouldn't listen. The bandit would most likely shout hosanna and start dancing on his desk top on receipt of the news that he was to replace the President as chief executive, if only temporarily. Temporary – hell, if Leyland Jordan got his feet across the threshold of the Oval Office it would take combined assault by all four services to turn him out.

The truck had finally gotten its act together and was grinding off up the incline. A horn beeped impatiently. Jean-Alice glanced in her mirror. A dusty sedan with two men up front was squatting on her tail. She wound down the window and gave them the finger. Dorfingers would just love that, she told herself with a grin, and on her way back from a conference with a Supreme Court Justice too.

She backed the Blazer into the parking lot and descended, swinging her tote bag jauntily. She had half expected to find a welcoming committee, a posse of FBI or Secret Service staking out the place, but the lobby was clear. The creep of a super leered at her from the service door. If you only knew, pal, she chuckled to herself as the elevator closed.

She turned the key in the lock quietly and pushed the door shut behind her gently to keep from waking the President. She paused, listening. Something was different about the place. He was gone. She could sense it. There was a dead feel to the apartment like the stillness of an abandoned house. Treading softly, she checked the bedroom on the chance that he had freaked out and was hiding up in a closet. She even looked in the shower stall. Nothing, not a trace anywhere. Gone and not even a smell of him left behind. Damn, she swore under her breath, returning to the lounge. Damn, damn, damn, a thousand and one damns! Not a note left or anything. He must have woken to find her disappeared, panicked and taken off. Probably figured she had gone to turn him in. Terrific, she told herself. Her first client lost and she had no idea how to contact him. Or even, she realized, where to start looking.

Had it all really happened? Maybe she was going crazy, hallucinating, inventing fairy tales inside her head. You heard of cases all the time. Or maybe it was all a hoax. Yes, that could be it. Some stunt dreamed up by the Republicans to make the President look an idiot. They were capable of it, God knows. Politicians were capable of anything. A mean hoax and she had fallen for it, hook and all.

Of course she had carried a torch for Jack Meade. What girl didn't, deep down? That boyish charm, it was fatal. They had guessed it and played up to it with the actor-double. Wherever they'd dug him up from, he'd been good. Smooth enough to pull the wool over her eyes.

Oh shit, she thought miserably, and she had felt such a spy. Like the case to end all cases. Her Prince Charming coming through the woods to her for help. The two of them against the hobgoblins. And now pop . . . ! The fantasy had vanished like a pricked bubble.

But she wasn't crazy. The President of the United States really had lain on her settee. It wasn't a dream, it had happened. She tried to recreate the scene in her head but the image proved stubbornly evasive. She picked up the blanket she had used to cover him and threw it angrily in a closet. She had better call Phelps before he went with the story to the Chief Justice. Phelps was going to throw a fit over this. Talk about a great way to start a career. She had gotten a justice of the Supreme Court fired up with a crazy fable about a presidential double and now she had not a single piece of evidence to back up her story.

Maybe after a while he would come back.

Yeah, and maybe not. Maybe he'd look himself out another lawyer. Maybe, maybe . . .

The meeting of the Chief of Staff's committee began badly. Blacker made his report to the meeting verbally. Hunter had not had time to brief the others on the fingerprint evidence from Miami and they reacted predictably. Protestations of amazement and disbelief were followed by disquieted silence. For a moment or two Blacker read actual fear in the expressions round the table. For the first time the group was facing up to the real possibility that the allegations against the President had some basis in fact.

Miriam Sheen was the first to recover. 'Conceivably the records might have been tampered with?' She glanced at Blacker for confirmation.

He nodded. 'It's conceivable. Unofficially FBI accepts the system is compromised. The majority of abuse comes from former agents who make up 80 percent of private investigators. A computer operator is supposed to enter a badge number for all requests. The Bureau has a unit that conducts audit trails but it has only nine officers to police half a million authorized users. Altering the database itself would be much harder but, like I said, it is a possibility. The only other explanation I can think of would be an error on the part of the operator entering up the prints.'

'A hell of a coincidence that would be,' General Vorspuy said sarcastically. 'A guy impersonates the President and it just so happens that his prints are mistakenly listed under the name of Jack Meade.'

Hunter spoke: 'I still think the chances of tricking the world with a successful impersonation of a figure like the President are so remote there is a strong likelihood this whole affair is simply a hoax intended to embarrass the new administration. Wouldn't you agree, Commander?'

Blacker took his time answering. 'No, I do not think it is simply a hoax,' he replied. 'But you're correct in a sense that it is a trick. Like counterfeiting.' He took out a dollar bill from his pocket and held it up. 'We all of us know what one of these looks like, or think we do, yet in parts of the country as high as one in twenty is some kind of a fake. Most of those fakes are so bad you wonder how a kid could be taken in by them. But they get by. Because they're green and the right size, they conform to our broad mental image of what a banknote should be like. Of course if you show people the fake side by side with the real thing they can spot the difference at once. It's the same with people. Witness identification is unreliable because the pictures we hold in our minds are too subjective. The trick in this case is that we never get to make the comparison, we're not allowed to see the two versions together. So each side is convinced its man is the real President.'

'You're forgetting,' the Chief of Staff countered, 'that at least three of those fooled by the impostor were persons close to the President. Or are you saying they too are in the plot?'

'That remains a distinct possibility,' snapped the Counselor tersely.

'I don't think so.' Blacker kept his voice even. 'The essence of the plot is that it is convincing. The three witnesses may be fools or more probably just not very observant, but honest all the same.'

'Of course it's a conspiracy,' the General concurred. 'The idea that one man can be behind all this is ridiculous. These witnesses, the uncle and Miss Lipscombe, have got to be lying.'

Blacker shook his head. 'Put yourself in the uncle's place; an elderly man with a couple of drinks inside him, he hasn't seen the President close up for the better part of nine months, hasn't been in the same room as him above a couple of times a year over the past decade. Sure he knows him, but does he know him well? Better than any of us? I'd say not.'

'There's another point,' put in the Admiral. 'The uncle was predisposed in advance to assume the person he was going to meet was the President. It did not occur to him to question the identity of the person who appeared. He would subconsciously have adapted the image in his mind to fit the appearance of the newcomer. In fact if now confronted with the real President he might genuinely refuse to accept *him*.'

Jay Leeder had a question. 'Admiral, what would you say are the odds against there being two identical people?'

The Admiral was silent a moment, marshaling his facts. 'We're really talking here about a question of discrimination. Even identical twins never present an identification problem to their own families. Yet white people commonly find it hard to distinguish blacks from one another, claiming they all "look alike". Blacks have much the same difficulty with pale skins even though hair differences might be said to provide greater clues.'

The subjects in this case, Hunter pointed out acidly, were not black.

'You're missing the point. The differences exist, it's just that you can't see them. Black people have no difficulty telling each other apart. Similarly with whites. Identical twins differ but we don't notice the clues.'

'So what you're saying is that these two men are not identical, they merely look to us as if they are?'

'Correct. Either the visual stimuli are too small to be detected or alternatively some feature that blunts our responses may overlay the pattern. Such as skin color.'

Jay Leeder was scribbling notes furiously. The Admiral continued.

'For a doppelgänger case to be reported it first has to be noticed. Doubles living in different countries or

223

communities are likely to escape attention. Age is another factor: two people might grow up identical in every respect – height, weight, hair color, facial features – but the similarity would pass undetected even if they lived in the same street because they happened to be born fifty years apart. These events may be rare but that doesn't mean they don't happen.'

'Granted that a doppelgänger is theoretically possible,' Miriam objected, 'even so the chances of it happening to a well-known person are infinitesimal, surely?'

'Can you be so sure? There are some four billion people in the world as of last count. With those kinds of numbers seemingly impossible coincidences become quite common. Besides which, celebrities attract attention. A close resemblance would come to the attention of the double more easily than that to, say, a car mechanic in Boise. Anyone could spot the profit in it. A look-alike might be drawn from the other side of the globe by the prospect of doubling up as a film star.'

'It still sounds far-fetched.'

'Only because the idea is new to you. Study the subject a while and I guarantee that when you walk the streets you'll start seeing resemblances all around you. Recognition is important to us. Experience teaches us to look for differences in people and rewards us when we find them. Haven't you always envied people with a supposedly good memory for faces? They've simply trained themselves to observe distinguishing features in those they meet. After which, memory is easy. We look for differences, not similarities. Which suggests again that we may be harder to tell apart than we think.'

'Fine, but even identical twins have different fingerprints,' Miriam pointed out. She switched her attention to Blacker. 'The question is where do we go from here?'

'We wait,' Blacker answered calmly. A ripple of anger ran round the table and he ignored it. 'The impostor has to make a move. The longer he delays, the stronger the

President's position becomes. If the impostor's claim is to have any chance of success he must make another attempt to press it, and soon. He has to come out of hiding. When he does we shall be ready for him.'

Across the city, Agent Colton squinted through the eyepiece of a 40-power telescope. Spellman had shuttered all but one of her attic living-room windows. He guessed she left open the one over her desk because it faced out toward the floodlit Cathedral. It would make a good backdrop against which to work.

Flakes of light snow drifted on the wind but mostly the night was clear. The angle of sight was offset approximately 45 degrees scanning a slice through the rear third of the room. In the 40-power lens it seemed like he was in there with her. Spellman was pacing back and forth, coming in and out of view. He would watch her approach, perhaps tossing her head angrily or mouthing something. There was no one else in the room that Colton could detect so she had to be talking to herself. Then she would halt, sometimes stoop, probably to consult something on the desk. A moment later she would straighten up and pivot, striding imperiously away again. One striking looking female. He particularly enjoyed her rear view. To his annoyance the edge of the window always cut off his vision just short of her tail. He was sure she had a great tail.

There were worse ways, Colton decided, of spending an evening.

II

Jean-alice woke with a start. The digital clock of her bedside radio glowed 6.50 a.m. She reached out for the light switch, then thought better of it. Instead she slipped from under the quilt, shivering slightly because the heat had not yet come on, and picked her way across to the window. Cautiously peeling back the edge of the drape, she peered down at the darkened street.

What she expected to see she wasn't sure. Perhaps Jack Meade loitering under a street lamp, gazing up at the apartment. The scene appeared exactly the same as it did every other day of the year. Last night's rain had washed away the worst of the snow. Lighted windows beginning to show in buildings opposite. A handful of early commuters setting out for work already and from down the hill a distant hum of the morning traffic building up on the Avenue.

She called the office and left a message to say she was unwell and wouldn't be coming in. The first day she had taken off sick in a year. Then she dressed swiftly and hurried downstairs. The lobby lights were burning. She checked her mailbox. Empty. She had harbored a faint hope he might have slipped a note through the door during the night. She turned away and caught the super watching her.

'Something you wanted?' she snapped viciously.

'Nope,' he answered, continuing to regard her with a leer as if enjoying a private joke at her expense.

It crossed her mind to question him if anyone had been asking for her but the prospect of involving him in her private life was too repellent. No note, no call and the mail not due for another hour. Depressed, she returned upstairs. She wondered if the phone were tapped. Impossible to tell with professionals. If government was determined to listen in on you they had the technology.

She dug out her running shoes from the closet. If her client were in the neighborhood, hoping to make contact, she could try to make it as easy as possible for him. And if nothing else the exercise would clear her head.

The rain had stopped and the city smelt clean and damp; a silvery mist clung to the bare branches of the trees. She set out along Massachusetts Avenue in the direction of the Naval Observatory, keeping to little more than walking pace and stopping often. Anyone who saw her would think she was in lousy condition but that couldn't be helped. Each time she stopped she bent down, letting her arms droop as if out of breath. Like this she could scan the street in both directions in case she was being followed. A couple of times she fancied a car was tailing her but she put that down to paranoia.

When she reached the Observatory she turned in the gates and jogged up as far as the turreted Victorian vice-presidential mansion where the guards at the entrance eyed her balefully. She followed the road on through the deserted grounds but no figure stepped out from the shadow of the trees. Dispirited, she retraced her steps.

Back at the Bible House she checked her box again. Three bills and an appeal from Stanford Law School. No sign of the super for once. She showered and made herself breakfast, all the time waiting for the phone to ring. It didn't.

She still had the tapes though, the tapes of their conversation together and the notes she had made. They counted for something surely? Yes, but would anyone believe it was the President's voice? There was voice analysis, of course. That was supposed to be highly sophisticated but maybe this impostor was good enough even to fool sensitive equipment. If he were a true doppelgänger. If such things existed. Once you accepted that premise anything was possible.

She sat down at her desk, switched on her computer and began to wind back the tape. The first task was to get the notes and transcripts worked up into coherent form, ready to be dispatched to Justice Phelps.

If Phelps would still help.

'She said she had all this from you, sir.'

Karen was telling the President about last night. They were in the Oval Office with the doors shut, tapes off. The fire in the grate gave off a scent of pine.

He was watching her face, his own expression inscrutable. 'I see,' he said carefully after a moment.

'I just thought I ought to tell you. Not that we did anything wrong. I mean, we were both free agents back then ... ' her voice faltered. 'It was understood there were no commitments either side ... '

The silence in the room was oppressive. Even so, she wanted to cry out, we were lovers. He was acting as if he had forgotten completely. Had she really meant so little to him? And if so why had he brought her back to be close to him? It wasn't fair to confuse her so. The sense of betrayal hit her again.

'And there are your letters, sir.'

A log slipped in the grate. Ah yes, the letters, he said. She had kept the letters, he supposed. 'Has my wife seen them too?'

She shook her head.

'Then I look to you to see that she never does. Do you understand?'

Karen nodded dumbly. She was beyond speech.

Foremost on the new President's agenda will be the proposed sale of advanced weaponry to Taiwan. The government of the island is seeking to purchase Tomahawk cruise missiles and advanced F–16 aircraft together

228

with sophisticated radar systems for defense against the mainland. Total cost of the package is put at over $5 billion. In the face of fierce opposition from the Communist mainland, the request had been sidelined by President Ivory. The Democrats are known to be strong supporters of the Taiwanese and President Meade is expected to approve the package in the near future, not least because it will secure some 50,000 American jobs in the defense industry. Reaction from Beijing is expected to be extremely hostile with the government there warning of the consequences of 'American adventurism'.

Another key decision pending in the President's in-tray will concern Pentagon proposals to resume nuclear warhead testing. It is expected the latter will provoke bitter divisions within the new cabinet as well as on Capitol Hill . . .

The President's first formal meeting with the Joint Chiefs of Staff took place in the Cabinet Room. Jay Leeder was present in his other hat as senior policy adviser. A uniformed guard at the door checked passes. He took his place at the long table next to Hunter and nodded across at the Pentagon contingent in their gold braid. Other seats around the walls were filling up with staffers and aides. By the time the President arrived with the Secretary of Defense and General Vorspuy the room was packed. Karen Lipscombe, who had been ordered to attend with her notebook, found every chair taken and had to stand.

General Clode, Chairman of the Joint Chiefs, opened the batting from the lectern. They had brought along some film, he said, to illustrate the points they intended to make.

'Just a minute,' the President interrupted. He pointed across the room to a male staffer. 'Who in hell are you?'

'Me, sir?' The young man gaped, scarlet faced at being singled out. 'Uh, Ted Shipler, sir . . . Mr President, Special Assist—'

The President cut him short. 'Where are your manners, for Godsakes? How come you're sat there on your ass while my executive secretary has to stand to take notes like a store clerk?'

The staffer's color deepened. He searched around desperately for his superior but he or she was firmly keeping their head down. 'Sir, as deputy assist ... I outrank,' he stammered. 'There's other guys junior to me ...' At the look of fury in the President's face, his protests dried up. Grabbing his files and papers, he scuttled out the door.

'You –' the President snapped his fingers at another staffer. 'Change places and give your seat to Miss Lipscombe.' The man hastened to comply. Karen slipped into the vacant chair. Under the Elvis headset her jaw was set and pale. She couldn't make the President out. He seemed to switch moods with her from one minute to the next. Everyone else was staring hard at their briefing books for fear of being next to catch the President's eye.

'I thought this was supposed to be a closed meeting?' Jack Meade rounded on Hunter and Jay. 'Half the West Wing seems to be in here, dammit.'

Jay Leeder blenched. Dozens of staffers had by now applied for and received all-access passes and made a practice of attending any meeting at which the President was expected. There was no way of telling who had invited them or if many of them had been invited at all.

'Admission procedures will be tightened up, Mr President,' Hunter responded, not letting himself be daunted. He made a brief notation on the pad in front of him. 'You want me to have the meeting cleared and start over, sir?'

The President glowered a moment while the room sat frozen. 'No, let's get on with it,' he growled. 'Continue, General.'

'Boy,' someone breathed as the lights went down. 'So now we have two first ladies to scrape to.'

*

Down in Florida, Troy Reece returned to the Naval Hospital. He found the staff less helpful than before.

'I'm sorry, sir, we have no patient by that name registered,' the clerk said firmly.

'Oh, come on.' Troy had missed his lunch and that made him short on patience. 'Unknown white male. Room 31C. I saw him in there with my own eyes. He was the one fished out of the river, remember? Or is it some big military secret?'

The swing doors to the wards banged open and a nurse came through adjusting her cap.

'Say, Phillips,' called the clerk. 'This guy's asking about the patient without a name. He discharged himself, right?'

Nurse Phillips narrowed her eyes. 'Oh yes, you were here the other day with a lady. I remember.'

Troy put on his friendliest smile. This was the one who had been helpful before. He fell in step, walking with her up the passage. 'I just wanted to speak with him again a moment but you're saying he's gone?'

'Uh-huh, he walked out day before yesterday.'

'Someone came to collect him? Who?'

'Nobody, he went out by himself.'

'You saw him go, then?'

'Not exactly. I was in the next ward, Chief Nurse was in the dispensary and he just slipped by.'

'He skipped out without telling anyone?'

Phillips nodded. Troy thought a moment.

'So what was he wearing? As I recall he was fished out of the river next to naked.'

She hesitated. 'He borrowed some clothes off another patient.'

Troy raised an eyebrow. Now they were getting somewhere. 'So he did have help, then?'

Nurse Phillips was showing signs of nervousness. She glanced back toward the desk but the clerk had wandered into the rear office.

'Not borrowed exactly. This other patient was in surgery. The man just took them.'

Troy eyed her narrowly. 'He stole them?'

'I guess you would say that. Look, I shouldn't be talking to you like this.' She pushed her hair back distractedly, darting more nervous glances around.

'It's off the record,' Troy assured her. 'Just let me get the story right. This patient, the one brought in from the river, who gave his name as Jack Meade, he stole a set of clothes from another patient and escaped? Were the police notified?'

The nurse nodded.

'What time did this occur?'

'I don't know exactly. Seven or 7.30, about then.' There were sounds of a trolley being wheeled down toward the lobby. 'Please,' she begged. 'I have to go now.'

Troy laid a hand on her arm. 'How come he wasn't stopped? Wasn't there anyone on the desk?'

'It was an officer's clothes he stole. A dental surgeon's.' She pulled herself free of his grasp and darted down the passage through the doors before he could question her further.

Troy walked back to his car frowning. He could sense his scoop slipping away from him. On the car phone he called his contact in the police department. Sure enough, an alert had gone out two days ago for a man masquerading as a Lieutenant-Commander Casey, wanted on charges of theft and credit card fraud. 'The warrants are still outstanding. Current information is that the fugitive may be hiding out in the Washington area. He used the cards to purchase an airline ticket to the capital. Fugitive's real identity uncertain. Secret Service are involved on account of the fugitive is believed to harbor obsessions about the President.'

'And this was Saturday?'

'Inauguration Day, correct.'

'Since when nothing?'

'Looks that way.'

'I hear the military took his prints when he was in hospital.'

'Yeah? Nothing on the screen about that. You could take it up with them.'

Troy dug out the local phone book he always carried with him and found the number of the Provost-Marshal's office. The officer who took the call predictably denied all knowledge of the case.

Troy redialed and spoke to Cal. He gave her a summary of events. 'Seems like we're at a dead end unless we can somehow locate our man again.'

Cal mused. 'I dated a guy in the PM office once,' she said.

'Great, would he help us?'

'I'm not sure. It wasn't what you'd call a clean break. Let me work on it but don't get your hopes too high.'

Doug Blacker had talked at the meeting last night of waiting for the impostor to make the next move, but he was not a person to sit on his hands. Dawn had seen him at Andrew AFB catching a flight down to Jacksonville aboard an Air Force jet. On arrival he spoke with the Commander of the Navy base and inspected the building used by the house staffers from the Meade transition team during the visit of the President-elect. A launch was made available to take him downriver to where the Rappaport yacht was still moored. The captain, an ex-Royal Navy officer, showed him over the vessel with pride. From his logs Blacker was able to establish the yacht's precise movements during the night in question.

He flew back to Washington aboard a scheduled flight, using the journey to study a chart of the St John's estuary. On arrival at the White House he sent for Lomax.

He spread the chart out on the desk and they bent over it.

'This is Mayport Naval Air Station and this is the course of the river. I wanted to check the facts in the Lipscombe letter. Could a switch have been pulled as claimed or is the whole thing impossible and a hoax?

'Now, according to the tide tables high water on the night in question occurred at 4.31. During the hours of darkness the yacht stood out to sea and steamed off the coast. Jack Meade claimed it helped him to sleep and the Navy said it made the boat less of a target. At 4.30 that morning the yacht reached the seaward limit of her cruise pattern off St John's Point. Anyone putting a body into the water at that hour could rely on the currents carrying the evidence far out into the ocean. All he had to do was open the scuttle and lower the body out. Jack Meade had actually made it easy for him by ordering the scuttles unsealed in the bedroom. First light wasn't for another fifty minutes. The Navy had a frigate riding escort but she was a couple of cables' length off; the chances of being detected were close to zero.'

'Only he makes one big mistake. The victim is still alive.'

'He might have intended that. In the event the body was ever washed ashore an autopsy would show water in the lungs consistent with a drowning accident. There'd be nothing to cause suspicion.'

'It would still look like Jack Meade, though,' Lomax protested.

'After days, perhaps weeks or months in the ocean? Even after only twelve hours' immersion the victim was so badly sun-burned and swollen as to be temporarily unrecognizable. It was a thousand to one against identification of the corpse being possible at all with average luck.'

But something went wrong, Lomax pointed out. 'Because the next day he washes up on the beach.'

He had asked about that down in Florida, Blacker said. 'The best explanation they could come up with is that there is some kind of rill running parallel with the shore around half a mile to a mile out this time of year. A body dropped overboard at high tide and caught in that would be churned about in the water but quite likely not travel a great distance in any one direction. It would hang in the current being buffeted back and forwards. Objects caught up like that can remain *in situ* for an indefinite period. It's pure chance when they finally get spun out oceanwards or back in the direction of the shore. This victim was very lucky. The people I spoke to said bodies normally float face down. They reckoned this one must have come to on entering the water and had sufficient strength to turn himself on his back. Otherwise without a jacket he'd have drowned for sure.'

'And we'd be resting easy in our beds – with the wrong president in the Oval Office,' said Lomax. He looked up at his boss. 'I thought we had agreed none of this happened. Are we changing that?'

Blacker flashed him a dark scowl. 'That suggestion is damn near treasonable and you know it,' he growled. 'When we started out I said this was a trick. A ruse to make us think there had been a swap and so throw out the genuine president. Nothing I learned today changes that. So, it's maybe possible a person could have survived falling overboard from the yacht and been washed back inshore. It's still all supposition. There's no proof any of it actually happened.'

'Sure, boss, I understand. I'm keeping an open mind, that's all.'

'It's still guesswork,' Blacker repeated stubbornly. 'The word of one crazy pulled from the sea, a fugitive on the run, against that of the President of the United States.'

'Besides which we haven't explained how an impostor would gain access to Jack Meade in the first place,' Lomax pointed out.

There was no answer to that. They still needed proof. Lomax was right; without plausible evidence to link the two men, they were no further forward. It was still all theory. Still treasonable.

It was 11 p.m. The committee was meeting for the third time. Lomax accompanied Blacker. The National Security Adviser's office had been swept for listening devices by Army engineers and pronounced secure. The Chief of Staff sat at the head of the table as before. Lomax sat on Blacker's left, the others took their places and Jay Leeder opened his notepad. Before they could begin, there was a call on the phone. Hunter took it and scowled at the Secret Service Chief. 'Your secretary. A message has come in for Agent Lomax. Important, apparently. They're sending it across.'

While they waited, Blacker delivered his report. The committee heard how yesterday a man answering to the impostor's description had been seen making a call from a booth in the capital; how that call had been traced to an address in Georgetown and that in turn had led to the offices of a law firm downtown. Agents had visited the offices and satisfied themselves that it was indeed the man they were looking for. He had left the offices in the company of a young woman lawyer, possibly to return to her apartment, and unfortunately there the trail had for the moment gone cold.

At this point there came a knock at the door and the messenger arrived with an envelope for Lomax. It contained the report on the fingerprints lifted from the mug in Jean-Alice Spellman's apartment. These were similar to those found on the phone at Hartsfield Airport, Atlanta and matched the prints of the Jacksonville patient.

The news electrified the meeting.

'So now it is only a matter of time,' said Miriam Sheen. 'We wait till they return and arrest them.'

Lomax sighed. People expected life to be too simple. 'We're not sure they're together any more. Our surveillance reports that Spellman returned alone.'

'And the President's double, this Commander Casey?'

'We can't be certain. We didn't even know for definite until a moment ago that he had been in the apartment. We suspect though that he left the building shortly after Spellman.' Lomax described how they had discovered the message from the offices of Dorfinger, Backhouse and Stern on the answerphone.

The President's Counsel eyed him coldly. 'You're saying he heard the warning on the loudspeaker and made his escape?'

'We've no means of telling but it seems likely, ma'am, yes.'

'It didn't occur to you to put someone on the switchboard at Dorfingers to prevent just such a warning being sent? I should have said that was an obvious precaution to have taken, wouldn't you, Agent Lomax?' she said witheringly.

Lomax flushed. 'Our first concern at that point was the safety of Spellman.'

'Indeed?' riposted Miriam. 'I was under the impression the primary responsibility of the Secret Service was the protection of the President.'

Blacker was on his feet at once before Lomax could respond. 'I agree with the Counselor, and I formally request the Secret Service be relieved of this mission on grounds of conflict of duties.'

'Shut up, the three of you, for Christsakes!' The Chief of Staff had had a tiring day and his temper, never good, was frayed. 'There's nothing to be gained by fighting among ourselves. The function of this committee,' he glared at Miriam, 'is to monitor progress and decide on strategy. Operational decisions are best left to the people qualified to make them.' He turned to Blacker: 'The Secret Service is doing its best under very difficult conditions and we are duly appreciative. Now can we continue?'

Blacker sat down again and nodded at Lomax to go on.

The visit to the apartment, Lomax explained, had been routine. Until they got inside they had no particular reason for thinking Spellman had done more than escort Casey from the offices of Dorfinger. 'She had spoken with him and we wanted to know what they discussed in case it gave us a lead on his intentions.' Once they began to suspect Casey had been in the apartment, he added, they had backed off to await developments. Secret Service agents had the apartment staked out but so far the impostor had not renewed contact.

'It may just have been a tactic to keep up the pressure on us. We don't know,' Blacker said.

Jay Leeder had a question. 'What if the contender should mount a legal challenge?'

'Could he do that?'

All eyes looked to the President's Counselor.

She nodded briskly, 'It's never been tried before but, yes, it's theoretically possible. He could retain counsel and bring an action through the federal courts. A judge might decide to strike it out, but with the fingerprint evidence . . .' She shrugged.

'The fingerprint records were fixed. Any judge would realize that much, surely?' said Vorspuy.

'I agree. But with that kind of evidence being introduced he might feel unable to dismiss the case without a hearing.'

The Chief of Staff squeezed his eyes shut as if in pain. 'Jesus, can you just imagine what the press would make of that? We would be laughing stocks the world over.'

Miriam agreed. 'On the other hand if his challenge is serious it may be the one thing that's holding him back.'

'In other words he's demanding we slip him back in as substitute instead of the current president and carry on as if nothing had happened? Which is preposterous. Aside from the legal position, what does he propose we do with the old president?'

'Come to that,' responded Miriam, 'what do we propose doing with this gentleman if and when we lay hands on him?'

'Lock him up under the mental health laws?' hazarded the General.

'Can the Secret Service detain him or do they need a warrant from a judge?' Jay Leeder wanted to know.

All eyes turned once more to Blacker.

'In the District, Secret Service do not need a warrant on the original detention unless the man is picked up in his home,' the Secret Service Chief said flatly. 'If we have cause to believe the President is threatened, we can pick the suspect up outside his home and take him to DC General Hospital. He is placed under the care of staff psychiatrists. Within forty-eight hours we have to file an application for detention and examination. If the psychiatrists conclude he is of unsound mind, they must report the fact to the district court within twenty-five days. That's the procedure.'

The committee debated this in silence for a minute.

'How about Mrs Meade? Has she expressed any doubts about her husband's identity?' the General asked.

Hunter shrugged. 'The President's wife hasn't seen him much these past weeks. She's been in hospital, he's been working day and night with the rest of us to put together an administration. They've been virtual strangers.'

'Sewall says the wife has been acting strangely,' said Miriam. 'Sleeps in her own room.'

'Which proves nothing. The woman's had abdominal surgery, remember. And anyway all first ladies have their own room, or so I understood.'

'Not all, no, and the surgery was a fortnight ago. She could have resumed marital relations by now. Sewall is fairly sure nothing's taken place.'

'So he's listening at the keyhole? Great, now we're spying on the First Lady in bed.'

'The question is, do we lie to her? Does she have a right to know?'

'Terrific. Suggest to a new wife she can't recognize her own husband in the sack? You want to be the one to break the news?'

The Chief of Staff interrupted. 'What I still don't accept is that there can be two different people in the country who are so alike it's impossible for anyone to tell them apart!'

'As was said at the last meeting, they don't have to be identical,' the Doctor responded in his calm manner, 'they merely have to be confusing. Certainly there will be differences but they may be insufficient for us to distinguish in the absence of direct comparison.'

'So you're saying stand the two up beside one another?' suggested the General.

'And everyone will tell you that the one with the crown on is the king,' said the Counselor. 'The President has been in the White House for half a week already. Are you seriously suggesting we go public with this kind of rumor? Hold a "guess the President" competition?'

There was another interval of silence.

'You could say he has been acting out of character,' ventured the General more thoughtfully. 'Throwing over Leon Perry like that.'

'He was right to drop Leon,' snapped the Counselor. 'It was a courageous decision and the act of a statesman. He needs to build fences, win over Congress, not indulge in confrontation as Leon would have done. A week ago we were calling it a bold and imaginative act.'

'It was damn poor reward for a loyal supporter as well as one of the biggest backers the party has seen this century,' said the General.

'He's President of the whole country, not leader of the party only!'

'Okay, okay,' said the Chief of Staff irritably. 'We're not here to discuss the dismissal of Leon Perry. The decision was the President's and that's an end to it.' He pointed a pencil at Blacker. 'You're very silent, what do you suggest?'

Blacker heaved a sigh. 'I've been trying to approach this thing from another angle, putting myself in the President's shoes.' He corrected himself and started again. 'In the shoes of the President assuming he had indeed been deposed by an impostor. An impostor who had been accepted by the establishment. I tried to imagine how I would act in similar circumstances, to see if that squared with what this character is doing.'

'And does it?' demanded the Counselor.

'Start from the beginning. The victim is fished out of the river, wakes in hospital, right? He attempts loudly and repeatedly to assert his identity. We have witnesses who all agree on that point. He is ignored and sedated against his will. Okay, the hospital said it was for his own protection but we know what that means. Witnesses also agree that what triggers his outburst is a news item on TV featuring Mrs Meade.' He met their gazes. 'I think we agree this all fits the pattern of expected reactions?'

'According to the hospital the victim was lucky to pull through,' Admiral Thomas observed. 'If it was a plot the impostor took a big risk in the ocean. It almost cost him his life.'

'Naturally he didn't intend it to pan out that way. He miscalculated the currents,' countered the General.

'Go on,' the Chief of Staff told Blacker curtly.

Blacker continued: 'He wakes up, realizes he is not being believed, decides his only option is to get out and find help. Again, reasonable in the circumstances. I'd have done the same. Now what comes next? It's Inauguration Day; he heads straight for Washington. On the way he tries to warn the Speaker but is treated like a madman. He calls his wife but can't get through.'

'Why doesn't he come to one of us?' said the General. 'Who's better placed to help him?'

'Any one of us would have bounced him straight into jail is why,' sniffed the Counselor.

'Someone else who knows him well then, Elaine for instance, or Leon?'

'Leon left the country directly after the Inauguration. Some Korean firm put him on a million a year retainer,' Jay Leeder reminded him.

'And Leon may hold a grudge against the President,' Miriam added. 'His testimony would be considered prejudiced. The impostor knows that. The same with Elaine. Besides, she's on the bottle by all accounts.'

Blacker waited for them to finish. He went on: 'According to the Lipscombe letter, by the time the patient escaped from the hospital he realized that a double had taken his place. This meant either by a conspiracy involving several of his closest advisers or alternatively by the doppelgänger having such a perfect likeness to himself that the entire nation was deceived. In either event his position was extremely dangerous. If he attempted to reach the White House on his own he faced a possibility of being detained again or even killed. It was equally unlikely the newspapers would believe his story. He tried to pass a message to his wife but believes it was intercepted.'

In summary, he said, all the actions of a man anxious, frightened and confused, uncertain who to turn to, whom to trust.

The Chief of Staff frowned. 'I don't see where this is getting us?'

'What it means is,' replied Blacker grimly, 'that the guy hasn't put a foot wrong so far, so either he is very clever or . . .' He let the rest of the sentence hang.

'Or else he is genuine,' the Counselor finished for him.

A phone on the table shrilled, startling them all. Again

it was for Lomax. When he put down the receiver his expression was taut.

'The breakdown of Spellman's calls just came in. She made only one during the period we believe the impostor was in her apartment.'

'Who to?' Hunter demanded.

'The residence of a Supreme Court justice, Aaron Phelps.'

There was consternation round the table.

'What in hell do we do now?' growled the General.

Miriam was the first to recover her composure. 'Do we know if she actually spoke to Phelps?'

'No, but according to the records she was on the line for several minutes.'

The General snorted. 'You'll put a wire on his phone of course?'

Impossible, Blacker answered. The phone lines of Supreme Court judges were secure. Maintained so by Bureau technicians. Any attempt at listening in would be detected immediately, with dire consequences.

The President's Counsel rose from her seat. 'Leave this to me,' she said crisply.

Up in her Bible House eyrie, Jean-Alice Spellman spent her second night of waiting for a call that never came.

Where would he go to hide? That was the question she kept asking herself. Where could an ex-president lie up with the Secret Service, the FBI, police and military searching the city for any trace of him? Unless he found somewhere and fast he faced certain arrest. He wouldn't have simply taken off into the blue. Therefore he must have had a plan, an idea at least of where he was headed.

The trick was to put herself in his shoes. Where would he go?

Back and forth between desk and door she paced, cudgeling her brains. Finally she gave it up and went into

243

the kitchen for something to eat. She could have murdered a pizza but her favorite take-away was over in Chinatown. She dug a Coke out of the fridge while she thought and switched on the TV to catch any news. As she did so a glimmer of memory came back. The two of them in the eatery near the office at lunchtime; a query she had put to him early on and hadn't gotten a straight answer to. Where had he spent last night? she had asked him. He had waved the question away, saying it wasn't important. Maybe it wasn't then but something in the way he said it had jarred with her. One of the signals lawyers learned to pick up on when a client wasn't being entirely frank. There had been more urgent matters so she had pushed it to a corner of her mind.

Yet for nearly eleven hours he had dropped out of sight with an army searching for him. So where had he been all that time? A hotel? No way, every hotel in the city would have been on the lookout for Lieutenant-Commander Casey. Same with the hostels. Last night had been bitter cold, he couldn't have slept rough in a car or the subway. In his state of health he'd have frozen to death. Conceivably he might have found a steam pipe to hole up next to, one that wasn't already taken by another hobo desperate enough to kill to keep it, and used the men's room in Grand Central or somewhere to wash up next morning. But the stations would be under guard too, likewise the airports, coach stations and other public places. The cops weren't fools.

Maybe he had picked up a hooker and gone back to her place? That was a possibility. It would account for the evasive answer. Hiding out with a hooker was hardly presidential behavior when you came down to it. Only she couldn't see it somehow. By 1 a.m. most of the hookers would have been off the streets, and anyway they looked for johns with cars or hotel rooms to go to. Besides he'd had no money. It would take a quite exceptionally golden-hearted whore to give a naval officer on the run a bed for the night for no charge.

That left a friend. A friend's house was the most likely. Jack Meade had lived and worked in Washington for six years. He would have one buddy at least he could call up in an emergency. Someone loyal prepared to stand by a friend. But who? It would have to be a person he knew well, someone who hadn't been compromised already by the impostor. Who wasn't a part of the administration, therefore. The question was, who could that person be?

Carrying the Coke she went back into the living room. On the shelf under the table by the settee was a stack of *Newsweeks*. It was a certain bet that Jack Meade's life and background would be covered about as thoroughly as it was possible to be. Research, that was the key. Make use of available data. She pulled over a lamp and, squatting down on the floor, took a pad and pencil and began to flip through the pile of magazines, starting from the bottom. The relevant articles were listed at the front of each issue. She scanned them swiftly, grateful she had completed that speed reading course at college. Every time she came to a name she jotted it down. The list grew and grew.

Somewhere among them had to be the person who was hiding the President.

12

It was a point of honor for the President's National Security Adviser that he was the first senior member of the administration in the office each day.

At six minutes to six in the morning his chauffeured car dropped him at the West Wing entrance. He had ascertained that this left exactly the required time to pass through security, proceed along the corridor, unlock his office door, remove and hang up his coat and be seated at his desk as his wrist-watch beeped the hour. Normally General Vorspuy would spend the next sixty minutes or so writing reports – he found he worked best during the quiet time before the other staffers clocked in – until a courier arrived from Langley with the President's daily intelligence summary. The General would then open his private safe, take out a key, unlock the courier's steel-lined briefcase and remove the pouch containing the summary. Actually there were two summaries, one for him and one for the President, the General's being thicker and more detailed. Having signed for the receipt of the pouch, the General then locked the President's summary back in his safe and made a note of the time of arrival.

Today, however, the General deviated from his customary practice. Instead of proceeding directly to his office, he went downstairs to the military switchboard in the lower basement.

'General!' An Air Force major in the communications watch room sprang to his feet. His left hand gripped a heavy black briefcase. This was the legendary football, so named because the military aide who carried it was supposed never to let it go. The aide himself was known as 'the bagman'. The football contained a code book and an electronic transmitter. In the event of a nuclear attack, the President would first verify his identity with the personal authentication card he carried, then consult the code book to select a nuclear strike option which would be transmitted directly to the bombers, submarines and silos.

'All okay?'

'Yes, General.' The major tried to keep the surprise from his voice. The General gave a grunt and went out again.

The bagman sat down again. Phew, what was that all about? he wondered to himself. Just checking presumably that he was here and alert. He sighed. Top brass.

The General returned to his office. His secretary had now arrived. He issued instructions to admit no one and hold all calls. As an additional precaution he locked the door.

The General was a lonely figure. Widowed two years ago, he threw himself into his work with single-minded dedication. He seldom left his desk during the day except to visit the basement Situation Room and for the 8.30 a.m. daily briefings with the President. Meals were taken at a small table set up at the other end of the room. Variety is the spice of life, he liked to remark.

He took a pad of paper and a pen. 'An Appreciation,' he wrote, 'of the Risks to National Security devolving from a possible presidential pretender:

'The President is Commander-in-Chief of the armed forces. He can order the deployment of forces and subject to congressional review, commit them to combat. He has launch authority for the ballistic missile force. He has regular access to the most sensitive intelligence in the military, signals, and political and economic spheres. He can appoint and dismiss officers and decide defense policy. The potential for harm is consequently enormous.

It may be helpful to look at this from three separate perspectives.

'1. The impersonation is initiated and controlled by a foreign power. On the face this would seem the most obvious scenario but it is difficult to see how it could ever be implemented. The present President was an outsider for much of the race, even within his own party, and only finally achieved power by one of the narrowest of recorded margins. Although there are obvious intelligence advantages to a foreign power in placing an agent in so sensitive a position, the practical limitations on a president's movements and communications are so severe as to make it virtually impossible for them to be exploited effectively.

'2. An alternative scenario has an impostor acting on behalf of an American fringe grouping with its own political agenda. The objectives here might be economic or nationalistic, involving perhaps restrictions of civil rights or immigration or an increase in defense capacity. In the latter instance the danger might stem from the destabilizing effect of such actions on the world community. Such an impostor might also initiate wild policy moves and aggressive actions against perceived enemies.

'3. The final possibility is a lone impostor acting on his own behalf. While this may be the least likely it must also be viewed as potentially the most dangerous since the motives of a lone individual would be next to impossible to gauge. While it may be assumed that a state-sponsored agent would not aim to commit national suicide by triggering a nuclear exchange, no such assumption can be made for a person acting alone.'

The General rested his pen and considered a moment. Then he resumed.

'Launch Authority. The possession of launch command authority for the nation's strategic weapon systems is the single greatest responsibility of the President. Certain safeguards do exist to prevent accidental launching.

Presidential authority is only activated in response to a request from a National Defense Command center. An unsolicited order would certainly be questioned by NORAD and refused unless there were outside evidence of an imminent attack. Also the Commander-in-Chief must actively select targets from the manual carried by his Air Force aide. In the event of the President acting irrationally this officer has instructions to deny access to the launching codes, remove himself and them to a place of safety and communicate immediately with the nearest National Command center.

'These safeguards would probably suffice during times of normal or reduced tension. A more serious situation arises once political strain causes Defense Condition to be raised. Current Defcon is 5 for standard peacetime. Defcon 1 is war combat status. At Defcon 3 or above, an order emanating from the President would almost certainly be sufficient to initiate launch procedures.

'In short, were a commander-in-chief determined to court national and perhaps personal suicide there would be a high likelihood of his succeeding.'

The General read through carefully what he had written. He could find no fault with his reasoning. He thought of the young man down in the basement with his code books and lists of cities and suddenly he felt afraid.

Jean-Alice awoke with a start, knowing she had over-slept. Eight o'clock and Tuesday. She had better go into the office like normal. He had found her there before; maybe he would try again.

She carried the radio into the bathroom while she showered. Top item of news was the unexpected death during the night of Chief Justice Roscoe from a cerebral hemorrhage, 'thought by informed sources to have been brought on by the strain of the Inauguration.' She wondered what Phelps would be thinking. The Chief Justice had been a fine lawyer in his time. Now he was gone and the top spot vacant. Perhaps Phelps would have other things on his mind besides the night before last's visit.

She climbed into a business suit and set off in the Blazer.

She knew something was wrong the second she walked through the door at Dorfingers. Darleen was watching for her, her sweet face twisted up with anxiety. 'Mr B. wants to see you right away in his office. You're to go straight there directly and I'm to phone and let him know you've arrived. Your room has been sealed. I tried to call and warn you but you'd left already.'

Jean-Alice's stomach knotted. Locking an associate out of his or her office was a preliminary to firing them. A regular precaution to prevent the abstraction of files and correspondence. And there was only one reason she could think of why Fenwick Backhouse would want her out of the firm.

She braced herself and forced a smile. 'Thanks, kid. If I don't make it back, tell the folks my last thoughts were of Mom and the flag.'

She strode resolutely through the full-height glass doors that separated the reception area from the partners' rooms. Outside Backhouse's office there was just time to extract her Sony cassette-recorder from her briefcase and slip it unobserved into her pocket. It might be as well to have a transcript of the coming interview on tape.

As managing partner, Fenwick Backhouse occupied a prized corner suite. On a clear day, he liked to point out to clients, he could see the Washington Monument from where he sat at his desk. He was sitting at the desk when Jean-Alice came in and he wasn't looking at the Monument. Jean-Alice didn't think she had ever seen him so angry.

He jumped up from his chair the moment she entered the room as if someone had stuck a tack through the seat. The secretary shut the door discreetly behind them. She would be listening outside, you could bet. Jean-Alice put a hand in her pocket and flicked on the record button. She was glad she had done so because without waiting for her to speak Backhouse strode round the desk and leaned into her face. 'Stupid, stupid little bitch! What the fuck d'you think you've been playing at?' he screamed.

Her job was as good as dead, she could see that. There was nothing to be gained by apologizing so she stood her ground. The important thing was to keep her temper and speak for the benefit of the tape. 'I'm afraid I don't understand you, Mr Backhouse, and do you mind not spitting in my face, please.'

His neck went purple and the veins on his temples throbbed like knotted worms under the skin. She began to be frightened he was going to have a coronary or else assault her physically and took an involuntary half-step back toward the door.

'Deliberately made a complete fool of me is what! With the President, the White House, the ABA! I had the Attorney-General on to me this morning asking me what the hell I think I'm doing using my firm's name to make wild allegations about the President of the United States!'

'If you are referring to statements made by my client, Jack Meade—'

'Jack Meade! Don't talk to me about Jack Meade. You don't know the first thing about Jack Meade. He is no client of yours. You've never met the man.'

'Jack Meade came to these offices two days ago. You had refused to meet with him. He retained me as his counsel. He made statements concerning the impostor currently illegally occupying the White House—'

'He did no such thing, damn you!' Backhouse swept her words aside in rage. 'I repeat, you've never met Jack Meade. You wouldn't know Jack Meade from Adam! I was at college with the sucker. D'you think I don't know when I'm speaking to him? Some charlatan trying to pull a hoax comes to the office and you haven't the sense to

251

see him for what he is: a cheat and a fraud. Instead you go around spreading ludicrous rumors, embarrassing the President. Do you have any conception of the damage your actions could do to the position of the United States? The world press . . .' He choked.

Jean-Alice wished she felt more sure of herself. It was perfectly true she had never laid eyes on Jack Meade before Sunday. Whereas Backhouse . . .

'Your actions have been scandalous, reckless, criminally irresponsible. You could very possibly face charges of treason as a result of your behavior. You have ruined my reputation and the reputation of this firm. It is perfectly possible I shall be asked to resign. My entire career destroyed and all due to the idiotic behavior of a sensation-seeking associate.'

Jean-Alice's chin went up. 'With respect, sir, you have only yourself to blame for refusing to see the client.'

The wall to the left of Backhouse's desk was the trophy wall where his testimonials and plaques were proudly mounted. In his fury Backhouse grabbed at a framed testimonial from one of the London Inns of Court and wrenched it from its fixing. Jean-Alice ducked as it was hurled in her direction to smash against a glass-fronted mahogany bookcase.

'There is no client! There never was a client! The man is deranged. He suffers from personality disorders and delusions. He is a fugitive wanted by the police . . .'

'I talked with him for six hours. I listened to his story. The man is as sane as you or I. And he is who he claims to be.'

'Then you're as mad as he is. A complete stranger walks into the office and tells you he is the President of the United States and you believe him. My God, you're the one who needs help, not him.'

The door clicked and the secretary ducked her head tentatively round.

'Get out!' Backhouse snarled. 'Get out. And you get

252

out too, Spellman. Get out and don't come back! Security will meet you at the front desk and escort you from the building. Any personal effects will be sent on to your home address.'

'You have no right to do this, sir,' Jean-Alice told him, holding on to her own temper. 'No right at all. I was simply doing my duty as an attorney. If you abrogate my contract I will sue you personally and the firm of Dorfinger, Backhouse and Stern for punitive damages.'

Backhouse's fury seemed to abate. He went back to his desk and sat down heavily. 'Do what you want.' He waved a hand dismissively. 'But I've a hunch you'll have other things to worry about besides losing your position here.'

Jean-Alice was not through yet. She paused in the doorway. 'You know what you just did, Backhouse,' she said contemptuously. 'You blew the biggest chance you'll ever have. The President asked you for help and you didn't believe him. For the rest of your life you're going to kick yourself for that.'

With a laugh Jean-Alice let herself out. The secretaries in the outer office gazed at her awestruck as she went through. In the lobby the security guards were waiting. Their manner was apologetic. 'Afraid we have to take you downstairs, ma'am.' Darleen was blinking back tears.

'Don't fret, girl. They haven't heard the last of this yet.' Jean-Alice kissed her.

One of the guards was at her side. 'Your office keys please, lady.' He held out his hand.

She unhooked them from her clasp and dropped them into his palm along with the swipe card for the main doors.

Dean Rosser, deputy to the managing partner, came walking briskly up to catch them. In his hand was a large buff envelope. He handed it to her. 'This is official termination of contract. Included is your final salary check and a check for severance pay due you under the terms of your contract.'

'Thank you. I intend to dispute the right of the firm to terminate and shall be issuing a writ of damages shortly.'

He nodded as if he had expected this. 'You will also find notice that the firm reserves the right to pursue you for damages in negligence. In addition a report of your behavior will be sent to the American Law Society.'

Jean-Alice nodded. 'I understand.'

Dean indicated the security agents. 'These men will accompany you home and recover any of the firm's property which may be in your possession,' he said flatly. 'This will include any files pertaining to cases belonging to the firm and over which the firm has intellectual property rights.'

'If you mean they intend to search my apartment, they'll need a warrant to do so.'

With a thin smile Dean handed her a second envelope. 'We anticipated,' he said drily.

She had not noticed the two men in dark suits sitting quietly in the reception area. Even when they got to their feet and approached she assumed they were clients of the firm. She even stepped back slightly to allow them to pass by. Only when they stopped in front of her did she realize her mistake.

'Ms Jean-Alice Spellman?' said the taller of the two. She knew then who they were, even before the tall man took out the wallet with the gold eagle embossed on it and showed it to her. They were government agents. And then she felt a moment of genuine fear.

'Ms Spellman, we are with the Secret Service. We would like to ask you a few questions.' The man paused. 'We also have a warrant to search your place of residence.'

Jay Leeder was on the phone. He had placed a call from his office to the National Archives Building down on

254

Constitution Avenue. He identified himself to a senior historian.

'We are trying to track down living relatives of a certain person.'

'When you say track down, do you mean locate physically? Or do you just want to know if any exist?'

'Both, I think.'

'And who would this person be?'

The President of the US, Jay told him.

'In which case I can save you the trouble; President Meade has no living blood relatives.'

'None at all?'

'No. The President was an only child, as was his father. Both his parents are dead. His mother had one brother and a sister. The girl died in infancy and the brother was killed at Anzio in World War II. Neither had heirs. The President's mother was a MacKenzie. Her father emigrated from Glasgow, Scotland at the turn of the century. He married his first cousin.'

'Oh? How about the uncle, Hinkson, then?'

'Mr Hinkson is no relation to the President although the President refers to him as uncle. He is the husband of the President's grandfather's niece, Janie Meade. She and her parents, an aunt and two sisters were drowned along with the President's grandfather, Alexander Meade, in the *Minerva* in 1938. Hinkson remarried after the war.'

'You're very well informed on the subject.'

'We research the family background of each one of our presidents, Mr Leeder. Standard practice in the Archives. We get a great many inquiries.'

'How far back have you taken this?'

'The President's family tree? In America on his father's side we can trace back five generations. One or two gaps in the collaterals but they're minor. On the Scottish MacKenzie side we've taken the line back to 1760 in Scotland.'

'And no breaks?'

'There are always inconsistencies in any tree: names get substituted, ages set down wrong, record clerks make mistakes. Like I said, nothing significant.'

'And you're certain the President has no living relatives, however distant?'

'At a certain remoteness everyone has relatives. All I can tell you for definite is that none of the President's great-great-grandparents have any other living descendants.'

'Isn't that unusual? Our grandparents' generation had large families.'

'And high mortality, particularly among children. They also tended to marry cousins frequently. Inbreeding reduces the spread of the tree. And then there were wars, of course. Families die out more frequently than you'd think.'

'How about Jack Meade's first marriage?'

'The President married Pascia Day O'Connor, film actress, in 1990. There were no children of the marriage and the couple divorced in 1994. O'Connor later remarried.'

Jay had one final question. 'The President's parents, are they both buried in Indianapolis?'

'Their remains are interred there, yes.' The archivist hesitated a moment. 'Their ashes, that is.'

'Ashes?'

'Mr and Mrs Meade were both cremated. It was their express wish. Their ashes are interred in the wall of the chapel of remembrance.'

One of the Secret Service rode beside Jean-Alice in the Blazer on the journey to the Bible House. The other agent and the two security men from Dorfingers followed in their own cars. Before they set off the agents carried out a search of the vehicle's interior. They pored over a street map of the capital.

'Is this your handwriting?'

'The circles and crosses? Some of it, I guess.'

'Mind telling us what they indicate, lady?'

'Restaurants, shops, friends' addresses, whatever you mark a map for.'

'Which addresses would those be exactly?'

'For God's sake,' Jean-Alice exploded, 'take the map away if you think it's that important.'

'Taking that attitude isn't going to help you any, ma'am.'

'Fine, I just lost my job back in there. Helping you or anyone else doesn't happen to be high on my priority list right now. So back off.'

'Just doing our job, ma'am. Don't make it harder on yourself.'

They drove out from the car park in silence.

At the Bible House the super still wore the same leer. 'Goddammit, why don't you put the cuffs on me while you're about it?' she muttered as they escorted her through the lobby.

'Keys,' the senior of the agents requested as they reached her front door. They drew automatics from under their coats. Jean-Alice's eyes popped.

'Stay back, please.' They waved her and the Dorfinger men aside and positioned themselves either side the door. 'Federal agents!' The one with the keys banged on the door.

'There's no one in there,' Jean-Alice said.

The agents ignored her. Unlocking the door, they flung it aside and rushed inside, crouching from room to room.

'Satisfied?' Jean-Alice demanded, following them. She stood in the middle of the living room, arms folded angrily across her chest, while the two rooted about among her books and papers. The Dorfinger goons had taken her cell-phone and unhooked her portable computer and were listing the law books and files.

'Sign here to acknowledge everything we're taking is property of Dorfinger, Backhouse and Stern, okay?'

She read through the papers. When she came to the list of files she crossed out the name 'Meade, J.M.', initialed it and handed it back.

The lead goon looked at the list where she had written on it. 'What you do that for? The list is complete. No exceptions. Now I have to write it out again.' He scowled.

The Secret Service had moved on to the bedroom. Jean-Alice could hear them opening drawers and closets. She waited sullenly till the goon had redone his list.

'No funny business this time,' he said thrusting it at her. 'You sign where it says is all. I got better things to do.'

'Me too,' Jean-Alice told him. This time she wrote, 'J.M. Meade is client solely of undersigned' and wrote her name underneath.

The goon snatched the papers from her, 'I said sign your fucking name is all!' he snarled. He scanned what she had written and his neck began to swell. 'Listen, lady, you gonna bring a heap of trouble on yourself. I got specific orders on this. Till you sign we don't leave, got it?'

'You've got all you're entitled to. Now get out of my apartment, apes, before I call the cops and have you thrown in the zoo.'

The goon reached inside his coat. 'See this?' He brandished a copy of her contract under her nose. 'Read the fucking print, lawyer birdbrain. Section 22, paragraph 3 (I). "All cases and clients introduced during the course of an associate's employment shall remain the property of the firm without exception."'

'The firm declined to take on this case. It's up to the client therefore who he chooses to represent him.'

'Says who?'

'Says the Supreme Court, is who.'

The goon snarled, 'We'll see what Mr Backhouse has to say on this.' He reached in his pocket.

Jean-Alice gripped him by the arm and swung him round. 'Call him from your own space not mine. Now walk. You too, asshole,' she told the other, pushing them in the direction of the door. They were struggling in an angry knot when the younger of the Secret Service men reappeared from the bedroom.

'What goes on,' the agent said. There was an ominous weight to his tone.

'The Gestapo here have got what they came for and are just leaving,' Jean-Alice told him, recovering her breath.

The lead goon was clenching his fists. 'She's holding back on that case you're interested in,' he said spitefully.

'Get out,' the agent ordered him.

'Didn't you hear? I said she's holding back . . .'

The agent pointed silently at the door. The goons subsided. Sullenly they collected the computer and box of books and trooped out. 'This one is down to you people,' they said. 'We had our instructions. You can take the flak for it.'

The agent shut the door on them. He turned to face Jean-Alice.

'I was handling them on my own, thank you very much. I didn't need you to interfere,' she said furiously.

'Sure,' he nodded pacifically. 'Sure. We could see that.' His badge had identified him as Agent Thule. He was in his late twenties, early thirties, fair haired and good-looking in a boyish kind of a way. Jean-Alice reminded herself to be on her guard. She had a weakness for big, handsome blonds.

'What you may not have realized, ma'am, is that the real Commander Casey is in hospital down in Florida. The man you spoke to was a patient who had stolen his clothes and ID. He has also been claiming to be the President of the United States. So you understand we were concerned for your safety, ma'am.'

'That's good of you, but as you can see, I'm just fine.'

'We'd like to take a statement from you anyhow.'

Jean-Alice affected surprise. 'Yes?' she answered, politely neutral, but her mouth felt dry.

He gestured in the direction of the living-room sofa. 'Suppose we sit down?'

'If it's a question of a formal statement, I prefer to go downtown to your office,' Jean-Alice countered.

'Fine by us, ma'am. You want to ride along in our car or follow?'

'Neither,' she answered crisply. 'We can make an appointment for a mutually convenient time tomorrow.' She drew a long breath. 'From where I stand it appears you people have made away with my client and in consequence I intend serving you with a writ of habeas corpus to compel you to release him. Because there are only two possible explanations for his disappearance: either your people have lost him, in which case they are liable in negligence for breach of duty of care; or you have hidden him away somewhere, in which case you can produce him again, and the law requires you to do just that.' Jean-Alice paused for breath.

Thule spoke between tight lips. 'Your client is running around in the stolen uniform of a Navy officer, claiming to be the rightful President of the United States. That could have serious implications for national security.'

Jean-Alice shook her head. 'You say he's masquerading as the President. He hasn't said that to me. Or to anyone else as far as I'm aware. He simply says his name is Jack Meade and he fell off a yacht. Come to that, how do you know the man you have in the White House is the real Jack Meade?'

She took out a menthol cigarette and fumbled around among the clutter on the desk till she ran down a box of matches and lit it. Thule glanced away out the window and sighed, 'Ms Spellman . . .'

'Jean.'

'Okay, Jean,' he looked back at her. 'Jean, about the one thing we are sure of in this darn affair is that your client is not the President. Hell, I was on duty at the Inauguration. I saw the man sworn in with my own eyes.'

Jean-Alice expelled a lungful of smoke and regarded him coolly. 'When exactly was that?'

'Dammit, you know when Inauguration Day is, same as I do!'

'And my client was fished out of the St John River eight days previously.'

Thule passed a hand over his brow. 'Are you sitting there and trying seriously to make me believe that the man on the run from the hospital is the rightful President of the US?'

'I'm not suggesting anything, Agent Thule . . .'

'Harry, okay? You're Jean to me, I am Harry to you.'

She bowed gracefully. 'It is you who are suggesting that my client is not Jack Meade and is committing an offense by claiming so to be.' She looked him squarely between the eyes. 'I say, prove it. You say you have the real Jack Meade in the Oval Office? Fine, put him up alongside my client and let's decide that way. Because the truth is there has to be something wrong somewhere, something you're not sure of, or otherwise you wouldn't be down here arguing with me.'

Thule made a gesture of exasperation. 'There is nothing wrong, as you put it, except a bunch of idiots at one of the inaugural balls almost got fooled by your client into taking him for the real president. We don't intend for that to happen twice. Okay?'

Jean-Alice shook her head. She wasn't going to let this pass. 'According to Jack Meade's own version, two of those you describe as idiots just happened to be close family relations.'

'An uncle by marriage, an old guy been drinking . . .' the Secret Service agent squeezed his fists together in an effort to hold on to his temper. 'A dumb mistake is all. Like I explained already this man is a danger—'

Jean-Alice cut him short, 'You have succeeded in

explaining nothing. The facts are that there exist two separate people, both claiming to be the rightful Jack Meade. One of them is the duly elected president of this country and nobody knows which is which. I'm not surprised you're beginning to panic. And it's against this background that my client has disappeared.' She stared at him grimly.

The second agent reappeared. He glanced at his partner and gave a brief negative shake of the head. Whatever evidence they had been hoping to uncover had not materialized, it seemed.

Thule gave up. Abandoning all pretense at keeping his temper, he stood up and fastened his jacket. 'Fine,' he said bitterly, 'I've done the best I can. You want to make life difficult for yourself, do that. But I warn you if your client is running around pretending to be President Meade and in so doing he places the President at risk, then this game is going to become rough – very rough indeed.'

Jean-Alice went to the window to watch them go. Not till she had made sure they had both gotten into the car and driven off down the hill did she allow herself to relax. She lit another cigarette and drew in a deep lungful of smoke. They were gone, for the present. How long though before they were back? They meant business, no doubt about that. She felt a fluttering in her belly. It was one thing taking on the authorities when you had the resources of a major legal firm behind you, a very different sensation when you were out on your own with no back-up. Aside from which, currently she didn't even have a client that she could lay her hands on.

She went to the window again and peeped out. It was likely, no, correction, it was a certainty she was being watched. The fact that she couldn't see anyone meant nothing. There might be agents behind any one of the windows opposite, lenses trained on her right now, watching, listening . . .

Listening. My God, suppose they had planted a bug. That would be why there had been two of them. One to occupy her attention while the other fitted up listening devices of heaven knew what incredible sensitivity. From now on she would have to reckon on every word she uttered being overheard.

That was fine. Unless her client returned unexpectedly the only person she would be speaking to would be herself, she reflected with grim humor. Except there was the phone. Suppose he tried to call her up, arrange a meeting? That must be what they were waiting for. Her heart sank. Certainly she would be followed every time she left the apartment. If he tried to make contact now he would be apprehended at once.

She must warn him. And to do that she must find him first. All under the noses of the Secret Service. She scanned the street again. A dark-colored sedan cruised slowly up the hill, paused by the entrance and continued on. More agents? Or just a driver looking for an address? Impossible to know.

The FBI had to obtain authority from a court to conduct electronic surveillance. Title 3 of the Omnibus Crime Control and Safe Streets Act, 1968. In normal circumstances that took time. Weeks sometimes on criminal cases when there was a heavy backlog. She racked her brain. Not all the books had gone with Dorfinger's goons. She still had her own.

She dug out a volume on privacy and squatted down with it. A feverish flick through the pages brought her up against the Foreign Intelligence Surveillance Act of 1978. Under the Act, any federal agency wanting to conduct surveillance for intelligence purposes of an American citizen, either at home or abroad, first needed to obtain the consent of the Attorney-General, then apply to a federal district judge. All requests had to be submitted through the Justice Department Counsel for Intelligence Policy. Licenses were generally granted for up to ninety days. Applications could be made to the court for extension of this period.

Appeals courts had upheld the legality of FISA orders on more than a dozen points.

She shut the book. Backhouse had been right, she had other things to worry about besides losing her job.

She couldn't phone, she couldn't go out. She was trapped in here. That was what the bastards intended. They were counting on Jack Meade growing so desperate he would have to run the risk of getting in contact.

She paced up and down, feeling more caged every minute. She would go mad if she didn't go out. And if she did they would follow her.

To hell with it, she thought finally. A run would clear her head. Let them come after her if they wanted.

She took the same route as before up into the Observatory. Maybe it was her imagination but the guards outside the Vice-President's mansion seemed to stare at her with extra hostility.

On the return leg she stopped by a phone booth and dialed up Dorfingers. 'Darleen? Hi, kid. Yeah, I'm okay. And thanks for looking out for me. I know you tried your best. Listen, could you do one thing for me?'

Back home, Jean-Alice showered and dressed hurriedly. Darleen had promised to call back inside the next thirty minutes. She let herself quietly out of the apartment and ran downstairs to the apartment below to rap on her neighbor's door.

'Melk, sorry to bust in on you,' she apologized. 'My laptop is down and I desperately need to block out some research.'

'You know I die any day for you,' Melk Zachinsky told her in huskily accented tones through his beard. 'You want Law on Line? Use your own password, okay? Make yourself like at home. I go out for coupla hours.'

'Gee thanks, Melk, I love you forever.' She flung herself down in front of his Gateway. She had used it before; in fact she and Melk had first met when he had banged on her door last year seeking help setting it up. He made a living translating aircraft systems manuals.

The phone rang. It was Darleen. 'Jeannie?' She sounded nervous and frightened. 'I got what you asked. Are you ready? I don't have much time.'

'Go ahead.'

Jean-Alice scribbled down the message, blew a kiss down the line and hung up. She checked the modem was on and dialed up the research service, tapping in the password Darleen had given her, offering up a quick prayer that Dorfingers had omitted to cancel it. They had. With a snort of triumph at her own cleverness, she proceeded to access Time-Life library, entering a search request for the name Jack Meade.

Slowly the listings began to fill the screen. The entries were in chronological order, starting with the most recent. The archive went back ten years. Jean-Alice decided to commence her search with the earliest. That way she figured to discover which were his oldest friends. The people he would fall back on in trouble.

She called up the first article. ACTOR IN OUTSIDE CHANCE, it was headed and dealt with Jack's original run for the Senate seat. She scrolled to the end but there were no useful names. She switched to the next listing.

By eleven she was up to 1993. Jack Meade, she was discovering, had generated a lot of coverage. She had a list of half a dozen names but none with a feel of the through-thick-and-thin buddy she was looking for. Leon Perry had been her best hope but a phone call had already established that he was out of the country. Her eyes were tired and she had a headache from staring at Melk's screen. She longed to take a break but she was afraid password authority might be withdrawn any minute. Also Melk would be returning soon and then she would have to take time out to chat with him and very likely tell him what she was up to. She pressed on.

Twenty minutes later she had her first bite. It was so short she almost didn't take it in. She had clicked the cancel button without thinking and had to go back again to read it properly. SENATORS SHARE HOME WITH HOBO, the bullet header read. And underneath, 'Jack Meade, Dem. Indiana, and Dwaine T. Lawrence, Rep. Illinois, inspecting living conditions among down and outs in the Washington subways, took breakfast with one of the system's senior residents.' That was all. She hesitated; maybe Dwaine would turn out to be the close friend she was hunting. She hit the select button again in the hope the next item on file would provide a follow-up.

'Former TV star and Democratic Senator Jack Meade, joined his Republican colleague . . .' she read on impatiently: 'Meade posed for photographers with Roy, who for the past three years has made his home in the steam tunnel below the Chrysler-Lincoln Hotel . . .' 'See box,' said a note below.

Jean-Alice found the box.

Set into the wall of the 15th Street side of the Chrysler-Lincoln, one of the capital's most prestigious landmarks, is an unmarked brass door. If you are lucky and it is unlocked, like today, you step through and pause a moment while your eyes adjust to the moist blackness within. You are standing in a steam tunnel, part of the network that fans out over mid-town carrying heat. Feeling your way by touch in the gloom, you descend an iron ladder. The wheeze of steam mutes the traffic noise and lays a film of moisture on every surface. At the bottom a greasy refulgence filters down through the sidewalk grilles barely illuminating the huge pipes that snake away to left and right along dripping tunnels into the darkness. A man known to the world simply as Roy lives in a kind of niche down here that he has lined with rags and newspapers. He likes it in the tunnel, he says. It's warm, he can heat up food on an uninsulated section of pipe, wash and dry his clothes, even take a shower sometimes via a rubber tube hooked up to a convenient relief valve. A guy who knows the tunnels can travel clear through to Union Station eighteen blocks away without once coming up for air, Roy claims. He does it many a time when this entrance is locked . . . Roy even has a TV in his mid-town *pied-à-terre*. Reception, he says, is dandy. That's how he got to know about Senator Meade. Greatest politician alive, the Senator, Roy thinks. Could be president one day. Sometimes Roy makes the trip up to Capitol Hill to watch the comings and goings. He has an interest in government, is surprisingly well informed. Senator Meade, he affirms, is a true American. Never passes him by without feeling in his pocket for a dollar . . .

Jean-Alice stopped reading. This had to be it. The place. Jack's hide-out. The Chrysler-Lincoln was only three blocks from the Mayflower where the presidential party had attended its final ball of the inaugural celebrations. 'Wash and dry his clothes, even take a hot shower . . .' A place to rest and recover while above ground 20,000 police and federal agents combed the city.

She read through the directions again to be sure she had them correctly in her mind. Then she shut off the machine. She scribbled a note of thanks to Melk and skipped back upstairs to her own apartment. The next problem was how to get across to 15th Street without bringing the cops down on Jack. One way would be to get over to Union Station and try somehow to get into the steam tunnel system and work her way uptown under street level. The dangers involved were all too obvious. Roy aside, the tunnels were home to a good many citizens she would prefer not to encounter.

She got out a map and studied it.

267

Midday. The Department of Justice. Armed guards from the Federal Protective Service scrutinized passes at the sixth floor courtroom where wiretap hearings were held, checking names against a list. Helen Hilker, the Department's Counsel, greeted Miriam Sheen inside. 'Glad you could make it,' she said.

'The hearing is pretty much a formality, right?' Miriam said as they took their seats in the small austere chamber. Aside from the stenographer and a clerk they were the only people present.

'Depends on the case, and on the judge,' Helen answered, keeping her voice low. The judge was drawn by rotation from seven alternating federal district courts, she explained. The court itself usually sat once a fortnight. 'Some judges rubber-stamp whatever we put up to them. Others make you spell out chapter and verse.' Today's judge was a first-timer, she added. Judge Shelley Greer.

At that moment the door behind the bench clicked and the judge entered.

'Your Honor, our experience is that where an individual suffers these sorts of delusions an attempt on the President's life can follow.'

Miriam was giving evidence. Judge Greer liked to have the details laid out for her. She was an imposing woman, polite but steely. 'But it is not the suspect you are asking to have placed under surveillance,' she pointed out.

'Your Honor,' Helen responded, 'it is the government's case that the suspect poses an exceptional threat to the President's person. The only lead the Secret Service has on him is through Spellman.'

'The problem, as I see it, is that your surveillance will be in clear breach of lawyer–client privilege.'

'We acknowledge that, Your Honor. Which is why government undertakes to use the information obtained by the surveillance solely for purposes of tracking down the suspect before he can harm the President.'

'I see. And is the President aware of this danger, Ms Sheen?'

'No, Your Honor.'

'And why is that? If the case is as serious as you make out?'

'It would only worry the President, Your Honor.'

'Quite, and yet you say this particular threat stands out as exceptional?'

Helen rose to her feet again. After summarizing the evidence succinctly, she continued, 'Your Honor, it is government's contention that the suspect's delusion that he is the rightful president, possibly engendered by his close physical resemblance, renders him an exceptional threat to the institutions of government as well as a clear and present danger to the President and First Family. We ask you therefore to continue the surveillance.'

There was a long pause. Miriam stared at the judge icily. What did she expect them to do, sit and twiddle their thumbs till the impersonator brought the Presidency down about their ears?

Finally the woman spoke. 'Very well,' she said, 'surveillance is continued for ninety days. On sole condition,' she added sternly, 'that no information so acquired be used in evidence for a prosecution.'

Dorfinger's financial controls were state of the art. Towards 2 p.m. a computer monitoring Internet accounts alerted a supervisor. The technician studied the screen a minute then dialed a number he had been given.

'Spellman,' he said. 'You still interested?'

'Tell us.'

'For the past hour someone's been using one of the firm's passwords to access an Internet server. My guess is it's her.'

'Any idea what for?'

'No way of telling this end. You'd have to get onto the server direct and ask them.'

'Got a pen?'

'Yes.'

'Take down this number. Use it to fax the details across. Do it now.'

'Listen, Mister,' Lomax snarled down the telephone. 'I have faxed you a copy of a Justice Department warrant authorizing electronic interception on that account. Also a waiver from the account holders, Dorfinger, Backhouse and Stern. You've got those in front of you? Fine. Sure, it's important or we wouldn't be demanding it. Demanding, got that? This is not a request, something you have an option over. You comply with the warrant else you are in contempt. Well, I'll be the judge of that.' He put his hand over the mouthpiece. 'Jerk tries to tell me the information is unimportant,' he said out of the side of his mouth to Blacker.

'Is that the what d'you call it, the service provider? I don't want the number, I want the name of the outfit. Then get onto your accounts department and call me back. In five minutes or I'll be on your tail.'

'Jesus Christ,' he said, putting down the receiver. 'These computer nerds. That's the third time today I've had the Bill of Rights preached at me.' Another phone shrilled. He snatched it up. 'Yes?' His face cleared. 'Right. Good, stay with her. I'll send you back-up.'

He turned to Blacker, a gleam in his eye. 'Spellman's on the move. She's called for a cab to take her to Union Station. I'm going over there myself.'

'I'll stay on the desk,' Blacker told him. 'You need anything, holler.'

'Hi, you've reached Jean-Alice Spellman's phone. I have some super-special visitors right now so please listen

270

carefully. This machine is broken. I'll be out at lunch till 3 p.m.'

Blacker listened to the message. 'What's it signify?' he asked.

'It's a code,' the Bureau technician told him. 'A warning the phone is insecure. Super-special is you people, at a guess.'

'Even I can get that much,' Blacker snapped. 'What about the lunch bit?'

'A suggested meet?' the technician shrugged. 'Who knows. You want us to wipe it?'

'Can you do that over the line?'

'Depends on the make of machine. If it's a three-digit command code that's no problem. More than three and it takes time unless she's left the machine on factory default. Otherwise easiest way is to go in.'

'We'll think about it and get back to you,' Blacker dismissed him. So Spellman was playing games now. Well, they would see.

13

The weather was closing in again. Jean-Alice had donned ski pants and a wool shirt for the trip, under a navy parka with Goretex outer shell and Timberland boots. Stuffed into her waistband was her gun, a .357 magnum, re-barreled and chambered down to take .22 ammunition. 'Looks like a big gun and handles like a small one,' a friend who was a cop had advised her. Jean-Alice had never used it.

Traffic in the downtown direction was solid as the cab neared Dupont Circle and it was coming on to sleet again. Leaning forward she rapped on the partition. 'I'm going to miss my train. Drop me off by the Metro station,' she said and stuffed money through the slot. She jumped out and sprinted for the sidewalk as the lines of vehicles started moving again. Down in the station, she ran through the gate and caught a southbound train to Farragut North. The moment the train pulled in, she leapt off and tore up the stairs to K Street. The Chrysler-Lincoln was three blocks away.

It was fully dark by the time she reached the wall of the hotel. She had the sidewalk to herself. A cold wind had gotten up driving before it a thin and bitter rain. Clutching the parka about her, she sought out the brass door. It was just as described. She tried the handle. It wouldn't budge. Damn! She pushed and tugged, twisting the catch every which way but the metal surface remained adamantly fixed. Jean-Alice swore. She had been so certain this was the place. Setting her shoulder to the door, she gave a furious heave. With a scraping sound the door burst open, precipitating her inward against an iron railing.

Recovering her breath, she felt in her pocket for her Maglite torch and pushed the door to again. About her she could hear the hiss of steam. Warmth began to return to her fingers. Deep shadows loomed all around in the darkness. She clicked the flash on and, peering, saw ironwork stairs spiraling downward. This then had to be the place the article had referred to. The question was – where now?

Gingerly, she descended the steps, her boots ringing hollowly on the iron rungs. Swinging the flash beam around, she made out a low archway leading to what was evidently a tunnel running along the block beneath a trunkwork of dripping pipes. Jean-Alice hefted the Maglite in her hand and moved cautiously toward it.

As she did so she heard a stealthy sound behind her. Instinctively she whipped round, reaching for the gun. A figure leapt out at her from some recess in the wall opposite. There was a fragmentary impression of bared teeth in a dark seamed face, then a violent blow struck her wrist sending the pistol flying as huge arms grappled with her. Desperately she tried to fight free but her assailant crushed her puny attempts at resistance. Locking his grip around her, he clamped a hand over her mouth, pinning her arms with the other. Jean-Alice bit down fiercely. The suffocating hand was snatched away with a yelp. She kicked back with all her strength, struck bone, scored another curse of pain and tore herself loose. In a blind bid for escape she caught her foot on a pipe and crashed full length.

Like a cat her assailant was on her again. Catching her by the ankle he hauled her back. She felt the weight of his body descend on hers, crushing her into the floor and tried frantically to squirm free. A fist smashed into the side of her head with a stunning blow. A second followed that made her teeth rattle and she lost the torch. Near dazed, she finally found her voice.

'Jack!' she screamed with the remaining breath in her lungs. 'Jack!'

The rain of blows ceased. The man was still lying on her, pinning her helpless. Hoarse breathing and a sour smell of sweat. His mouth was in her face. 'What's that, woman?'

'Jack! Jack Meade! Please, I'm looking for Jack Meade!' she gasped. 'Are you . . . are you Roy?'

'Who the fuck's askin'?'

'Spellman. I'm his lawyer. He came to see me . . . Sunday, it was. Please . . . I can't breathe . . .'

There was a pause then with a grunt her attacker heaved himself off her. Jean-Alice sucked air gratefully.

'Who'd you say you was?' the unseen figure suddenly blurted again threateningly.

'Spellman, Jean-Alice Spellman . . . Jack . . . Jack Meade's lawyer. He . . . he ran out yesterday. I'm trying to find him.'

'Which one?' His face thrust into hers, hot and angry. He caught her by the arm again. 'Which Jack you mean, woman?'

Her brain raced. 'The real Jack,' she answered swiftly, trying to speak calmly. 'The President, not the other one.'

The grip on her arms tightened so that she cried out under the pain. 'Roy? Are you Roy? You know where he is, don't you? You've got to get me to see him. I can help him.'

He squeezed tighter, the nails biting into her flesh. 'Where you get my name, woman?'

'Through Jack. He said you were a friend, someone he could trust. *Ow*, you're breaking my arm!'

'Why'd you turn a gun on me?'

'I was nervous, goddammit.' Jean-Alice wasn't going to admit she'd been scared.

'You got ID, woman?'

'In my pocket.'

Abruptly the fierce grip on her arms released and she was turned roughly on her back. Hands patted her down, searching.

'This it?'

'The wallet, yes, inside.'

A flashlight clicked on her face, dazzling her.

'None of that!' He slapped away her hand as she tried to shield her eyes. He studied her features a minute. The light snapped off again.

'Wait here,' he commanded, rising. She sat up, rubbing her bruised limbs. 'I'll take the gun and the fancy flash. You stay put if you know what's good for you. You gets lost in the tunnels you never find your way out.'

He was gone.

Jean-Alice waited in the tunnel. The darkness was blacker than ever, full of small sounds which might have been water dripping, dirt falling from the roof or animals moving stealthily nearby. Rats, Jean-Alice thought, massaging her bruises and trying to wipe the dirt from her face and clothes, forcing herself to concentrate on Roy returning.

Suppose the President didn't believe her? Suppose he didn't trust her any more? Suppose he told Roy to get rid of her?

After what seemed hours she heard sounds of someone approaching up the tunnel and tensed as the light fell on her again.

'Come, woman.'

In the blackness of the tunnel he led her by the hand. 'You use a flash and people know you're down here.' He did not say who they might be. Himself he had gotten used to the dark. Twenty-five years he had lived down the tunnels. 'You get so you can smell your way around.'

He stopped. A small amount of light filtered down through a vent in the street above. Enough for Jean-Alice to make out an iron door set into a rough brick wall.

'You built this?'

'Yup,' Roy grunted as he stooped to insert a key in the lock. The bricks were leftovers dumped by contractors when the Metro was being constructed, he told her. 'Snuck 'em in nights three, four at a time. Door come off an ol' locker bin down near Union Station.'

He swung the door back. 'You gotta understand,' he said, pausing in the entrance. 'Jack's pretty sick right now.'

Jean-Alice stepped inside. She gasped.

Light glittered, refracted from a thousand facets. She found herself blinking in sheer amazement. The chamber she had entered was vaulted like a cellar spanning eight feet by perhaps twelve. Walls and roof had been roughly daubed in white plaster into which were set shards of broken mirror that glittered in the light from the single bulb like a cave of iridescent shells. Carpet offcuts padded the floor in a medley of colors. The furniture was junk and garage sale; a leather office chair patched with duct tape, a white plastic garden table, an ancient portable TV. Under one wall was a home-made shower and a portable commode. Opposite, a stone ledge with a mattress served for a bed. Jack Meade lay on the bed, breathing fitfully. He was dressed only in a shirt, unshaven, his skin flushed and clammy with sweat. From a hook on the wall hung the dinner suit she had last seen him wearing.

Kneeling at his side, sponging the sweat from his face and glaring at them with an expression of mingled fear and suspicion, was a middle-aged woman.

For a long minute no one spoke. Then the woman got slowly to her feet.

'I'm Elaine Manken,' she said calmly.

It took Jean-Alice a moment to place the name. Then she got it. Of course: 'The President's personal secretary that was, right?'

Elaine's jaw tightened. 'I still am, as it happens. This is

the President here –' she indicated the figure on the bed. 'You, I take it, are the lawyer.'

Jean-Alice confirmed her status.

'How did you find us down here?'

'It was a journey without maps,' Jean-Alice said. 'Don't worry, I wasn't followed.'

Roy broke in. 'He's sick,' he said in his unnaturally hoarse voice. 'President's sick. He needs a doctor. She won't let me send for one.'

Elaine tossed her head angrily. 'A doctor might turn him in. We can't take the risk,' she said adamantly. 'I've seen him like this before. He gets these attacks when he's stressed. He'll pull through.'

'He needs help,' Roy insisted stubbornly. 'He's gonna die else.'

'He is not about to die and there isn't a doctor we can trust.'

'I know one,' Jean-Alice said. 'I'll fetch him over.'

Simon Cheng was nearing the end of a three-year internship at DC General. He had been dating Jean-Alice Spellman off and on for ten months. More off than on recently. Relationships were hard to sustain for young professionals starting out. When he recognized her number on his bleeper he was pleased.

'Long time no hear, girl.'

'Cut the crap, Si. I need help.'

'No shit, what's up?'

'You free?'

'As of this minute, you mean? Hell, no. I'm tied down here for another hour. Can it wait?'

'Half-eight then. Meet me on the corner of 16th and Massachusetts. And bring your bag of tricks.'

'Hey, hold on a minute, Jean . . .' he protested but she was gone. He hung up and dialed the apartment but all he got was the machine.

A Checker cab dropped Simon on Massachusetts Avenue. Jean-Alice had the door open and was dragging him out almost before he had paid the fare.

'What's this all about?' he demanded.

'Did you bring your kit?' she repeated brusquely.

'Yes. Yes I did but—'

'This way, hurry.'

Roy had unlocked the hotel door. Somewhere in the past he had managed to acquire a key of his own. She bundled Simon down the stair, ignoring his protests.

'But what are we doing, Jean? Where are you taking me? What's it about, for God's sake?'

'Mind your head,' she told him, pushing him through Roy's door.

Simon uttered a startled exclamation at the sight of the glittering ceiling, the wild-looking man with his shock of greying hair and loose heavy arms, the sullen, well-dressed woman by the bed.

'This is Roy. He lives here,' Jean-Alice said briefly. She drew Si to the bedside. 'This is Elaine.' The two nodded at one another. 'And this is Jack. He had a bang on the head a few days ago and now he's down with a fever.'

Simon stared at the man on the bed. 'Who is he? Some friend of yours?'

'Never mind that. Can you help him?'

Simon knelt, feeling for the man's pulse. It was stronger than he had feared. He lifted the shirt; there were no obvious injuries. 'You say he had a fall, a blow to the head?'

'That's what he told us. He fell off a ship and was nearly drowned.'

'When did this happen?'

'Just over a week ago we think.'

'He's been like this since? You have to get him to a hospital.'

'No, you don't understand. He was treated. In a Navy

278

hospital. He was fine after a couple of days. They kept him sedated but he escaped. That was in Florida.'

'Florida?' Simon echoed.

'Yes, Florida. He caught a plane up here and . . . and met with some people. He had . . . legal problems and came to see me. That was Sunday. Then yesterday morning he fell sick.'

Simon opened his bag and took out his ophthalmoscope. He peeled back the patient's eyelids and shone the light in each in turn. 'Pupils react to light. No sign of internal bleeding.' Gently he felt the man's head. 'No contusions either that I can find. He may just be suffering from exhaustion and have caught an infection from these damn tunnels while his resistance is low. Anyhow we can't take the chance. He'll have to go into hospital for tests.' He listened to the patient's chest for a minute, then straightened up. 'Does he have insurance?'

Elaine and Jean-Alice exchanged glances. 'No hospital,' Jean-Alice said.

Simon frowned. 'He has to get away from this place. If not the hospital how about your apartment?'

She shook her head. 'Not safe. Agents have it staked out.'

'Agents? What agents? What're you talking about? Have you gone paranoid?'

'They lost the bitch! Two teams, five operatives and Spellman gives them the slip like they were fucking amateurs.'

Lomax had returned from Union Station empty-handed and furious. Furious with his agents, even more so with himself.

'The best chance we had of nailing this bastard and we blew it. Shit! Shit! Shit!'

Blacker was no happier. Wearily the two of them sat down to analyse what went wrong.

279

'First question,' Blacker said: 'did she give us the slip or did she just get lost in the crowd?'

Lomax had brought along a hot dog. The smell of hot sauce filled Blacker's office. He sighed. 'God knows,' he said frankly. 'Could be either. Last anyone sees of her is hopping out of a cab at Dupont Circle. The agent with Suter in the tail car ran down into the station after her but the train was just pulling out. He assumed she was making for Union Station and took the next one in pursuit. When he reaches the station there's no sight of the woman. Could be a genuine mix-up. Could be she duped us. At this point we have not the smallest goddam idea.'

'Simmer down,' Blacker ordered him. 'Go back and take it from the beginning.'

'Easy,' Lomax grunted sourly. 'Spellman spends the rest of the morning on the Internet. Then she takes off.'

'Deduction being she located what she was searching for?'

Lomax shrugged.

'Which could be one of two things: either a piece of information she needs to help her client or an idea of where he could be?'

'Yeah,' Lomax agreed. 'She went out jogging again already, remember. I figure she doesn't know where he is.'

'Could be she jogs every day.'

'Not according to the super. He says she is a gym person. Likes racket games, tennis, squash. But yesterday and today she jogs, which is out of routine. Also the weather is lousy, snow on the ground in places. The way I make it,' he repeated, 'Spellman doesn't know where the client is. She goes out for a jog in case he is in the vicinity wanting to make contact. He doesn't show. Before she returns to the apartment though Spellman stops at a pay-phone and calls up Dorfingers.'

'Dorfingers told you this?'

'One of our people was following and had the number traced before anyone else could get in there. Plus Dorfingers confirm a call was put through at that time.'

'Their calls are taped?'

'Logged but not taped. Calls are only taped on an individual basis if the partner or associate concerned thinks a case warrants it.'

'Go on.' Blacker was listening.

'She phones up Dorfingers. Talks for forty seconds. Time enough to give a short message only.'

'Or request help.'

'Which is what I reckon. The receptionist, Darleen, admits to taking the call. Claims Spellman was worried over personal items she had left behind in her room. Says she told Spellman she would have to speak with the office manager and he was out at lunch. Nothing else.'

'She lying, you think?'

'Impossible to say. She is a crony of Spellman's so it's on the cards she would be willing to do her a favor. What we do know is twenty minutes later another call is logged from Dorfingers back to Spellman's apartment building. Call is made from a phone in a client conference room which was unused at the time. No way of telling who made it. Could have been anyone in the firm. Duration of call is nineteen seconds only.'

'Go on.'

'Within three minutes of taking the call, Spellman is logging onto America On Line using a Dorfinger password issued to an associate currently vacationing in the Caymans.'

'Lucky bastard,' Blacker muttered absently, regarding the steady rain falling outside. 'So to recap: according to your theory Spellman, under cover of going for a run, phones the office and sweet-talks her girl friend into getting her a password?'

'Yeah, assuming hers has been invalidated. Actually it hasn't, Dorfingers forgot, but she wasn't to know that.

She spends the next two hours, twenty-three minutes and six seconds on AOL.'

'Doing what, for Godsakes?'

'Look at it from her angle. She met Casey, the President as she thinks, on Sunday. Brought him back to the apartment. He's exhausted, been on the run, fresh out of hospital, he passes out on the couch. We found a blanket, remember? Spellman makes an appointment with someone at the Supreme Court. We don't know who, probably one of the justices . . . '

'President's Counsel is working on that,' said Blacker.

'Anyway, Spellman returns, her client has vamoosed. Probably, she subsequently figures, scared off by us. Where he is, she has no idea. There is no drop, no meet. He fell asleep before they got around to contingency planning. She's in the same position as us.'

'You think she can locate Casey where 20,000 police and federal agents have failed?'

'She's spoken with him, though. Could be he let slip a clue, something he said, a name, a place. Enough to trigger an idea.'

'Why should she turn to the Internet then?'

'Can't be certain yet. Getting AOL to release information is like asking a nun to give milk. Setting up her own website maybe? Play Hunt the President – full video action! Requires Windows 97 or above. $29.99. Please have your credit card number ready.'

'Very funny,' Blacker growled.

'Just kidding, boss,' Lomax apologized. 'AOL are still digging in their records, they say. From hints they let out, they suspect she was using a browser program to trawl the archives of major publications like *NYT* and *Washington Post*.'

'Damn computers,' Blacker muttered savagely.

Admiral Thomas meanwhile had taken certain steps. On his own initiative he had sought an interview with a Dr

Webber, formerly of Jack Meade's medical team. Dr Webber practiced in New York and the Admiral flew up to speak with him face to face.

'I should start by stating that this entire conversation is strictly confidential and highly secret. Disclosure of any part to a third party could result in prosecution. Do you accept?'

'Understood, Admiral, with the proviso that if anything you tell me should bear upon the health of our mutual patient, I cannot bind myself not to disclose it if I deem it to be in his or her best interest.'

'Agreed. Now according to the notes I have on file, shortly before the Inauguration you carried out certain surgical procedures on the President-elect. That is correct?'

'January 5th to be precise, yes.'

'These procedures were carried out at the Westbury Clinic?'

'Yes.'

'Had you examined him previously?'

'Naturally. Senator Meade consulted me on two separate occasions prior to surgery to determine the extent of treatment necessary.'

'Can you remember how the appointments were made?'

'The Senator's secretary, Mrs Manken, always phoned me personally to arrange a time. The Senator was anxious to maintain privacy.'

'I would like you to think very carefully about the next question, Doctor. Can you be absolutely certain that the patient you operated on was the same person you had examined earlier?'

Dr Webber was silent for a minute. 'I'm not exactly sure I understand you, sir. The patient I operated on was undoubtedly the President-elect, that is, Senator Meade. He was escorted into the clinic by the Secret Service. A guard was even present in the theatre during every minute of the operation.'

'There was nothing about him that struck you as different, altered in any way?'

The doctor hesitated. 'I think it's no secret that Senator Meade had previously undergone aesthetic surgery.'

'A nasal alteration, right?'

'Rhinoplasty, yes.'

'But not performed by you?'

'No, I was given to understand the operation was carried out in California.'

Admiral Thomas phrased his next question carefully. 'When you conducted the operation, did you notice anything to indicate that surgery not mentioned in the patient's notes had been carried out at any time? Any scarring or stretching for instance?'

The doctor smoothed his carefully silvered hair with a well-manicured hand. 'I noticed nothing. I repeat, the patient had undergone rhinoplasty some years previously, since when there had been further sagging of the musculature and connective tissue. I made adjustments, took a few tucks. Perfectly normal procedure and there was no secret made of it at the time. At the Senator's request a press statement was issued giving full details.'

'You were not surprised at being asked to perform the operation?'

'Why should I have been? Thousands of such procedures are carried out every month.' He gave a sardonic chuckle. 'And unless I am mistaken you have personal experience, Admiral.'

The officer flushed. 'Yeah, sure okay. Like you said, no big deal. I remarried, you know how it is.' He fingered his jawline.

They talked some more.

'The fact is we no longer possess the records.'

'How's that again?'

'We no longer have the records. A week after the

operation the Senator called me up personally to request that I surrender them to him and naturally I complied.'

'Jack Meade called you to ask for his records?' The Admiral struggled to hide his dismay. 'Are you certain it was him you spoke to?'

'Positive. He also asked that I destroy any duplicates and back-up copies. We agreed this was the only way to ensure complete security. As a matter of fact I was glad to comply since it absolved me of further responsibility. I imagined he handed them over to you, Admiral.'

'Can you recall what day exactly you received this call?'

'I believe it was the second Saturday in January, that would be the 13th.'

Among the host of letters arriving on Karen's desk was a missive from the American Institute for the Blind. All the differently abled organizations were delighted by such a positive appointment. It had taken her this long to get around to replying to them. This one was appropriately couched in Braille. It was seldom that she had occasion to use Braille nowadays, thanks to the Elvis system. Feeling out the words, letter by letter with the tips of the fingers was a chore. Simpler and quicker to have the computer do the work. She switched on the Braille reader and set it to print. The machine beeped. 'There is a document in memory. Do you want to save it?'

'What document is that?' she asked.

'Document has no name,' the machine responded blandly.

Karen's brow furrowed as she tried to recall when she had last used the reader. 'Display document,' she instructed, turning her head to bring the IR port of the Elvis into range of the transmitter. She blinked as the display scrolled up before her gaze. '*My dear Karen,*' she read, '*I am addressing this to you for the single reason that I have no one else to turn to I can trust . . .*' Her pulse began to race.

At first she tried to tell herself that it must be a hoax, a cruel trick by the same people responsible for the hate mail she had been receiving. A real sick joke that would make the President's blind secretary think she couldn't recognize her own boss. Put it out of your head, forget about it, girl, she wanted to say, but it wasn't possible.

She read the document through mechanically, then again from the beginning to take it in properly. The text seemed to dance before her eyes as she struggled to piece together how it had gotten there. It couldn't have come in on e-mail because the reader was not hooked up yet. It was definitely addressed to her and was a Braille original because the coding was there to be read in the top left corner. It had been prepared at the Center for the Visually Impaired here in Washington. So the original had been fed through the machine, then removed and the message left for her to discover. No, not left for her. The document had been sent to her but intercepted. Whoever had intercepted it had not been able to read Braille: a sighted person, therefore. So he or she had used Karen's reader to translate it into text. This was probably the only one in the White House. What the person hadn't known was that because all blind are extra-careful about losing data, the machine automatically retained a facsimile of the last printout in memory.

So, whoever it was knew the contents of the message but was not aware that Karen now knew. Hold on, you're fantasizing, she tried to tell herself, the place is getting to you. It had to be a hoax. It had to be. Only what to do? What to do?

Her lips were already framing the command 'Print'. She hesitated, then commanded 'Braille print'. The machine beeped chirpily in response. The printer whirred and began softly stamping out the indentations on the paper. It seemed to take forever. Her heart was thudding even though she knew no one else round here could read the code. She dug out a foolscap envelope and with a shaking hand addressed it to her mother in Carmel with a scribbled note: *Mom, please take care of this for me. Keep it somewhere safe and don't tell anyone. K.* As the last sheet came off the printer she ripped the pages off the tray, stuffed them inside the envelope and sealed it up.

Calmer now, she sat back in her seat and scrolled through the document one last time on the headset. 'Delete,' she ordered when she was done. With a final bleep the text cleared. Now the only evidence that remained was on its way to Carmel.

Simon Cheng had prescribed antibiotics and analgesics. 'See he has plenty of liquids. Bottled water only and fruit juice. If his condition deteriorates you'll have no choice but to take a chance and get him to a hospital.'

'And have someone recognize him?' Elaine shook her head. 'You have to treat him here. This is the only place we can keep him safe.'

Simon looked at Jean-Alice and shrugged. He had made out the prescription in Roy's name. 'I'm putting myself on the line for you here, Jean.'

'I know, Si, and I'm grateful. I'll explain when I can. Right now you just have to trust us. Elaine's right, he's safer here.'

'I hope you're right. And see you get some rest yourself, girl. You look beat.'

'Soon as I've seen him settled down, I'll get on home. That's a promise.'

Roy went out for the medication. 'Better I go,' he told them. 'Safer. Cops see one of you ladies heading down the tunnel, they get suspicious.'

'Go then, but hurry.'

Roy was back inside twenty minutes with the medications. Together the two women propped Jack up and helped him to take them with water. Afterward he lay back and seemed to sleep a little easier. Toward eleven he woke, aware and less feverish. He recognized Jean-Alice but seemed perplexed by her presence. She endeavored briefly to explain how she had tracked him down. He sounded relieved but still desperately anxious.

'The impostor . . . we must act,' he gasped, clutching her hands. 'Every day he's in there, he grows stronger, harder to dislodge.'

It's okay, they told him. We're making plans. Sleep now and build up your strength. We'll talk again in the morning.

The warning buzzer in Brad Sewall's office alerted the Chief Usher that the President and First Lady were returning to the mansion from an official dinner. A welcoming light from the great overhead lantern shone down on the presidential limousine as it cruised slowly in under the North Portico. The Secret Service were on hand the moment the convoy halted, positioning themselves to shield the President and his wife against a marksman trying for a snapshot from a building across the square. Inside the North Entrance Hall mobile screens of bullet-proof polycarbonate had been rolled across the long front windows. With the new generation of .5 inch sniper rifles capable of punching through toughened glass at mile-plus range certain rooms within the mansion itself were no longer considered safe.

To Sewall, tiredness only seemed to accentuate Caro Meade's beauty. Her coat was unfastened; underneath, her limbs shimmered like ivory through a tracery of black lace and her eyes were huge and luminous. Dorothy Fine was with her. The President, followed inside by his aides, was already moving off in the direction of the West Wing, talking to Hunter and Jay Leeder.

Caro gave Sewall a wan smile. 'The President has some calls to make. I shall go up to bed. Did those fabric samples I ordered arrive yet, do you know?' Sewall said he would check and see.

'If they have, could you send them upstairs? I'd like to study them in the morning.'

Dismissing Dorothy for the night, the First Lady took the elevator to the second floor. 'Oh, Gina, I'm so exhausted,' she told her maid as she sank down onto the chair in her dressing room. 'I must have shaken hands with 200 people tonight.'

'Shall I run you a bath, ma'am?'

'Yes, please, it'll help me to sleep.'

Gina scurried off then returned to help her off with her clothes.

'Gently with the gown, lace rips so easily.'

'Yes, ma'am.' Gathering up the skirts of the dress, Gina lifted it carefully over the First Lady's head. She was hanging it in the closet when the communicating door to the bedroom opened with a soft click.

Both women looked round startled. It was the President, fully dressed.

'Thank you, Gina,' he dismissed the maid quietly. 'You can run along. I'll take care of Mrs Meade now.'

'Yes, sir.' Gina threw a quick glance at the First Lady for confirmation and scuttled from the room.

For a moment neither moved. The President regarded his wife with appreciation. Caro reached over for her gown, which lay on the chair.

'Let me get that.' With a quick step he gathered it up.

She nodded uncertainly, uncomfortable in her near nakedness as she stood facing him. She felt a desire to cover herself.

'I was going to bathe,' she said coldly.

He stepped closer. She felt his hands touch her hips lightly, move upward, and closed her eyes. 'Wearing this?' There was a catch in his voice. She could sense his excitement as he slipped the straps down over her shoulders.

289

'Not tonight, please, Jack. It's too soon. Remember what the doctor said.'

He was kissing her now, his lips hard still from the surgery. She felt a wave of disgust. 'I'm tired,' she pleaded, crossing her arms over her breasts.

'I'll be careful, trust me,' he told her, pulling her hands away. He was becoming impatient and she felt a twinge of fear. It made her angry.

'Why don't you ask Karen Lipscombe for it?' she snapped, pushing him off.

The package had been delivered to the First Lady's office in the East Wing. It took Sewall some time to obtain a key and locate the samples. He returned to the mansion and took the service elevator to the second floor.

The Secret Service were on duty as he stepped out into the lobby. The President had quit for the day and rejoined his wife.

He tapped at the door to the First Lady's suite.

There was a gasp from within. Then the First Lady's voice. 'Is that you, Sewall?'

'Yes, ma'am. I have the samples you requested here. Shall I leave them with the maid?'

'No, no, wait just a moment.' Her voice sounded strained. He stood out in the hall, hoping he hadn't embarrassed her. Finally the door was opened by the First Lady. Her face was flushed and she was wearing a dressing gown belted tightly around her.

'Please put it through in the bedroom,' she told him without glancing at the package. 'And then send my maid back to me.'

Sewall complied. The bedroom was empty, the bed neatly turned down and undisturbed. He placed the package on a chair and came back out. 'Good-night, ma'am.'

There was no response from the First Lady. Caro

Meade had vanished into the bathroom and he heard her lock the door as he let himself out.

Outside the Chrysler-Lincoln it had stopped raining. Jean-Alice and Elaine walked west along K Street till they came upon a near-empty eatery. They took a table in back out of view from the street. Jean-Alice sought out the rest room. She washed and felt better.

Back at the table they ordered food. Elaine asked grimly for a tomato juice on the rocks. They talked in hushed voices.

'How about you, aren't you under surveillance too?'

'Of course, that's why we couldn't bring Jack back to my place again after the fiasco at the ball. Luckily we had the idea of Roy's for an emergency. Anyway the Secret Service think I'm just a lush. I don't answer calls or switch on the lights and they assume I've passed out with a bottle. Then I can slip out.' Elaine spoke bitterly. Jean-Alice sensed the pain of her personal struggle. This crisis had been the saving of her. 'Don't worry,' the President's secretary added sardonically, 'I'm clean now. I won't let anyone down.'

'Elaine?'

'Yes?' She stared into her drink.

'Elaine, look at me. I need to know, are you certain?'

'Of what?'

'You know what I mean. Are you certain as you can ever be? One hundred percent sure that it definitely is him, the President?'

Elaine's stony eyes narrowed suspiciously. 'Of course I am. There's no doubt in my mind. None at all.'

'But how do you know? What is it that makes you sure? What's the give-away?' She waited for an answer. 'Don't you see? People are going to ask. You've seen the double on TV. Right now he looks more like the real thing than Jack himself does, particularly given Jack's condition at the moment.'

Elaine scowled into her glass. 'I worked ten years for the man, isn't that sufficient? It's him, I tell you.'

The sudden whoop-whoop of a siren made them tense. A squad car went racing up the road. They listened to the sounds fade in the distance and slowly relaxed again.

'We need to decide where we go from here.'

Elaine swallowed a gulp of juice. 'You really think we can mount a legal challenge?'

'I hope so. I've researched the possibility and discussed it with Judge Phelps of the Supreme Court. He agrees we might have a case. Whether we would win it is a different matter.'

'That's not much use.'

'It isn't absolutely necessary for us to have a winning case so long as it's strong enough to worry the opposition. The object of the exercise is still to force them to confront Caro Meade with the President.'

Elaine looked bitter. 'I wish I had your confidence.'

They parted outside the restaurant. They arranged to visit Roy's place in shifts to check on Jack tomorrow. Elaine would try to get up a list of people who might be counted on to support his claim. Testify to his identity. Jean-Alice set off on foot. She was afraid to take a cab for fear it might be traced. It took her forty minutes to get home. By the time she reached the Bible House she was too tired to care if she was being watched or not.

Exhausted, she took a hot shower, then made herself a mug of coffee and added a slug of bourbon to it.

At all costs she had to head off any attempt at violence. Should she call Phelps? Seek his advice? But she still had no more proof than before. And who would believe the thrashing and delirious inhabitant of the steam tunnels was the real President of the United States? Even with Elaine's testimony.

About Elaine she wasn't sure yet. Elaine was totally loyal to the President, that was certain. But Jean-Alice sensed a deep vein of bitterness there. An unappeased hatred for those who had pushed her out. And revenge was not on Jean-Alice's list of priorities. That might cause conflict later. Time would tell.

At least she was no longer in this on her own. That was something.

Down in Florida, Cal finally showed up at Troy's place as he was turning in for the night. Her manner was excited. 'Sorry it took so long. The date put in for a reprise and I had to string along.'

'I hope it was worth it,' Troy sniffed, pouring them both drinks. 'So what did your beau have to say?'

'That's just it. The story checks out, the missing patient, Commander Casey and the stolen clothes but there's more.'

'On the fingerprints?'

'How did you guess? Well, you're not going to believe this. According to my friend someone almost dropped an all-time big bloomer. They actually misidentified the guy's prints with, wait for it, Jack M. Meade.'

Troy half choked on his whiskey. 'You got to be kidding.'

'No, I swear it's true. I didn't believe it either at first. Nor did he when he was told, he said. Apparently they got a mismatch on some computer and it threw up Jack Meade's name in error. To make it worse some genius even forwarded the reply up to Washington, can you believe?'

'Let's get this straight,' Troy said, speaking carefully. 'A man is pulled out of the river. In hospital he claims to be Jack Meade, the President-elect, and when his prints are taken they are found to match the President's.'

'Could it be a genuine error? It's a common enough name. Suppose the patient's name really is Jack Meade, same as the President?' Cal suggested. 'That might account for his obsession.'

'It doesn't explain away the physical resemblance,' Troy pointed out quietly.

'It might be a hoax,' Cal said later. 'Someone else heard about the guy claiming to be the President and decided to have a little fun?'

Troy leaned over the table. They had sent out for pizza. 'You don't know these fingerprint systems,' he said, chewing. 'There are safeguards, passwords, procedures to guard against error. Every match is checked and double-checked.'

'Systems make mistakes, computers too. My bank manages it all the time.'

'Sure, but that's different, don't you see? Fingerprint classification is incredibly detailed. For a mistake to arise our man's prints would have to be identical to the President's, and that's impossible.'

'If you rule out error and it's not a hoax, then that only leaves one possibility,' said Cal slowly. 'That the patient who escaped from the hospital was the real Jack Meade.'

They stared at one another aghast.

14

It was after nine when Jean-Alice awoke. It had taken her a long while to get to sleep last night and when finally she did she dreamed of being hunted through dark tunnels by Backhouse in a golf cart. She ran a shower and felt better. At least she now had a client again.

She was eating breakfast when the entryphone buzzed. It was Si.

'For Godsakes,' she snapped weakly for the benefit of any eavesdroppers. 'Go away and leave me alone.'

'Listen, girl,' he interrupted. 'I know you don't want to see anyone. But you need help. It's either me or I call your family. Your decision.'

'Okay,' she said in a tone of defeat. 'You win. Come on up.'

'Your temperature is up three points. You have a chest infection,' Si grinned.

'Yeah, I guess. I feel like I'm dying already.'

'Bed and Bufferin will take care of it. When you're stronger in a day or so, I'll prescribe an intimate massage.'

She made a fist at him. *'Don't make me laugh, idiot! Did you bring the stuff I asked?'* she hissed.

Si pointed to his medical bag.

Agent Thule was on watch across the road. He had noted Si's arrival in the log.

'Sounds like the Doc is leaving,' said his colleague whose earphones were hooked up to the tape deck monitoring the infinity bug in Spellman's living-room phone.

Thule bent to the eyepiece of his 'scope. He could make out the back of Spellman's head over by the apartment's front door. He watched her crossing toward the work desk still with her back to him.

'Phone is up. She's making a call. It's the modem. AOL access number,' the technical sang out. 'Better buzz Lomax.'

Dressed in Si's clothes and a man's dark wig, Jean-Alice took the stairs to the lobby. The snoop of a super was nowhere around. Usually this time of day he was holed up in the basement watching the soaps. She went boldly out the front door. Si's shabby white Datsun was parked outside. Jean-Alice had borrowed it before. It had a crappy starter. She let it roll down the slope, slammed in the gear and heaved a sigh of relief as the engine caught.

Ten minutes later up in the apartment, Si got up from the desk, leaving the modem on line. Being careful to keep his face away from the windows, he turned on the CD player. Russian choral music drenched the room. Jean-Alice's current weakness. Si removed the wig she had lent him and noiselessly let himself out the front door. He had brought along with him a knitted beanie hat and a sheepskin coat from Afghanistan. He looked like a student as he went out the main door tagged onto a couple of kids from Poland.

Agent Thule spared him a cursory glance as he passed down the road and went back to his study of the attic floor.

Si went around the corner where he met Jean-Alice sitting in his car. They drove up to the Observatory together where they exchanged clothes in the car.

Si had good news. He had stopped by Roy's already to check on the patient. There had been a big improvement. The fever was gone and he was sitting up, taking food.

'Considering all that he's been through he must have one heck of a constitution.'

'You have to be pretty fit to survive the campaign trail, I guess. All those months of hopping flights and going without sleep.'

'To say nothing of twelve hours in the ocean,' Si added.

He dropped her off at 17th Street on his way to the hospital.

'She's sick,' said Thule. 'She went out and got herself soaked in the cold searching for him. She's exhausted, stressed, she's lost her job and she's being hunted by us. She's tried to find the President without any luck. She thinks she's failed him. Her doctor has diagnosed a chest infection.'

'Nice pair of lungs at that,' Lomax observed, gazing at Spellman's photograph. Thule glared at him.

'Where did she go when she gave us the slip yesterday? That's what I'd still like to know,' Blacker said.

'If she did run Casey to earth, she's doing damn all about it,' answered Lomax. 'She hasn't stirred from the apartment in twelve hours.'

'I've half a mind to bring her in anyway,' Blacker growled.

'If we do, we kiss goodbye to any chance of using her to lead us to him.'

'Think I can't work that out? Just don't lose sight of her again or it's more than your jobs are worth.'

'Right you are, boss,' Lomax answered pacifically.

'This is more than just the Presidency, it's about me, myself, my identity.'

Jean-Alice was amazed by the change a night's rest had worked on Jack Meade. He had used Roy's meager facilities to bathe and Frankie had shaved him again. Humphrey the valet had been in and left fresh clothes

297

including a suit from Saks Fifth Avenue. Jack tried it on and was pleased. 'Always used to buy suits off the rail. This fits me as well as a tailor-made.' He frowned. 'What is she using for money, do you know?'

'Elaine told me she can still draw checks against the election account. The White House forgot to bar her signature, apparently.'

He nodded approvingly. 'Then the first thing we must do is send a draft to Commander Casey to reimburse him for those things I took.' Meantime though, he wanted to talk about other matters. He had been analysing his situation, he said. He had come to a number of conclusions.

'I know this much, he's an actor, or was. He has to be. There's no other way he could pull off this trick without professional training. It takes observation, character analysis, role creation, diction study, all kinds of skills. An amateur wouldn't know where to begin.'

Jean-Alice listened while he tried to explain.

It had all begun back in the campaign. For a long while he had been conscious of a sense of being watched. 'I don't mean the public, that's different, you get used to it. This was something else. And altogether more sinister. A shadow worming its way into my life, is the only way I can describe it. At first I thought it was a stalker. That happens, as you know.'

Jean-Alice could guess.

It began with little things, he said. Items disappearing. Notes, diaries, photographs. A sheet of scrap paper covered in practice signatures, his own, found tucked into an appointment book on his desk as if someone had been interrupted. A bill for a suit he had never ordered; photos of himself in the company of people he didn't recall having met.

'Our security advisers investigated, naturally. We assumed it was someone working for Ivory's people. The campaign was getting pretty rough by that stage. For weeks I had been getting by with hardly any sleep. Perhaps the strain was making me forgetful. Sometimes I'd be up on stage to address a meeting and find my mind a total blank. Hunter was trying to make time for me to relax but it was next to impossible.'

Jean-Alice was beginning to see now. 'Now you think this person, the man who is posing as president, he was gathering material, understudying you?'

He nodded. 'And now he is me. He's taken over. Squeezed me out. That was what I could sense him doing. I didn't realize it at the time. It's like . . .' he cast around for words: '. . . like doing a scene and someone else brings a minor character suddenly to life. You sense the energy being drained out of your part. The play shifts to focus around this other individual and you're helpless to prevent it.'

Actors were trained to steal other people's personalities, he said. 'That's what the impostor has done. He's stolen my part and now he's playing me. Appearance, personality, my life, my job – like a thief he's taken them from me one by one.' Even his wife, he added.

'And you have no idea who it might have been?'

He shook his head then straightened his back and looked Jean-Alice in the eye. His jaw was determined. 'But that's over,' he said quietly. 'From here on we start fighting back.'

Now the President took charge. 'With our friend Roy's permission, we are going to make this our nerve center of operations. Communications are the first essential of any campaign. Security next. We need to recruit someone with an understanding of technology. Any suggestions?'

Frankie put up a hand. 'How about Conroy Martin? He handled the phones in the campaign bus.'

The President glanced at Elaine. She shrugged. 'He took a job with CIA.'

'He's young, idealistic,' Frankie said. 'One of us. We could trust him, Mr President.'

299

Check him out, the President ordered. But don't take any chances. We can't afford to make mistakes. 'Next, objectives.' His gaze swept over the meeting. 'The mission of this group is to restore me to the Oval Office. All other considerations are secondary.' The attack would be two-pronged, he went on, ticking off the points on his fingers. 'One, legal. Jean-Alice Spellman will coordinate a challenge to be mounted through the courts against the impostor in the White House.'

Jean-Alice felt her spirits lift. Things were moving at last. For the first time since Jack Meade had walked into her life, an age ago it seemed, she could believe they stood a chance.

'The second line of action involves establishing lines of communication into the White House itself. Elaine, this is where you come in.'

Jay Leeder was a political economist by training. At the University of Miami he had published a controversial study of the New Deal charging that the Federal Reserve by hiking interest rates had brought about a catastrophic collapse in the money supply, destroying the American banking system and plunging the country into depression.

Jay's thesis caught the interest of Bob Rappaport of Jacksonville, one of the Democratic Party's largest backers. Rappaport was seeking ways to wean the Democrats from their traditional high-spending, big government policies, seeing in them a major obstacle to re-election. He offered Leeder a consultancy and introduced him to Irwin Hunter. At the time Jack Meade was coming under fire for a lack of substance in his political agenda. Jay's youthful iconoclasm would play well with the media and besides he possessed Rappaport's backing. At a meeting aboard the financier's yacht he was invited to join the team.

He was telling his story to Siobhan Fitzgerald of *Face*

the Press over lunch at Bice, a toney Italian eatery off Pennsylvania Avenue, using his carefully cultivated air of absolute candor. Producers and journalists liked facts. Give them the details and they would eat out of your hand. Who knew, they might want to do a profile of him soon?

'So anyway, I took this one to the President.' They were discussing the bond market.

'You have walk-in privileges?' she asked innocently.

He grinned. 'You know I don't. I report directly to Irwin Hunter and you're right, I am exaggerating my own importance. Potomac fever.' Play it humble, arouse her interest. She wasn't a bad-looking dame. Older than him but great legs.

He was still congratulating himself when her next words almost made him choke on his food. 'So what's this I hear about Jack Meade slipping the leash on Inauguration Night?' she asked innocently.

'I can't believe I'm hearing this,' the Secretary of State exploded. 'We have already affirmed the goal of non-proliferation. It has been a stated central plank of our foreign policy and yet here we are seriously considering resuming nuclear testing.'

The President was in the West Wing Oval Office with his senior policy advisers. For the informal after-lunch discussion the President sported loafers and a green Bill Blass blazer that made him look cool and aloof as he sprawled, one leg over the arm of a sofa, with easy grace.

Chesney Goss from Defense occupied a high-back chair by the fire. A heavy-jowled former CEO of a major construction group, his face darkened as he vigorously defended his department's proposal. 'Resumption of testing will serve direct notice on hostile states we mean business in addition to providing our scientists with vital verification of the potency of our own systems, many of which are untried.'

'Phooey! The Pentagon is blowing smoke. They've tried this on with every new administration for the past two decades. Even Ivory turned them down. It would be a slap in the face for our allies and give the green light to every dictator around the globe to press ahead with the development of weapons of mass destruction.'

Susan Maytag, a horse-faced foreign policy adviser, spoke of the erosion of America's moral authority. A unilateral resumption of nuclear testing would signal the end of SALT 3 and a return to the Cold War. Other members of the President's inner circle joined in. The condemnation was universal.

Irwin Hunter munched on handfuls of peanuts from a bowl on the table. Similar arguments had raged most nights throughout the campaign. Then it had all seemed a game, now it was for real. The destinies of 300 million Americans depended on decisions reached by a dozen people here in this room, himself among them.

Karen Lipscombe entered without knocking and deposited a stack of papers on the President's signing table in the alcove to the study.

The President looked up. 'What've you got there, more work for me?'

The headset mask swiveled. 'Testimonials for the Girl Scouts Associations, Mr President. You're due to meet with them here ten minutes from now.'

The President groaned. 'Since when? I didn't know about this.'

'It's on your schedule, Mr President. Perhaps I forgot to point it out to you,' she added tactfully.

The President frowned. 'Every time I get stuck into some issue I have to break off to deal with trivia. How the country gets governed at all beats me.'

Hunter as ever had a suggestion. 'Perhaps this is something the First Lady could handle? It wouldn't take more than a few minutes of her time. Then the Scouts could have a brief meet with the President right at the end.'

The President brightened. 'Great idea,' he said. 'Call Mrs Meade for me, Karen. Ask her if she'd mind helping out this once.'

As Karen went out, Jay Leeder entered. He looked flustered. 'Excuse me interrupting, Mr President, but there's an urgent matter come in for the Chief of Staff's attention.'

Back in her office, Karen Lipscombe dialed the second floor. She got Dorothy Fine.

'The First Lady is tied up right now,' Dorothy told her. 'She'll get back to you.'

Karen passed on the request from the Oval Office. 'The President is in the middle of an important policy meeting. He would be truly grateful if Mrs Meade could see her way to obliging him in this.'

'I'll see,' Dorothy answered in a tone that said no already.

In a minute she was back. 'The First Lady says to tell you she's sorry but she doesn't see this as her problem.'

'Dorothy, I'm caught in the middle here. As a personal favor to me, would you have another try at persuading her? These are nice girls who have come a long way and this is their big day. All the First Lady has to do is talk with them till the President can get free. It's a lot easier than some of the stuff she undertook during the campaign.'

'Karen,' Dorothy responded coolly, 'do I have to spell it out? The First Lady is not about to do this. She says it's not in the agreement. Now do you understand?' The phone went dead.

'It was Trish Beale, would you believe?' Jay said.

Hunter gaped at him.

The two of them were back in the Chief of Staff's office.

'It was Trish Beale, Barney Nikolis' deputy. I spoke with Nikolis, he checked with his sources and they confirmed. If you can believe it the way it plays is this: the Beale woman is a party to the shenanigans at the Mayflower. She witnessed the President, as she thinks, escaped from his escort, giving the squeeze to little Miss Cyber Secretary. So to avert possible press revelations, Beale calls up a media contact and privately assures her there is no truth whatever in speculation the President had an inaugural assignation in a hotel room with a female friend. Or that he became intoxicated and fought with his escort. And then, this is the best bit, Beale, the dizzy dame, adds her own explanation: it wasn't the President at all but a look-alike.'

The color had drained from Hunter's face. He looked as if he were going to puke. 'She said that!' he gagged. 'She knows about Casey and the rest? What idiot told her?'

'Nobody. Nothing. She doesn't know the first thing to do with the business. It's just Trish's way. She spouts whatever comes into her head. It was pure goddam coincidence she lit on the truth.'

Hunter groaned and put his head in his hands.

'I told Fitzgerald it was a load of baloney. A media attempt to run a reprise of the Kennedy thing. I think she believed me. I'm praying she did.'

'She had better have believed or you and I both will be explaining personally to the President how people are saying he's been replaced by a substitute!'

Jay swallowed. It didn't bear thinking about. 'What are you going to tell Blacker?'

'I'm not telling Blacker anything and neither are you.'

*

'You're not going to believe this,' Lomax said.

Blacker grunted. He was not in a good temper. 'Try me,' he said.

'They can't find the log.'

'Which log?'

'The security log from the yacht. Rappaport's yacht that you went to see. The boat the President is supposed to have fallen overboard on.'

Blacker swore in disbelief.

'Yeah, it's a fact,' Lomax continued. 'I've been pushing Lester for a sight of the thing since Sunday. Finally I went downstairs and Lester, you remember Lester? Used to head up Hillary Clinton's detail. Big guy, likes to dress sharp. Trod on Princess Diana's foot at a state dinner and got himself transferred back to general duties.'

'I can place him,' Blacker grunted. 'But he wasn't in charge down Jacksonville. It was Luchinsky.'

'No, you forget, Luchinsky had to pull out. Something about his mother being sick. Lester was left in charge.'

'And now he's lost the log?' Blacker was incredulous. 'How, for Christ's sake?'

'That's what I've been trying to find out.' Lomax picked his teeth with a loose paper clip. 'Which wasn't easy on account of everyone covering their butt. So far as I can make out, the log was officially listed lost on the Wednesday. That's after Jack Meade has departed back to Washington.'

Blacker's frown deepened. 'I don't buy that for a start.'

'That's what I told Lester. "What you mean is," I said, "Tuesday was when you gave up looking for it. You figured by then with the President-elect back in Washington no one was going to lose sleep over a missing log." Matter of fact even then the idiot didn't mark it "missing" only "unavailable". Anyway so far as I can establish, the log first went AWOL on the Saturday. Lester is checking the rosters an' he can't find the log among the others.'

'Saturday the 13th, the day the President-elect's double is found on the beach?'

'The very same.'

'This is the log for the President-elect's suite we're talking about? Or the entryport log for the boat?'

'No, the Secret Service log for visitors to the suite in the stern. The main log, the exit-entry for the whole boat, was Navy responsibility. Any movement in or out of the suite was logged on a hand terminal by the guards at the door. See, the way I figure, just suppose some guy did step in to take Jack Meade's place, well that guy has got to have come from somewhere. It isn't as if he can beam down onto the yacht from outer space. He's going to have come aboard physically and stayed behind. So what we want to know is who slept on the boat that night?'

'What does Lester think happened to the log?'

'Lester is so scared for his pension he can't hardly think straight. According to him the log was definitely in place Friday night. He's ready to swear his name to that. Next morning the day team started over afresh as usual. It wasn't until Lester went to make up his report around in the evening that he realized yesterday's data was missing. Data from each day is held on a removable disk. Lester couldn't locate it anywhere, not in the computer, not in the safe. It had vanished. He says he wasn't panicking right then. The disks are write-protected so the data was safe. He thought most likely some idiot mislabeled the disk. Easily done,' Lomax admitted, breaking off a moment. 'That's the trouble with these new systems. The old-style book log you could just turn back a page to find out who was where. With a computer disk you have to run it in order to see what's inside.

'Anyway,' he continued, 'the squad from the previous night were all off duty and gone ashore. Lester reckoned to have them sort it out when they came back on. Only they couldn't. They spent all next day trying to figure out what had gone wrong. Lester says they searched every disk down there. In the end they gave up. By then the President-elect had gone back to Washington. He figured he'd gotten away with it.'

'Little he knew,' Blacker sniffed. He thought a moment. 'Where were the disks kept when not in use?'

Lomax looked up at the ceiling, 'This is another good bit. After the President-elect turned in for the night, the disk containing the log was placed in his safe inside the suite. Seems it was the only secure facility.'

'Then one of the President's staff could be responsible?'

Lomax shook his head. 'That was the first thing Lester thought of. Trouble was by then Elaine Manken had been dismissed. She and the President were the only ones with keys to the safe.'

The committee had decided to have the CIA carry out a picture analysis. The results were brought to the Chief of Staff.

'Photographs.' Lindeman, the CIA representative, leaned forward over the papers in front of him. He had a heavy rasping voice and slow intonation that gave weight to his words. 'At the request of the Secret Service our technical division people studied 423 photographs of Jack Meade; 311 of these were taken during the presidential campaign between dates—'

The Chief of Staff interrupted. They were meeting in his office. Besides the CIA man and himself only Blacker, Lomax and Sheen were present. 'We're short of time here. Spare us the detail, huh?'

'Er, yes sir . . . approximately 300 photographs taken of the candidate spread evenly across the campaign were compared with photographs taken during the Inauguration. For comparison purposes a selection of pictures from Mr Meade's earlier life, including his term as senator and some of his acting stills were used.'

He paused for comment. Nobody spoke and he continued: 'Analysis techniques are similar to those used for criminal identification purposes and location of missing persons. Particular features such as shape and set of ears, eye sockets, chin depth, jaw and cheekbones are measured and the resultant data compared using computer enhancement. Typical accuracy exceeds 93 percent.'

Again he paused and looked up.

What about plastic surgery? Miriam wanted to know.

'The system was designed to defeat attempts at disguise. All measurements relate to underlying structures of the face and head which would be unaffected,' Lindeman answered.

From a box at his side he selected three eight by twelve glossy black-and-white prints and placed them face up on the table for everyone to see. 'The results of the analysis divided broadly speaking into three groups. For convenience we label these Tom, Dick and Harry.' There were mirthless grins round the table. 'According to our experts all the photographs exhibit strong similarities, such as might be expected between identical twins for instance. Nevertheless using computer enhancement our experts are of the opinion that the photographs surveyed reveal two distinct individuals.' There was a sharp intake of breath from Hunter. 'The third group, labeled Harry, includes photographs where the differences are not susceptible to classification or are too confused to make identification certain.'

He passed round sets of the three pictures. All of those present stared at them. So far as Blacker could tell they were all of the same man. Lindeman began to explain the differences, which though not detectable to the layman were apparently sufficiently clear for the experts to state that there was an 80 percent probability they were of two different people. At least it was only two, Blacker thought to himself.

'The principal distinctions are to do with the width of the eyes and the measurement between the lobes of the ears. The overall length of the head, that is from the point of the jaw to hairline, is another marker but not distinguishable in all shots due to the way the hair is worn. Our people point out that even these different characteristics would not show up in every shot and can be disguised for instance by dressing the hair carefully and using glasses which are worn in approximately half of all photographs.'

The Chief of Staff pulled himself together. 'These two distinct individuals, Tom and Dick as you call them, are they found together all across the timescale of photographs or is there a clear division?'

Lindeman sucked in his breath. Evidently he had been anticipating the question. His stubby fingers tapped the folder in front of him. 'In my opinion . . .' he wetted his lips with his tongue. 'In my opinion the individual Tom is to be discerned solely in the earlier photographs, that is those prior to the Inauguration. Dick is found mainly in those taken during and after the Inauguration but also in a number of instances he is present in shots taken during the campaign.' He paused unhappily. The others round the table waited. 'In other words the pattern is confused,' he concluded lamely.

'You mean to say you're telling us,' the Chief of Staff said furiously, 'that all this and you still can't be certain?'

Karen Lipscombe still had to find a place to live. The President wanted her to stay on at the White House but that would not do. She was already chafing at the confinement plus she hated living out of suitcases. She wanted her own things around her. The hard part was making time to view. Prior to the Inauguration she had seen two places, both in Georgetown, expensive and wrong for her – narrow twisty stairs, doors at different heights, raised lintels – guaranteed to have her flat on her tail at every other step. Now Elaine Manken of all people had come up with a modern apartment by Dupont Circle that she said belonged to her cousin. She was offering Karen first refusal. It was evidently her way of extending the olive branch. Viewing was set for Friday.

At the nightly meeting the numbers were the same as previously except that to the left of the President's Counselor sat her assistant, a younger woman with sleeked-back fair hair, a blonde Amazon with quarter-back shoulders. According to the White House rumor mill, already working overtime, these two liked to lock the door of Miriam's office after lunch and climb into an upstairs sleeping loft where they enjoyed physical relief together. A story at least as likely to be true as that they were considering now. Her name was, Blacker racked his brain, Koi, that was it, Ms Koi, like the carp.

Hunter opened proceedings with a curt nod.

Blacker described how the Secret Service had contacted leading theatrical agencies for details of any actor who might reasonably be considered for playing the part of the President. No one person had so far been singled out as being a near double of Jack Meade but there were several described as bearing an acceptable resemblance. Video profiles of the actors concerned were being studied.

'Judging by the standard of those we've examined,' Blacker added, 'it's hard to believe any of them would pass scrutiny, even with the help of make-up or surgery.' He would however keep the committee informed of any developments.

Next, Jay Leeder related his researches into the President's family tree. So far as could be ascertained, he said, Jack Meade had no close relatives alive. Of his immediate family all were dead and either cremated or consigned to sea burial. The sole exception appeared to be the President's grandmother, believed to have been interred in the Boston area in 1953. Efforts to locate the exact whereabouts of her grave were continuing. It was simply a question of checking through church records.

The meeting brightened perceptibly at the news. 'So all we have to do is to compare a DNA sample from the body with one from the President. I take it that doesn't present any problems, Doctor?'

The Admiral studied his hands on the table. The deeper he got into the affair, the less he liked it. 'Technically, no,' he admitted reluctantly. 'The procedure is standardized. We already possess samples of the President's blood taken at his recent check-up.' He coughed, meeting the gaze of the others uneasily. 'We keep running up against the ethical question here. President Meade is my patient and I am being asked to sanction tests and release information without his knowledge or consent.'

The Chief of Staff spoke sharply. 'We've been through all that. We agreed that everything is being done in the President's own vital best interests.' There were murmurs of assent from the others round the table.

'And what if the tests don't match?'

Miriam Sheen supplied the answer. 'In that event,' she said tartly, 'the person would be shown to be an impostor usurping the position of your real patient and it would be your clear duty to make the truth known at once.'

Hunter added blusteringly, 'It's irrelevant anyway. We know perfectly well the President is who he says he is. What we're looking for is a quick and simple test which will prove it.'

The Admiral shook his head. 'It isn't as simple as you seem to think,' he said. 'All a contra-indicative test will show is that the man through there,' he inclined his head in the direction of the West Wing, 'is not the biological son of his parents. He may be completely unaware of this fact, for which there could be a lawful explanation – a secret adoption for instance. A barren woman, the baby of some young unmarried girl quietly taken in. These kinds of things happen far more often than you think. Believe me, as a doctor I know.'

311

Faces fell. The earlier optimism in the room had evaporated. 'What it comes down to is you're saying we can't rely on the DNA test either?' said General Vorspuy gloomily. The Admiral nodded.

'Unless the test proves positive,' Blacker pointed out.

Nobody made any reply to that.

'The odds against an unrecorded adoption would be rare, I imagine,' Hunter spoke uncertainly after a moment. 'Putting it another way, the downside risk is small while the benefits of having this whole business cleared up once and for all are enormous. I vote we proceed with the test. Anyone else in favor?'

One by one the others muttered their assent or silently raised their hands for Jay Leeder dutifully to note down in his minutes. Only Blacker remained mute.

'That is settled then,' observed Hunter with satisfaction. 'The test goes ahead as quickly as possible. Do we have any idea of the timescale involved, I wonder?' he glanced inquiringly at Admiral Thomas.

Blacker interrupted. 'There's one point we have to consider first and that is who is to authorize the exhumation.'

There was silence in the room for several seconds. Leeder scowled at him. 'It would have to be done undercover,' he said with a shrug. 'As a black operation if necessary.'

'Black operation is right,' Miriam agreed. 'It would certainly be an illegal act. Opening up the grave of the President's grandmother without his knowledge makes Watergate look like a Mother Superior's tea party.'

312

15

Directly across the street from the Capitol, an oval plaza
fronts a cross-shaped building of gleaming white marble.
Flanked by twin massive allegorical figures, a broad
staircase climbs to a double colonnade of thirty-two
Corinthian columns three stories high. Chiseled under the
bas-relief in the pediment is the inscription 'EQUAL
JUSTICE UNDER LAW'. The pediment itself, the guidebook
informs the visitor, represents 'Liberty Enthroned' and
the sculpted figures 'The Contemplation of Justice' and
'The Authority of Law'.

Everything about the building is designed to impress.
Passing under the colonnade, the visitor enters through
the immense front doorway whose four sliding panels of
carved bronze each weigh six and a half tons. A wide
columned hall with a coffered ceiling and busts of chief
justices leads to the courtroom. Twin elliptical staircases
span five floors from basement to library without apparent support, the marble and bronze steps seeming to
float in the air as if weightless. In the courtroom, the nine
justices are seated on a raised bench before yet more
columns of veined Siena marble that ring the chamber.

Within this temple of justice, the third branch of the
American government exercises its mandate as guardian
and interpreter of the Constitution.

No institution in the capital guards its privacy as
fiercely as the Supreme Court. Tourists may prowl the
Capitol and observe debates, peer into the state rooms of
the White House. Though visitors are grudgingly permitted to peep into the famous court chamber when not in

313

session, the justices' suites, the meeting room where all decisions are made, remain firmly off limits.

Miriam Sheen appreciated this fact as she faced Associate Justice Aaron Phelps. She also knew that lawyers gossiped like actors, which in a sense was exactly what they were. A visit to a justice in his private chambers by the President's legal Counsel when the post of chief justice had just fallen vacant could have only one construction. The news would be all round Capitol Hill by lunchtime.

The interview had proceeded predictably. When she had broached the selection of the new Chief Justice, Phelps had feigned distaste. 'You are canvassing my views? So soon as this, with poor Roscoe hardly cold?' he said with a cultivated shiver of distaste.

Miriam was not fooled. 'There has been speculation in the press already. The President will be concerned not to press the post on anyone unwilling to shoulder the burden. At the same time it's important not to allow the impression of a vacuum. That could lead to open competition, which would be undignified.'

Miriam watched a shadow of alarm creep into Phelps' carefully neutral expression and knew she had gauged him correctly. Phelps badly wanted to see his bust among those of former chief justices in the entrance hall. 'I need to ask if you have any objection to your name going forward. Of course if you prefer not . . .'

'No, no. That is,' Phelps licked his lips, 'if called to serve I . . . I trust I should know my duty.'

From a basket under the desk there came a snort. Bobo the dog urging his master on. Miriam smiled encouragingly. 'Of course it's early days yet, you appreciate.'

'The Senate, yes.' Phelps was already thinking of the day. 'I don't foresee trouble there. Confirmation would be purely routine.' He gulped, 'I am really most grateful to the President. It's a great honor. A truly great honor,' he added.

'It would assist the President for you to set out your views on what you see as the substantive issues facing the court.'

'A position paper, as it were,' Phelps muttered. 'I suppose I could let you have something along the lines.'

'Call it a statement of values. How long would it take you?'

'A week, ten days. Is there a particular hurry?'

'The President would like to come to an understanding without undue delay,' Miriam answered smoothly. 'Before the rumor machine swings into action.'

Phelps' eyes glinted behind the pebble glasses. 'This haste wouldn't have anything to do with stories that Jack Meade has a double fronting for him,' he suggested craftily.

The President's Counsel had been waiting for this. Phelps knew about the double because he had spoken with Spellman; that was why he was being offered the job – to keep him quiet. She didn't miss a beat. She feigned a momentary look of astonishment; how could a public figure allow himself such a gaffe? she seemed to be indicating. Then she gave a brittle laugh. 'If that's your idea of humor, Judge, I recommend you don't let the President get to hear of it. Unless that is you want to kiss goodbye to being the next chief justice.'

Aaron Phelps cringed with embarrassment. Trust that idiot Spellman woman to have passed on a story without checking. He should have known the idea was too way out to have a shred of truth in it. Now he had made a total idiot of himself in front of the President's Counsel. If the Sheen bitch repeated what he had said . . .

'I assure you,' he gabbled frantically, 'there was no intent to insult . . . merely repeating a rumor . . . stupid thing to say . . .'

'Quite.' Miriam Sheen snapped the locks of her briefcase and rose, straightening her jacket. 'Don't get up, Judge,' she said in clipped tones. 'I'll see myself out.'

'Er, please,' he stammered, 'please, tell the President . . . proud to be of service in any capacity . . .'

Miriam threw him a wintry smile. 'We'll be in touch.' The door closed behind her.

Justice Aaron Phelps slumped back in his chair. He thought over her words and gnawed his lips.

As she was driven back to the White House, Miriam Sheen permitted herself a smile. That creep Phelps would kill for the post of chief justice. And that gave her a lever to employ against Spellman. With luck now they could keep the lid on her while they figured out who was the rightful president.

'Godsakes, Troy!' Wade Guinyard, editor of the *Meteor*, exploded. 'What kind of a paper d'you think this is? You're not writing for the *National Inquirer*.' Wade was a big man, overweight and normally cheerful in outlook. Just now he was anything but. 'I mean just look at this . . .' His stubby fingers whacked the keys of his terminal, scrolling Troy's article up the screen. '"President's double escapes from Navy hospital. Mystery doppelgänger rescued from ocean." You can't expect us to run crap like this. It belongs with "Pregnant by Aliens from Outer Space" and "Elvis found in Denver detox clinic." How many times do I have to tell you this is a serious newspaper. We entertain, yes, but we do not print garbage. "Jack Meade sought for Inauguration Day Theft" does not come under the heading of responsible journalism.'

'C'mon, Wade, I have put in leg work on this like nothing else,' Troy protested. They were talking in the editor's glassed-off cubicle in back of the main office. 'I have researched every angle. I have spoken personally to witnesses. I have expert testimony, tapes, photographs. Every fact checks out. Call the Sheriff's office if you don't believe me. Speak to Fitzroy Grape out at Mayport. I mean you only have to look yourself at the blow-ups.

This guy has to be some kinda relation of the Prez. It's all in there, Wade, the yacht, the guy on the beach, the patient in the hospital. How come they won't release his prints? There's a connection here, Wade. I haven't figured it all out yet but I'm close. I just need you to run with it.'

'A connection, sure. A connection that exists in your head. You need to lay off the swamp juice, change your brand of smoke or something.'

'Ask Cal if you won't take it from me. She went with me to the hospital. She saw the guy lying there. She took the shots. Just call her in and ask her.'

Wade's lungs wheezed as he took a long breath to hold onto his temper. 'This is not nut country, Troy. Our readers don't expect to see the new President trashed on the front page his first week in office. Show a little respect, for God's sake.'

'Okay, okay, point taken,' Troy tried to placate him. So yes, maybe he had overplayed his hand a little. This was the police desk, remember. 'I wanted to grab readers' attention. But I can plane it down. Polish off the edges. You want serious, I'll give you serious.'

'Troy,' Wade sighed, 'you're not getting it. We are not running this story. Period.'

Troy was not getting it. This was his big story. His once in a lifetime scoop and the man was wimping out on him. 'Jesus, Wade,' he cried, 'what's the matter with you? The biggest break to come our way in a decade and you're spiking it?'

'I'm not spiking it, I'm just not running it. It's a crazy dumb story. It'll make us look ridiculous.'

'It'll make us famous, for God's sake. Wade, use your dumb brain for once. You can't let this go. It's the best thing I ever wrote.'

Wade's face darkened. 'The heck I can't. Well, here's what I think of your masterpiece, lover man.' His fingers hit the keyboard again. Troy's text winked and vanished. Troy's mouth hung open in disbelief. 'It's for your own

317

good, Troy,' said the editor exasperatedly. Writers were all the same, the best of them got a wild hair once in a while and went a little crazy. 'Now get out of here and file some copy I can use before I lose my temper good.'

Scarlet with fury, Troy stormed back to his desk in the outer room. Cal was waiting for him. She came over.

'Well?' she said. 'How'd it go?'

Of all the enigmas surrounding the President, the most puzzling was the First Lady. The second floor was her domain, her private space, and she determined to keep it that way. Since Barney Nikolis' public dressing down on the first morning no staff member save Dorothy Fine and Karen Lipscombe had trespassed upstairs without an official summons. Even Hunter phoned before taking the elevator.

Hunter especially found it frustrating. It was as if he had to view the Presidency through a glass wall. Whole sections of the President's day remained a blank.

He told Blacker about his problem. 'Every afternoon at 1.30 unless he has an official function Jack Meade leaves the office. He doesn't go upstairs right away. He takes a swim.'

'I know.' Blacker was fully aware of the President's habit. So was everyone else in the building. A gift originally to FDR from the children of America who had collected dimes by the million for its construction, the heated swimming pool between the mansion proper and the West Wing had been a favorite of John Kennedy's. Richard Nixon had ordered it torn out to make way for the press, to universal regret. During the Ivory administration Congress had voted to allocate funds for a purpose-built press center and the pool had been restored using corporate donations.

'He swims nude they say.'

'It's his pool.' The President had issued strict orders that he was not to be disturbed during his swim. Not even the Secret Service were permitted to enter, giving rise to rumor that the President frolicked naked in the pool with his secretaries as Jack Kennedy was said to have done.

'He takes lunch upstairs alone or with the First Lady, no calls or visits allowed till he comes down again at three. They've both made that clear.'

'They're newly married. What d'you expect of them?'

'I know, I know. It's just that I can't get a handle on the way he thinks any more. It's like he can withdraw into a place I can't reach him. I work out a policy decision with him, agree an appointment, then he goes upstairs and when he comes down again he's changed his mind. Is it her or what?'

Blacker shook his head. 'My impression was she doesn't care much for politics one way or the other.'

'Well, they can't spend all their time up there screwing. Can't you find out from the Chief Usher? I never get a chance to speak to the man. It's like I'm fighting shadows.'

Blacker stood up. 'My job is to protect the President. Not spy on him behind his back.'

'Terrific,' the Chief of Staff returned. 'Just so long as you're certain it's the President you're protecting.'

Karen Lipscombe closed her shorthand book, snapped a thick rubber band around to hold it shut and laid it carefully back from the edge of the pool. The notes were not especially secret; they never did any important work in these stolen half-hours by the poolside. The shorthand was really just an excuse for the President to have a companion in here with him. He got too easily bored to swim alone.

She screwed up her eyes. Without her Elvis set, the President's head was just a dark blob against the shimmering water. Stretching, she poised herself, raised on tiptoe, straightened her arms and dived gracefully in to join him.

She held the plunge, letting herself glide long and deep, reveling in the feel of the water warm against her skin. The tips of her fingers broke the surface. As her head came clear she became aware of the sound of clapping.

'Well done, that was a beauty.'

She laughed with pleasure, smoothing back her hair. 'I remembered to keep my legs straight this time.'

When they had first begun their swims together he had chided her on sloppy diving technique. Now it was a standing joke between them. The President had banned his Secret Service from the poolside. With no observers present they could forget his position for a few short minutes, splashing and laughing in the water like two ordinary people. They would kick water in each other's faces or pretend to drown and be rescued or even sometimes have head-ducking sessions, all in a spirit of fun.

When the play was over, Karen climbed out of the pool, collected her towel and made her way to the changing cubicle. There was one each for men and women. Simple stalls with a single shower and toilet each. The pool was just for the use of the First Family and not designed for communal use.

She showered briskly and toweled herself dry. Feeling along the changing room for a hook, she hung up the towel and located the hair-drier. Switching it on, she bent her head into the warming stream of air.

All at once she became aware of a figure in the room with her.

The bright light and white walls of the cubicle left her completely sightless. There was a blur of light before her and somewhere in the heart of it a solider core but she could not see anyone. Strangely it made her feel less frightened. She knew it was the President. She sensed his presence and was aware that it was he. Because she could not see him it somehow did not matter that she was naked. She stood facing the doorway where his voice came from, still holding the drier in one hand, not trying to cover herself.

'Yes, Mr President?' she said and her voice quivered only slightly. They might have been back in the office.

'You left your notepad by the pool. I brought it.'

The shadow against the light stepped closer but remained indistinct. She could detect his breathing, quick and low.

'I'll see you back in the office,' he said and was gone.

Blacker returned through the West Wing. The time was 1.45. As he passed the flower shop the door opened and a woman came out. It was Karen Lipscombe.

'Good afternoon,' he said. 'How are you today?'

At the sound of his voice her face lit up. The headset swiveled. 'Mr Blacker, hi, nice to run into you. How are you keeping?'

Blacker searched for something to say. 'Did you manage to find somewhere to live yet?'

'Oh no, I simply haven't had time to look. And the First Lady is being so kind letting me stay on upstairs.'

'I guess it's nice for her to have the company,' he hazarded.

'I'm not much company for anyone. By the time I get through work I'm not good for anything but sleep. Actually I hardly see Mrs Meade. She and the President are usually having their dinner by the time I go up.'

Footsteps clattered up, hurrying up from the depths of the West Wing. 'Karen!' a woman's voice shrilled.

Karen heaved a mock sigh. 'Duty calls,' she apologized.

'Well, nice to have seen you,' he mumbled awkwardly.

'Likewise.' She flashed a radiant smile at him as she swept away toward the Oval Office. A lady happy in her work, he thought enviously. He glanced into the flower shop where banks of blooms were being readied for a reception later in the afternoon. There was a door in back, which gave access to the pool. The President would be in there now. Had Karen been with him?

Maybe those rumors were true after all. He hoped not.

'It doesn't look right,' Jodi DuCharme was telling Karen in her office next to the President's. 'It doesn't look right at all.'

'I take your point but I still think you're being hyper-sensitive.'

'You're being naive, Karen. This is the White House. He's the President and you're a single, attractive female. You know how people invent stories.'

'There's nothing to invent a story about. I just go in there, sit by the side of the pool and take dictation while he swims. Afterward I take a dip.'

'He's in the nude, that's the point.'

'You said he's the President, if he wants to be undressed it's up to him.'

'Oh come on,' Jodi protested, 'this could cause trouble and you both know it. This is not Camelot, times have changed.'

'Look,' Karen told her. 'He's in the water. I'm wearing a swimsuit. It's no big deal. I've no way of telling if he's wearing trunks or not.'

'People are talking,' Jodi repeated stubbornly.

'Let them talk. If they want to be malicious I can't stop them. You'd think a blind person would be given some benefit of the doubt,' she snapped.

Jodi retreated to the outer office. You did what you could to help people and all you got for your pains was your head bitten off.

Alone at her desk, Karen phoned through to the ushers' office. 'Mrs Meade said I might have the use of a car tonight to check out an apartment in town.'

Certainly, ma'am, the usher on duty answered. What time for?

'Half-seven please. I shouldn't be more than an hour.'

'No problem, Ms Lipscombe, we'll book it out to you for the evening. Just mention to the driver if you expect to be back after midnight.'

It was so easy living in the White House. So pleasurable. But you have to get accustomed to fending for yourself again, young lady, she reminded herself firmly.

The *Springs Free Times* was part of the new revolution in journalism. The *SFT* wasn't based out of any particular township. Its loyalties and readership were centered on a ring of amorphous shopping centers and satellite developments that had long since shed their ties to the cities that had spawned them. In a culture without roots, it served people whose sense of belonging was defined by freeway corridors.

Its news was at once parochial and global with a regular dash of scandal. Its proudest moment had been an exclusive interview with Michael Jackson and the backspacing of the career of an Under-Secretary of the Army photographed cavorting with his sergeant-driver.

The *SFT* was in short the antithesis of everything Troy had grown up to respect.

'A supermarket giveaway sheet,' he growled disgustedly as Cal drove him west on Route 10. 'I don't know how I let you talk me into this.'

'Because every other paper of repute has turned us down flat,' she reminded him. 'And because *SFT* has a circulation of 600,000 and rising. Which is more than can be said for the old *Meteor*.'

'And the nation is going to take the story seriously when it's printed alongside tales of school teachers seduced by TV evangelists, I suppose?' he responded bitterly.

They bowled along into the afternoon sun. 'I think this

is the place.' Cal swung into a 20-acre parking lot radiating from a multiplex cinema. She stopped the car opposite a Macy's and Troy let himself out. 'Welcome,' he cried, 'to the hub at the end of the universe. The limbo of civilization.'

'The only editor between here and Atlanta prepared to back us works out of this place,' Cal told him severely. 'So either stop clowning and be prepared to give her your best shot or we might as well quit right now and not waste her time.'

Troy held up his hands in surrender. 'Lead on.'

Troy was surprised by the *SFT* offices which, compared with those of the *Meteor*, were shabby and cramped. The screenwriters on the way in looked positively antiquated.

'The majority of our staff are part-timers,' Mrs Kitto explained. 'We only employ eight or ten contract workers. Aside from myself,' she added. 'We also commission a large amount of material freelance. Such as yourselves,' she smiled.

The most prominent feature of the editor's office was a TV set tuned to a local news channel. While they spoke Mrs Kitto continued to devote half her attention to the screen, flipping channels with the remote and occasionally interrupting the conversation to comment on a breaking story. Her lacquered black hair was elaborately coiffured. Troy wondered if it mightn't be a wig. Her age could have been anywhere between thirty and fifty. Her trimmed-up physique suggested regular workouts and she dressed out of designer stores. She wore expensive gold jewelry. She probably drove a Mercedes. Everything about her indicated competence, ambition and ruthlessness.

She brushed aside his attempts to provide background. 'You said on the phone you had pictures?'

From the folder Cal produced the photos snapped in the hospital. Mrs Kitto ran a cursory eye over them and

324

switched back to the television. 'They'll do. Now your man's skipped out on you, is that right?'

'We don't know for certain. Could be a cover put out by the military while they're holding him somewhere else.'

'I like that. It has pull. Our readers like to see Washington on the spot. Think you can substantiate?'

Troy started to explain about the fingerprint evidence. 'How the President's name . . .'

A phone bleeped on the desk. Mrs Kitto volleyed instructions into the receiver. 'I'm listening,' she said, still talking. 'You can involve the President? Jack Meade? How about Caro? No? Pity.'

'The baseline is,' Troy told her, flicking a quick look at Cal for support and taking a leap of faith, 'we think there could be some sort of a family tie-in here that the White House is covering up on. Like a long-lost brother or cousin or whatever. The resemblances are too uncanny to explain away by any other means.'

Mrs Kitto sat up in her chair. She snapped her fingers like a whip cracking. 'President's secret twin rescued from ocean. I like it. I like it very much. We'll run it.' She seized the phone again. 'Bring me in a contract form and make out a check for $25,000.'

Troy felt as if his heart had turned suddenly into a ball of ice. The headline she proposed was outrageous, appalling. There was a stunned look on Cal's face. What had the woman said? Twenty-five thousand? Split between the two of them? Shit, he could spring on a new car at last. He could . . .

Mrs Kitto was speaking again. 'We'll pay the same again for each further installment. With a bonus 50 percent if the story runs in the national press and 100 percent if it makes a major TV newscast.'

Troy's mouth had gone dry. A sudden vista of wealth avalanching toward him made him sick to his stomach with nervousness. Cal was now looking as if she was going to pass out. She seemed to be having trouble with her breathing. Hell, he was having trouble with his own breathing. Suddenly his anxieties over the sensationalist treatment of the subject seemed to recede.

Twenty-five big ones per installment. The story would run to three shots, no problem. Maybe more if they dug around enough. Hell, they could spin it out for a week if they wanted. A hundred and fifty thousand. Two hundred thousand, even. Double that if the networks picked up the story. Add another 100,000 for syndication bonus. Half a million dollars. Two hundred and fifty thousand each. Real money within his grasp at last.

This was it. The big one. The scoop he had always dreamed about. And the *Meteor* had turned it down. More fool them. He and Cal were free now to sell to the highest bidder. No more writing up car wrecks and Saturday night stabbings. One good lead a year was all that was needed from now on. One good lead and this scandal sheet with its shabby offices and debased ethical standards was going to make them rich, rich, rich.

Publish and be damned, that would be his motto from now on.

The address Elaine had given was a high-rise, newly converted. Fitting out was still not completed. There were protective coverings on the carpets and decorators' ladders in the stairwells. Elaine had said the apartment was south facing. It had the sun and a view of the river.

Elaine opened the door to her.

'Hi, I'm a little early. The traffic was so easy.'

'Did you bring anyone with you?'

'Only the driver. The White House sent a car. It's waiting out front. Why, is that a problem?' Karen was puzzled.

'It's not important.' Elaine closed the door behind her immediately and locked it. The lobby smelt newly painted but Karen had barely time to notice before Elaine

326

was hustling her on through. 'This way.' Her manner struck Karen as distant. Perhaps she was already regretting her offer of help.

Elaine led the way into a drawing room. It was grandly decorated with an immense crystal chandelier and long windows hung with elaborate velvet drapes. Karen's heart sank. 'Oh, I didn't realize the apartment was so formal. I don't think I can afford all this.'

Elaine gave a mechanical smile. She had remained by the door, holding it open apparently waiting for someone.

'Karen?' The voice seemed to come from the rear somewhere. A man's voice, resonating unnaturally in the empty apartment with an eerily familiar ring.

Karen stiffened. 'Who is that?'

A man walked briskly into the room. He was light haired and medium height and he wore a dark business suit. His carriage, the way he moved his hands, held his head, above all his voice so closely resembled Jack Meade that for a moment Karen thought it must be the President. Instinctively she reached for the controls of her Elvis to sharpen the focus. Something felt wrong, very wrong, and fear knotted inside her.

'Sir?' her voice faltered. 'Sir, is that you?'

'First answer me this.'

He approached. Jack's walk. To the life. He was on edge, she recognized the signs. 'Why didn't you respond to my letter, the one I gave you at the ball?'

'What ball? I . . . I don't understand?' Karen's head swiveled in dismay, from Jack Meade's double to Elaine and back. Conflicting images jumbled in her mind. 'Please,' she whispered, 'please, what do you want? Why have you brought me here?'

'All in good time,' he told her. 'First though I need you to listen. To listen and answer questions. There's been a conspiracy. Elaine and I are trying to get to the bottom of it. You can help us.'

'I can?' Her hand went to her mouth in disbelief.

He continued. 'The inaugural ball. I put a letter into your hand up in the suite at the Hilton. It contained an urgent message asking you to warn my wife that I had been deposed and a double substituted in my place. Did you carry out my instructions, and if not why not?'

'The letter in Braille . . . about the . . . the substitution?' she gasped. 'It was from you? I don't understand. I found it on my reader.'

'What? What are you talking about?'

'I went to my Braille reader and it was in the memory. Yesterday. I couldn't understand how it had gotten in there. I thought it must be a hoax.'

'I slipped it into your hand that night at the ball,' he repeated stubbornly. 'You must remember. I kissed you, for God's sake!'

'Yes, I . . . I remember being in the suite and you . . . holding my arm and . . . kissing me. I hadn't my headset on. I couldn't see what was happening. I was confused,' Karen babbled. 'You never gave me any letter that I knew.'

She told them how she had gone later to the Braille reader, discovered the letter and destroyed it.

Elaine said, 'And you had no idea how it got onto the machine?'

'I told you I thought it was a hoax. Someone resentful because of my job.' She felt awkward speaking of it to Elaine.

Jack Meade shook his head. 'There was a jostle in the doorway at the moment of handover. The letter must have fallen to the floor and been recovered by the Secret Service without your realizing.'

'Which means the impostor in the Oval Office knows you're still alive,' Elaine said.

'Maybe, maybe not. It doesn't follow the Secret Service will have told him.'

Karen broke in. 'Please, I don't understand. Are . . . are you trying to tell me what was in the letter is for real?'

'Of course it's for real, you idiot,' Elaine snapped. She took a deep breath, calming herself. 'I'm sorry,' she apologized. 'It's hard to accept, I know. It has been for all of us.'

'But it isn't possible,' Karen said feebly. This couldn't be happening to her. If only she could see like ordinary people.

'Of course it's possible,' Elaine said urgently. 'This is the President you're talking to. Don't you recognize him?'

'I . . . I . . .' Karen couldn't find an answer. 'I don't know,' she said miserably.

Jack Meade's voice interrupted. 'Leave it for the moment, Elaine. We're asking too much of her. It's not fair,' he said quietly. 'Let her have time to make her decision.'

'Sir, time is not on our side,' Elaine protested.

Jack brushed it aside. He had more pressing concerns. 'Karen, how is my wife? He hasn't harmed her, the impostor? She is all right, isn't she? Tell me she's safe.'

'She's fine, Mr President.' The response came out automatically. She swallowed. 'The First Lady is just fine,' she repeated jerkily, adding, 'She seems a little strange sometimes.' Like me, she thought. 'They have separate rooms.'

'As long as he hasn't hurt her,' Jack said in a strained voice. The last words had mattered to him desperately, she could sense.

Biting her lip, she made a last appeal. 'Sir, I don't know who you are. I've been working for the President this past month. You know I'm not able to judge. How can I know the truth? You need to speak to someone senior to me, someone in high office. The Chief of Staff maybe or . . .'

'But you do know me, Karen,' came the quiet response. 'You know me very well. Better than you can possibly know the impostor in the Oval Office.' Karen felt a pang strike right to her heart.

'Please, what is it you want me to do?' she whispered.

She felt the touch of his hand. 'It's Caro I'm afraid for.' His voice shook. 'She's all alone up there in the residence with him. If the impostor finds out I'm alive and panics, her life won't be worth a nickel. Karen, I'm relying on you to protect her. She has no one else.'

The White House car dropped Karen Lipscombe off at the South Diplomatic entrance. She ducked under the awning out of the steady rain and ran inside, hugging her coat about her, before the doorman could get to her, afraid her legs might give way before she made the sanctity of her own room. For once in her life she was grateful for the concealment of the Elvis.

All was quiet in the mansion. The President had not yet returned. The uniformed guards on duty nodded indifferently as she passed. Karen gained the third floor without having to speak to anyone, locked the door and threw herself down on the bed, clutching the pillows for comfort.

Two presidents. Confused images of the past besieged her racing brain. That night on the yacht, the inaugural ball and just now in the apartment with Elaine. Two presidents. Two Jack Meades. It wasn't possible, yet it had happened.

16

Blacker had managed to snatch a spell of rest on the cot in his office. One of the perks of the job, if you could call it that. He felt as if his eyes had been closed no more than a minute before Lomax was shaking him awake again.

'God, what time is it?'

'Just after five. You told me to call you.'

'Any word on Casey yet?'

'Negative. No joy from Spellman either. Stayed home all night. No calls, no visitors.'

With a grunt Blacker rolled out of bed. He stumbled through to the bathroom to relieve himself and picked up his electric razor. The face that stared back at him from the mirror was gray and pouched from fatigue.

'Boss, I had an idea,' Lomax called from the other room.

'What's that?'

'While you were asleep,' Lomax shouted to make himself heard above the razor, 'it suddenly came to me. This impostor guy, he must have been somebody before he assumed the President's identity, okay? And to have any hope of pulling off a successful switch, he'd have had to study the real President's behavior thoroughly, right?'

'Yes, go on.'

'Well, seems to me he would want to get as close to the President as possible prior to pulling it off. Which suggests he might have posed as a member of the election campaign. I'm not sure but I have the impression the candidates are that desperate for staff they'll take on most anyone who offers. A job on the central committee, say, would give him the perfect opportunity to watch the candidate at work, study his mannerisms and at the same time load up on a mass of detail – who his friends were, who was in for what job, what the slants were on policies.'

Blacker stopped shaving. 'Go on, you're making sense.'

'He would have to conceal their physical resemblance but that wouldn't be so difficult. Hair coloring, a mustache or beard, a skin tinter perhaps. He'd try to work his way into some position where he wouldn't attract notice but could watch what went on. Best of all would be some job that gave access to the candidate from time to time.'

Blacker had finished his shaving and was splashing water on his face. 'I should have thought of that. Get on to the Deputy Chief of Staff, tell him we want a list of everyone who worked on the Meade committee for the election campaign. A high proportion will have been offered jobs working for the new administration. That's why they signed up in the first place. We're interested in anyone who turned down a posting or failed to show on the day for one they accepted.'

It took twenty minutes to contact Jay Leeder and obtain from him the number of the present custodian of the Meade campaign committee records. Finally Lomax put the phone down and turned back to his chief in triumph.

'The Meade campaign still maintains an office in town, in the Watergate complex of all places. The secretary is a Mrs Huston. I'm meeting her there at 7.30. She understands it's to do with a confirmation check that somehow got overlooked.'

Lomax rang through at nine to report. He had never realized, he said, how many free helpers these political committees attracted. It looked as though every activist in the country had at some time or another passed through the Washington Central Democratic Committee. The computer listed more than 7,000 names.

Blacker agreed to send down some more people. 'This is a long shot. We can't afford to tie up resources without you getting a result.'

Don't worry, Lomax told him. He had a hunch about this one.

In the Oval Office, the President consulted the White House phone directory. He found the number he wanted and dialed it himself. A woman's voice answered.

'Secret Service command post.'

'Chief Blacker, please.'

'I'm sorry, Chief Blacker is unavailable. He's in a meeting with General Vorspuy. Who is this calling?'

'It's not important.' He rang off.

He dialed Hunter down the corridor. This time the Chief of Staff's secretary recognized the President's voice.

'Sir, Mr Hunter is over in a meeting with the National Security adviser. I can have him call you directly.'

'No, don't bother,' he told her. 'It's nothing urgent.'

Enough of this game. He picked up the operator phone.

The response was immediate.

'Yes, Mr President.'

'Tell Colonel Coffey I want to see him.'

'Right away, Mr President.'

It was that easy.

Rex Coffey, Chief of the White House Military Office, straightened his tie and flicked a non-existent hair from the shoulder of an immaculate uniform.

'I'm going across to the Oval Office,' he informed his secretary. 'The President wants to see me.'

His secretary looked suitably impressed. 'I'll hold your calls, Colonel.'

Rex picked a document from the pile in his out-tray to

take with him. A circular dealing with staff seating aboard Air Force One, it was in no sense urgent. In due course a messenger would have trucked it across to the West Wing with the twice-daily load of internal mail but Rex knew that anyone wandering around the West Wing without papers of some kind in his hand looked like a flunky. Rex was very conscious of his dignity.

He walked out from the East Wing and along the glassed colonnade overlooking the Jackie Kennedy Garden. There were no tourists today in the elegantly vaulted marble corridor running between the presidential library and the Vermeil Room. Outside the oval-shaped Diplomatic Reception Room he encountered a uniformed woman NCO hurrying in the opposite direction.

Rex stopped her. 'Where d'you think you're going, Corporal?'

The woman skidded to a halt and saluted. 'East Wing, sir. I've a package for the First Lady's office, sir. They said to run it over right away.'

'How long have you worked in the White House, Corporal?'

Her chest heaved, 'T . . . two weeks, sir.'

'Then you should know by now,' Rex said crushingly, 'that standing rules forbid service personnel using the formal floor rooms as a cut-through. Go back down through the basement.'

'Yessir, sorry, sir.' Abashed, the woman saluted again and hurried off back the way she had come. Rex followed, humming a satisfied tune.

Rex had political ambitions. For some time now he had been casting around for the right opening. Recently he had found it, a nice safe seat in the House of Representatives. The present incumbent was not quite ready to retire yet but the local Republican party had indicated privately that Rex was very much the kind of figure they were looking for to step into his shoes. Rex could wait. He had three more years' service to do with the military. He was a light colonel. Promotion to bird colonel was two years away provided he kept his nose clean and his record unblemished. More than anything Rex wanted to retire as a general officer. The spread between the retirement pay of a light colonel and a brigadier-general meant the difference between ease and penury. Especially when combined with a congressman's salary.

Promotion to field rank was in the President's gift. It was customary for a commander-in-chief to reward officers in his immediate circle for their loyalty with a jump in rank on retirement. It was important therefore that Rex seize every opportunity to ingratiate himself with Jack Meade. One such opportunity had just presented itself.

He had been worrying all weekend over the Commander Casey affair. If wind of it were to come to the President it might easily prejudice him against the military, with dire results. To his surprise though he had learned that the story was being kept from the President for some reason. Most likely because the Secret Service feared it made them look incompetent. Most presidents ended up mistrusting and hating the service anyway sooner or later. Here perhaps was an opportunity for Rex to exploit this and at the same time cast himself and the military in a favorable light.

The West Wing was full of people. Jumped-up staffers, munchkins, here-today-gone-tomorrow people. Rex preferred the East Wing. The East Wing was his domain. On the east side he was confident of being shown proper respect. The Secret Service on duty outside the Oval Office recognized him however and nodded.

He entered Karen Lipscombe's office.

It had been a nightmare day for Karen. Keeping up appearances in the office, striving to act normally in front of the President when all the time she was secretly aware

335

it was nothing but a fraud, taxed her acting ability to the limits. Now that she had been face to face with the real Jack Meade, heard him and spoken with him, it seemed impossible that she could ever have been taken in. Surely she should have detected the lack of warmth in the impostor's manner toward her? The truth was that of course she had noticed but had blamed it on his marriage. Small wonder the man had reacted oddly when she repeated Caro's remarks about their affair. That must have come as a shock to him.

If only she had trusted her instincts at the beginning. She had tried to tell herself that it was just mood swings that made the President seem cold towards her one minute then affectionate. But when the real Jack touched her, spoke her name, kissed her, there could be no possible doubt. As it was, she was tormented by feelings of betrayal.

Each time she entered the Oval Office now, she was acutely aware of jarring anomalies in the persona of the man behind the desk. The looks, the voice, the mannerisms were still perfect in detail, yet the total effect fell repellently flat as if a mask had slipped, momentarily disclosing the ugly truth beneath.

The loathing she felt for the impostor was only equaled by her hatred toward him for having tricked her into failing Jack when he needed her. She felt soiled and dirtied. By including her in his deceit he had contaminated her.

It took all her courage now to answer the impostor's summons. She forced herself to wear her brightest smile, for fear he would otherwise detect a change in her manner. But how long could she keep up the pretence?

'Any idea why he wants to see me?'

Rex had formed his judgement of the President's new secretary on first meeting. Karen Lipscombe did not play politics. She served one master – Jack Meade. Period. Rex was glad of that, it made her easy to work with.

'Sorry, Rex.' The blonde head with its robot helmet faced him, unblinking. She never shook her head, he had noticed, or nodded. She did have a pretty smile, when she chose to use it. Today, though, she seemed preoccupied. 'Sorry, Rex, no. He just picked up the phone and asked for you. You can go straight in. There's no one else with him.' She reached out to touch a button on her computer keyboard, which, Rex knew, projected a copy of the President's schedule onto the Elvis screen in front of her eyes. 'The Secretary of Commerce is due in eight minutes from now.'

Rex turned to the door. He felt a momentary knot of anxiety in his gut and stilled it. Straightening his back, he reached for the doorknob.

'You wanted to see me, Mr President?'

'Yes, Rex. Come in, sit down,' the President welcomed him. He indicated a chair beside the big desk. Rex seated himself stiffly.

'Rex, I wanted to touch base. I know you run the military side here in the mansion.'

'Any time I can be of help to you, sir,' Rex said. What was on the President's mind? he wondered.

'A couple of minor points I'd like to clear up.' The President made a show of consulting a list on the desk in front of him. 'You, I take it, are in charge of selecting the aides to the presidents? Military aides, that is.'

'Well, sir, there's a standard procedure. Basically the Military Office receives notification of proposed appointments from the Pentagon. We submit the names to your office for approval or rejection. Then we notify the Pentagon of the decision and the appointments are duly announced.'

'I see. And if I wish to nominate a particular officer to serve here in the White House?'

'No problem, sir. You let me have the officer's name and I pass it on.'

'The Pentagon doesn't object?'

'You're the Commander-in-Chief, sir. It's your right to make appointments as you see fit. Except where ranks are subject to confirmation by Congress. It's possible if the officer concerned was vitally needed elsewhere that the Pentagon might request a postponement, but that would be exceptional. I'm sure you'll always find the Defense Department anxious to be of service, sir,' he added. Rex permitted himself to relax slightly. He had the measure of the summons now. The President wanted to repay a campaign debt by granting some supporter's son or daughter the coveted gold braid of an ADC. 'Was there someone you particularly wanted to see brought into the White House, sir?'

The President gave a brief, sour smile. 'No, as it happens there isn't. That's to say there's a name down on the list I'd prefer to see taken off – Woodbury, Captain Bruce, USN.'

Rex suppressed his surprise. Woodbury and Jack Meade had been room-mates at Naval Academy. 'Fine, sir. I'll see to that.' He didn't ask why. If the President wanted to tell him he would do so. All he said was, 'Is there a name you would care to suggest instead, sir?'

'No, just take Woodbury off. I don't want an issue made of it. Just leave his name out, okay?'

'Understood, Mr President.'

'Excellent.' The President appeared to relax. He leaned back and put his feet on the desk. Every president did that. It was a kind of ritual. He frowned up at Rex. 'Colonel, can you think of any reason why the Chief of Staff and the National Security Adviser should be conferring behind my back with the Chief of the White House detail?'

'With Chief Blacker? No, Mr President.' Rex's face was a picture of surprised innocence. The likely reason for the secret discussions suggested itself to him at once. He knew better than to admit as much straight away, though. The President might imagine Rex too was a part of the conspiracy. Presidents were notoriously paranoid. Instead he temporized. 'I could try to find out for you, sir. I keep my ear pretty close to the ground.'

'I'd be grateful, Rex. I don't want to seem overly suspicious but I like to be kept informed of what's going on.'

'Leave it me, Mr President,' Rex smiled. Ever since his arrival in the executive mansion he had been waiting for an opportunity like this. A chance to make himself indispensable. He would keep the President dangling for a day or so, then start feeding him the story, a few details at a time. Long before they were through, he, Rex, would have become the President's most trusted adviser.

As he left the Oval Office he could feel those stars on his shoulders already.

Towards midday, Lomax phoned again. This time he sounded tired but optimistic. He had three agents with him checking through the lists and one of them, Mary Jo Wojno, was a computer whiz. She had written a program to weed out any female names and those listed by the Secret Service as having received a pass for the viewing stands at the Inauguration. 'Because by that time we know that our man was in Jacksonville Naval Hospital.' On the downside all the possible names that Mrs Huston could recall as having worked in the proximity of the candidate during the final weeks seemed to have checked out as genuine, either currently working for the government or otherwise accounted for. It seemed the committee had been very security conscious about whom they took on, carrying out checks through their own security arm, especially when it involved working in the inner circle of the campaign. Presumably they were worried about leaks. Politics was a dirty business.

'I don't need you to tell me that,' Blacker growled.

'Yes, sir, part of the problem is that by the second week in January the campaign committee was running itself rapidly down. Most staff had either been laid off or moved on to jobs with the transition team. No one was properly in charge any longer and individuals came and went pretty much as they pleased. Consequently it's hard to pinpoint when a person dropped out of sight.'

'I can't spare you any more men,' Blacker told him. 'Our resources are stretched enough hunting for Casey. You'll have to make do with what you've got.'

It was late afternoon when the phone rang on Blacker's desk. It was Lomax again, triumphant this time.

'We've found him, sir! The impostor! Name of Callaghan, Prescott Ellis. Political adviser, aged forty-five, unmarried, lives in Seabrook. He was working in the campaign committee offices just like we guessed. The only difference was he was on loan from the State of Indiana, which meant he didn't figure on the computer printout. Mrs Huston says he had a desk here but didn't have much to do with the rest of them. He told her once he used to write speeches for the President back in the days when he was a senator. First off he worked as a pollster, then switched to building speeches according to the "pulse" system. That means crafting every sentence the Candidate utters to strike a particular resonance with the audience. Kind of like pressing buttons to make the gays, the Poles, the gun lobby, light up. Callaghan was very good at it, apparently. The President liked to run all his major speeches by him for the okay. Had frequent access to the Inner Office, also accompanied him on the stump, flying in the campaign jet, staying in the same hotel.'

'So where is the guy now, then?' Blacker interrupted.

'Mrs Huston says he was offered a place on the White House staff as a senior speechwriter but declined. Claimed he wanted to go back home to Indianapolis but the general view in the office was that he was miffed at not being named leader of the team. He actually signed out formally a month ago but dropped by the office occasionally to pick up mail. Also he was called in a couple of times to advise on particular speeches, or so Huston understands. The last time she saw him was on the afternoon of the 10th. He was clearing his desk finally and came in to say his goodbyes.'

Blacker sniffed and stared at the notes he had made. 'How does the description match up?'

'Pretty much exact. Around the same height and build so far as I can judge. I had to be very indirect getting the staff here to make comparisons in case I aroused their suspicions. One girl did volunteer that Callaghan was "heavy looking" in the body but that could easily be put down to clothing. Hair color auburn with a touch of gray. Quite smart that. Looks very individual but washes out quickly. And a small mustache. Again it changes the appearance radically but is simple to remove in a hurry.'

'Photographs?'

'That's another odd thing,' Lomax said. 'The office is full of them. You know how political people are. Walls of pictures of the Candidate, the President with this group and that. But virtually nothing of Callaghan. Apparently he just never seemed to be around when the cameras were produced. A reputation as a modest, self-effacing type but nothing you would call strange. He does feature in some of the wide-angle Convention shots and I'm bringing back samples for the lab guys to blow up but the definition is lousy.'

'So what makes you think he's our man?'

'A remark of one of Mrs Huston's helpers. She said they used to laugh at Callaghan behind his back on account of the way he was so obsessed by the Candidate. Even used to walk like him, she said. It was a kind of standing joke in the office.'

'I'll be over,' Blacker told him and called for his car.

*

'This is Mrs Huston, sir. Deputy Director Blacker.'

Mrs Huston was a formidable lady in a tailored gray suit and bouffant hair. Blacker shook hands. 'I appreciate the help you're giving us.'

'Always happy to cooperate with the Secret Service. I imagine you can't tell us what this is about?'

'Wish we could, ma'am. Now I understand this man Callaghan used to work for you?'

Mrs Huston inclined her head graciously. 'Technically he was employed by the Indiana state government. He was on loan to us and we reimbursed Indiana for his salary.'

'What exactly did he do here?'

'He was on the speechwriting team. His specialty was composing bullets. The speech pulse system identifies key segments within a speech. Passages which strike an emotional response with particular groups. It's a highly refined technique. A speech can be tailored to have a precise impact on an audience – sort of like touching nerves. If you stroke the right spots the speech will draw votes regardless of content.'

'You mean all flavor, no meat?' said Blacker, sniffing.

Mrs Huston drew her eyebrows together freezingly. 'It is just one of the tools all campaigns use. Prescott was good at it. I can show you a sample if you like.'

She produced a page of typescript on which certain passages were highlighted in different colors.

'Each color corresponds to a different voter section. It's highly scientific.'

Blacker studied the page. It seemed to mean nothing to him. 'You said he was good at his job. How, exactly?'

'Certainly the President was very pleased with him. He used to take Prescott along on trips whenever the speech might be important.'

'Yes, but what was it that made his work stand out?'

342

Mrs Huston chose her words carefully. 'He was adept at tailoring bullets to the Candidate's speech rhythms.' She paused. 'Put simply, he understood the way the President spoke.'

Blacker had one final question. When was the last time Callaghan would have seen the President?

Mrs Huston shook her head. That was hard to answer. Like she had told Agent Lomax, Callaghan had continued to help out after the date he had officially left the campaign. She knew for a fact that he had worked on speeches for the President on more than one occasion. Asked when these might have been, she said she could not be certain but she believed Callaghan had been summoned down to Florida to help with the Inauguration speech.

On the freeway out to Callaghan's address at Seabrook, Lomax filled his chief in on what they had learned.

'He left nothing behind, but that's standard. The former offices were closed down and emptied after the election. The rump of the outfit set up here after the Inauguration to maintain the organization on a caretaker basis for the next three years till the re-election campaign begins. This letter arrived for him. I opened it up. It's from his sister in Albuquerque, saying she hopes it will catch him before he moves to Seattle and how their parents are hurt he didn't find time to visit home before moving west.'

Blacker took the letter and read it. 'Get on to her. Say you're an old friend of her brother's who's lost touch. Ask her if she has a current address for him and try and find out when they last saw each other.'

Lomax shook his head. 'I already tried,' he answered. 'His family hadn't heard from Prescott Callaghan in more than five years when out of the blue they had a call from him last month telling them he was doing well and hoping to come down to see them before he moved to his new job.'

The address the Campaign office had given them was a studio apartment in a converted older property. Evidently the speechwriter had lived modestly. Lomax rooted out the caretaker and showed him his badge.

'Moved out a fortnight ago,' he reported back gloomily to his chief. 'No forwarding address. Paid off all the bills and ordered a firm of professional cleaners to go in afterward. Caretaker says they left the place immaculate and it re-let the same week. New people move in tomorrow. Says Callaghan only used the place to sleep and was away a lot. Never had any visitors that he knew of. Only laid eyes on him a half-dozen times.'

He produced the key and they let themselves in.

'Notice anything about this place?'

Blacker sniffed. 'Smells kind of funny?'

'It's clean. Real clean.' Lomax ran a finger along the edge of the table. 'Every goddam surface has been wiped down. Most likely with an ammonia-based cleaner. That's what you can smell still. I'll bet we don't lift a single print off the entire place, unless the landlord's shown anyone else round since.'

They moved among the sparse furnishings, opening drawers, checking closets. All was pristine, any trace of previous occupancy expunged.

'The landlord said the guy who rented here wore gloves a lot. Something to do with a skin complaint. I tell you this man is smart. He picked this place because of its size and layout. Easy to clean down. Easy for him to come and go without being seen. This is a man who doesn't leave things to chance. He wears gloves all the time around the apartment to avoid leaving prints and then to make doubly certain when he leaves he wipes the entire place down.'

'Also,' Lomax continued, 'he chooses somewhere the

landlord doesn't declare the rental so there's no paperwork, no ID check. Yes, he's smart okay.'

Blacker swore to himself. At every step the trail grew colder.

'We're wasting time,' he said. 'Let's get back.'

'He's our man,' Blacker said. 'I'm sure of it.'

Under his desk lamp he was examining the photographs Lomax had brought back from the Watergate offices. The FBI technical laboratories had taken away several and promised to do their best by way of enhancement, but according to the expert all were taken from too great a distance to be of help in a facial comparison. Blacker had sent for video footage of every major address the President had given prior to his Inauguration but privately he was not optimistic. He had a hunch that a man who had buried his trail with such care would have stayed out of camera range.

Finally came a report from the field office in Denver where the Secret Service maintained a permanent unit. Agents had just returned from interviewing Callaghan's family at their home in Albuquerque. Aside from a letter a month ago they had had no contact with him for the past five years and only sporadically before that since he left college. According to the sister, her brother was an adopted child and the relationship had never been close. The only photograph she could supply dated from his early teens in high school, all others having been lost when their trailer home burned down two years ago. The sister did however confirm that her brother had been considered a dead likeness to Jack Meade when he was playing Bruce Delahaye in *Winchester County*.

Back at the mansion, the President was due to depart for a reception at the Organization of American States when a query came up over a letter that he wanted recalled for alteration. Karen checked with the log she kept of all presidential correspondence. Sure enough the letter in question had already gone down to the mailroom. She called and spoke to the supervisor on duty. The final afternoon mail drop had been franked and sorted but not yet dispatched. Jodi and the other secretaries had left for the evening, so Karen went down to the basement herself.

The mailroom took up a big area. This was where the models of the executive mansion in toothpicks were received, the tapes of first-graders singing 'Happy Birthday, Mr President', the gifts of pumpkin pie and hand-knitted vests, the requests for neckties and hair clippings, all part of the 20,000 letters and packages addressed to the President and his family each and every day. One hundred and fifty full-time and up to 500 part-time staff, mostly retired civil servants, opened and read every message, of which a representative 150 were sent up to the Oval Office daily. The rest would receive one of a dozen or more pro-forma replies.

'Please, please,' Karen begged the mail clerks. With groans and sighs of resignation, they cut open the bundles and started the laborious process of sorting through by hand. It took twenty minutes to locate the envelope. Showering them with gratitude, Karen snatched it up. Back in her office, she retyped the letter with the new wording, tore the copy off the printer and took it upstairs to the second floor.

The Secret Service man on duty at the elevator told her the President was in his bedroom and the First Lady around somewhere on the floor. Karen hesitated. The thought of encountering the false president up here in the residency was doubly repellent. The door to the yellow Oval Room opposite was open. She peeked inside, hoping to find Caro Meade. The room was empty. Opposite the fireplace, twin flags guarded the double doors to the President's room. Steeling herself, Karen tapped. She thought she heard an answer from within and turned the handle.

346

She took a step inside the room. It was empty. The TV was on in the corner, turned down low, and it was that she must have heard. The clothes the President had been wearing lay on a chair where they had been tossed. The bathroom door stood open, bright light reflecting off the tiles. He wasn't in there. She felt a momentary relief. The letter could be left on the table for him to read. She could return for it later when he had gone out. Then she noticed the far door too was ajar. It connected through a walk-in closet with the First Lady's room, and all the warnings Jack Meade had given her last night flooded back in a rush.

On tiptoe she crossed the room and listened. She could hear the murmur of voices, but faint as if coming from out in the corridor. Maybe it was the guards in the hall. Softly, she rapped on the door with her knuckles. No response. She pushed the door open a little more to see inside. Karen had never been in here before. The First Lady's bedroom was decorated with peach and floral draperies and the carpet was peach to match. The bed was another four-poster but slender and more elegant than the one the President slept in. On one side of the marble fireplace stood a small sofa with a pretty Sheraton desk against it. A faint scent of Obsession, the First Lady's favorite perfume, clung to the air. There was no sign of Caro Meade or the President.

She could hear the voices more clearly. They were coming from the First Lady's dressing room beyond. A man and a woman. Karen's heart began to thump.

'. . . I must tell you I spoke with your doctor today . . . no reason why we couldn't resume physical relations.'

'I don't want to talk about that just yet. It's too soon for me.'

'I understand how you feel. It's hard to feel . . . romantic . . . guards, eyes everywhere, people listening all the time. I can't relax either . . . like a prisoner. They won't even let me walk in the grounds.'

Caro Meade's response was inaudible but evidently an agreement, for the impostor's voice resumed.

'. . . been thinking, why don't we fly down to Camp David at the weekend? Just the two of us? . . . more privacy there . . . guards keep their distance . . . be like before the election.'

Again the response of the First Lady was too low pitched for Karen to make it out properly. If not ecstatic it was nevertheless clearly some form of assent for the impostor concluded with a remark to the effect of having Rex Coffey make arrangements.

Karen was still straining to hear more when the door to the dressing room opened suddenly and the President emerged. She held her breath. He plainly hadn't seen her standing so still. He went straight to the desk and began rummaging in the drawers. For several seconds she stood riveted to the spot. Then to her dismay, before she could manage to speak, he raised his head and this time glanced in her direction. At the sight of her a look of alarm came into his face, swiftly replaced by a dangerous anger.

'Mr President?' Instinctively Karen sought refuge in her oldest stand-by. Blindly she swiveled her head this way and that as if unable to pick him out. 'Mr President, are you in here, sir? It's Karen. I have the letter with me.'

There was a long pause. Her words seemed to hang on the air. Then he spoke. 'Over here, Karen.' The tone was calm but she fancied she could detect the raw edge of anger still beneath.

She twisted to face him, forcing a smile. 'Oh, there you are, sir. I'm sorry, I didn't see you properly. My eyes must be tired.'

'Is that the letter?'

'Yes.' She held it out.

'Put it here on the desk,' he ordered. 'I'll look at it later.'

She almost fell into the trap. At the last moment she checked herself and fumbled deliberately past a chair.

'Here, let me have it.' He took it from her. She sensed him relaxing, deciding he had gotten away with whatever he was doing.

'Thank you, Mr President. Good-night.'

'Wait, Karen,' he called her back as she was closing the door.

Her heart came into her mouth. 'Yes, Mr President?' She turned to face him again.

He gestured. 'Your eyesight, it isn't usually this poor downstairs. Is something giving you trouble?'

She had her excuse ready. 'Oh no, Mr President, it's just that you're used to seeing me in familiar surroundings. I'm easily confused in strange places. I try not to get caught out.'

'Another time, remember to knock. These are private apartments. My wife particularly hates to be disturbed. So do I.' The menace in his tone was unmistakable.

'I'm sorry, Mr President. It won't happen again,' she apologized.

She went weakly upstairs to her room.

Today was Thursday. In two days' time the impostor would take Caro Meade with him to the Maryland woods and consummate his possession of her.

The log from the yacht had been found.

Blacker hurried to the command post. Lomax was just coming off the phone. He was jubilant. In a few succinct sentences he related his discovery.

'All this time we're chasing Callaghan, we're still following up after the log, the missing log from the yacht. Mary Jo Wojno, the software whiz, has been trying to reconstruct the files. Some idea she could mine data from the temp files or some such, but no luck. But it set her off wondering were there any other logs kept of comings and goings? And she thinks, the yacht is tied up on a naval reservation. Anyone entering or leaving has to show a pass or produce identity. So she contacts Navy security.'

'And?' Blacker demanded impatiently.

'Turns out base security is lax. I mean by White House standards. Pretty much anyone can drive in. They got cameras on the gates. Used to keep the film a month but budgetary pressures mean now they recycle the tapes every seventy-two hours. What the officer does say is that for the visit of the President-elect they set up a special inner secure zone. Seems they fenced off the Bachelor Officers' Quarters and the dock, put a guard post on the gate with entry only by special electronic pass. The same passes that also got you onto the boat. Using the Navy data, she's rebuilt the files for our missing logs.'

'And?'

'Prescott Callaghan was on the base Wednesday through Saturday.'

Blacker took a long deep breath. At last they looked as if they were getting somewhere. And about time.

Meanwhile the team had a second break. The head of the unit Lomax had sent to turn over the apartment in Seabrook reported back: they had made a find. A cassette tape discovered when the living area couch was moved. Very likely it had been inadvertently kicked underneath and later overlooked. Otherwise the place was squeaky clean. Like an operating theater, according to the searchers. The tape was the only item. They had dusted it for prints and obtained one lift, which had been sent off for identification.

Lomax brought the tape in to Blacker.

'Have you played it back?'

'Voices, a conversation. Like it's a recording of a meeting to do with the election campaign. References to caucuses, turnouts in the primaries, voting patterns, all that political stuff.'

'Recognize any of the voices?'

Lomax nodded. 'One is the President for sure. Another the Chief of Staff, I think. For the rest,' he shrugged, 'technical say it's a quality recording, probably made using a Sony Professional. Kind of equipment reporters carry.'

'So not a snoop job then.'

'Could still be. These recorders are not large items. Also they're standard issue in many offices I would guess. Voice-actuated. Leave it on a shelf or in a drawer somewhere and it's easy to say it was left on by mistake if anyone notices.'

'So Callaghan bugs the Candidate's office to keep up to speed on the inside dope ready for when he takes over?' It made sense, Blacker thought. If any of it made sense.

'See if you can chase up your friends at the Hoover Building,' he told Lomax. 'I want a sight of anything in the files on Prescott Callaghan. And have them expedite that print. If they can cross-match it with one of Callaghan's we may be able to wrap this thing up.'

Lomax returned gloomy. 'Nix,' he reported. 'A fat zero. We checked the NCIC and the Triple I sub-system both. There's no record on a Prescott Callaghan with local, state or federal agencies anywhere, or with the Canadians either. He's never been picked up for a traffic violation, never had his car stolen, been mugged or written his congressman. He's not on the records of Justice Department, Drug Enforcement, Customs or Immigration or Missing Persons. The all-time honest Joe Citizen.'

'How about prints?' Blacker cut him short. 'He was a state employee. Surely they would be on file with Indianapolis?'

'I'm hoping so. We're still waiting on it. Indiana have a mandatory policy but there seems to be a hold-up. Could be he's managed to avoid compliance.' Part of the trouble, he added, was that with so many appointees from the President's home state up for government positions in the new administration, the local bureau was run off its feet. 'I spoke with IRS. They're willing to release Callaghan's tax records but first they have to have an affidavit from us that he's a threat. I had your secretary draft one.'

Blacker scribbled his signature on the paper and handed it back. He rubbed his eyes and forced his tired brain to think. Tonight the President was due to host a banquet for his first visiting foreign head of government, the Prime Minister of Canada. That meant extra security, additional worry. As if they hadn't enough on their plates.

FBI Central Records were organized into five categories. Category 1 held names of anyone connected to an FBI investigation: criminals, suspects, victims, witnesses and associates. Category 2 was for FBI agents and applicants. Category 3 listed appointments to sensitive government positions. Category 5 was administrative. The remaining category, Category 4, was the subject of controversy. Its stated purpose was to list those people who were 'the subject of unsolicited information or who offer such information, or request assistance or make inquiries concerning records'. In other words if a person contacted the FBI wishing to know whether there was a file maintained on him, the act of making the request was sufficient to cause a file to be opened: Catch-22.

The wall clocks of the Secret Service East Wing office showed 8 p.m. The team of agents summoned by Lomax filed in and took seats. Two had been pulled off a long-term Treasury investigation, the other three had worked protection for the former First Lady.

The briefing lasted an hour. Two of the team, he instructed to leave for the West Coast to follow up Callaghan's claim to have relocated to Seattle. Details of bank transfers, mail-forwarding instructions might all yield clues to his current whereabouts. 'In each case try to talk personally to whoever had contact with Callaghan. He may have let slip a chance remark about his intentions. If instructions were by mail, obtain possession of the originals, not copies. At banks particularly, ask for sight of any files and check for notes. Clerks will often attach a contact number to a client's personal sheet or add an observation of their own. Remember Callaghan will have been striving to put across a genuine impression and may have said more than he intended.'

The next pair he allocated to Indianapolis. Indianapolis was where Callaghan had first encountered the President as a senator. Before that any resemblance between the two could have been of no more than passing interest to an impostor. Indianapolis had to be where he took the first steps. 'Indianapolis is going to be where Callaghan kicked off his plan. Work back to where he first arrived in the city. Who were his friends? How did he spend his leisure time?'

The last two agents were women. Lomax set them to the task of tracing Callaghan's records. 'Start with his last known address. Talk to the landlord again. What references did Callaghan give? Has the landlord kept anything that might have belonged to him? Has there been any mail, or phone calls? Call up the phone company records. Try the neighbors in the building, local stores. Did he have a girlfriend, a lover? Find out if he had a car. How often did he use it and where is it now? Get onto the IRS, Social Security, the credit card companies and the bank. Look for any signs of big payments coming in that might indicate if he has backers. I want a complete pattern of his finances and how he lived. The Democratic people should be able to provide you with any travel he may have done for them during the election. Ascertain what dates he was with the Candidate and where. The same goes for the transition period.'

All the agents took detailed notes. All had queries at the end. Lomax dealt with them as best he could. He had just finished and dispatched the teams on their way when Blacker returned.

The Secret Service chief took the cassette tape from his pocket and tossed it on his desk with a grunt.

Lomax flicked an eyebrow. 'You played it to them?' Blacker nodded. Lomax waited for more. Nothing came. 'So what did they say? Is it genuine?'

Blacker slumped down in his chair and scowled. 'It's genuine, okay,' he said. 'They knew all about it.' Apparently, he said, the Meade election team had been determined to prevent insider accounts of the campaign being published later as had happened after previous elections. 'So they commissioned a writer to listen in on their discussions and write a definitive account for them. Sort of pre-emptive strike, if you like.' The deal with the writer had fallen through for some unconnected reason and Callaghan had taken on the job.

Lomax blinked at him. 'You mean Callaghan had a legitimate right to this?' he tapped the cassette.

'That and a hundred like it. According to the Campaign office, I spoke with Mrs Huston just now, Callaghan had a whole boxful as well as a trunk of notes. He used to sit in on some meetings and take shorthand dictation. Said it gave him a better feel for the debate.'

Lomax snorted derisively. 'Besides a perfect cover for observing the President in action.'

Blacker said nothing. He swiveled his chair around and stared at the draped window. 'What is it about this guy, Eddie?' he said softly. 'Each time we seem to get a grip on him, he slides out from under us again. We could be chasing a moonbeam for all the good we're doing.'

'Oh, and I almost forgot,' said Lomax. 'The report came in from NCIC. That print on the tape.' He paused.

Blacker glared at him. 'Well, did they get a match?'

Lomax shrugged. 'They got a match okay.' He gave a short laugh, 'Yeah, you're gonna love this one. The print matches up to a set listed under the name of John MacKenzie Meade.'

'Meade? Like from Jacksonville?'

'Uh-uh.' Lomax unwrapped a stick of gum and popped it in his mouth. 'Not the Jacksonville Meade. This set are on file with the Pentagon. This is the Washington Meade. The Meade who touched that tape is living right here in the White House.'

At the Troika meeting that evening, Blacker related the success the Secret Service had had over at the Watergate. It was the first good news since the crisis began and morale in the room lifted.

'I remember Callaghan, we all do,' the Chief of Staff declared. 'Auburn haired, a little taller than the President perhaps, wore a mustache, walked with a limp. Smart soundbite man, kind of unhealthy paunchy look, over-weight and bad color, sweated a lot, girls in the office used to complain . . . funny-looking eyes.'

'Built-up shoes,' Blacker said. 'A stud in the heel of one shoe, it produces a permanent limp so long as it is worn. An old actor's trick. Dyes his hair, wears colored contact lenses and a padded under-vest beneath his shirt. In hot weather it makes him perspire.' He shrugged. 'Glue-on false dentures to change the shape of the mouth, distort the speech, face-tinting skin dye, criminals use the same tricks when they think they may be caught on video camera.'

Hunter interrupted impatiently, 'Yes, that's all very well for a one-off event, a few minutes, a couple of hours even, a day at most, but we're talking weeks, months here. Even a professional actor couldn't be expected to carry off a deception that long.'

On the contrary, Blacker said, a deception grew easier the longer it was practiced. 'It would be the first days that were riskiest for him. After that you were all accustomed to seeing him the way he was. In the theater, on

Broadway, actors are accustomed to sustaining roles for every bit as long. It becomes second nature.'

A silence followed. Phones could be heard ringing and the sound of carpenters' hammers close at hand.

'He had a knack of throwing words together that made them sound spontaneous. We offered him a job but he turned it down. Not senior enough, or so he claimed. It doesn't seem possible that he could be mistaken for the President but I suppose it must be if you say so.'

'Tracking the impostor down should be a straightforward enough task, I take it?' growled the General. 'Now that you have a name and presumably other details.'

Blacker shook his head. 'No, that is where he's been clever. He hasn't left a hole. On the contrary he has very carefully filled it in. That was why he reopened contact with his family after a gap of five years. And why he invented a job and new life in Seattle. He guessed that with a limited number of alternatives, he would come under suspicion so he provided himself with a plausible exit. It's proof he's concerned about, you see. By dispatching Callaghan off to the West Coast he's hidden him well. We may suspect but we can't prove. We know that he transferred Callaghan's bank account out there and my guess is that the Seattle police will come up with some further trace of him, a phone call, a temporary address. Enough to sustain the concept of a separate existence. It's all he needs.'

17

Lomax left a message for Blacker and took a red-eye flight to New Mexico.

The trailer park where the Callaghans lived was named Las Brisas. The air was sour with traffic fumes from the multi-lane highway on the other side of the boundary fence. There would have been less noise under an airport flight path. The Callaghan trailer was Number 138. It looked new. Insurance money presumably from the fire. The shades were still drawn over the windows. It was only 7.15. Too bad, he thought and rapped on the door.

A redheaded woman in a soiled yellow kimono opened, tousled and puffy eyed from sleep. 'Do I know you?' she said.

Lomax flipped open his wallet. 'Federal agent, Miss. It's about your brother. May I come in a minute?'

'Prescott? Oh, you were one of the ones who phoned.' She reached behind her for a pack of Virginia Slims and stuck one in her mouth. 'Okay, if you must.' She slouched back inside.

Lomax followed, shutting the door behind him. The living room smelt of last night's Chinese take-away. In the window stood a green parrot in a cage. The woman was over by the kitchen range, lighting her cigarette on a burner. Lomax sat on the couch and watched. This would be the sister, Patsy. Younger than Callaghan, aged around thirty-five. Not much like him to look at. But of course, he was forgetting, Callaghan was adopted.

'Coffee?' She spooned granules into a mug. 'Maxwell House.'

'Fine by me.'

She opened the door of the fridge under the counter and knelt to rearrange the contents. She rose again with a carton. 'Milk?'

'Please.' She wasn't wearing anything under the kimono, he decided.

'So,' she said placing the mug on the table and dropping down beside him. 'What else d'you want me to tell you?' She tore open a Sweet'n Low and emptied it into her drink. From its corner the parrot observed the proceedings with a gleam in its eye. 'His name's Clint,' the woman said.

It was more a question of going over details again, Lomax explained. Routine.

'Shit,' the woman yawned. 'Don't you people talk to each other? I already told the other guys once.'

'For the record, okay. First off, is it correct you haven't laid eyes on your brother in quite a while?'

She nodded. 'Not since he left town the last time.'

'Which was what, five years ago?'

'Something like that, I guess.'

'Can you be more precise?'

The woman wrinkled her brow. 'Prescott wasn't around much after he left school. Said there was nothing to keep him here. He was right at that. He spent some time in California. Came back when things didn't work out for him there. That would be 1995.'

'Whereabouts in California exactly?'

'San Francisco to begin with, then LA.'

'What was he doing there, do you have any idea?'

She looked at him sarcastically. 'Becoming a movie star, d'you think? He never told us.'

'And then he went off to Indianapolis?'

'India-no-place, yeah. He did pretty good for himself too. Got a job working with Jack Meade as a speechwriter.'

'You didn't try to get in contact with him? You didn't phone or write at all?'

She shrugged. 'Called him up a couple of times. He was busy mostly. Said he'd call back. Never did.'

'How about letters?'

She shook her head. 'Never was much of a one for writing.'

'And you never thought of traveling to Indianapolis to visit him?'

'Where'd we get the money? From him?' She gave a short barking laugh that made the parrot squawk suddenly. She put her legs up on the couch and leaned back. She was looking at him under her hair. 'Say, you know you're kinda cute.'

'No one from here ever went to see him? No one else from the family? A friend maybe?'

The woman frowned. 'Don't you ever ease up? I told you, no. We were never that close, him and me. Ma was too sick. Marcia Williams that went to live in Cincinnati was going to look him up if she got the chance but she didn't.'

'How was that?' Lomax asked.

'Because she got herself killed,' the woman said uninterestedly, poking a pecan nut through the bars of the cage at the parrot.

'Was she close to your brother?'

'I wouldn't know about close. They went together at high school. Then Prescott left town. He always wanted to get on. Guess he did at that,' she added wistfully.

'So this Marcia Williams wanted to get in touch with Prescott. She have an address where to find him?'

'Senator Meade's office, where else? Prescott was getting on, I tell you. He helped run Jack Meade's election for the Senate and after that he worked on the presidential campaign. He wrote all Jack's speeches. He and Jack were like that –' she held up crossed fingers.

'And you don't know if they did in fact meet up ever?'

'Nope. Marcia got herself killed. Some bastard busted

into her room and choked her to death. Dumb bitch left the door unlatched.'

Lomax finished his coffee. He got up to go. 'Thank you for your assistance, Miss Callaghan. You've been a help. We hear anything we'll let you know.'

The woman put down her cigarette. 'Ma isn't here,' she said rising languidly. 'They took her into hospital. You want to come in the bedroom with me? Like I said, you're kinda cute.'

The Illinois trip was the President's first out of town trip since the Inauguration. The first ride on Air Force One. Correction, he had ridden the plane before. Several times, as it happened, but this was his first as president. This time it was his plane. Hunter elected to stay at the White House. He hated flying and anyway he had work to do, people to see. With the President out of the way he could clear some of the backlog. Jay could handle this one.

The presidential party helicoptered off from the South Lawn. Jay was happy as a pig in mud. He and Barney Nikolis and congressional liaison, Harry Huenerheim, traveled with the President aboard Marine One to Andrews AFB where the presidential jet awaited. Karen Lipscombe accompanied them. The stated purpose of the trip was to promote his economic plan. Unofficially it was to repay a campaign debt to Mayor Reynolds. The image team had wanted to play down the connection with Reynolds, an old-style ward pol with reputed close links to organized crime. The President had swept their objections aside. Reynolds, he said, was the most important politician in Chicago and Chicago was the most important city in the state of Illinois. Cynics recalled that it was Reynolds' support that had brought in the crucial 20,000 Marion County votes that had tipped the balance of the election. Lunching with the Mayor was the President's way of saying thank you.

The band played 'Hail to the Chief' as the President

went aboard to join Senator Kobel, a trio of congressmen and, a surprise last-minute guest, FBI Director Judge Watson. The press corps were already packed in the rear section of the 747–200B with a score of Secret Service between them and the VIP section up in the nose.

Overspill journalists from the press corps and extra staff were accommodated on the back-up plane, a second similarly equipped Boeing 747, designated Air Force Two. Experienced members of the White House entourage preferred to have seats on the back-up because it was less crowded. A lucky senior staffer might even get to use the presidential suite for the trip. Already airborne and shadowing the presidential flight was a third aircraft, an E–4B variant of the Boeing 747 series recognizable by the distinctive dorsal blister housing satellite/SHS communications antennae and operated by the USAF as an advanced airborne national command post. Popularly dubbed the 'Doomsday Plane', with a battle staff of thirty-three under a full general, its mission was to provide a command and control platform for the US leadership in time of war.

Already on the apron at Chicago's O'Hare International Airport was the transport aircraft, which had carried the two armored limousines, Stagecoach and its reserve. A fifth plane had flown in additional agents and advance men who were swarming over the Convention Center, erecting the bulletproof podium from which the President would speak, screwing in place the presidential seal, setting up the flags and the teleprompter and sound system.

As the plane lifted off over Maryland an Air Force officer circulated with gift packs. Opening hers, Karen found a certificate in her name confirming her status as a passenger aboard Air Force One. From the accompanying information sheet she learned that the airplane accommodated an airborne equivalent of the Oval Office, a senior staff room, a conference/dining room and a presidential stateroom complete with twin beds and private bathroom in addition to seating for seventy passengers and twenty-three crew. There was even an operating theater.

For Karen it was a relief to be out of the White House. She dreaded the President's company now. Even his voice seemed to ring false with her, like a ghastly caricature of Jack Meade's. Her great fear was that he might somehow guess she had discovered the truth about him. As it was, she thought he had half begun to suspect. Ever since the previous night when he had come upon her in his room he had been curt toward her. As if he definitely thought she was spying on him. His manner was moody and hostile towards the other staff too. There was an ominous air of tension as if events were building up to a crisis in which anything might happen. If only there were some easier way of getting in touch with Elaine or Jack.

Karen's sense of strain was not lessened by the presence on board of the infamous Judge Watson of the FBI, invited along by the President at the last minute. Why, she hadn't been able to find out. He had supported Ivory blatantly at the election, all but accusing Jack of being a Communist and agitator. It was commonly believed that he instructed his agents to dig up scandal on prominent figures, which he then used for blackmail purposes.

Others too were speculating on the invitation to the FBI Director.

'Well, I'll say old Jack is certainly enjoying his new toy.' Senator Kobel dropped into the seat next Jay Leeder. 'He's back in the steerage fraternizing with the media. Your boss certainly knows the right way to stroke those guys an' gals. They're trying to make him move the press section up in front of the Secret Service next trip.'

'They can try all they like,' said Jay and the Senator laughed.

'You're right there. Jack may look like an actor still

but he's nobody's fool. He'll keep those animals back of the plane where they can't see what their betters get up to – or overhear what we say about them.'

Jay grinned. He liked Saul Kobel, a stout, red-faced politician who looked like a farmer and had been an early enthusiast of the Jack Meade for President movement.

The Senator leaned closer and dropped his voice. 'Whose idea was it to invite Judge Watson along for the ride?'

Jay glanced across the cabin to where the squat, powerful figure of the FBI Director sat by himself. Instinctively he too spoke quietly, 'The President's, I presume. I guess he feels he needs to strike a balance.'

The Senator gave a dry sniff. 'You mean flying the law and order flag at the same time he drops in on Mayor Reynolds.'

'I was thinking more in terms of placating the party's right when entertaining a liberal-minded senator,' Jay riposted.

Kobel chuckled at the dig. 'Point taken. I just wondered is all. Ronnie Reagan once told me the great thing about Air Force One, you can have real private conversations up at 35,000 feet.' He gripped the arms of the seat and levered himself up. 'Nice to talk to you, Jay. Reckon I'll go pay my respects to the old scoundrel. You never know, he might have something on me too.'

Jay watched him cross over, pause beside the figure of the Judge and shake his hand. The Senator had not been wholly joking in his remarks, Jay knew. There were people who said the FBI Director was becoming a second Edgar Hoover, too powerful to be dismissed even by the President. He wondered also about the reference to private conversations. It was odd that Jack Meade had not mentioned to himself or Hunter that he had invited Judge Watson to make the trip. Perhaps it was just as a counterweight to Mayor Reynolds.

The First Lady was sitting up in bed with a stack of newspapers. Gina had just brought in her breakfast on a tray. Dorothy Fine sat on the foot of the bed. Trish Beale, the First Lady's press secretary, had pulled up a chair. Boxes of eight by twelve gloss color photographs of Caro Meade shot by the White House press team littered the coverlet. Ninety percent of inquiries to the First Lady's press office concerned clothes or fashion details.

'Will you look at this, the garbage they print about me!' The First Lady smacked a paper angrily. 'Listen: "Caro Charteris Meade attended Miss Motcombe's School for Girls in Virginia. Fellow alumni remember her as a wild one. According to one authoritative source she was required to leave after diving naked into the swimming pool before a visiting crowd of spectators." I mean how can they write such lies?'

'It's outrageous,' agreed Dorothy. 'How can they think it's true?'

'Get on to them, Trish. Find out who their source is. If it's a friend of mine I want her name. She'll never see the inside of the White House. And take away the paper's pass, they need to be taught a lesson. These things are really hurtful.'

Trish promised to see what could be done.

'Who on earth makes up these tales?' said Dorothy to her as they departed for the East Wing. 'It's pure spite. Can't they be got for libel somehow?'

'I doubt it,' Trish said drily.

'My God, you're not suggesting it's true?'

Trish shrugged.

'Well you were at school with her. If anyone knows it must be you.'

They entered the elevator. Trish waited for the doors to close before answering. 'I was there, yes, but I didn't attend the pool gala. I was in the sick bay so I only know what they said later.'

'And what was that exactly?'

364

Trish shrugged again. 'Okay, so it was an all girls school but there were parents present, brothers, boy-friends and stuff. It was a relay race. Caro was last to go of her team and they were lying behind. She said afterward she was fed up with the idea of swimming the last lap all by herself. It was boring. So she peels off her costume the instant before she dives in and does her two lengths stark naked.'

'She didn't? Good grief.'

'It was all over so quick no one could've seen anything except her butt. She climbed back into the costume again before she got out the pool. It wasn't really such a scandal.'

'But what did she do it for?'

'For laughs. Who knows? She always was something of an exhibitionist. She went through three schools.'

The elevator reached the ground floor. 'But she said it wasn't true,' Dorothy protested as they waited for the door.

'Sure. Which means she's most likely edited it out of her head. She always told the most incredible stories about herself. Kind of reinventing herself as she went along. She used to claim she was adopted at ten months and Jackie K. was her natural mother. Also that at fifteen she was her uncle's mistress. The way she told them you half believed. She's a sweet girl but flaky. God help the guy who marries her, we used to say.'

Spellman was sneaking out on them, Agent Thule was sure of it. 'Yesterday that modem of hers was running twelve hours without a break and the CD system played the same six disks over and over,' he told Suter. 'She's making us look a bunch of idiots.'

It didn't take a genius to work out how the trick was being pulled either.

That morning when Simon parked his battered car outside the Bible House, Agent Thule was waiting around the corner of the street, snucked up under a blanket in the rear footwell of a Secret Service vehicle.

'Looks like the Doc coming out now,' Suter's voice crackled over the radio. 'Starting the car, driving off toward you.'

Thule crouched down under the blanket. In the rearview mirror he glimpsed the Rabbit turning down into the street. It drove past him and pulled into the side a few spaces down. He raised his head cautiously to watch. The driver wore Simon Cheng's clothes and was waiting with the engine switched off. Ten minutes later the radio crackled again. 'Bunch of students coming out. One could be Cheng, can't be sure at this distance. Heading your way.'

Agent Thule continued to observe in the mirror as a figure on foot approached down the street. Close up, it was evident that this person was in fact Cheng in an Afghan coat. He got into the Rabbit with Spellman. Thule watched as they exchanged clothes. He could see them chuckling together at their cleverness. The laugh would be on them before they were through. The Rabbit started up and nosed off down the street. Thule scrambled out from under the blanket and slid behind the wheel.

'Target Spellman headed east. In visual contact,' he reported over the radio. Now to see where she led them.

Down the hill, a third agent was waiting on a motorcycle, already alerted by radio to the success of the trap. As the Rabbit drew abreast, he kicked his machine into life and weaved into the traffic flow in pursuit. Between them, the two vehicles tailed Simon's car eastward across town.

Jean-Alice was fully conscious of the dangers of being tailed. She and Simon kept a lookout as they drove. They spotted neither vehicle following but Jean-Alice was not convinced. The Secret Service were not idiots. She told

Simon to drop her off on Massachusetts Avenue by Scott Circle. There were many large hotels in the immediate area and she was confident of losing any pursuers in one or another of them.

Agent Thule saw her get out of the car. The motorcycle had temporarily dropped back to avoid being noticed. Thule pulled over into the nearside traffic stream to keep her under observation while he radioed the agent on the bike to close up.

'She looks to be headed for the Governor's House Holiday Inn.'

'Stay on Bataan. I'll cut round behind and relieve you,' his partner's response came over the radio.

Thule cruised slowly along Bataan Street at a respectful distance behind Spellman. All at once the lawyer turned about, retracing her steps up the way she had come. Agent Thule looked hurriedly away to avoid being recognized. He glanced back in the rear mirror and was just in time to see her sprint across the Avenue in front of the Australian Embassy. 'Dammit, I think she made me! She's doubled back to the north side.'

'I'm coming through onto Bataan now,' his partner called. 'I can see you. Where is the target?'

'I think . . .' Thule strove to avoid a collision with a delivery van while staring into his mirror after Spellman's disappearing figure, 'I think she went into the Holiday Inn. The bitch is onto us for sure!'

With a rasp of exhaust, the motorcycle slewed past the nose of Thule's car, weaving expertly in and out the traffic, ignoring the horns of angry drivers as it cut across the circle. The Holiday Inn stood on the corner of 15th and the agent ran his bike past the cabs in the entrance drive and braked opposite the doors. 'She went inside,' he said into his headphone. 'You pull on round and watch the front in case she tries to be cute again, while I cover the rear.' Without waiting for a reply, he twisted the throttle and sped off.

Inside the hotel, Jean-Alice brushed through the lobby to the café. There was a line waiting for breakfast. She darted out the side entrance at the same moment the motorbike came past. The agent was traveling too fast to stop in time. He overshot and had to keep going. He saw Spellman turn onto O Street, mingling with the crowds on the sidewalk. He roared on up the street, made a left into Church Street, left again on 16th and raced back south to try and pick her up. He missed her again on O and made a fast run around the block onto 17th, growing angry now. As he leaned into the turn, his rear wheel found a patch of oil in the road and skidded from under him. He wrenched frantically at the handlebars to stay upright but the momentum was too great. With a screech of metal the bike crashed into the side of a stationary limousine. As the agent rolled clear and stood up, cursing, he thought he might have glimpsed Spellman up the street disappearing into a side door in the wall of a building.

Air Force One was skirting Lake Erie west of Cleveland. Congressman Joe Albruzzio had just requested Jay Leeder if he might take a look inside the presidential airborne executive office.

'Just a quick peep is all. You know, so's I can tell the kids I was there.'

No problem, Jay assured him. He would be happy to conduct the Congressman over personally.

'Sure appreciate that. Just so long as it's no trouble. I know how busy the President is. I'd hate to disturb him.'

'He was up in his private suite a while ago. I'll just check.'

He led the way forward and tapped softly at the office door. There was no response. 'It's okay,' he said, standing aside. 'C'mon in.'

'Gee, some place, huh?' Albruzzio whispered in awed tones, surveying the flags, the presidential seal on the bulkhead, the array of communications equipment, the gray secure phones. 'You could run the country from here. No need to go back to Washington.'

'In fact that's exactly what it's designed for,' Jay told him. 'In the event of a war emergency, such as nuclear attack, Air Force One can act as an airborne National Command Authority. From here the President can direct the armed forces and there is equipment to tie into commercial radio and TV networks to broadcast messages to the population.'

He heard a click behind him as he finished speaking and turned. The President had just entered from the door to his stateroom. Behind him stood another figure. Jay felt his heart skip a beat as he recognized the rigid features of Judge Watson. A momentary frown passed over Jack Meade's face but it was instantly replaced with a forced smile.

'Well, Joe. Taking over my office already?'

Jay apologized at once for the intrusion. 'I'm sorry if we disturbed you, sir. The Congressman asked if I could show him round.'

'Much appreciate it, Mr President. It's a real privilege to fly with you, sir.'

'Not at all. Nice to see you, Joe,' the President beamed. 'I'm here because of people like you and I won't forget it. Same as I won't forget when I was feeling real down after that poll in Massachusetts and you sent me an e-mail message saying "Hang on in!"'

He was shepherding them both toward the door they had entered by as he spoke. Before they realized it, they were out in the passenger section again.

'Ain't he the great man though?' Albruzzio enthused as the door closed behind them.

'What else did you say in the message?' Jay asked him, curious.

The Congressman wrinkled his brow. 'Gee, I don't know. I generally send some kinda boost to every

369

candidate. Between you an' me I'm not certain what I did that occasion. But that's not the point, is it? He says I did and that's what counts.'

Maybe it was, Jay supposed. He was wondering more though what the President was doing with Judge Watson. And he remembered again Saul Kobel's remark about Air Force One being a great place for private conversations.

It crossed his mind that he ought to warn Irwin Hunter.

To round off the article Troy wanted a statement by someone in authority. He rang the White House Press Office. He was on the line twenty minutes.

'No dice?' said Cal when finally he put the phone down.

Troy lit a cigarette moodily. He had been passed from desk to desk, the responses beginning polite, then becoming incredulous, finally abrupt. In every case he had encountered disbelief, derision even. The White House declined to dignify the allegations with a response. For the first time since all this started Troy felt discouraged.

'Barney Nikolis' office said to go ahead and print, they enjoyed a laugh good as any.'

'There must be someone who'll listen. How about the Vice-President?'

'And have my head chewed off? Thanks a bundle. I've dealt with Leyland Jordan in the past. The man makes a flame-thrower look a soft touch.'

'Chief of Staff Hunter? Or you might try the First Lady's office?'

An idea came to Troy. He picked up the phone again and dialed Directory. 'Hi, yeah, it's a Washington DC number, name is Manken, Elaine Manken.'

'The ex-exec-sec?' Cal quipped. 'Smart one.'

*

Elaine Manken's private number in Washington was unlisted. Troy passed the problem to a contact of his, an ex-Bureau man who supplemented his pension doing private work. The request was a cinch. Inside the hour Troy was dialing again.

'What did you say your name was again?'

'Troy Reece, ma'am, with the Jacksonville *Meteor*.'

'That's Jacksonville, Florida?'

'Yes, ma'am, I just wanted to ask your opinion of—'

Elaine replaced the receiver, cutting him off in mid-sentence. She sat for a moment in thought. Then, collecting her coat and purse, she hurried out of her apartment. There was a mini-market on the corner of the street where she regularly shopped for basics. She bought milk and some crackers. On the way back she stopped by a phone booth. It took her only moments to get through to Jacksonville. She asked for Troy by name.

'Troy Reece speaking.'

'This is Elaine. My phone is not secure. Give me a number where I can reach you that can't be traced.'

Troy thought fast. 'My assistant, Cal's cell-phone. There's a message service for emergencies.'

'I'll call you back on that number in exactly fifteen minutes.'

The call came through on schedule. Troy took it sitting in his car outside the *Meteor*'s office. Elaine Manken was wary at first. She sensed a trap. Troy gave her the full story, everything they had. He held nothing back. When he revealed about the fingerprints, he heard her suck in breath.

'Do you have proof of this?'

'Of the prints story? A tape of the Navy Provost-Marshal officer's evidence, sure.'

'The tape is authentic? And verifiable?'

'Both. And witnessed by another officer.'

'Would you be willing to bring it to Washington?'

371

'I might. Why would you want it?'

'Because the man you saw in the hospital is the rightful President of the United States.'

Troy choked on the phone. 'Where do I reach you?' he managed to splutter.

'I'll let you know when and how. In the meantime be sure and keep any documentation safe. Make copies and put them somewhere they can't be found. The evidence could be vital to the President.'

'How do we make contact again?'

'This is the number of a pager. Dial it and I'll get back to you directly.'

She rattled off the digits. Troy scribbled them down and read the number back. The phone went dead. He opened the car door and walked back to the *Meteor* building.

Down at Chicago International Airport, teams of security agents were already scouring Runway 3A for bombs and debris. Air Force One would shortly be entering an approach pattern and all other traffic in or out of the country's busiest airport hub was being held or diverted. The airport authorities had protested at the messed-up schedules and loss of revenue for their customers. Why couldn't the President use downtown Midway, the same as New York made him use Newark instead of jamming up JFK? No way, the President's advance team answered, O'Hare International was the media choice. Mayor Reynolds backed them. The President of the United States was here as his guest and he was damned if he was going to have him fly into a rinky-dink suburban airstrip like a convention charter.

Aboard, the President had sent for Karen Lipscombe to join him in the executive office. His Day-Timer was open on the desk.

'You know Judge Watson, our fine FBI Director?'

'It's an honor, Judge.' Karen suppressed a spasm of

distaste as their hands touched. The Director's grip was cold and crushing, like putting her fingers into a turtle's beak and about as dangerous.

'Likewise,' he growled in his gravel voice with no trace of a smile.

'Karen,' the President said. 'I've prepared a short statement in connection with the Judge here. I'd like you to have it typed up and distributed to the press in back of the plane.'

'Yes, sir.' Karen sat down at the table, her pad at the ready. She felt an unaccountable foreboding.

Hunter, at work in his office, took the call. It was Jay Leeder, the alarm evident in his voice through the crackle and hiss on the scrambler downlink from Air Force One. The President had just informed journalists traveling aboard he intended nominating FBI Director, Judge Watson, to a second term in office in a complete about-face on campaign promises. 'Not only that, he's gone and promised Watson a 50 percent budget hike!'

'Whatever possessed the President to do a thing like that?' demanded Miriam furiously. 'Judge Watson is incompetent, he's corrupt, he's prejudiced. He stands for everything we pledged to change.'

'Judge Watson is reappointed – with a promise of a 50 percent budget hike, the Pentagon gets the green light for A-bomb tests, Langley has its charter confirmed; it's a pattern,' Hunter observed tautly. 'The Bureau, the military, CIA, he's bought their loyalties. You have to hand it to him, he's being very shrewd.'

'We never had a hint of this. How'd they manage to keep it secret?'

'Easy. Rex Coffey. Back-channel communications through the Military Office. There's no other way they could have pulled it without us finding out.'

'Why would Jack negotiate behind our backs?' said the General. 'And what's Coffey's game?'

'Power play, dummy,' the Counselor told him witheringly. 'He wants his first star. Rex delivers the Judge. The military get the test ban lifted. Rex jumps to field rank. Am I right?' she glanced at Blacker.

Blacker nodded. That wasn't the worst of it, he added. 'As Bureau chief, Judge Watson has right of direct access to the President. The first whisper comes to him that we're engaged in investigating the President, he'll lift that phone. Don't think he won't.'

'He probably has a file on each one of us already,' said Miriam.

'You'd better believe it,' Hunter told her. The FBI Director's private filing system of sensitive information was an open secret. And the key to his long survival.

The General shook his head. 'The President does all this without speaking to us? Why? It's completely out of character.'

Miriam snorted. 'That's exactly the point.'

Karen had to get word through to Jack Meade. There were only twenty-four hours left to get the First Lady away. Elaine had warned her, though, against using the White House phones except in direst emergency. Surely this was one?

The Camp David tryst was definitely fixed. She had sneaked a look at the President's Black Book this morning. Moreover the President had not asked her to accompany them. He didn't want any distractions.

She phoned the White House from the plane and spoke to Jodi. 'All okay back there? You bet we're having a swell flight. Air Force One is incredible, fantastic. You shall have your turn, I promise. We should be back on the helicopter around four. Rex Coffey's office will warn you of any schedule changes.'

She replaced the receiver and hesitated. Should she call

the number Elaine had given her? Suppose it was traced? Jack might be placed in danger. An idea came to her. She dialed her mother.

'Hi, Mom, it's me. Guess where I'm calling from? That's right, Air Force One. We're approaching Chicago. How about that?'

Predictably her mother was thrilled. Karen let her gabble on a minute, then interrupted. 'Mom, can you do something for me? I don't like to make too many private calls on this phone. Could you call this number.' She dropped her voice. 'Ask for Elaine, say I won't be able to meet with her Saturday through Sunday because our friend is going to Maryland. Got that?'

'Is that Camp David? Lucky you. Sure, I'll call Elaine for you. Nice to talk to you, honey. Take care of yourself.'

One thing about Mother, she didn't ask questions. Karen could only pray the message would be understood.

The President stared at Elaine in disbelief. The rest of the company held their breath excitedly as she described the phone call from Florida. The news was incredible, almost too good to be true. A gift from God just when they needed it most.

'Fingerprints?' the President said dazedly. 'My fingerprints?'

Elaine nodded, 'That's right, Mr President, the military took your prints while you were in the hospital. They were looking for means of identification.'

'I said I recalled something like that taking place.' He glanced at Jean-Alice. 'I told you about it that first time we met.'

'That's true, you did, sir. I remember now.'

Elaine continued: 'The Pentagon's Military Personnel Center in Alexandria failed to come up with a match. Since your prints would have been automatically on file from your military service, we assume the impostor switched them for his own. Somehow he must have penetrated the system and doctored the files. It sounds impossible but there's no other explanation, Reece says.'

'I agree. I'd assumed something similar myself.'

'When the Pentagon's response came back negative, it occurred to the officer in charge down in Jacksonville to try the state files. Presumably the impostor didn't know about those. To everyone's amazement they got a match.'

'Miami. That was the first time I had my prints taken.'

'It was? That could be interesting,' Jean-Alice put in.

'It could? Why?'

'It suggests a basis of accuracy. Even by itself it makes the evidence stand out, dramatizes the event. It could be good for us.' Jean-Alice made a note.

'This is brilliant! Just brilliant!' The President punched the air exultantly. 'Exactly what I've been praying for. Scientific evidence, exactly the proof that we've been lacking so badly. No one can ignore us now.'

Frankie hugged herself. 'I can't wait to see their faces in the White House when we spring this on them.'

'We'll issue an ultimatum,' the President declared. 'I want you to set up a meeting with Hunter for tonight,' he told Elaine.

'Suppose he won't play?' suggested Jean-Alice.

'Then we tell him we'll go to the Speaker of the House,' the President said confidently. 'Dan Webster will listen to me. He's backed me from the beginning.'

'Why should he now, though?' Jean-Alice interrupted. She saw their puzzled expressions. 'I'm sorry to dampen your hopes, sir, but doesn't it occur to anyone that the Troika has probably known about these prints for over a week?'

There was a sharp silence.

The President frowned at her. 'But this is proof, don't you see, Jean?'

'With respect, sir, this is evidence, not proof. The Troika will claim the computer files were tampered with.

They must believe that's what happened, otherwise they'd have had no choice but to arrest the impostor and they haven't done so.'

Again the silence.

'If they won't believe fingerprints, what will they believe?' Elaine scowled. 'According to you, nothing is any use.'

'I didn't say that. Look, the fingerprints are useful evidence. Properly presented in court and backed by witness testimony, yes, they would count for a lot. The White House can try to explain them away but they would count a heavy stroke in our favor. Juries like fingerprints. But on their own they are not enough. And certainly insufficient to make the Troika hand over the keys to the Oval Office.'

After the burst of elation a gloom settled back over the company. The President ran a hand through his hair. He looked sideways at Jean-Alice and suddenly he chuckled. 'My God, you lawyers.' He shook his head, laughing to himself. 'Always bringing us back to reality. Of course you're right, Jean, we haven't won yet. But,' he grinned round at them all, 'this news gives us a hell of a weapon to do so.'

One of the phones rang again. Elaine answered it. The rest of the room saw her face darken and their spirits, which had been raised by the President's words, fell again. Elaine rang off. Jean-Alice watched her composing her features to break the bad news, whatever it was.

'Well, who was that?' the President demanded impatiently.

Elaine shook her head. 'It was Karen Lipscombe; at least, it was her mother with a message. Karen's aboard Air Force One. I think what she was trying to tell us is that the impostor is taking the First Lady up to Camp David tomorrow for a holiday – alone.'

There was an appalled silence. Everyone grasped the

import at once. The effect on the President was devastating. The color drained from his face. For a second Jean-Alice feared he was about to collapse again. 'No,' he whispered. 'Sweet Jesus, no.'

'He may change his mind. It would depend on his work schedule. We could try to confirm the story,' Elaine suggested helplessly. The President shook his head mutely. Everyone knew it was pointless.

'At least we know the First Lady is safe for now,' Frankie said tactlessly and Jean-Alice saw the President wince. Who could blame him? Jean-Alice thought. Exactly twenty-four hours till his new wife was snatched away to a cabin in the woods with a substitute. How then would they tell her that the man in her bed was not the real president? It didn't bear thinking about.

No one else dared speak. The President closed his eyes for a minute, breathing deeply. Finally he opened them. 'One step forward, another back,' he said. 'It's always the way. No one said this would be easy.' He looked at Jean-Alice. 'You've talked the most sense of all of us today. What do you suggest?'

'Sir,' she said, 'I think we should mount a legal challenge at once. Today. We can draw up a deposition and I can file it for you, but we need to act fast if we're to block the President's plans.'

He nodded grimly. 'I agree. The legal route is our only way out. Right, everyone, let's get to work. The deposition has to be at the Supreme Court before close of business today. Jean, I want you to prepare for a meeting with Miriam Sheen.' He smiled briefly. 'Don't look so worried, she's almost human.'

Jean-Alice tore back to the Bible House in a cab and ran up the entrance steps. To hell with anyone watching the place. They would know she had slipped out somehow, but too bad. It hardly mattered now they were about to take the President's case public before the courts.

Inside her apartment, she grabbed the phone as she struggled out of her clothes and made an appointment for thirty minutes' time with a firm of lawyers downtown who were handling her suit for wrongful dismissal against Dorfingers. She changed, brushed her hair back and ran out to her Blazer, her heart keeping triple time. In her briefcase was a copy of the deposition she and the President had prepared together. This was hard evidence, fingerprint evidence to back the President's claim. The authorities would have to act now, surely?

And if not she was going to force them.

At the lawyers', she strode up to the firm's reception desk. 'It's urgent I call Justice Phelps at the Supreme Court,' she addressed the young black paralegal crisply. 'Can you let me have a phone for five minutes?'

'Certainly, ma'am.' The young man had seen her before. He knew she worked with Dorfingers, a prestige firm. He was unaware she had been fired. 'This way please.' He showed her into a bookcase-lined clients' room. 'Shall I have the switchboard connect you to the Supreme Court?'

'Please.'

He went out, shutting the door carefully. Jean-Alice sat down in one of the easy chairs, putting her briefcase on the table. Thirty seconds later the phone on the table buzzed. She snatched it up.

'Justice Phelps' office.' A woman's voice.

Jean-Alice racked her memory. 'Zeta?'

'Who is this?'

'It's Jean-Alice, you remember me?'

'Jean? Why, yes of course. The Justice was speaking of you only the other day. How are you keeping? You're with Dorfingers, aren't you?'

So Phelps either did not know or had not told of her sacking. That was a relief. 'I'm fine. Zeta, I haven't time to chat right now. I need to speak to His Honor quickly. Can you put me through?'

'I don't know, Jean. He's in conference, the Wichita case.'

Good grief, was that still running? Jean-Alice thought. 'Zeta, please can you interrupt and ask if he'll come to the phone?'

'Oh dear, I'm not sure I can. Is it real important?'

Jean-Alice ground her teeth silently. I wouldn't ask you if it weren't, would I? 'Yes, yes, it is important. Extremely so.'

She snapped the lock of her briefcase as she spoke and ripped out the President's deposition. Opening the door a crack, she beckoned urgently to the paralegal out in the hallway. 'I want you to fax this through to Justice Phelps right now. The number's on the header.' She thrust the document into his hands and shut the door again.

She picked up the phone again, drumming her fingers on the table as she watched the sweep hand move round the dial of the gilt sunburst clock on the wall opposite. How long did it take to walk into the Judge's room next door and ask a simple question? She wished she had brought a cigarette.

Zeta came back on again, 'Oh dear, I'm so sorry, Jean . . .'

Jean-Alice didn't let her finish. 'But His Honor doesn't want to speak with me. Listen, Zeta, there's a fax just gone through to your office. I want you to rip it off the machine, then go right back in there and give it to the Justice. Tell him Commander Casey's name will be all over the newspapers tomorrow. Have you got that? Commander Casey.'

Zeta put down the phone. She sounded like she was in shock. People did not speak to Supreme Court justices like that. Not even to their secretaries.

There was a wait of two or three minutes, which seemed like an eternity, then Phelps' quavering tone came on the line. 'Now understand this, Spellman—'

Jean-Alice cut in. It was her big day for interruptions.

'Listen to me, Judge, and listen good because I don't have a whole lot of time to waste. Zeta has just handed you a fax. I recommend you read it at once. It contains forensic proof of everything I told you the other day. The story is true. The President has been replaced by a look-alike and there is fingerprint evidence in support, together with sworn testimony of close associates.'

'In exactly five minutes from now a messenger will hand-deliver to your office a summary of my arguments. I repeat, I have the real Jack Meade with me. I have close credible witnesses prepared to swear that my client is the true president. I have technical and forensic proofs, including fingerprint evidence, that will stand up in court.'

'I . . . I . . .' Phelps made incoherent noises down the line.

'Justice, I am appealing to you because I earnestly believe this is a matter which needs to be kept from the press. It can and should be decided in closed court.' Jean-Alice paused for breath. She prayed the paralegal wasn't listening at the door. Lowering her voice, she continued, 'But believe me, Justice, if I don't get action, if I have to go national because it's the only way to get results, then I will. We are just hours ahead of press disclosure as I speak. I'll get back to you when you've read my deposition.'

She cut the connection, punched the button for an outside line, redialed and got Frankie waiting for her over in a callbox on Capitol Hill. 'Okay, girl, let's go, go, go!'

The phone rang in Blacker's East Wing office. It was Miriam. 'I've just had Phelps on. Spellman's been in contact with him. She's offering to bring in Casey – Callaghan.'

'Phelps?' Blacker couldn't place the name momentarily.

Miriam made an impatient sound. 'Justice Phelps of

the Supreme Court. The Chief Justice-designate, as it happens. He was the one Spellman went to before, the time your people searched her apartment. Spellman has laid a formal deposition on Phelps, alleging fraudulent imposture on the part of the President. She claims to have witnesses, plural, former close employees of the President ready to swear to her client's identity. Plus – and get this – "incontrovertible fingerprint evidence"; her words. So someone has tipped her off about that screw-up down in Miami. Now she says the impostor is ready to surrender to the authorities in return for safeguards. He'll give himself up to Phelps personally at the Supreme Court and submit his claim to forensic tests.'

'When, today?'

'She's going to call him again to fix a time. In return we are to call off the hunt for him and guarantee the safety of the First Lady. If we don't agree to their terms they'll go public with their evidence. Dammit, Blacker, Spellman's been in contact with the impostor all along. She's made a fool of us. You should have brought her in at the beginning.'

'On what charge? We've been through this, Counselor. Spellman's done nothing illegal. You're the President's lawyer, for Christsakes, you should know that much. Our only chance was to watch her. It still is.'

18

Jean-Alice dialed the White House from the Blazer. She asked to speak with Miriam Sheen, the President's Legal Counsel.

'I'm aware whom you purport to represent.' Ice and steel.

'I've conferred with my client. He is willing to surrender to the custody of the Supreme Court, subject to conditions.'

'And they are?' The Counsel poised her pen.

'One: surrender will take place inside the court building.'

'Accepted. We're as anxious as you not to turn this into a circus.'

'Two: my client will not be treated like a criminal. He will not be physically restrained. No handcuffs, belts or leg irons. He will obey any reasonable directions but your people will not lay hands on him or subject him to intimidation or humiliation.'

'Hmm.' The President's Counsel pinched the bridge of her nose. 'Okay, granted, but we reserve the right to search your client for weapons.'

'There won't be any. My client seeks legal redress not personal vengeance.'

'Three: I will have round the clock access to my client. I will be present at all interviews, searches, interrogations or hearings involving him. I will be permitted to take notes and recordings, bring in or take out of the building such books, documents, files and/or any other equipment I deem necessary for the conduct of my client's case. I may be searched for weapons but that is all. The same will also apply to any assistants I may choose to enlist.'

'Agreed, only providing that the name of any assistant be submitted to us in advance for clearance.'

They dickered to and fro on further terms.

'The accommodation provided will be secure and so far as possible in keeping with my client's dignity.'

'Your client will be held in a basement strong-room,' Miriam said bluntly. 'For the President's security as well as his own safety.'

'That is unacceptable.'

'I'm sorry. That's how it has to be. The Secret Service is adamant. In any case there is no other secure accommodation available.'

'You're forgetting I've worked in the building. There is a two-bedroom guest apartment for visiting jurists on the seventh floor behind the justices' suites. It is secure from both our standpoints. I will overnight in the second room and there is a private sitting room we can use for conferences.'

'Will you be calling the First Lady as a witness?'

'I haven't made a decision, Counselor. It may not be necessary. Will you be calling Mrs Meade yourselves?'

Miriam made a noncommittal response. Each recognized the other's thinking. Whichever side found their case slipping would have no choice but to summon Caro Meade to make a choice between the two. The First Lady was the key. She had been all along.

'Have you considered what the effect on her would be?'

'Better than being married to the wrong man for the rest of her life, Counselor.'

'I'll have to take this under advisement.'

'Please do. And get back to me as soon as possible. We need to know if this agreement is to proceed or not.'

Jean-Alice was playing tough.

*

Blacker spoke to Hunter. 'She'll use the press. She must have found someone to buy her story. She'll want to have them standing by when she brings in Callaghan to the Supreme Court so's we can't touch him.'

'Then we're finished,' the Chief of Staff said matter-of-factly.

'No, we still have time.' Blacker was glancing at the clock, thinking fast. Four o'clock. Spellman had half an hour on them so far, no more. 'Spellman may have seized the initiative temporarily but these things still take time to organize. Spellman will want a camera crew as witnesses. Then she has to pick up Callaghan. She won't want to keep him hanging about exposed where he might be recognized; she'll wait till the last minute. Call Phelps and have him tell Spellman the White House insists on conditions. Counsel for the President can play out negotiations till the Supreme Court closes at 6 p.m. Spellman won't want to schedule the event for evening. She'll want daylight, people around, time to bring in the networks if she has to, time to plan and get it right. She'll wait.'

'I thought you said Callaghan wouldn't risk it, coming out into the open?'

'We can't prove he is Callaghan yet,' Blacker paused. 'It's even possible he may not be,' he said carefully.

'What do you mean? Who else could he be, for Christsakes?'

'We can't be sure. He could be anyone.' Blacker paused. 'Conceivably even the President,' he added.

Hunter's color faded. He moistened his lips before he spoke again. 'Do I read you correctly? I thought you told us this whole business was a fake?'

'The possibility must be faced.' Blacker picked his words carefully. 'We know Callaghan was on the boat the night the President-elect is said to have disappeared. We know there exist two men, each identical with the other. If it is a trick, it's a trick that could have worked.'

The Chief of Staff eyed him grimly.

'Then you have less than twenty-four hours to prove it didn't,' he said ominously.

Agent Thule showed a photograph of Spellman to the head of hotel security at the Chrysler-Lincoln. A former detective named Brady, he had twenty years' service with the Bureau behind him. He studied the snapshot and shook his head. 'No,' he said, 'haven't seen her here. Striking-looking woman, I'd have remembered.'

Thule asked about the brass door in the wall on 16th Street. The detective shrugged. 'We keep that locked. It's a service entrance for city maintenance staff. Before I took charge there used to be trouble with undesirables holing up in the steam pipes, panhandling on the sidewalk. I put a stop to all of that; we'd had complaints from guests. I brought in the city police to root them out, then had the ducts sealed off but they still try to sneak back in. Every so often we mount a clear-out drive.'

Down in the tunnel, Roy froze beneath the stairs. He had just returned below from escorting Elaine out to go to meet Troy and Cal. She had taken a cab to the airport and he had hung around on the sidewalk as he sometimes did, till he caught sight of Brady coming around the corner. He didn't recognize the man with him but he knew a law officer. Lucky he had locked the door after he and Elaine came out. He moved off up the street to the entrance to the hotel's underground garage. The security guard was reading a comic in his glass-fronted box. He did not look up as Roy flitted in under the arch and crouched beside the ramp in the shadow of the metal doorpost. Set into the start of the ramp was a gully to carry off rainwater, which would otherwise run down into the garage below. At this end the gully funneled into an eighteen-inch drain. Lying flat, Roy squeezed himself through legs first and let himself drop.

When he stood up again, he was inside the tunnel once more. Drips from the drain he had entered by trickled away through a grille in the floor. Moving with complete assurance in the dark, Roy crept up the tunnel toward the stairs next to his home. If the men came down the stairs he wanted to be near enough to hear what they were planning and help the others escape if necessary.

Brady and Agent Thule climbed down the ladder and stood up in the echoing chamber below. Brady shone his flashlight around the walls. Agent Thule peered into the dripping tunnel.

'Be careful,' Brady warned. 'These sewer rats can hide up in some dark corner and the first you realize it is when one of them sticks a knife in your back.'

'How far does this run?'

'Anyone's guess. According to the city cops, clear on through to the subway. The authorities installed grilles to keep the transients out of the system but they saw the locks off.'

'Can you gain entry to the hotel from out here?'

No way, Brady told him emphatically. 'This is nothing to do with the hotel proper. The door is an access point for the maintenance authorities responsible for the sidewalk drains and electrical conduits. They're forever losing the damn keys. Now the locks will have to be changed again and all the low-life who've taken up residence smoked out.'

'It's possible Spellman could have escaped down inside the tunnels then?'

The detective made a face. 'I doubt it, this is no place for a woman on her own. More likely she was hoping to find a back way to slip into the hotel without being seen. But like I said you can't get in from here. There used to be a hatch through but we bricked it up.'

The traffic noise up above was making it hard to

distinguish what the men were saying. Roy crept a little closer, pressing himself into a recess between two pipes.

Brady turned around to climb back up the stairs, the flash jinking across the damp stained brickwork. Abruptly Thule caught a movement in the shadows. 'Hey, look over there!' he called sharply, reaching for his gun.

Brady brought the beam back, playing it on the spot. 'I don't see anything.'

'There was someone. I saw a hand.' Thule edged closer, his gun out pointing. He raised his voice: 'Federal agents! Come on out, whoever you are!'

There was no answer. The two men stood still, listening. The boom of traffic resonating from the street above drowned out all smaller sounds. Brady swept his flash across and back. 'There, under the pillar!' Thule snapped. The beam fastened on a patch of shadow beneath a low arch against the far wall. He crouched, arms extended with his Glock pistol in a two-handed grip. 'Come on out, hands on your head.'

There was a scrabbling sound and slowly a figure crawled out, holding its arms empty in front of it. 'That's right, keep the hands up. Okay, now turn around,' Thule ordered as the captive straightened up. Shuffling its feet awkwardly, the figure obeyed. It was a man.

'You got some ID on you, feller?' Thule said with distaste.

Brady let out a snort. 'Godammit, I know him,' he growled. 'This is Roy, one of the types I was telling you about. Used practically to live down here. Hell, I thought we got rid of you last year,' he said angrily.

Roy screwed up his eyes against the light and made an unintelligible sound in response.

'Did you see a woman come down here a little while back?' Thule asked him. 'A white woman, young, around five foot eleven tall.'

The man only stared at him blankly.

'You'll get no sense out of him,' Brady said. 'Okay, you can get the hell on out now,' he told Roy. 'I had a bellyful of you last time. Go on, get up the stairs.' He motioned with the flash.

'Hold it,' Thule interrupted. He was still holding the Glock out, finger on the trigger, pointed at Roy. 'Empty out your pockets. What's that you're carrying? Yes, there. Bring it out, real slow.'

For the first time the man spoke. 'It's a gun.' He had a deep, slow voice.

'Let it drop carefully. Good, now back off. Stop there.' Crouching, Thule reached forward to take the weapon. A .357 magnum, a big gun. He broke it open to extract the shells. Relined to take .22 ammunition. 'You got a license for this, Roy?'

The big man shook his head.

'Where'd you get it?'

'Picked it up in the tunnels. Kept it for protection.'

Thule sniffed the barrel. 'Smells like it's never been fired.' He passed the weapon across to Brady. 'What do you want to do with him?'

'Bring him up to the surface. I'll call V Street and have the police send a car for him. If he goes away for possession of an illegal weapon it'll keep him out of my hair for a while.'

Roy offered no resistance as they led him up the stairs and handed him over to the hotel security guards. Brady thanked Thule for his help. 'Sorry I couldn't be any use to you over the Spellman woman. I'll pass the photo around inside. If she does show up, we'll alert the White House.'

A Metropolitan Police black-and-white took Roy up to Third District Headquarters on V Street, where he was duly charged with possession of an unlicensed firearm. Asked if he wanted a lawyer, he gave the name Jean-Alice Spellman. The arresting officer found her in the book. He phoned the Bible House and left a message on her

389

machine to the effect that a client of hers, one LeRoy Robinson, was in custody and requesting bail.

The call was noted by the Secret Service but by then Suter had gone off duty. Agent Thule had not filed a report on the incident and the agent on watch took no action.

The co-pilot of Marine One, the presidential helicopter, radioed that he had the White House in sight. They would be touching down within approximately three minutes. The Secret Service were already waiting on the South Lawn and the SWAT team was in position on the roof. Blacker was about to go down when the phone rang on Lomax's desk.

'This is Gloria Loosemore of the Loosemore Theatrical Agency. Mr Lomax asked my help locating an actor look-alike able to stand in for the President.'

'Have you anything for us?'

'I put some feelers out on the West Coast with people who knew Jack Meade when he was in the business. They all mentioned the usual bunch of stand-ins and comics doing impersonations. Okay for daytime TV shows and Elks reunions but not what you're looking for. Only one person recalls handling an actor who sounds as though he might fit. A guy with real talent, he says, only unfortunately the poor sap's career never had a chance to develop because in screen tests he showed such a strong resemblance to Meade.'

'I see. And this man was a real look-alike?'

'Apparently. The person who told me said the man kept being turned down for parts on account of the similarity. It was the time when Jack Meade was playing Bruce Delahaye twice weekly on CBS.'

'So where is he now, this man?'

'That's the bad news. Eventually he became disillusioned and left the profession. I'm doing my best to have him traced but so far nothing.'

'Did he have a name?' Blacker asked.

'Yes, that much I did establish. He went under the name of Prescott Callaghan.'

Blacker left his office and walked briskly across underneath the mansion. As he climbed the stairs to the West Wing, his radio informed him the President had arrived in the Oval Office. In the corridor outside, four agents of the Personal Protection Unit scrutinized anyone approaching for indication of a concealed weapon. A fifth sat at a small table in the secretaries' office next door. At the sight of Blacker they stiffened.

'Colonel Coffey just went in,' Mark Peck, the Section Chief, responded to his commander's mute interrogation. Every few minutes it was his job to peer through the spyhole in the white-painted door and check that no assassin had broken in undetected. The precaution was justified; world leaders had died at the hands of close associates or even members of their own families.

Blacker stooped to look through the fish-eye lens. The two men were seated by the fire. Rex was leaning forward, concentrating on whatever it was his commander-in-chief was saying. The Chief of the Military Office certainly seemed to have enhanced his access to the President all of a sudden.

Assuming it was the President in there. As long as he had held this job, Blacker's philosophy had been simple. The protection of the President first and foremost. Nothing else mattered. Until now. Piece after piece of the puzzle was being slotted into place, but whose picture would it finally reveal? Three days ago Blacker had been confident; today he was no longer certain.

'They're biting!' Jean-Alice screamed triumphantly over her mobile from the Blazer as she headed back across town to Roy's. 'I spoke with the President's Counsel and she's agreed to terms. There are a couple of details outstanding and we need to discuss those, but the broad structure is in place.'

'That's terrific news.' The President sounded genuinely excited. 'Now we're making progress. Elaine has gone to meet her journalists off the flight from Florida. She'll check them into a hotel and set up a meeting with me later.'

'Fine, sir. Good idea. Their testimony can only help you.'

'Did you ask about my wife?'

'We touched on her. Miriam Sheen is phoning me back. I'm waiting on her call.'

'Keep me informed. Remember, my wife's . . .' a faint hesitation '. . . my wife's well-being is paramount.'

'I understand, sir.' Jean-Alice cut the connection. The phone rang again almost immediately.

'This is Miriam. There's a problem. Can you come over?'

'To the White House?' Jean-Alice tried to make it sound casual.

'To the East Wing entrance. The guards will be expecting you. Do you need transport?'

'I have my own. I can be with you in ten minutes.'

She swung the Blazer around at the next intersection and headed down onto Pennsylvania Avenue. Thank heavens she had elected to wear her business suit. The Versace would never have done.

Jean-Alice had never been inside the White House before. An agent signed her in at the gate and she was given a temporary badge. She followed him into the paneled entrance hall. Portraits of first ladies adorned the walls. 'This way, please, ma'am,' the agent said, and led her downstairs to the lower basement level.

'Are we going to the West Wing?' she asked as they entered a long, lighted tunnel.

'Yes, ma'am, this passage connects the two wings beneath the mansion.'

So they were smuggling her in the back way. That was sensible. The tunnel was busy with traffic. Men and women, many wearing uniforms, hurried by them in both directions. Messengers trundled carts loaded with mail and documents. At intervals there were uniformed guards, protecting, she supposed, entrances to the mansion. They reached the far side and mounted the stairs. Jean-Alice found her palms sweating with rising excitement. She was about to step into the heart of American government.

The atmosphere inside the West Wing was different, intoxicating. A potent blend of power and urgency wafted through the corridors like musk. Faces recognizable from nightly news bulletins emerged from doorways or passed by exchanging profundities. Senior staffers gossiped importantly on corners. Even the secretaries looked glamorous.

The Counselor's office was not so big as the power suite of a partner in a prestige law firm. It held a settee, two armchairs, a coffee table, an English walnut longcase clock and an inlaid bombe desk by Buhl, both probably on loan from the Smithsonian. Behind the desk a flag stood between two full-length windows overlooking the South Lawn. That view was what made the room so special. Backhouse would have killed for it. The room might not be huge but it was right down the corridor from the President and its occupant had walk-in privileges. Miriam Sheen was just starting out. With reasonable luck she was tipped to finish up as Attorney-General. She could move straight on to senior partner of a top firm on the outside or to a seat on the federal bench, maybe even the Supreme Court.

Miriam was prettier than expected, Jean-Alice thought, taking a seat across the desk. No, prettier was the wrong word, but small boned and fine featured, which counted for nothing beside the snake-like fascination of the trap-taut mouth and the eyes chipped from obsidian glass. The

393

eyes regarded the world with a stare that was totally focused. This woman would never miss a single beat. Never give a second chance.

Absolute dedication to the task in hand. That was how you got to be number three to the President. Jean-Alice was reminded that no more than twelve years separated her from this woman.

'One question, Counselor.'

'Yes?'

'Is this some kind of a stalling ploy, because if so . . .'

Miriam shook her neat head of curls. 'It's no stall,' she enunciated crisply. 'I had full agreement from the Chief of Staff for the procedure you outlined. It's Phelps who's put a brake on the program.'

'I don't consider his objections valid. Under the Constitution Article 3, Section 3, the Supreme Court retains original jurisdiction in controversies to which a public minister shall be a party. I consider that covers this case.'

'Perhaps, the point is debatable. The issue here however is that the court has declined to exercise authority. Phelps cites *US* v. *Richard Nixon* as arising out of a subpoena from the federal district court. Frankly, I think he is covering himself but there isn't time to dispute it. The question is, how do we proceed?'

'Agreed. Do you have any suggestions?'

'Off-hand, no. I can try to work on something. And if you have any proposals I'll listen to them.'

Jean-Alice was thoughtful. She's being smart, trying to put the onus on me to come up with something so as to gain an insight into the weak points of our case, she told herself. Out loud she said, 'One option would be to follow Phelps' advice and retire the case to a lower court.'

Miriam fixed her with a steely look. 'I take it you are prepared to face a criminal charge, then?'

394

Jean-Alice fenced. 'That would depend on the nature of the charge.'

The President's Counsel lowered her gaze a fraction. 'If I understand the thinking behind your original proposal, your intention was to arrive at a speedy resolution to this dispute – and in doing so avoid damaging publicity?'

'As rightful president,' Jean-Alice began. Miriam's chin lifted at this but she did not interrupt. 'As rightful president, my client is conscious of his duty to preserve the prestige of the United States at all times.'

'Which a trial in an inferior court would hardly do.'

'Even if you could frame the necessary charges – no easy matter.'

The two women regarded one another a moment. A phone rang on the desk. Miriam picked it up and listened briefly. 'I'm nearly through. Very good, five minutes,' she said, glancing across at the clock. She replaced the receiver.

Jean-Alice sat up straighter in her chair. She had an instinct she was being set up for something.

Miriam put the tips of her fingers together and pressed hard. Jean-Alice recognized a technique for dispelling tension. She had similar tricks herself.

'Phelps did suggest involving the Electoral Commission,' Miriam volunteered.

'I don't see where a breach of election rules has occurred. No one disputes Jack Meade was fairly elected.'

'It's possible a commission could be specially constituted.'

Jean-Alice frowned, her brain in overdrive. 'Based on the Supreme Court?'

'Phelps would take the chair. Each side would then nominate an additional member. Not necessarily a lawyer but a figure of prominence.'

'Had you anyone in mind?'

'Not yet, no. The idea only just came to me. I'll have to give it some thought.'

'Me too.'

Miriam glanced at the time again. She rose and came round from behind the desk. 'Fine, let's go.'

'Are we done?' Jean-Alice stood.

'Not quite. There's someone I want you to meet with.'

She ushered Jean-Alice out. The corridor was crowded. Miriam moved imperiously through the throng, heels clicking on the marble floor, Jean-Alice in tow. Staffers skipped out of her way, hurling greetings in her wake, 'Hi, Miriam.' 'Afternoon, Counselor.' Miriam ignored them. Her attention zeroed on a hapless special assistant: 'Torval, your proposition is late. Have it on my desk by six.' The young man went red, then white and bolted away. Everyone else avoided her eye.

Jean-Alice drew a few glances of cursory appraisal, no more. Power was the only attraction here. You either had it or you didn't. She caught a whiff of Poison and half-turned to look back. A white-blonde Valkyrie had fallen in behind her like a prison wardress. Before Jean-Alice could speak, a commotion of some sort broke out up ahead and the buzz of talk fell suddenly silent. Miriam was still pressing on toward the front, the Valkyrie pushing Jean-Alice on to follow. The Secret Service were barring the passage outside what must be the door to the Oval Office. Jean-Alice felt a sudden thrill quiver low in her stomach.

Miriam stopped right alongside the guards and turned to face right. Jean-Alice followed suit. She was watching the big mahogany door, waiting for the President to come out. There was a click and the next door along opened suddenly and a man stepped out straight in front of her. It was the President. He had used the secretaries' office exit. They were face to face. Jean-Alice's jaw dropped with an audible grunt. The blood rushed to her head.

Flaming with embarrassment and surprise she gaped dumbly at the familiar figure before her.

'Hi,' he smiled and held out a hand. 'Jack Meade. Who're you?'

Jean-Alice stared, speechless. She had the weird impression he was taller than the others around him with an altogether greater presence. Energy and power seemed to flow outward from him with an almost physical force. But that was ridiculous, she tried to tell herself, it was just that the White House setting made him seem larger than life, the fact of all his minions focusing on him. She tried to concentrate on his appearance but his face seemed to flicker distortedly before her gaze. She was aware of certain features: eyes, teeth, the famous smile, the crinkling lines around the mouth and the wave of the hair, only it was hard to hold them together somehow. Part of her brain urged that this was a critical moment. It was vital she note dissimilarities, points of contrast, but the sheer impact of the presidential presence overwhelmed her senses.

She became aware of the awkward pause, of people tittering behind her. The President was regarding her with tolerant amusement as she struggled for speech.

Miriam Sheen came to her aid. 'This is Jean-Alice Spellman, sir. Ms Spellman is a lawyer. She is currently working very closely with Justice Aaron Phelps.'

'How d'you do, Mr President?' The spell broken, Jean-Alice managed to return the President's handshake.

'And how is my old friend, Justice Phelps? He is a great jurist, an inspiration to freedom lovers everywhere.'

'He's fine, sir . . . and his little dog.' More titters behind. Dear God, what was she saying? It was just babble. Words coming out of her mouth with no meaning, like an idiot. She must get a hold on herself, she must.

She blinked rapidly twice, willing herself to see him whole. And then she did. For the space of three or four seconds she and the current President of the United States eyeballed one another at half a yard's distance.

Sweat broke out on Jean-Alice's hairline and on the palms of her hands. Her heart began to hammer in her chest.

This was everything she had dreaded. And worse.

Back on V Street, Roy had been placed in a holding pen, pending the arrival of his lawyer. The arresting officer entered details of the illicit weapon on the computer linked to the National Crime Information Center located in a brand new thousand-acre facility in a remote Appalachian valley at Clarksburg, West Virginia. NCIC was staffed around the clock by 2,500 personnel. Right-wing anti-government terrorists had already tried to bomb it. Its twenty million records ranged from auto theft and grand larceny, through missing persons to foreign fugitives and Secret Service protection. A sub-system, the Interstate Identification Index, linked to records at state and local levels.

When details of the serial number flashed up on the screen, the officer noticed that the gun had originally been registered to a Jean-Alice Spellman, the same name as that given for the suspect's lawyer. The gun had not been reported stolen. That could be an interesting point to raise with Spellman when she appeared to bail out her client.

NCIC databanks could be accessed by over half a million authorized users from 100,000 terminals across the nation. One of these was located at the Secret Service liaison desk in the FBI's Hoover Building where Spellman's name had been placed on the watch list two days previously. The computers picked out the connection and flagged it for the attention of the FBI special agent in charge.

The agent got on the phone to V Street. The arresting officer was just finishing his shift. He gave the Bureau a bald outline of the case, adding that the suspect had been detained at first instance by security at the Chrysler-Lincoln. The agent knew Brady at the hotel. They had worked out of the Miami field office together for a while. It took only a short while to get from him details of Roy's private den in the tunnel under the hotel. A few minutes' trawl through the Bureau's files threw up the story of Roy's friendship with Jack Meade as a senator. The implications were obvious.

As this was a special investigation, the information was passed at once to the fifth floor. Its arrival coincided with the return of Director Judge Watson from Air Force One and was brought at once to his attention. Immediately the Judge read the report, he used his secure line to the Oval Office to speak to the President. The two men conferred for several minutes. When they were done, the Judge summoned his personal assistant and issued orders.

The special agent who had sparked the excitement was told on no account to pass the information to the Secret Service. He was to leave his desk and proceed immediately to the Chrysler-Lincoln to liaise with Brady. Meanwhile down in the basement, an FBI SWAT team was suiting up to enter the tunnels. Mission orders were to seal off Roy's bolt-hole, detain and arrest anyone in the vicinity regardless of rank or authority. The suspects were believed armed and dangerous; agents were warned to open fire at the first sign of resistance. The raid to be carried out with maximum dispatch and total secrecy with any prisoners brought back to Bureau Headquarters and held in strict security pending instructions from Judge Watson.

The Secret Service possessed its own terminals connected to NCIC. Because Spellman's name was on the watch list, the item was automatically flagged. The agent on duty contacted V Street only to be told the arresting officer was tied up on the phone. The Secret Service database contained nothing on Roy but a check with DC records confirmed that a .22 caliber weapon was registered in the lawyer's name. The agent retried V Street and this time spoke to the officer on the case. The officer was in a hurry to get off. He couldn't see what the fuss was about, he said. So far as they could tell the gun had never been used. There was no reason to doubt the suspect's claim that he had found it dropped through a grating on 17th Street.

The agent then checked in the logs and saw that Spellman had last been spotted on 17th Street in the vicinity of the Chrysler-Lincoln Hotel. The entry had been made by Agent Thule. He tried to reach Thule but he had gone off-duty. Lomax was out of town and Blacker in a meeting with the Chief of Staff. No one at the Bureau would return his calls. All the agent could do was wait.

Dinner at the White House had been scheduled since before the election. Essentially it was a thank-you for the Democratic party's heavy-hitters. The First Lady was concerned to have everything go off right. She sent for Chief Usher Brad Sewall.

'These people are our loyal friends. They've made sacrifices to put my husband in the White House. It means a lot to them to be invited back here and the President wants to be sure they have a good time. Show them we care about them still, that we haven't forgotten them now he's the President.'

Sewall was used to first ladies panicking before a big night. Everything would be taken care of, he assured her.

The afternoon of the dinner was dreary. The rain showed no signs of letting up. Caro Meade grew more and more agitated. She sent for Sewall again.

'How will we stop the carpet being ruined by guests' feet?'

Rubber mats would be out along the North Portico

and outside the Diplomatic Reception Room, Sewall told her. Long black runners to keep the carpets dry. He had ordered extra doormen with umbrellas detailed to the south entrance, extra coat racks and checkers to take care of dripping raincoats. The military would have additional personnel on duty to help with car doors and direct traffic. There was a regular set of plans for storm weather and they would cope.

As the afternoon wore on, the First Lady's behavior grew increasingly frenetic. She was particularly concerned that proper respect be paid to Senator Kennedy.

'The Senator will partner me in to dinner and be seated on my right,' she informed the Chief Usher.

Sewall expressed polite surprise. He had understood the Vice-President would be leading the First Lady in.

'Oh no,' Caro Meade laughed. 'The Senator is head of the family and Leader of the Party. Leyland Jordan knows that. I am the hostess. The senior guest sits on my right and afterward at the dance, the President will lead off with Mrs Kennedy while Ted will partner me.'

Sewall sought clarification from the First Lady's Social Secretary, Sherrilyn Hufford. Mrs Hufford looked perplexed, 'I don't think that is how it is going to be. My understanding is that the President wishes to honor the Vice-President and the Speaker of the House of Representatives. Senator Kennedy may be the grand old man of the party but he wasn't one of Jack's backers. Quite the reverse.'

'You'd better run it by the Oval Office,' said Sewall. 'We're going to need a ruling on this. The First Lady has the ball and she's running with it.'

'She must have flipped,' Sherrilyn muttered, running her eyes down the acceptances list. 'Just as I thought, Senator Kennedy isn't even coming. He wrote he would be attending a family ceremony up in Boston.'

Sewall went to see Dorothy Fine. 'Looks like someone forgot to tell Mrs Meade.'

'I did tell her.' Dorothy made a gesture of exasperation. 'The Senator was most gracious. He wrote her a personal letter apologizing. I showed it her last week but she doesn't seem to have taken it in. She's gotten this fixation in her head that the dinner is being held especially so the family can honor her.'

Sewall left her and Sherrilyn to sort the matter out between them. He went back to the state floor where the butlers were setting out the vermeil flatware in the State Dining Room. The antique ivory color for the wood paneling had been chosen to complement the gold curtains. Silver tureens of carnations were being readied in the flower shop to be centered on the E-shaped table just before eight. Between the Red Room and the Blue Room a bar had been set up. The President and his wife would mingle with their guests while cocktails were served before dinner. Afterward the carpet would be removed from the East Room and there would be dancing on the polished oak floor with coffee and liqueurs in the Red and Green Rooms for guests wanting to sit out. Sewall had ambivalent feelings about the dancing: seven presidents had lain in state in the East Room, including Abraham Lincoln. The last one was John F. Kennedy.

Upstairs in the family quarters, Grace Tute, the housekeeper, was organizing the First Lady's wardrobe with the help of Gina, the First Lady's personal maid. The dresses and gowns were stored in protective bags in closets on the third floor. Plastic tags indicated designer, color and coordinating accessories, purchase date and occasions worn. A selection of gowns were laid out in the rose and white Queen's Bedroom for her to choose from.

The First Lady herself had sought refuge in the exercise room next her office, converted from the former bedroom of Tricia Nixon and Caroline Kennedy. She emerged to make her selection for the evening, then ordered hot milk to be brought to her in the third-floor solarium, her current favorite retreat. Gina and Grace carried the unwanted garment bags back up to the closets. Returning from one trip, Gina reported that her mistress was prowling about upstairs, 'checking out the guest rooms'. Maybe, the staff speculated, she was planning to invite friends over.

Shortly afterward however, the First Lady came hurrying down again. She went straight to her bedroom and announced she was on no account to be disturbed. All staff were to vacate the residence while she rested.

Sewall was attending to the requirements of the orchestra when his pager sounded three bleeps, the coded signal from the Secret Service warning that the President had returned from the Oval Office and was entering the mansion. The staff exchanged glances. Intuition and long experience in the comings and goings of the First Family warned that something was wrong. Sewall moved toward the door in time to see the President hurry through the Cross Hall to the elevator accompanied by Admiral Thomas and his military aide and two nurses.

Moments later Dorothy Fine came running up from the East Wing also making for the elevator to the second floor.

A buzz of excited comment broke out in the room behind. Sewall turned back.

'Get on with your work. You haven't time to chatter,' he rebuked them curtly. An abashed silence fell.

Everyone knew that some disaster had taken place. Minutes later the news was confirmed. Sewall was summoned to the telephone. It was the President.

'Will you come upstairs, please. There's been an accident. The First Lady has had a fall.'

'I'm fine, truly I am. It was just a stupid fall. I landed on the settee and I wasn't hurt at all. I'm not even bruised.'

Caro Meade was sitting up in bed in a dressing gown. Her face was dead white with a hectic flush to the cheeks. The President was sitting next to her. Admiral Thomas was standing by. He looked grave.

'I leaned out too far and tipped over the banister. The mat must have slipped. I wasn't injured. I wish I hadn't told anyone. I wouldn't have if I'd known you were going to make such a fuss.'

Her manner put Sewall in mind of a child that has fallen off its horse and revels in the attention.

Jack Meade turned to him. 'Obviously my wife won't be attending dinner tonight. It'll mean rearranging—'

Caro flashed him an angry frown. 'Don't be ridiculous! Of course I'm coming. I shall be perfectly okay when I've had a rest. I'm fine now, just tired. What sort of fool do you think it will make me look if I stay away?'

The President looked despairingly at Admiral Thomas. The Admiral shrugged. 'There's no sign of injury that I can find. No loss of consciousness. Mrs Meade has been extremely lucky. Even so there is a risk of shock. I strongly advise that she keeps to her bed this evening at least.'

'Precisely,' agreed the President. 'You feel fine now but the stress of playing hostess could be dangerous. You're only just out of hospital, remember.'

'How can I forget when you keep reminding me?' The First Lady sighed. 'If everyone in this place insists on treating me like an invalid I shall soon turn into one.' She threw back the covers and swung her legs to the floor. 'I'm getting up to start changing,' she said defiantly. 'And if you gentlemen choose to stay and watch, that's fine by me.'

'Dorothy Fine says she fell. She was leaning over the rail of the grand staircase trying to see into the hall below and lost her balance and pitched over. It's a fifteen-foot drop; she'd have snapped her neck if the cleaners hadn't

404

pushed a settee back against the rear wall just there. It broke her fall and all she suffered was some bruising and shock.'

'If it was a fall.'

'Dorothy Fine swears it was. "A stupid accident", were her exact words.'

'How does she know? Was the woman there when it happened?'

'No, but she's talked with the First Lady. And she swears that's all there was to it. She's worried people will start saying Caro Meade threw herself off the stairs deliberately.'

Blacker and Sewall met upstairs. Dorothy Fine joined them in the second-floor center hall by the elevator. Together they went to view the spot where the accident had occurred.

'So the sequence of events goes like this,' Blacker said. 'It's 5 p.m., late afternoon, the First Lady has been resting in her bedroom. Right?'

'She takes a nap most afternoons,' Dorothy explained. 'Medical orders. She was working hard all day on preparations for tonight's dinner.'

Blacker continued. 'She wakes. For some reason she thinks she hears voices, correct?'

Dorothy nodded.

'She puts on a wrap. She had undressed earlier?'

'Mrs Meade liked to shower on rising. And she is positive about the voices.'

'Voices on the stairs. How can she hear them from where she is?'

It was the First Lady's habit to sleep with the communicating door between her bedroom and the President's open a crack, Dorothy Fine explained. This afternoon the door from the President's room into the west hall was also ajar. 'I assume the maids must have left it open.'

405

More likely the valets laying out the President's dinner suit, Sewall suggested.

'So Mrs Meade hears voices then, and goes out to investigate. The hall was in semi-dark?'

It was, Dorothy and the Chief Usher agreed. Standing instructions to the house staff were to stay away from the second floor until summoned by the First Lady's ring. The guards likewise. Believing the voices were coming from below, the First Lady went out onto the landing and leaned over the banister.

Blacker tested the rail and leaned over to examine the hall below. He straightened up and surveyed the First Lady's secretary. 'Dorothy, how near are you in height to Mrs Meade?'

'Near enough. The First Lady is exactly five foot eight inches, I'm five eight and a half.'

'Fine. You mind helping us carry out a test?'

'So long as you don't want me to throw myself over the edge.'

'Not yet. I want you to lean out as the First Lady might have done and tell us what you can see.'

'Here is okay? Shall I take my shoes off?'

'Please. Now imagine you hear a noise. What d'you do?'

'Lean over to see.' Dorothy put her hands on the banister rail. 'Like this?'

'How far round can you see?'

'Not a lot. The wall is in the way. I'd have to lean further over to catch anything on the next landing down.'

Blacker thought a minute. 'Okay, let's say you are determined to learn who it is down below. What would you do then?'

Dorothy studied the stairs. 'If I were desperate enough I might try climbing over the rail and leaning out to see round the wall that way.'

'Care to give it a whirl for us?'

Dorothy raised herself on tiptoe to put the edge of one knee on top of the rail. 'Not easy in this skirt.'

'The First Lady was dressed how, in a nightgown?'

'Sleeping pajamas. So no problem for her.'

'Okay, that's all. You can put your shoes back on.'

They moved back into the west hall. Blacker thanked Dorothy for her help. He and Sewall returned down the stairs.

'You think that was how she came to fall?' the Chief Usher said when they were out of earshot.

'It's possible. The rail was too high for Dorothy to overbalance and tip down and Mrs Meade is not so tall as her. So the only way the accident could have happened is if she deliberately climbed over the rail and leaned out to see someone on the second landing down.'

The elevator door opened at the state floor. Karen Lipscombe stood waiting to enter. She looked startled to see them. 'I heard about the First Lady's fall. Is she hurt?' she said to Blacker.

He was obscurely pleased at the quick concern in her voice. 'A few bruises, a bit shaken up seems to be all. She had a lucky escape.'

'Admiral Thomas has seen her,' Sewall added. 'He says she'll be fine once she's over the shock. She's resting now.'

'Oh, I guess I won't go up then. I wouldn't want to disturb her.' She made as if to return, then abruptly swung back. Beneath her helmet her face was strained and anxious. 'You will look out for her, won't you?' she pleaded suddenly to Blacker. 'She's . . . all alone up there, you see.' Her voice trailed off. She bit her lip.

Blacker's heart went out to her suddenly. He wondered what she knew. 'We'll take care of her. The First Lady won't come to any harm, I promise you.'

He watched her disappear back in the direction of the West Wing, then turned to Sewall again.

'So an accident?' he said quietly.

The Chief Usher flicked him a sideways glance. 'If you like to call it that?' he answered.

Blacker raised an eyebrow in query.

Sewall glanced around. The nearest guards were over by the main doors. 'If it was an accident she took good care to be sure of a soft landing. Maybe even positioned the settee herself,' he said.

'Why would she want to do that?'

The Chief Usher shrugged. 'A cry for help perhaps? Or maybe she needed an excuse to get out of something she didn't want to do – like flying up to Camp David for instance?'

19

Jean-Alice drove back to her apartment. She felt drained emotionally as well as physically. She wanted to change out of her lawyer's clothes, take a hot shower and unwind before reporting to the President. Images of her meeting with the impostor still raced through her mind. How was it possible for two people to be so alike? When the President finally came face to face with his rival, how would he react? Or Caro Meade if she had to make the choice?

The resemblance was so uncannily exact, it was scary just to think about. Small wonder the First Lady even was confused. On the positive side it made the President's situation that much more believable. The simple fact of a double's existence meant the possibility of a substitution had to be accepted.

With an effort she brought her thoughts back to the present. The deposition was filed. The legal process set in motion. The impostor would have to be told. What would his reaction be? Had he instructed Miriam Sheen to spin out the proceedings, play for time while he exercised conjugal rights over the First Lady? Suppose Caro Meade could be brought to support his cause against the rightful president? What would that do to the real Jack Meade? Who would believe him then?

There was no point in speculating. The vital thing was to press on, give the impostor no time to regroup. She reached the Bible House and ran up the steps. Inside the apartment, the message light was glowing on her telephone. She pressed the Replay button, listening while she unbuttoned her clothes. The first message was from her cousin Rachel in Hawaii, then came the second: 'This is Detective Grover, Metropolitan Police, V Street for Ms Spellman . . .'

The FBI team was led by a special agent in charge with a gray face and heavy beard shadow. Pierce, his name was, the Judge's special assistant and hatchet man. Most of his career had been spent in the Intelligence Division, hunting spies.

Pierce had been briefed personally by the Judge. 'The Republic is in danger,' the old man told him. 'We have to nip this business in the bud before it spreads and infects the nation.' A bunch of them, part malcontents, part fools, but with a traitor and fanatic at their head, he said. 'He has them convinced he's the rightful Jack Meade and the man in the Oval Office is an impostor.' Surgery accounted for it mainly, and acting skill. Once the story got out the damage to the nation's image would be incalculable.

Pierce got the picture. After the briefing he went downstairs to the Hoover Building's basement armory. From an evidence vault he selected a couple of handguns and an assault rifle seized on previous operations and all guaranteed untraceable. Throw guns, to be tossed down beside corpses to provide convincing proof of resistance.

The FBI drove to the hotel in unmarked vehicles. Pierce went inside. 'FBI.' He brandished his badge in the under-manager's face. 'Where's Brady?'

The manager blenched. 'I'm sorry, Mr Brady is not on the premises.' There had been an incident, he apologized. A prominent sports personality staying in the hotel had got into a fight with his girlfriend. She required hospital-ization. Brady had driven her to a private clinic.

Pierce ground his teeth. Liaison was breaking down already. People needed their priorities straightening out. 'Who else knows the layout of the tunnels?'

The manager looked amazed. No one in the hotel did.

They left that to the city police. It was their job. Pierce swore and hurried back outside to the waiting vehicles. They would have to search out the hiding place themselves. He ordered his men to equip themselves with flashlights and follow him.

'Where's Roy got to?' asked the President. 'I haven't seen him for a while.'

The phone rang before anyone could answer. Frankie picked it up.

'Get out!' Jean-Alice screamed frantically into the phone. 'The police have arrested Roy. He's given them my name. The place is going to be raided any minute. Get out of there, now!'

Pierce's men poked cautiously among the pipes and corners of the filth-encrusted entrance chamber. Finding nothing they cautiously entered the tunnel. All at once, the agent in the lead halted and held up a hand. Everyone stood still, listening.

'That was a phone.'

'The place must be around here somewhere. Find it,' Pierce snarled.

There was no time to snatch up the phones or equipment. They saw the flashlight beams reaching toward them as they tumbled out of the hatch and dove for darkness and safety. Frankie was first, then the President, Humphrey last. Ducking under a drain, they fled into the tunnels.

Jean-Alice tore down to 17th Street in the Blazer. One look was sufficient. The entire block including the Chrysler-Lincoln was sealed off, police and FBI everywhere. No way of telling if the President and the others had managed to escape in time. What the hell were the authorities playing at? Possessed by fury, she dialed Miriam.

'I thought we had an agreement, goddammit?'

'We do. What's your problem?'

'Your dumb gorillas are trying to arrest my client.' Jean-Alice gave the Counselor a crisp description of the scene.

'I know nothing about this, believe me. I'll try and find out what's going on.'

Jean-Alice drove around the block, hoping to spot one or other of her friends, but without success. She tried to call Elaine on her mobile but the phone wasn't responding. Finally Miriam rang back. She sounded worried.

'I spoke with the Justice Department. The raid was authorized by the President direct through Judge Watson.'

Jean-Alice felt her stomach knot. 'You're saying he knows – about the challenge to his identity?'

'He must. How, we don't know. I did manage to establish they haven't detained your client. Not yet anyway. They're still hunting for him in the tunnels.'

Lomax flew back to Washington.

He had slept on the plane. Lomax could sleep anywhere. It was a knack. In the White House, Mavis, Blacker's secretary, said he was in with the President. She handed him a stack of faxes and memos. Lomax took them off to his desk and put them aside to read later. He called up Cincinnati PD and asked for the homicide division. He spoke to a Detective Slaney.

'Marcia Williams, single, white, female, murdered 1998. Recently arrived from Albuquerque. Ring any bells?'

'Williams . . . Williams . . . nope, can't say as it does.' The Detective sounded harassed. Damn federals, he was probably thinking. 'Have to check the files and call you back,' he said wearily.

Lomax gave him one of the black numbers for the Secret Service switchboard which ran straight through to the office so callers didn't know they were phoning the White House. He was going through his paperwork when Slaney rang back.

'Williams, Marcia, right? Age thirty-seven. I got her now. Happened out Hamilton way. Not my case but my partner, Garcia, he worked on it. He's here now. I'm handing you over.'

Sure he recalled the case, Detective Garcia told Lomax. Poor woman been in the city less than a week. Strangled with her own tights. 'She was nude and there were indications of a break-in. We figured she panicked a burglar and got whacked.'

'No suggestion there might have been another motive?'

Garcia pondered. 'I dunno,' he said at length. 'The building had been refurbished recently. Security was of a good standard, I remember. It wasn't that ritzy a place but safe, know what I mean? Which was why Williams took it, apparently.'

Go on, Lomax told him.

'Well, the theory was she had left the alarm off and forgot to double-lock. The door was fitted with a police bar. I didn't buy that. I mean a lone woman in a strange town, worried about security, yet she goes to bed leaving the door unbolted. Doesn't make sense.'

'You saying she might have let her attacker in?'

'It crossed our minds. Lonely woman, visits a singles bar, picks up a stranger, they go back to her room. Turns out he's a weirdo likes to choke his women. Only he went too far. Wouldn't be the first time.'

'You're saying you recognized a pattern?'

'Not necessarily in this case. Only that it could have been.'

'Was the victim violated?'

'Not according to the autopsy.'

'You say the motive might have been theft. Was there much missing?'

'The place had been turned over. Cash and jewelry

413

gone. Not that she had a lot. Could've been our freak with the taste for ligatures covering his tracks. Maybe it's happened before with him an' he figures she's got no more use for the dough. Your guess as good as mine. All her personal stuff gone too.'

'Personal stuff?'

'Letters, diary, addresses, ID. Like as if he was worried she might have something on him. Could be this wasn't the first time for the two of them.'

'Your people charge anyone in connection?'

They pulled in a couple of probables, Garcia told him. No joy. Either they had alibis or there was nothing to tie them to the woman. 'Is this important? I can dig out the file if so.'

'It's important.'

Lomax reported to Blacker. The Secret Service Chief heard him out in silence. 'So our man's a killer now?' he grunted when Lomax was done.

Lomax hunched his shoulders. 'Callaghan disguised his appearance to infiltrate the Meade campaign. His physical resemblance to the Candidate would've caused comment else. So he uses techniques he learned in acting school to make himself look different. Which is fine till he gets a phone call or a letter from Marcia Williams saying she's staying in Cincinnati and hopes to get over to Indianapolis to see him real soon.'

'Upon receipt of which he flies down and strangles her.'

'Or drives. Indianapolis–Cincinnati is barely a hundred miles. That's what worried him. There was a strong likelihood of Williams making good her threat. The way I read it, he waited till he figured she had gone to bed and buzzed her doorbell. The building had a video key system. So Williams throws on a robe, I'm guessing again, and unbolts the door. Once inside the bastard waits till her back is turned and strangles the poor bitch.'

'No frills, brutal but effective,' Blacker muttered.

'And cunning. Notice how he gives the cops a double motive. First he makes it look as if the victim was killed by a frustrated lover. Then he ransacks the room for anything that might lead to him and takes anything of value, suggesting burglary.'

'Cincinnati PD never questioned him about the killing?'

'His name never even came up.'

Lomax sprawled back in the chair. 'Williams was a panic reaction. No, not panic, this guy doesn't panic. He's too cool for that, but unpremeditated. It wasn't part of his longer plan. The woman threatened to expose him. She didn't mean to but he couldn't afford to take the risk, so he silenced her. He would have done the same to anyone else who got in the way. It could be he attempted to dispose of the rest of his family for similar reasons. That fire in their trailer is too much of a coincidence. They were luckier, that's all.'

When Karen Lipscombe returned to her office in the West Wing, Rex Coffey was waiting for her. 'Hi,' he greeted her. 'How was your trip today?'

She looked up, the automatic focus of the Elvis lens whirring. 'Hi, Rex. Yes, it was fine, thank you.' Her tone was clipped, businesslike. 'You've come to see the President?'

'I have some information he asked for. He said you'd slip me in between appointments.'

She nodded. The President had spoken to her on his return. 'Colonel Coffey can see me any time without appointment. Just send him in. The Chief of Staff doesn't need to know either.' And no sooner was the President returned than here was Rex with a smirk on his face, sliding into the Oval Office behind the backs of the other staff. What were the two of them up to?

'He'll be a few minutes yet. Another finance bill meeting.'

'I'll wait. And meantime—' Rex laid a small package on the desk – 'For you, compliments of the Military Office.'

'Oh, why thank you. What is it?'

'Little gifts we make to senior staffers such as yourself who fly with the President. Sort of glad-to-have-you-aboard present. Go ahead, open it.'

Karen tore open the bubblewrap envelope. It contained two small red leather boxes. She opened one. 'Wow!' Inside was a gold fashion pin bearing the Air Force One presidential insignia. 'How beautiful. Is this really for me?'

'Of course. There's a second one for your mother or sister or friend, whatever.'

Karen opened the other box and stared again. 'What did I do to deserve this?'

'Lots of little things that make the job of the Military Office easier.' Rex admired the softly gleaming blonde hair as the President's secretary bent forward to examine the jewelry again. He could suggest a date now but no, that might be chancing his luck.

Karen shut the boxes up carefully and placed them back in the envelope. 'Rex, you're very kind, but I can't accept these. It wouldn't look right.'

Before Rex could press her, the phone on her desk buzzed. 'That's the signal for you to go in.'

'What you want me to do with these?'

'Pick them up again on your way out. I'm sorry, Rex, it was sweet of you but they're not my style.'

So the cyber-secretary wasn't bribable. That was something to know anyway.

When the door to the Oval Office had shut behind Rex, Karen sat still a moment, her brain working furiously. The two men were engaged in plotting, she was certain. Rex must have found out something. As head of the Military Office he was perfectly placed to pick up gossip and spy on people. The White House switchboard was under his control, the operators drawn from the Signal Corps, likewise the chauffeurs of the limousines, the social aides who mingled with guests at official functions, the mess staff, the crews of the planes and helicopters. There was precious little Rex Coffey didn't get to hear about. He made it his business to find things out. Karen doubted that Rex would actually ever be a traitor. More likely it was the impostor using Rex's ambition to make him do his dirty work for him.

Camp David was part of Rex's empire. The presidential retreat in the Maryland hills was guarded and maintained by marines. The compound was considered so secure only the President's doctor and his military aide, the bagman, accompanied him. And his wife.

Once Caro Meade had accepted the impostor into her bed would she ever be persuaded he was not her true husband? Suppose by then she was carrying his child? Karen prayed her message had gotten through to Elaine.

And now there was the First Lady's accident. If that was what it had been. Suppose Caro Meade did suspect after all? That would be terrible for her. Imagine the terror, the agonies of doubt she would be experiencing. Who would believe her? With everyone in the President's entourage apparently deceived, whom could she turn to without being branded crazy? Caro would think she was going mad. She would make frantic attempts to convince herself it was a delusion, trying to force herself to act a normal wife, alternating with mood swings of despair and violent rejection. All of which would account for her outbursts of irrational behavior.

Karen cast her mind back to last night and the conversation she had overheard. The First Lady had expressed reluctance to make the trip to Camp David. Suppose her nervousness was due not to concern for her health but to fear of the President? Was that the explanation behind the suspiciously timed accident this evening? Was it a frantic attempt by a terrified First Lady to stave off the moment when she must submit herself physically to the alien figure impersonating her true husband?

What if it were true? And what if the impostor had guessed? If so, Caro Meade's life wouldn't be worth a candle.

How to find out? If only there was some way to eavesdrop on what he and Rex were saying in there.

She considered the tapes. The taping system was controlled from Karen's desk. It could be switched to cover the Oval Office or the study or both together. The moment she thought of it, Karen dismissed the idea. Activating the taping system illuminated a warning light on the presidential desk panel and simultaneously triggered an audible alarm. There was no way to listen in without the President being aware.

The door from the Oval Office opened, startling her.

'Karen.'

'Yes, Mr President.' It took her a conscious effort to use the title now.

'Colonel Coffey is taking me down to show me over the shelter beneath the basement. I suppose we'll be around fifteen minutes.'

'Yes, sir. Your next appointment is at 5.50: Mr Nikolis.'

He glanced at his wrist-watch, 'Phone his office, have Barney delay five minutes.'

'Just as you say, Mr President.'

The two filed out, picking up the President's Secret Service escort in the passage. Was there a look of sly triumph on Rex's face as he passed Karen's desk? She felt a sense of dull defeat. The trip to the bomb shelter was unscheduled. Another outlying part of Rex's empire. A place of absolute privacy. And yet she must contrive to find out what they were planning.

She rang Barney Nikolis' secretary. 'Oh dear, Mr Nikolis is anxious to run the text of the press statement on the reappointment of Judge Watson past the President. It's due for release to the networks at six.'

Desperation suddenly lent Karen cunning. 'Send the statement across to me and I'll take it in to the President for you.'

Five minutes later, the document in her hand, she was making her way down to the lower basement. Two agents from the Presidential Protection detail on guard outside the elevator made her wait while they phoned down. Karen crossed her fingers, praying the President wouldn't tell her to wait.

'He says to bring it along down.' The guard replaced the phone and pressed the switch to open the door. He stepped into the stainless steel car with her. There was only one button on the control panel. 'If you're at the bottom it comes up, if you're at the surface it goes down,' the agent explained. 'Hold on to your stomach, ma'am.'

With a lurch the floor dropped away. Karen felt as if she were on a fairground monster ride. The fall seemed to go on and on. She braced herself against the side. 'How deep do we go?' she gasped.

'Six hundred and sixty-two feet. Er, that's classified, incidentally.'

'Is that enough to be safe from a bomb?' She tried to grin.

'Depends on the bomb, I guess. This was constructed during the Cold War. It would be used when there wasn't time to get the President out to the helicopter.'

Karen prayed it would never need to be used in earnest.

The car was slowing. The weight returned to their bodies. Karen had to clutch the handrail again to prevent herself falling. With fewer visual clues than other people she was vulnerable to disorientation and dizziness.

*

The shelter was much larger than Karen had expected. Two levels of spartan accommodation. Vault-like corridors lined with double tiers of bunks. Washing and cooking facilities. Cold stores, food stores, even a morgue. Walls and ceilings painted in muted pastels designed to prevent you going mad during the six months or however long it took for the radiation to fade or the rescue teams to dig you out. Karen thought she'd rather die, frankly.

'And this, Mr President, is the recording studio from where you would address the nation in time of emergency.'

She located them as Rex was explaining how the President would speak to the American people from a soundproofed room off the studio. 'If we can go in here for a moment, sir. There are items relating to national security that cannot be divulged to third parties.'

He ushered the President inside and closed the door. Karen was left alone in the passage. The two guards had remained one floor up by the elevator. Save for the wheeze of the air conditioners and de-humidifiers the complex was silent as a tomb. She wandered back into the studio. Its dubbers and mixers had an eerily dated look as if they had never been used. Presumably they hadn't. Banks of blank TV monitors stared from one wall. She reached out to touch a screen and felt a thin film of dust on her fingers. A window in the wall opposite overlooked the room where Rex and the President were seated across a standard issue table. She could detect facial movements and Rex seemed to have brought along a cassette tape recorder but not a sound emerged from beyond the glass.

She took a chair at the producer's station under the monitors. Her back was to the window but she could see their reflection in the dead screens in front of her. She was reminded of her last job before she came to the White House. A world away, it seemed now. With no conscious intention her fingers found the audio control knob and clicked it on. There was a crackle as the speaker circuits warmed up. Guiltily she flicked the sound down again. As she did so she caught Rex's voice: 'They definitely appear to be negotiating with the impostor. This is a tape of Hunter and Sheen together yesterday.'

Frantically Karen spun the control, cutting the sound. In the empty silence she could hear her own heart hammering. Rex knew about the other Jack Meade, the impostor, he called him. He was warning the President. Evidently he had tapes of others in the administration who were involved. Karen felt a blank terror shot through with despair rise suffocatingly about her. With trembling fingers she switched the control on again, upping the volume one click at a time till the whisper of sound from the next room crept back over the speaker, so faint she had to strain to catch it.

Rex's voice again: 'Elaine is a part of it. This guy, he's gotten himself a lawyer, some woman named Spellman, and the pair of them have been in contact with Hunter and the others. The Troika has the Secret Service trying to run him down but no luck so far.'

The President's voice, tight but controlled: 'I spoke with the Judge again. The Bureau think they may have a lead. Do you have names of anyone else in the plot?'

'No, sir. It seems the conspirators also tried to get at your wife through Lipscombe but Blacker's people intercepted the message.'

'Karen? Karen met with Elaine two nights ago. Some story to do with an apartment for rent.'

Karen bit her lip at the sound of her own name. She clicked the knob up another stop. Damn, she wished now she'd accepted Rex's bribe.

In the reflections above she saw the President shaking his head, then the breathy whisper over the speaker: 'I can't understand what they hope to achieve by this.'

'It may not be deliberate treason as such, Mr President.

421

The Troika could believe they are acting in your best interests. It's possible they hope by cooperating to lure this impostor into giving himself up. I guess it will take a formal inquiry to get at the truth.'

'I can't believe Karen would betray me.'

'No, sir, but she could be manipulated.'

There was another pause, a longer one. The President seemed to be chewing his nail, thinking, then Karen tensed as she heard the words . . . 'and their next step will be to attack me through my wife'.

A sound of footsteps out in the corridor jerked Karen around: one of the guards coming down to see what was going on. She deadened the sound and, rising, slipped out from the studio. The guard caught sight of her. 'Hi, we gonna be much longer down here, you know, ma'am?'

The door to the broadcasting room opened at that moment. The President emerged, Rex following. The President glanced about sharply. 'What's the matter? Is something wrong?'

Karen felt a flush rising up her throat into her cheeks. She caught her breath, praying it wasn't noticeable, and tried to speak normally. 'No, Mr President, nothing. The guards were wondering how long you were going to be, that's all.'

The President's expression was unreadable. 'Is that the press release?' He took the document from her hand and skimmed it. 'This could have waited,' he sniffed. 'We're all through,' he said to the guards. 'Let's go back up.' He touched Karen on the arm, motioning her to precede him.

Karen had to steel herself to stop from flinching.

Frankie and Jack were nearing exhaustion. Humph was having to help them along, half carrying them. Ever since leaving Roy's they had been fleeing desperately down the tunnels without a break. Twice the FBI had almost had them trapped in a dead end before one or other of them

had found a hole to scramble through. Then the flashlights had lit on their trail once more and off they went
again at a stumbling run in the dark with only the
occasional glimmer from the street lamps above to guide
their way.

They came to a junction, hesitated and turned right.
The tunnel sloped steeply downward. They had gone
only a few steps when lights blazed ahead suddenly. 'FBI!
Halt or we shoot!' All three dived for the sides, trying to
squirm in among the rats' nest of pipes and cables.
'Back,' gasped Humph. 'Crawl back up. And keep low.'

'Halt!' the voice shouted again and this time there was
a stab of flame and a deafening sound. A burst of shots
blasted down the tunnel, stunning and terrifying them all.
Humph let out a yelp which was drowned by an ominous
hiss of escaping steam from a punctured pipe.

'Humph!' Frankie screamed. Peering in the gloom,
Jack could make out his valet lying on his back, an arm
cocked against the wall. Steam and water played across
his motionless form. Under cover of the vapor and spray,
the President crawled to Humph's side and tried to feel
him for injuries. To his surprise and relief, the big man
groaned and rolled over. As he did so there was another
burst of firing and bullets pinged and whined off the
pipes overhead.

'Humph, where does it hurt?'

'My hand, I think. It feels numb. I hit my head when I
fell.'

'Can you crawl as far as the corner?'

With grunts of pain Humph began heaving himself
along the floor. The lights were closer now. Jack pulled
Humph down beside him as more shots rang out. This
wasn't arrest, this was a killing. A burst smashed into the
pipework behind them. The shots were so closely spaced
they virtually shredded the iron lining of a four-foot-
diameter drain. There was a piercing sound like a
locomotive whistle followed by a violent crack. The

ancient pipe split in two, spewing water into the tunnel in a thousand gallon a minute torrent. There were yells from down the slope as the attackers found themselves engulfed in a waist-deep torrent and the lights were extinguished.

Levering himself to his feet, Jack grabbed Humph by the arm and staggered away up the tunnel. A figure clutched at them. 'Mr President, it's me, Frankie. What happened?'

'Humph's been hit. I'm not sure how badly. The tunnel is blocked. We're safe for the minute at least,' he gasped out.

Frankie took Humph's other shoulder, easing the burden. 'This way. I've found a ladder. I think it lets us out.'

It was a quarter after seven before Karen Lipscombe finished work. The President was upstairs with the First Lady getting ready for the dinner. The other secretaries had already departed. Instead of returning through the colonnade to the mansion, she turned left and went out through the basement exit of the West Wing onto West Executive Avenue, the strip of concrete that was now a government parking lot. Tonight it was jammed with catering and service trucks for the reception. Ducking her head against the steady drizzle, Karen hurried up the ramp to the Old Executive Office Building and pushed through the swing doors.

This ornate gray granite pile built in the style of the Second Empire resembled nothing so much as a tired wedding cake. It housed the overspill of the Executive Office of the President, the offices of the Vice-President and the National Security Council in 550 sumptuously appointed rooms. It also possessed the best automats and vending machines in town. White House workaholics could get cash, pay bills, and send flowers to the spouse

424

they no longer had time to see or grab a baloney sandwich, all without leaving the precincts.

Karen descended to the basement. She found a Riggs National Bank machine and drew out $200. In practice she had little real need of cash these days. Living expenses in the White House were billed monthly, and in her case paid anyway by the President: 'No, Karen, I won't hear of it. It's my fault for engaging you at such short notice.' She never had time to get out and shop.

The cash was an excuse to come over.

In the basement were other staffers attending to similar household functions. The building, like the West Wing, operated twenty-four hours a day, seven days a week. They glanced in Karen's direction with idle curiosity and several nodded politely. The President's cyber-secretary was already part of administration legend. It was not possible for her to pass unrecognized.

From the top of the basement steps, Rex Coffey watched the progress of the blonde head. From the cash machine, he saw her move on to an automat supplying gifts by Lord and Taylor. For a fee purchasers could have their order delivered by Federal Express with a message included.

He wandered down to join her. 'Hi,' he said.

She jerked round guiltily. 'Who? Oh, it's you, Colonel.'

'Rex, please. I'm sorry if I startled you.'

'You did a little. I was concentrating on this machine. They're so darn complicated.'

'Aren't they though?' he agreed. 'But useful if you're in a hurry.'

'That they are.' She gave a strained laugh. 'I must run, Rex. Good-night.'

She swung away, tripping up the stairs. Rex watched her go, admiring the fearless way she moved. It couldn't be easy for her, even with that seeing-eye apparatus.

Karen was halfway back to the West Wing when she realized she had forgotten to collect her receipt. She turned and hurried back. When she reached the machine there was no sign of it or of Rex either, and her heart did a flip.

Rex Coffey chose his staff for the Military Office with care. Certain qualities were needed to work in the White House, he explained to applicants. Such as integrity and discretion. Above all, loyalty. Absolute unquestioning loyalty. To Rex Coffey.

Back in his East Wing office, he gave Karen's receipt to his secretary. 'Call them up,' he told her. 'Explain you're the purchaser and you need to confirm the wording of the message. I want to know who the recipient is.'

His secretary didn't raise an eyebrow. She was well versed in the ways of White House politics. It took her only a minute to get through to Lord and Taylor. Affecting to be Karen speaking from the West Wing, she spoke to the dispatcher. 'I need to double-check on the wording of the message,' she explained. 'I have the receipt number.'

'No problem, ma'am. I can call it up on the screen for you. Yes, here we are. Karen Lipscombe, White House/OEOB: two pounds assorted Belgian chocolates; premium rate – delivery guaranteed within two hours; recipient – Mrs Elaine Manken, Apartment 2b, 67 Tracy Place, Kalorama Heights, Washington DC.'

'And the message?'

'"Urgent we speak. Washington Monument 2200." signed K.'

The secretary covered the phone while she repeated it to Rex. Rex thought a moment, then scribbled rapidly on a scrap of paper.

'Hello?' the secretary said. 'Yes, I'd like to change that message, please. New text reads as follows: "Spoke with CM. Must see husband. Will be at Washington Monument 2200." Signature as before.'

426

Somehow between them Frankie and the President got Humph up the ladder. They propped him against a wall. He was losing blood and the pain was getting to him. He didn't make a sound though. 'Leave me here,' he said between gritted teeth. 'I can look after myself. You get out of here, Mr President. Save yourselves.'

The President wasn't listening. He was busy binding Humph's injured hand with handkerchiefs and a necktie. 'See if you can find a cab,' he told Frankie tersely. 'We need to get him to a hospital.'

Lomax was back at his desk when the phone rang. It was Detective Garcia from Cincinnati again. 'Hi there, Agent Lomax?'

'What can I do for you?'

'The Williams thing, you working on a case with the same MO?'

'We ain't exactly sure, yet,' Lomax hedged. 'Could be. I was waiting for the papers to come through before I got back to you.'

'Right, well it's just that you maybe can put more resources on it than ever we could. For instance there were some prints we obtained from Williams' room that we never got a match for.'

'You found fingerprints?' Lomax almost yelped.

'One only,' Garcia told him. 'Male thumb, never identified, on the doorframe of the bedroom. The building was newly decorated so it could've belonged to some guy working there. No match but still I figure, it's worth a shot. Guy could be out there at it still. I'm wiring the file through. Lemme know how you do.'

Lomax put the phone down thoughtfully. He went through to tell Blacker.

'What d'we do if it's him, the President?'

'Calm down,' Blacker told him. 'We've been through that already.'

'I know, but that was only a patient escaped from a hospital. This is different. The prints this Garcia is sending over are of a killer. What do we do if they match the guy down the hall?'

'We are Secret Service. Our job is to protect the President.' Blacker spoke patiently and quietly. 'So far as we are concerned still the real Jack Meade was sworn in on Inauguration Day and is occupying the Oval Office. Anything else is treason. We go ahead and have those prints matched up against the ones that were taken in Jacksonville. With luck we'll have the proof we need that Ms Spellman's client is a murderer. I look forward to seeing her face when I break the news to her.'

'And if not?'

'If not is another story. We'll face that only if and when we have to.'

Lomax went back to his room.

Troy and Cal's flight had been on time. Elaine checked them into the airport Holiday Inn. It had been decided they would be more secure out there than if she brought them into the city.

Swearing them both to secrecy, she gave them a succinct account of the crisis which had engulfed the Presidency. Tomorrow, she explained, a hearing was scheduled at the Supreme Court when Jack Meade would present his case against the impostor. The two of them would be present as sole press representatives. Beyond that nothing was guaranteed.

They parted and she caught a bus back down to 17th Street. It was late and she had promised to relieve Frankie. They were taking turns to do duty with the President so he was never left alone. To her dismay there was a heavy police presence outside the Chrysler-Lincoln with fire trucks and ambulances standing by. Motorcycle cops were waving motorists on past a line of FBI vehicles.

Elaine stopped one of them. 'Excuse me, officer, would you mind telling me what's going on?'

'Drugs raid, lady. The bad guys took to the subways but the FBI smoked them out. Nothing to see here.'

Elaine moved dazedly up the street, wondering what to do. At the next intersection a silver blue Blazer with peeling paint flashed its lights urgently at her and there was Spellman hanging out the window, waving to her frantically.

The first two cabs Frankie stopped took one look at Humph's condition and sped off. As the third drew up, she and the President bundled the wounded man inside before the driver had time to realize and yelled at him to take them to DC General.

'Better you stay outside, sir,' Frankie whispered at the Emergencies entrance. 'I can handle Humph.' She fetched an orderly and helped the valet onto a trolley. The President waited in the cab, anxiety gnawing at him. He stiffened as a squad car cruised up and stopped. Two uniformed cops got out and began questioning people at the entrance. He leaned forward and tapped the glass. 'Where to?' the driver grunted.

'Kalorama Heights, Tracy Place.' Elaine's apartment. It was the only address he could think of.

Blacker had worked out a plan. When the prints were received from Cincinnati, he and Lomax would personally hand carry them over to Bureau Headquarters for comparison. The comparison prints he had had made up were in the names John and James Doe. Only Blacker knew which were the President's and which those taken from Commander Casey.

They drove across in Blacker's car. On 10th Street North they turned into the Hoover Building main entrance underpass and showed their passes to the guards on duty at the steel barrier designed to deter suicide bombers driving laundry vans packed with C-4. Security was heavy. In the underground parking level an agent toting a machine gun backed them into a bay.

As they walked toward the elevators, Lomax nudged his arm. 'Rex Coffey's motor,' he muttered in an undertone, indicating with his eyes a GM sedan standing by itself.

Blacker merely grunted. He had too much on his mind to worry what the Head of the White House Military Office was doing at Bureau Headquarters this late on a Friday night.

A plainclothes agent from Secret Service liaison met them in the lobby. He handed Blacker an electronic pass to work the exit gate and conducted them to the fingerprint identification division. The internal layout of Bureau Headquarters mirrored the impenetrable mind of its founder. A maze of corridors and dead-end junctions. Blacker was always glad of a guide. They handed over the prints to the duty SAC.

'A comparison job, they said on the phone?'

'Uh-huh. We want you to tell us if the print lifted at the crime scene by Cincinnati PD is a match for either of these two we have on file.'

'Shouldn't be difficult.'

The SAC's cubicle overlooked an open plan office with twenty or more operators seated at terminals. He called one in and handed him the prints. 'Put these up on screen for matching, Joe. Do it right away.'

'Sure,' the clerk nodded.

He was gone twenty minutes. 'Sorry it took a while. Both the comparison sets are pretty similar.'

'They are?' Blacker flicked an eyebrow.

'Yes, sir. Ten ulnar loops on both. I guess that's why you have a problem of identification. Certain patterns carry greater inherent individuality than others. If you have ten ulnar loops on your fingers, from a criminal viewpoint it's an advantage because statistically it's the most common pattern. Identification puts extra demands on computers and manpower.'

Blacker and Lomax exchanged glances. Experts, they were all alike.

'You got a result for us though?' Lomax tried to keep the impatience out of his voice.

'Oh sure, no difficulty. It took longer but there's no doubt. No doubt at all.' He handed Blacker back the files with a smile. 'John's your man, okay. Sixteen-point match.'

Not a muscle twitched in Blacker's expression. 'Thanks,' he told the clerk.

Lomax waited till they had returned to the basement and were sitting in the car. 'Goddammit,' he burst out, 'ain't you going to let me in on it?'

Blacker started up the motor and swung the car out and up the ramp. Not until he had negotiated the electronic gate and they were out in the street did he answer.

'John Doe is the President.' His voice as he spoke was utterly flat and devoid of emotion.

'Jesus,' Lomax whispered chokingly. 'Didn't I say it would be? Jesus, Jesus,' he repeated as if he couldn't believe his own words. 'What do we do now?' he asked.

'We keep our mouths shut while I figure out is what,' Blacker snarled at him.

Back up in the Hoover Building, the SAC on the fingerprint division left his cubicle and went down to Joe the operator's desk.

'You made back-ups?' he asked.

'Of those Treasury files? Sure, Chief.' Joe was a civilian, a support employee not a badged agent, but his loyalty to the Bureau was total. Fifteen years working in Headquarters and he needed no telling how the FBI covered ass. His fingers rattled over the keypad, calling up the data Blacker had given him. Orange on blue the prints scrolled up the screen.

'Okay,' the SAC ordered. 'Now run a match with NCIC. Let's see who Treasury's John Doe really is. And give it priority.'

'You're the boss.' The keys rattled again.

There was a wait of several minutes. Two hundred and fifty miles away circuits were being cleared on the database at Clarksburg to permit the priority search. Then abruptly the screen went blank. A message appeared: INFORMATION RESTRICTED TO ASSISTANT-DIRECTOR LEVEL.

The SAC puzzled for a moment. Then he picked up the phone and dialed the fifth floor.

Blacker got out the blueprints of the yacht again. It was necessary to be absolutely certain.

Anecdotal evidence placed Prescott Callaghan on the yacht Friday night and again on the Saturday. Friday's log, as reconstructed, recorded him as visiting the boat in the late evening and departing again shortly after midnight. Apparently this was a normal pattern. It was the President-elect's practice to send for his speechwriter last thing at night to run through the latest version of the inaugural address with him.

For the following day, Saturday, the logs as reconstructed did not show Callaghan boarding or leaving the ship. But that would not have been too difficult to arrange. The passes issued by the naval base were the swipe card variety with a photograph of the bearer and magnetic strip with ID details. It would be simple for Callaghan to borrow or steal someone else's card. Especially late in the evening when many people would be enjoying themselves in the bars. No one at the ship's side would question a photograph if the card itself was valid.

Aboard the yacht, Callaghan took the ladder down to

the main cabin level. As one of the President-elect's close entourage he would be a familiar face to the Secret Service agents on duty in the corridor; very likely he greeted them by name. Instead of going directly to the President-elect's suite door he stopped off to speak with Elaine Manken on some pretext or other, entering the suite via the connecting door from her office.

Blacker pressed the intercom to summon Lomax.

'What's this?' Lomax frowned at the papers laid out on Blacker's desk.

'A plan of the yacht. Main cabin deck looking aft. No need to bother about the other sections for the moment. This is the owner's suite in the stern. Here's the door out to the corridor. Agents were stationed here and here. And this was Manken's office.'

'The secretary who got fired. I get the set-up. Now what?'

'Okay, let's try and see how it might have worked. Put ourselves in the shoes of the impostor. It's evening of Saturday around 11.30 p.m. He's just arrived on board, most probably on a pass borrowed or lifted from another staffer.'

'How come he isn't picked up?'

'Navy is responsible for perimeter security. Which means the guards on the dock and at the yacht's entryport don't know any of the staffers by sight. He signs aboard and descends the ladder to the main accommodation deck here.' Blacker tapped the plan with a pencil. 'At the foot of the ladder he meets his first service check. Anyone entering the stern corridor section has to identify himself and submit to a weapons search.'

'He is still using the phoney ID?'

'I don't think so. Not at this point. As one of the President-elect's close entourage his face would be familiar to the agents on duty. He wouldn't be asked for ID. They know he arrives every night at this time. They don't need to check his credentials. They frisk him, josh a minute, pass him on down toward the man on the door. Only instead of going directly to the presidential suite door he stops off to speak with Elaine Manken on some pretext or other.'

Again why? Lomax wanted to know.

'I'm not sure and to be honest I've no proof yet he did so but I've a strong hunch. If he went straight into the suite the Secret Service would be expecting him to come out sooner or later and he couldn't afford that. Paying a call on Elaine would seem entirely natural, staffers were in and out her office all the time. From there he could slip into the suite the back way and no one the wiser. The other advantage of stopping by Elaine is it gives him a chance to check if the President is alone or expecting anyone else. I surmise, but I can't be certain, that he came prepared to strike on several consecutive nights waiting until conditions were right.'

'Makes sense,' Lomax agreed, studying the plan and scratching his chin.

'So entering the suite via the connecting door from Elaine's office, Callaghan finds the President alone. He waits till his back is turned and whacks him on the head . . .'

'What with? He's been searched for weapons, remember.'

'Some item in the suite he's marked out before. A lamp, an ashtray, anything so long as it's heavy. Alternatively he might use an ether pad. He could bring that through sealed in a glassine pouch.'

'Wait a minute. Didn't the report from the hospital in Jacksonville mention the patient showing traces of phenobarbitone?'

'You're right. I forgot that.'

'Callaghan could easily have slipped some into the President's coffee, say, without him noticing.'

'I agree, but the patient had a cracked skull when he

434

was found so it looks like he opted for brute force. Either way the President-elect is unconscious and he drags the body into the bedroom.'

'Suppose Elaine comes in while this is happening?'

'This is only taking seconds. In the bedroom he tapes his victim up and gags him, then strips off his own clothes and disguises. What would that involve? The padded vest comes off with the clothes. Cheek inserts, denture plate, contact lenses pop straight out. How long does that take? At a guess I'd say no more than two minutes tops. Even bet he knows down to the second because he'll have done practice runs, timing himself. This is not a guy who leaves things to chance. All that's left is to pull on Jack Meade's robe and wash off the skin tint and hair dye, shave the mustache. He stuffs his clothes out of sight and heads for the bathroom.'

Shaving off a mustache would take more than a few seconds, Lomax observed. 'And suppose he cut himself in his hurry. More likely he'd do that ashore before he left. Glue on a fake. It's dark, precious little chance of it being spotted.'

'It's possible. We may never know. Personally I think he would have waited. Once he's in the bathroom he can afford to take his time. Anyone knocks on the door of the bedroom, he sings out in Jack's voice to wait a minute. Who's going to disobey that? I guess also he would pick up the phone and tell Elaine to hold all further callers.'

'And then he tips the body out the scuttle.'

'Not immediately. It's still late evening, remember. There are people about up on deck. He needs to wait till it's quiet. And he has another worry. The yacht is still some way inside the estuary. If he dumps his victim right away, chances are the corpse will wash back up some-where inside the waters of the base. Callaghan wouldn't want to risk that. Only he didn't know about the inshore current.'

Lomax tapped his finger on the cabin that had served

as the President's bedroom. 'It's plausible. The only part I don't buy is the timing. It's taking too big a risk keeping the body around. He couldn't count on keeping Meade quiet that long. Suppose someone came in and Meade woke up and made a noise? I reckon he'd get rid of the evidence right away.'

'And risk the body coming up under the boat? I doubt it. He probably administered a knockout shot to keep Meade under. Phenobarbitone is easy to obtain, no problem to smuggle a syringe past the guards. Put the body in the toilet. Who's going to look in there that time of night?'

Lomax proposed a final difficulty. 'His clothes, Callaghan's. I don't mean those he was wearing, he'd have tipped them over the side, but he'd been living on the base three days. What happened to his kit? He wouldn't have brought it on board with him and there'd have been questions asked if he'd left it behind wherever he was sleeping.'

Blacker told him about the dumpster out back of the kitchens. 'I checked with the base again. Callaghan had a single room in the BOQ. They were in short supply and he pulled rank to be on his own so it must have been important to him. The way I see it he packed up his stuff every night before setting off for the yacht and hid it in the dumpster, retrieving it later if events failed to work out. He leaves his pass out in the room with a note saying he's quit and gone home. So long and thanks everybody for a great time.'

'Why hasn't he signed out at the gate like everyone else?'

'Who cares? Security are content so long as they've gotten their pass back. They only worry about people coming onto the base. They can mark him down: Checked Out/Pass Surrendered. In the morning the dumpster is removed taking his kit with it.'

436

'Neat.'

'Like I said, he's no fool. He plans. Question is, what do we do now?'

20

The black sedan with pennant fluttering drew up outside the West Wing. Three passengers in back, driver and escort up front. The escort was out and opening the rear door before the vehicle stopped rolling. Judge Watson climbed heavily out followed by two of his senior agents. Blacker was waiting to receive them inside the entrance as protocol demanded. The two agents solemnly surrendered their weapons.

'Director.'

'Blacker.'

In single file, the three followed the Secret Service Chief down to the Oval Office. The guards in the passage stood aside at their approach. Blacker tapped on the door and opened the handle. 'The Director of the FBI, Mr President,' he announced and stood aside to allow the others in.

'Judge,' he heard the President say, 'good of you to come.'

Blacker shut the door after them and came away.

Karen Lipscombe was scared. The presence of Judge Watson next door in the Oval Office filled her with dread. Her fingers trembled as she typed out the presidential finding delegating authority for the investigation to the FBI. She took it through for signing, trying to avoid the Judge's cold gaze as she crossed the room. His stare was like a basilisk. Just looking at him she felt poisoned.

She went back to her desk and uttered a small prayer. Events were slipping beyond her control. She picked up the phone and dialed the emergency number Elaine had given her.

The phone rang and rang.

With a sardonic smile Pierce handed Blacker an envelope. Inside was a single sheet of paper headed with the President's seal and bearing Jack Meade's familiar black ink scrawl. Typed by Karen Lipscombe, it directed Blacker to turn over to the FBI all '– files, papers, transcripts and records in the matter of the person fraudulently posing as Jack MacKenzie Meade'.

The Bureau had taken over. The Secret Service was off the case.

Blacker pressed the intercom to call in Lomax. When he appeared Blacker passed him the note without comment.

Lomax read it. He raised his eyebrows and shrugged. He opened the door to his room. 'All in there,' he said with a wave.

Pierce stepped through and ran his eyes over the littered desk. 'I'll send my people along to pick this up.' He smiled mirthlessly back at the two Secret Service men. 'No offense, boys, but this is more our line than yours.'

'Just what I been telling myself,' said Lomax. 'Best of luck,' he added jauntily.

Pierce scowled. 'We don't need luck at the Bureau.'

'Screw up on this and you will,' Lomax told him.

'So that's the verdict,' Hunter said.

The Troika was in shock. This was what they had dreaded. The sum of all their fears. The worst case. The man in the White House was an impostor.

'There might be another explanation.'

'Such as?' said Miriam.

'We've only just had this data in,' Blacker reminded her. 'There hasn't been time to evaluate it properly.'

'You mean the prints might be forged or something?' said the General hopefully.

Or something, Blacker said. Forgery was a non-starter. Enforcement technology was simply too good. 'Used to be they could transpose prints on tape. Now experts can pick 'em out by the absence of moisture between the ridges.'

'So to recap,' the President's Counselor summed up. 'We have fingerprint evidence to prove the President has been replaced by an impostor. Right?' She looked at Blacker.

'That's about the size of it, yes,' he admitted. 'The print from the Williams girl's apartment matches those taken from the President at his Pentagon induction three weeks ago.'

'And?' queried Vorspuy. They had listened out the account once. He had yet to be convinced.

'And the President's schedule for that date confirms he could not have committed the murder. He was across in California.'

'I remember, we flew together from Indianapolis on the campaign plane,' Hunter agreed. 'He wanted time to prepare for a TV debate.'

'So it's not possible for him to have left the print?' the General persisted.

'Oh for God's sake,' interrupted Miriam. 'The real president couldn't have left that print. The print was left therefore by someone else. Someone who has since switched roles with the President. And the person with the obvious motive is Callaghan. He couldn't risk her turning up in Indianapolis and blowing his disguise.'

'I don't believe it,' the General whispered, but his tone said, *Oh God, it's true then. It has to be.*

'And now the President knows we know,' Miriam said flatly. They still referred to him by his title. Force of habit. 'He has the Judge's men hunting Spellman's client even as we speak.'

'He knows and this meeting is technically illegal.' Blacker said. 'It's the FBI's baby now.'

'If he's not the real president, his orders have no force.'

'His orders have force while they're obeyed,' Hunter told her. 'That's why he's brought in the FBI. Rex Coffey he has in his pocket already. All our phone calls go through the military switchboard. It's even betting he has Judge Watson's goons bugging our cars and offices.'

That was truer than they guessed, Blacker thought.

'So what do we do now?' said Miriam crisply.

Hunter took charge. 'That's what we have to decide.' He cast a glance at Blacker. 'Doug, we're grateful for what you've done. This is our problem now. When we reach a decision we'll let you know.'

Blacker shrugged. He was happy to be out of it. He rose to go. 'There is one thing.' He paused. 'If the rightful president is after all Miss Spellman's client, then it is the duty of the Secret Service to protect him. Which means my agents could have to face down the FBI. I need a clear mandate before that happens.'

They all looked at him. They understood what he was saying. Now they faced a shooting war.

'The President of the United States – and the First Lady!' The two-man color guard advanced, the marine band crashed into the opening notes of 'Hail to the Chief' and the procession led off into the dining room. Watching from an alcove, Sewall perceived a shadow of irritation flick across the President's expression. What was that about? he wondered, trying to think of any lapse in protocol. Twenty years in the White House had taught him the value of preparing his defense in advance.

Caro Meade looked ethereal, a cameo in a pale, figure-hugging gown, her dark hair caught up and entwined with glistening pearls, her skin translucent almost, eyes glowing in the haunted face. There had been gasps of spontaneous applause when she entered the hall down the grand staircase. Sewall hoped she would have strength to last out the evening.

Leyland Jordan gave his arm to Joan Webster, wife of the House Speaker. His face was inscrutable as they followed in the wake of the First Couple. Half the people in the room, he knew, would be saying to themselves, 'Look at old Leyland there, walking behind the Actor like a puppy dog. Wonder how he enjoys that, ha, ha?' Let the bastards sneer. His turn would come and he would have his revenge on them.

'*What time did this happen?*'

'*Was she hurt at all?*'

'*Is the First Lady hospitalized? When will she be released?*'

The press center was buzzing as Trish Beale made her announcement. Hacks were jumping, waving recorders, scribbling notes on publicity handouts, expense sheets, anything they could find to write on. '*Cut the crap, will you,*' the CNN man screamed down his phone to Atlanta. '*We need to go live on this, now!*'

Trish Beale struggled to make herself heard: '. . . slipped on the Grand Staircase outside the private apartment early this evening, sustaining mild bruising and shock. The First Lady was examined immediately by Admiral Thomas, in charge of the President's medical detail. No injuries were detected. Mrs Meade has subsequently been able to attend a dinner-dance honoring the Vice-President and the Speaker of the House of Representatives . . . received no treatment. Hospitalization completely unnecessary . . . a minor fall . . .'

Pandemonium broke out in the hall as a barrage of questions was hurled at the podium, drowning out her words.

Jean-Alice and Elaine returned to Jean-Alice's apartment. They couldn't think what to do but wait for news. Jean-

Alice tried calling Miriam again but the President's Counsel was still in her meeting and would not take a message. She called the Justice Department, who denied all knowledge of any arrests. She wondered whether to go and see Roy, try to obtain bail for him, but the President's safety was more urgent. In desperation she rang Phelps at his home. 'My client had agreed to give himself up. For the authorities to seek to detain him now is a total breach of faith.'

'I fail to see how I can help,' the old man responded querulously. 'The agreement provides for your client to surrender himself at the Supreme Court building. Until then he remains your responsibility.'

Then Frankie rang in from the hospital to Elaine's mobile.

Humph was in surgery; his injury was not life-threatening. The bad news was, the President had vanished.

'We'll keep searching the streets,' Elaine told her. 'You stay where you are in case he returns.'

Jean-Alice rang off. She switched on the TV and caught the tail end of the First Lady's accident. She stared at the screen in dismay. Good God, how would Jack Meade react when he learned of this?

The White House switchboard was Army owned, its thousand-plus operatives drawn from the Signal Corps. With the FBI on their side, Rex had no fears of anyone listening in to his messages. He contacted the Pentagon and, invoking the President's authority, spoke to the adjutant to the Deputy Chief of Staff of the Army. The adjutant was a bird colonel. Like Rex he hoped to make general officer one day. It did occur to him he should perhaps check upstairs but he knew better than to cross the powerful Head of the White House Military Office, who had the President's ear.

Minutes later at Fort Lesley J. McNair down at Anacostia, a grumbling platoon of light infantry were

443

suiting up under the urgent snarls of their NCOs. Woodland pattern battledress, kevlar helmets. As they shouldered their M-16 rifles and formed up, the sergeants passed among them distributing ammunition.

'What's it about, Sarge?' one man asked.

'Ask no questions, you don't get told no lies.' The grizzled Staff Sergeant smacked two loaded mags into his hand. Outside in the square, troop-carrying Hummers were gunning their engines, filling the air with diesel smoke. The platoon scrambled aboard, forty men fully equipped and armed. The Lieutenant climbed in beside the driver of the lead vehicle. 'Let's go.'

'Where to, sir?'

'DC. The White House.' The officer's response was curt. Keep your goddam mouth shut, it said.

The driver shrugged to himself. What the hell, it was none of his business. He was paid to drive was all. Let other people do the worrying. He swung the Hummer up toward the gates.

Elaine's building was a converted townhouse. The President told the cab to wait while he tried her apartment. In the hallway, the doorman frowned at his filthy and disheveled appearance. Clearly he noticed no resemblance to the Jack Meade in the White House. Ms Manken was out, he said curtly. The President said he would leave a message.

The doorman was watching a newscast on a portable TV. The President caught his wife's name. 'What was that? What were they saying about an accident to the First Lady?'

'Oh that,' sniffed the doorman, 'that was nothing.' Before he could elaborate, a delivery boy entered. 'Package for Manken.'

'Okay, give it here.' The doorman signed the receipt. He checked the envelope on the package. 'Huh, White House.'

The President was still staring at the screen, listening to Trish Beale's press statement. At the words he swung round. 'Let me see that.' He snatched the envelope off the package. The address of the sender was clearly given together with Karen Lipscombe's name.

'Hey, what you think you're doing? Give that here!' the doorman shouted as the President ripped out the card.

The Troika sat in silence. They had been debating Blacker's thunderclap for an hour without result. The same ground over and over. What do we do next? How do we explain this to the American people? How do we face the President himself when he gets here?

'He'll understand the position,' the General said. 'Surely?'

Hunter sniffed. 'I wouldn't.'

Miriam agreed. 'We have to offer him our resignations.'

The sudden shrill of a phone interrupted. The Chief of Staff picked it up. 'For you, General,' he said irritably, pushing it across.

The National Security Adviser took the receiver. 'Yes?' He listened a moment. His expression glazed. 'When did this happen? I see. Very well, I'll be along directly.'

He replaced the phone and looked round the table. 'That was the Pentagon,' he said in an abnormally quiet voice. 'The President has just ordered that Defcon status be raised to Level 3.'

'Let me get this straight,' Hunter said. 'The football system, it doesn't go via the Pentagon?'

The committee was still in session, anxiety written large on every face.

The General shook his head. 'No, the satchel carried by the bagman contains codes and equipment to enable the Commander-in-Chief to communicate directly with

445

the missile control officers in the silos and submarines.'
He saw their dismayed looks, and elaborated. 'The
system is predicated on an attack warning transmitted to
the President by NORAD. The timescale is so short, you
see. Say our warning systems detect a missile launch by a
hostile submarine 200 miles off Newport News. The
flight time could be less than three minutes. It would take
too long to route launch authority through the Pentagon
for confirmation. A sneak attack would knock out our
command and control before a retaliatory strike could be
mounted. So the presidential order is transmitted direct
to the men in the bunkers.'

'He says "fire!" and that's all there is to it?' Hunter
sounded aghast.

'It's not as simple as that. There is a code sequence. He
has to select a target option . . .'

The Chief of Staff brushed aside his objections, 'But
stripped of fancy language – any time the President
wanted . . . he could call over the bagman, punch in a
code and goodbye Moscow? Or Tripoli. Or Beijing?'

'The President has first to validate his identity. He
carries a laminated ID card . . .' The General was
sounding flustered.

'But that's only to confirm to the silos the source is
genuine, right? That the order proceeds from the
Commander-in-Chief, yes?'

The General nodded, swallowing. 'The procedure is
automatic. The President confirms his authority with the
card and transmits the selected code. If the two sequences
match up with the prearranged instructions to the missile
commanders, then they will initiate launch.'

The Counselor intervened. Her face was pale but her
voice was incisive as always. 'Presumably this all takes a
little time. Didn't I read somewhere that missiles are no
longer pre-targeted? Or is that automatic too?' she added
sarcastically.

'That's correct, as far as it goes. Missiles are no longer

pre-targeted. However one of the effects of raising our Defcon posture to Level 3 is that elements of the strategic deterrent are readied for immediate use. That is to say a range of targeting data is pre-fed into their guidance computers. The code issued by the President instructs them which coordinates to select.'

'Mutually assured destruction,' Admiral Thomas shuddered. 'Madness.'

'In the absence of a workable anti-ballistic defense system it's the only viable deterrent. A balance of terror. Neither side has anything to gain from Armageddon. So far it hasn't failed us.'

'Raising the level to 3, what does that entail specifically?' Hunter wanted to know.

'An increase in the numbers of Trident fleet ballistic missile boats at sea. Patrols may be extended, missile silos closed up, guidance systems pre-targeted. Reserve unit personnel warned for stand-by status. Increased security at military installations. Extension of combat air patrols and anti-submarine measures . . .'

'These I assume would be detected by any opponents, the Russians or Chinese say?'

'Almost immediately. Just as we would with them. The extra guards at overseas military bases, increased air and naval activity, these are well-known signs that everyone watches for. In fact in the past they have been used by both sides to transmit signals of displeasure in times of confrontation.'

'And Moscow will respond similarly?'

The General nodded. 'Yes, they will bring their strategic missile forces to the same condition of readiness the moment their satellite reconnaissance detects changes in our defense posture. They have very likely done so already.'

'So the system is self-fulfilling,' observed the Counselor. 'We raise, they raise.'

'That is so. But then it works the other way too. We

lower our Defcon, they follow suit. And even Defcon 1 only puts the armed forces on a war footing; that doesn't automatically mean the shooting starts. Even if fighting were to break out, it wouldn't necessarily involve an exchange of nuclear weapons. In fact everyone would do their utmost to avoid it.'

'Until one of us makes a false call,' observed the Admiral quietly.

There was dead silence in the room. No one round the table dared to voice what was foremost in every mind. That a short while ago a man who might or might not be the legitimate president, who might alternatively be an impostor, even a murderer, had put himself in a position to unleash thermonuclear war, literally at the touch of a button. It was a scenario too scary to contemplate.

Now it had to be faced.

Elaine phoned Kalorama to ask the doorman on duty if there were any callers for her.

Had there just? the doorman told her disgustedly. Only some crazy off the street who had torn up a package addressed to her from the White House and run off. It took Elaine some time to get the story straight. The President had taken the card with him and the guard could not remember the name of the sender except that it came from the White House.

'Has to be Karen Lipscombe,' Elaine said to Jean-Alice, frantically dialing Directory for the number of the delivery company. It took several minutes to get through to the dispatcher who had taken the order. 'I'm sorry, the card got torn off,' Elaine explained. 'I'm Ms Manken, can you tell me who the donor was and if there was any message?'

How to locate and protect the real president before Judge Watson's men got to him first? That was the problem facing Blacker. The big FBI search operation downtown had apparently drawn a blank. Wherever Jack Meade was, he was somehow still evading capture. His luck couldn't be guaranteed to hold out, though.

Who would he go to in trouble? Blacker needed a lead and fast. There was the Spellman woman. But she seemed to know nothing and he had agents watching her anyway.

Then there was Karen Lipscombe. She was the person Jack Meade had first approached. She had been looking worried the last couple of days. Suppose she had found out about the impostor herself? Would she know Jack's whereabouts? It was a long shot but worth a try.

He pressed a button on his interphone. Where was the President's secretary as of this moment? The answer came back within seconds. Karen Lipscombe had departed the White House through the OEOB in the past five minutes. On foot.

SAC Pierce had brought half a dozen agents into the East Wing with him on pretext of carrying out Lomax's files. Lomax raised his eyes at their number but the Bureau always did like to do things mob-handed in his experience. If they had the men to spare it wasn't his business. He showed them where the files where. Pierce said they needed cartons and dispatched a man to fetch some.

'Where's Blacker?' he asked.

'He went out.'

'Where to?'

'That's his business.'

Pierce's man returned with two more agents. Between them they wheeled a metal filing cabinet on a trolley. They set it down and grinned. Lomax left them to it and went to check on the operations room. As he left he heard Pierce calling in Blacker's absence to Bureau Headquarters.

*

449

Lomax went downstairs in the East Wing. The ground floor was taken up with the staffs of the First Lady and the Military Office. There was no sign of Rex. By the steps to the basement four men from the Signal Corps were endeavoring to manipulate an enormous wardrobe safe out into the passage leading to the Secret Service armory. Unable to get past, Lomax retraced his steps and went out through the colonnade into the ground floor of the mansion proper. He was wondering what had become of Blacker. It wasn't like him to desert his post for long periods.

The public rooms of the mansion seemed uneasily quiet. He decided to go down to the basement passage. If Blacker was in the West Wing he might return that way.

It was the first time Karen had been outside the White House on foot since her arrival. It felt strange to be out in the real world again. Nobody watching, nobody knowing or caring you were the President's secretary. For a moment there was a heady sense of freedom at actually being able to go anywhere she wanted. Then she remembered the business in hand and sobered up.

The quickest way down to the Monument lay straight across the Ellipse. Karen had been long enough in the city to know that was not a sensible option. The 53-acre oval field south of the White House, site of the zero milestone and the national Christmas tree, was also a magnet for less desirable citizens unaccountably drawn to the executive mansion. Washington was statistically more dangerous than Belfast or Jerusalem. And the blind were especially vulnerable to attack. Which was why Karen carried a spray can of mace ready in the pocket of her coat.

Crossing over 17th Street, she turned left and headed down toward the river, keeping to the broad sidewalk under the bare trees, past the Corcoran Gallery and the Continental Hall of the Daughters of the American

Revolution. On the corner of Constitution Avenue she turned left again and crossed over to the park.

It was much darker here than under the buildings, still and eerily beautiful. Although it remained cold, a mist had crept up off the Potomac, casting a watery haze around the park lanterns. To her right the illuminated Monument loomed like a ghostly incandescent finger of stone against the dark sky. To the north the gardens of the White House seemed frosted with silver under the floodlights. Cars swept by, hissing moisture from beneath their tires. She reached the Monument parking area and turned in.

Within a few yards the traffic sounds faded behind her, blanketed by the mist and trees. There were only two or three vehicles to be seen. None appeared occupied. Small stones crunched loudly under her feet. The city seemed suddenly far away. Karen gripped her mace can in her pocket and swiveled her head slowly, hoping for a sight of Elaine. The mist diffusing the light made it difficult for the Elvis to compensate. Outside a range of four or five yards her vision degenerated to a milky blur. She tried switching over to infrared but the droplets of moisture suspended in the mist only made it worse.

She checked her wrist-watch, holding it up to her ear. One of the small annoyances of being partially sighted was it took two hands to tell the time. '*Ten-oh-three p.m.*' The tinny voice was oddly reassuring in the vacant park. Elaine would be along soon, with luck. Karen shivered and clutched her coat about her. One advantage at least about the cold, it kept the muggers indoors.

She began to walk back in the direction of the Avenue, instinctively avoiding the fringes of the park with its pools of darkness between the lamps. At least there she would be relatively safe and she would be able to spot Elaine driving up. She tried to rehearse what she was going to say. This time she would not be taken by surprise.

451

A blaze of headlights dazzled her suddenly. A vehicle was swinging in off the Avenue. Karen drew back waiting for it to continue past her but with a screech of wheels the driver wrenched the car round in a U-turn and fish-tailed back out the way he had come.

Elaine sat in the front of the Blazer with Jean-Alice. 'Head down for the Lincoln Memorial,' she directed. 'We can stop there. It's a longer walk but safer. If we run into a trap we can escape across the bridge to Arlington.'

Mist drifted like smoke across the park as they drew up. The floodlit Memorial loomed over them, glorious and unearthly in its beauty. Jean-Alice remembered learning it was as tall as a nine-story building. If so the appearance was deceptive. The brooding figure of the seated President gazed out toward Washington's Monument and the illuminated dome of the Capitol down the Mall. At their feet, the reflecting pool was a black mirror, frozen and lifeless.

The cold air stung their throats as Jean-Alice lowered her window. 'There's no sign of anyone around. I vote we stay with the wagon. It'd take us forever to search the park on foot.'

At that moment her mobile shrilled, startling them both.

'Jean?' The voice was Miriam's.

'Yes, I've been trying to call you the last half-hour.'

Miriam didn't waste words. 'We've found the evidence. There's no longer any doubt. Your man is the right one. We need you to bring him in – now!'

'What? I don't understand. Where to?'

'Here to the White House of course. Where else?'

'But I told you, he's on the run from the Judge's men. We don't have the first idea where he is!'

'Then, for Christsakes, you have to find him!' Miriam's voice was sharp-pitched with urgency. 'Listen, the President knows. He's bringing in the FBI to take over here and he's raising Defcon. Do you understand what that means?'

'Defcon? You mean the missiles?' Jean-Alice's teeth were chattering. She was struggling to hold the phone and take in what was being said.

'Events are slipping out of control. You must get your man over here. Immediately.'

'Yes, yes, I mean . . . I'll do my best,' Jean-Alice stuttered. Suppose it was a trap?

Miriam read her thoughts. 'I'm going to call Phelps. I'll make sure he's there to guarantee your man's safety. Now get cracking!'

The line went dead.

The Hummers attracted little attention as they batted through the late evening traffic downtown. Military vehicles were commonplace around the White House. On the Lieutenant's direction they turned off short of East Executive Avenue and drew up on 15th Street alongside the Treasury Building.

One of the less-kept secrets of the White House is the tunnel connecting the Treasury Building with the East Wing. With entry and exits at sub-basement level, the Treasury tunnel functions as a useful back way to sneak visitors into the executive mansion without being seen by the press. Because it was built originally as a bomb shelter during World War II, the tunnel came under the jurisdiction of the Military Office. The Secret Service monitored it with cameras and alarms but the tunnel itself belonged to Rex. The only entrance to the White House to be under his authority.

Rex ran through the tunnel and up the stairs to the ground floor of the Treasury Building. In the entrance hall the guards from the Secret Service uniformed branch regarded him curiously. Rex ignored them. Uniformed branch were mere janitors, despised by everyone. Then through the doors he caught sight of an Army truck pulling up outside in the street. Excellent. Perfect timing.

He pushed through the doors. The lead Hummer bore a unit flash of a black mamba snake against a starry background; underneath the legend WE STRIKE IN THE DARK! A young lieutenant jumped down from the cab. 'Hold it there, Lieutenant,' Rex called.

'Colonel, sir,' the officer snapped a salute. 'Lieutenant Winger, Charlie Company, First Battalion, Sixteenth Infantry, reporting as ordered, sir. One platoon with full field kit.'

'At ease, Lieutenant,' Rex responded. 'Your men equipped with flashes?'

'Flashes, sir? Flashlights?'

'Yes, dammit.'

'Sir, we're trained for night operations. Our motto is *We Strike in the Dark*, sir.'

Rex repressed a smile. He had almost forgotten what it was to be young and keen. 'Okay, Lieutenant, mount back up. I'll explain the mission as we go.'

Doug Blacker cursed the mist. It was unusual for the time of year but then Washington weather was notoriously unpredictable. Luckily the traffic was light. He headed down 15th Street towards Constitution Avenue, intending to make a sweep around the White House precincts in the hope of spotting Karen.

The sensible course would be to call in and put out an all-points alert. If he did so the whole world would know about it. If, as he guessed, Karen was on her way to meet the President. Scare him off at this critical juncture and the consequences could spell disaster.

If he hadn't checked his rear mirror as he passed the First Division Monument on the corner of the Ellipse he would have missed her. As it was he caught only a glimpse. A woman on the edge of his field of vision, disappearing in the direction of the parking area. Maybe

Karen, maybe not. Whoever it was she was taking a risk. There had been a woman tourist murdered thereabouts this time a year ago.

He jammed on the brakes at the intersection, twisting round: this time he got a better look even though she was further away. The figure had blonde hair under a helmet head-dress of some kind. Damn, he swore to himself. He had driven right past. To get to her he'd have to cut round inside the Ellipse. Grimly he put the wheel over.

Karen was feeling increasingly nervous waiting alone in the car park. She decided to push on to the Monument. Turning her back on the road, she set out across the turf toward where the floodlit obelisk rose from the encircling mist like a spire of solid light against the surrounding night. She could feel the frosted grass crunching beneath her feet. As she drew nearer the luminance made it paradoxically harder for her to see. Droplets of moisture suspended in the mist scattered and refracted the light from the arc lamps, creating a diffused haze ahead of her. She adjusted the Elvis controls at her belt, switching out of color mode into monochrome. The black and white images heightened contrast, which improved matters slightly.

She paused a moment to get her bearings. Ahead the ground rose slightly. The mist seemed to clear for a spell and there was the Monument visible in its entirety, austere and beautiful, the ring of surrounding flagpoles like guarding spears from a forgotten army. No sign of anyone waiting that she could tell. The entrance was around the far side. She moved hesitantly on across the short-mown grass.

The Lieutenant was familiar with the park area. When he understood what Rex wanted done, he offered suggestions.

'If we drop off on 15th Street, sir, across from the

Mall, we can form a line and sweep in from the north-east. Then we can drive the target down toward the tidal basin, sir. We'd have her trapped then.'

And anyone with the bitch, Rex thought savagely. The President was going to be delighted with this.

Miriam Sheen ran through the deserted West Wing corridor and out into West Executive. Her car was waiting, engine running. The driver saw her exit and reversed to meet her. Miriam sprang in the back, calling instructions. The car swept across Pennsylvania Avenue, headed north-west for Rock Creek.

Rock Creek was just under two miles. Traffic was light, fortunately. On Miriam's orders her driver threw the car about like a joyrider. He came round Dupont Circle in a controlled slide, the rear tires burning rubber as the back broke away. He caught it neatly and six minutes after leaving, he turned into P Street against the traffic flow, rammed on the handbrake, put the wheel over and the car slid stern first into the driveway of Phelps' large house as if it belonged there.

Phelps was watching TV. CNN was speculating on possible successors to the Chief Justice. He gaped as Miriam was shown into the room.

'Get your coat, Justice,' she told him. 'We're going to the White House.'

'At this time of night? Surely you are not serious, Counselor? Our arrangement is for tomorrow.' And from his bed on the couch Bobo growled in support of his master.

Miriam rounded on the dog with a gesture of impatience that sent the pooch scuttling under the furniture in terror.

'Arrangements have changed, Justice. There's no time to waste. In the past hour the Secret Service has obtained proof Spellman's client is who he claims to be, the genuine Jack Meade and rightful president. The person in

456

the Oval Office is an impostor. Worse, he is also very probably a murderer. We suspect he has learned we are onto him and is preparing to move against us. We have to act fast. Spellman is bringing Jack to the White House to confront the First Lady.'

Phelps' bony hands twisted in fear. 'These are matters for the Executive. My presence would be inappropriate at this juncture,' he stammered. 'Later on when affairs are resolved . . .'

Miriam cut him short. 'You're coming back with me right now, Justice,' she told him brutally. 'We need you to administer the oath of office. Jack wasn't sworn in at the Inauguration, don't you see? The impostor took his place on the stand. Jack's orders have no validity unless he's sworn in and only you can do that, Justice.'

Up by the Ellipse, Blacker swung the car off the Avenue into the Monument parking. He got out and looked around. No sign of Karen Lipscombe. No sign of anyone. Ahead and to his left rose the Monument, lonely yet enduring, quintessential symbol of the nation. He saw it every day and had never thought about it till tonight. He transferred his gun to the pocket of his topcoat and pulled on his gloves. The best gun was no use with a numb trigger finger. Then he set off across the grass.

When he had gone about halfway, he halted and dropped to his knees. Bending low was a trick he had learned back in training. It set shapes against the lighter background of the sky and helped distinguish them. He scanned round 180 degrees. Still nothing. This damn mist hid everything. He was about to straighten up again when he noticed a mark on the grass in front of him. He stared at it closely and saw there were others. Stripping off his right glove, he felt the ground carefully. Footmarks, impressed into the frosted grass. Heel and toe, small feet. A woman's feet.

Still keeping low, he broke into a run.

It was almost three-quarters of a mile along the path by the pool to the Monument. Jean-Alice kept to a cautious speed. Once they saw a police patrol away in the distance by the wall, otherwise they encountered nobody. They crossed 17th Street and motored onto the grass. Still they had the park to themselves. Too late for the tourists, too cold for anyone else. The Monument was drawing nearer. Still there was no sign of the President.

Jean-Alice turned the wheel over, heading up north toward the cover of the trees. 'Better to park up out of sight and do the rest on foot. We don't want to draw the cops down on us.'

They stopped under some bushes and bailed out of the car. Together they started walking toward the Monument. On foot it appeared much further off. As they approached it seemed to grow in size, looming above them, enormous, totemic. Feeling insignificant and exposed under the lights, they passed between the flags and approached the shaft.

'If we climb the steps we can stand in the doorway,' Elaine suggested. 'The shadows will swallow us and we'll be able to see anyone coming.'

'Good idea,' Jean-Alice agreed.

It was colder up on the steps but the view was better. 'Where on earth can he have gotten to?' she said.

Elaine's teeth chattered. She peered around nervously. 'I think we should go back down,' she said.

'Wait,' Jean-Alice said suddenly, 'there's someone coming.'

Into the circle of flags from the north stepped a figure. As he came into the lights they saw it was the President.

Karen saw them at the same time. The Elvis picked out three dark shapes. Two against the pale marble of the Monument, a third on the grass. She halted, frightened, screwing up her eyes, straining to make out who the lone figure was. But the backwash of radiance from the

458

floodlamps swamped the definition circuits. The other two shadows appeared to be moving about on the steps. They were descending to the ground, coming to meet her. So was the third. She took out the mace can and held it across her chest. Her pulse was racing and her eyes beginning to throb as they did when she was frightened.

The shadows were moving toward her across the lighted circle. She could make them out more clearly now: two women, it looked, and a man. 'Elaine?' she called out uncertainly, 'Elaine, is that you?' She took a step toward them.

Just then there was a shout from behind. Her own name. 'Karen!' someone was calling.

A few yards from the steps, Jean-Alice, Elaine and the President froze motionless, staring at one another. Karen was clearly recognizable on the edge of the ring of floodlights whose reflected beams gleamed on her spill of bright hair. But behind her now the figure of a man was chasing after her from the shadows. Chasing and shouting, brandishing what looked like – was – a gun.

'Shit!' Jean-Alice was the first to recover. She grabbed Elaine's hand and began dragging her back in the direction they had come. 'Mr President! This way, sir!' she shouted to the President. Karen did not know which way to run. She stood transfixed like a rabbit caught in the open by a flash beam, her helmet headpiece twisting one way then another.

Then from behind the running figure and down from the direction of the river, more men came into view, moving in open line formation at a disciplined trot. They seemed to be carrying weapons. Jean-Alice's heart lurched into triple time. Those were rifles! They were soldiers. Someone had called in the Army.

The President was hesitating. 'Sir, over here!' she shouted to him again. 'It's a trap!'

The figure nearest Karen was now closing in on her fast. Behind them, Rex saw one of the soldiers level his

459

weapon. Oh God, he thought, no. There was a flash and a long cracking echo reverberated off the high walls of the Monument. The man nearest Karen dropped to the ground. For a dreadful moment Jean-Alice thought he had been killed. Then she saw the man scramble to a crouch, hurl himself across the intervening few yards to where Karen stood paralysed with shock and tumble her to the ground.

The President took a step in their direction. There was another shot. Whether fired by the man on the ground or by the soldiers over by the Mall, Jean-Alice couldn't tell. She heard the clatter of magazines being loaded and rifle bolts cocking. God, this was about to turn into a free-fire zone. Letting go of Elaine, she caught a hold of the President. 'Leave it!' she shouted, shaking him. 'There's an army out there, you can't fight them all!'

The President resisted a moment, then seemed to think better of it. He set off after Elaine at a jolting run. Jean-Alice caught them up at the edge of the lights and slipped a hand under Elaine's arm. The President took the other side. They could hear shouts behind them and whistles being blown. The whole park was alive with soldiers, Jean-Alice thought angrily as she struggled to keep the gasping Elaine on her feet. Dark shapes showed up ahead. They were nearing the bushes. Somewhere here they had left the car. She braced herself for a final effort.

Rex had dropped to his belly with the rest of the platoon when the shooting started. He could hear the soldiers around him chambering rounds into their weapons. This isn't supposed to happen, he thought. 'Hold your fire!' he yelled hoarsely. Christ knew who was shooting out there. It could be anyone. And a target in the dark was as likely as not to be an innocent tourist. And he, Rex Coffey, had no authorization to be conducting military operations down here.

'Hold your fire!' he shouted again. 'Lieutenant, where in hell are you?'

'Here, Colonel.' A figure appeared in the dark at his side. 'Sir, we have been fired on.'

'I'm aware of that, Lieutenant. Who was it shot at us?'

'Sir, I don't know but we have captured two of them.'

'You have?' Rex's heart took a leap. If they had apprehended the impostor ... He envisaged himself escorting his prisoner back to the White House to be confronted with the President. Son of a bitch, they'd make him a general on the spot for this.

'Show me,' he said grimly.

Covering Karen with his body, Blacker squinted into the night, trying to spot which way the three figures had run. 'Are you okay?' he demanded tersely of the girl.

'I think so, yes. Please, my headset,' she pleaded, putting her hands up protectively. 'Can we get up now?'

Blacker rolled off her. He got cautiously to his feet, gun at the ready and looked around. For the first time he saw the soldiers. Who in hell had whistled them up? And from where?

Two men in battle kit raced up and covered them with their M-16s. 'Drop the weapon! Drop the weapon!' they shouted.

Blacker straightened slowly. He held his hands apart shoulder high and let the gun fall deliberately slowly. He didn't want to give anyone an excuse for shooting. 'US Secret Service,' he shouted. 'My credentials are in my inside pocket.'

One soldier moved forward, the other stayed back covering him. 'Take the ID out. Use one hand only. Do it slowly,' the soldier nearest ordered. Blacker obeyed. He drew his badge out and held it up for them to see. 'Toss it over,' came the order. 'And keep those hands up.' More men were coming up around them. More weapons trained on them. Blacker felt fury blazing inside him. He

461

threw the badge over. 'Now you, lady,' the voice shouted.

'Show him your pass,' Blacker said to Karen.

'Shut up, you,' the voice ordered. 'C'mon, lady. Hurry it up.'

With trembling hands, Karen fumbled inside the neck of her coat. She pulled out the pass and with difficulty worked the chain over the Elvis set. 'Now toss it to me. Okay. Remain where you are.'

Another figure loomed up into the light. 'Who's this? Are these your prisoners?'

'Oh shit, Rex,' Blacker's anger at his humiliation boiled over. 'I might have guessed it was you. Are these goons part of your screw-up? What in hell d'you think you're playing at?'

Rex stared at the two of them. His face twitched pallidly in the floodlights. He seemed as angry and amazed at events as Blacker was. With an effort he pulled himself together. 'We're taking you into custody,' he said stiffly. 'I am acting on the orders of the President.'

'The hell you are,' Blacker told him contemptuously. 'The only person you have authority to arrest is yourself.'

'Why did you shoot at my men?'

'I didn't, you asshole. One of your hoodlums was shooting at me.' *The idiot, he could have killed the real President*, he almost snarled. But he bit back the words. Not now, not yet. And not before these people.

One of the soldiers had picked up Blacker's gun and was sniffing the barrel. 'Sir, this weapon has not been discharged. I saw at least two unidentifieds take off that way—' He jerked a thumb westward. 'Maybe three,' he added.

'Then get after them, you fools!' Rex snarled.

21

On the state floor of the White House, the evening's entertainment was over. The President and his consort were bidding farewell to their guests. As Jordan approached, Jack Meade took the Vice-President by the arm. 'Leyland, will you and Eunice stay behind to take a nightcap with us upstairs?'

Leyland was about to decline when his politician's instinct warned him otherwise. 'I'd be honored, Mr President,' he replied formally.

'Excellent, I'll ask Speaker Webster and his wife to join us.'

Jordan's granite eyes hooded momentarily. Himself, the Speaker and the President. What did the Actor have up his sleeve now?

'Leyland and Eunice, I want to start with an apology.'

The five men and women were gathered by the fire in the Yellow Oval Room on the second floor that in summer opened out onto the Truman portico. Caro Meade had just excused herself, pleading fatigue. The Oval Room was the prettiest in the White House, in Leyland Jordan's opinion. The President's study under Roosevelt and Truman, it had been Eisenhower's trophy room, displaying his many cases of medals and decorations. Mrs Kennedy had Frenchified it; now Caro Meade was planning to leave her mark here. Time would tell, Jordan thought sourly.

'I want to start by saying sorry,' the President repeated, standing in front of the mantelpiece. Behind him hung Rembrandt Peale's portrait of George Washington. The colors – the United States flag and the President's flag – flanked the doorway opposite leading to the President's bedroom. Jack Meade's expression was one of grave and genuine concern. The trouble with actors was they were trained to fake their emotions, Jordan reminded himself.

'I want to apologize for the way the formal announcements were made this evening,' the President continued. 'I have instructed Colonel Coffey and the Chief Usher that in future whenever they announce myself and the First Lady, they are also to call the Vice-President and Mrs Jordan if you are present. It's a gross discourtesy to the Second Citizen to have you slide in after us without any kind of recognition. I feel very embarrassed at the way you were both treated tonight and I assure you it will not happen again.'

The others looked dumbfounded. It crossed Jordan's mind for a moment that the remarks represented a complicated sneer on the part of the Actor, so astonished was he. But the President's manner appeared perfectly genuine. Jordan managed somehow to find words of gracious dismissal of any insult.

'Well, I appreciate the generous attitude you take, Leyland, which is what I would expect of a man of your stature. Even so, it was a disgraceful oversight and should never have occurred.'

'Now,' he said, rubbing his hands. 'Ladies, I'm going to take your husbands away from you for a little while. I want to have a talk together up the end of the room while you stay here comfortable by the fire. There are some items of strategy that we have to plan out together.'

Jordan's warning hackles rose as they crossed the carpet. He had practiced the technique frequently himself. First the soft words, stroking the victim's vanity, then the demands.

'So you see my plan is this. I'm determined the Republicans shall not get in in '08. To see our programs through, to effect any real change, requires a minimum of four terms. And that means it is essential that we build Leyland up so we can have a follow-through, give the Vice-President's office real substance, not just the face-saving jobs that get trotted out at the start of every other administration.'

'I think the only danger of this from Leyland's point of view, and he may put this as a valid criticism, is that if you screw up then you are going to take him down with you,' the Speaker opined ponderously.

'If I screw up I take Leyland and the whole party down with me.'

'Well, I think it's a fair offer and I will say it's high time. I mean, Leyland,' the Speaker turned to him, 'you deserve a turn at bat if anyone does. I don't think anyone would deny you that.'

Leyland Jordan couldn't believe what he was hearing.

'I'm going to bed now,' the President told the Secret Service. He had said goodbye to his guests, personally escorting them to the elevator. The night man pressed the bell button to the ushers' office twice, signaling that the President was turning in, to switch off the lights and hold all except emergency calls.

The Judge called the residence. While FBI technicians checked the line was secure, he spoke personally with the President. 'Sir, the Bureau is standing by. We await your order.'

The President had instructed the stewards to leave the sitting-room window undraped. He looked out, savoring the view of the Memorial and the lights beyond. His brain was crystal clear, deadly. 'I want one thing understood: my wife is not to be disturbed. On no account are your men to enter her suite in the residence. Is that clear?'

'Perfectly clear, Mr President.'

'Then you have my authority to commit.'

In his own room the President moved purposefully. On the night table were a couple of files for his attention sent up by Hunter. He glanced at them. Nothing that wouldn't keep till morning. He spun the combination lock on his personal safe. Inside, in one of the drawers was a 9mm automatic. He slid it into the pocket of his coat and shut the safe again. Just in case. Still fully dressed, he tapped softly at the communicating door to the First Lady's bedroom. There was no response. Noiselessly he tried the handle. The door remained fast. It was locked on the inside.

A spasm of fury shot through him. Had the bitch guessed the truth finally? Events were slipping beyond his control and his enemies closing in from every side. His teeth bared in a silent grimace. His hand went to the gun, then slowly relaxed again as he fought for calm. No, he must keep his head. The game wasn't over yet. President of the Republic and Commander-in-Chief of the mightiest military machine the world had ever known, his powers were still awesome.

He pressed the bell to summon the night guard again. 'Tell the bagman I want to see him.'

With the heightened alert status the Air Force aide guarding the football was spending the night on call outside in the hall. He responded at the run. 'Mr President?'

'Come in, son. Shut the door and sit down.' The President pointed to a chair. He squeezed the young officer's shoulder reassuringly. 'Nothing to worry about. I just want to take a peek inside that satchel of yours.'

'You sent a message to Elaine telling her to meet you? Tonight at the Monument?'

'Yes, the impostor had found out. I didn't know what else to do.'

'You damned little idiot,' Blacker told her savagely. 'You might have gotten yourself killed.' He was furious. With her, himself, with the President and with Elaine. With the whole damn world come to that.

Blacker had recovered their IDs together with his gun. Then he and Karen made their way back to the car. Blacker sat her inside. 'Let's get some things clear,' he said. 'That was Elaine Manken at the Monument?'

'Yes.'

'And the other two with her?'

'One I didn't recognize. I hadn't met her before. The other was Jack Meade.'

'The rightful president?'

'Yes.'

'You are absolutely positive on that? No doubts at all?'

She shook her head, 'None. On my life that was the real Jack Meade.'

Blacker looked at her sternly. 'How can you be sure? It's not as though you could see him clearly.'

She did not flinch. 'I met with him face to face two nights ago. Elaine arranged it. We were an hour together. It's not just appearance; the way he talks, moves, the things he says. Once you see the real thing, you can't be fooled again.'

Her words carried the absolute ring of sincerity.

He started the car. 'Come on. We have to find the real Jack Meade before Rex and his Boy Scouts do.'

The underground parking bays of Bureau Headquarters reverberated to the throb of motors. Four SWAT teams had been assembled for tonight's operation. Two from the capital itself, one from Baltimore and another flown in from Philadelphia. Twenty-five agents to a team. One hundred all told. In addition the FBI's fifty-strong crack Hostage Rescue Team had been drafted in from the Metropolitan Field Office at Quantico, Virginia. A hundred and fifty agents all trained in paramilitary combat.

Against them the routine White House Secret Service detail on duty consisted of one hundred uniformed guards, rated low effectiveness, and thirty-five plain-clothes agents of the First Family Protection detail. Where it counted the attacking force would have a three to one superiority. Plus the added advantage of surprise. Privately the Judge was confident the contest would be a pushover. The uniformed guards, formerly the White House police, lacked the qualifications and training of the Secret Service. And even the Treasury agents seldom saw real action whereas the Bureau's agents were out on the streets 'gunning and running', as one of them put it, every day of their lives.

In deadly silence the agents donned urban combat suits and kevlar helmets and fastened the velcro straps on their body armor. The SWAT teams were armed with shot-guns or Heckler & Koch MP5 sub-machine guns. Many also toted 9mm SIG automatic pistols. The MP5 took a 30-round magazine and could be set to fire single shot, three-round bursts or full auto. FBI SWAT troopers routinely set theirs on burst mode. All weapons were loaded and locked, safeties on.

This was a mission like no other. The Judge had personally briefed every individual taking part. First and foremost – no bloodshed. They were going up against fellow Americans. Fellow law-enforcement at that. The Secret Service was not, repeat not, the enemy. There was a high-level error and the President had personally, the Judge stressed that word, had *personally* requested the FBI, his trusted agents, to sort matters out.

They were going in fast and they were going in hard. Bureau tactics called for overwhelming force and fire-power to awe the opposition into surrender. That was how it was going to be. The teams were only to fire if fired upon or in pursuit of their objectives.

Those objectives were clear. The mission had been lucidly explained. They were to take control of the White House and ensure the safety of the President. Every man knew exactly what he was to do. The stakes also were clear. The Presidency itself was at risk. It was down to them.

Blacker took a left turn onto the Avenue and cruised west, he and Karen scanning the gardens for signs of Jack Meade. They turned off onto Bacon Drive past the wall and the Lincoln Memorial. The park was empty and still under the lights. He swore under his breath.

'How did we let ourselves be taken in so easily? We assumed it was impossible for two people to look exactly alike. We checked out everyone else, all the candidates for office, and the appointees. It never occurred to us to question the identity of the President himself. He just stepped straight into Jack Meade's shoes and like idiots we accepted him as genuine.'

Karen gazed at him. Competing emotions, horror at her near escape, anger and humiliation at her own stupidity, tore at her. 'I let myself be fooled too,' she said.

It was so easy, Blacker thought angrily. A new administration, off-balance and unstable. A plan, requiring only ruthlessness and nerve to carry out. A switch that went undetected because no one was looking for it. 'We all betrayed him,' he said. 'Or very nearly so. You at least realized the truth.'

Suddenly his earpiece squawked. 'Blackfoot! Blackfoot!' His code name. Lomax's voice. 'Come in. Come in. Urgent. Blackfoot, respond.'

Half dragging Elaine between them, Jean-Alice and Jack Meade found the Blazer among the bushes. With numbed fingers Jean-Alice fumbled for the keys and they pushed Elaine into the rear, scrambling aboard after her.

'Right, let's roll it!' the President yelled.

Jean-Alice needed no urging. She slammed the stick forward and floored the throttle. The passengers jerked back in their seats as the five-liter engine surged under full power. In the rear mirror Jean-Alice glimpsed a soldier in combat kit run out from the bushes. He was carrying a rifle. He dropped to one knee, aiming straight at them.

Shit, she thought aloud. She wrenched the wheel round for all she was worth, cutting blindly across four lanes of traffic in a frantic blare of horns. Lights blazed, there was a shrill scream from Elaine as something huge filled the nearside windows. A sixteen-wheeler was thundering down on them, vacuum brakes blasting uselessly. The Blazer rocked on two wheels. For an instant Jean-Alice thought she was going to lose it, then they righted and slithered sideways across the road. She fought the kicking wheel, trying to turn into the skid, aware of cars screaming down on them. A gap loomed in front. A side street entrance. She aimed the nose at it and stamped her foot on the pedal again, praying the treads would grip. Miraculously the Blazer powered forward. Behind them the articulated truck had jack-knifed sideways and was careening helplessly down upon the knot of paralysed soldiers. Then mercifully the scene was blotted out as they shot up the side street.

'Son of a gun,' Jack Meade struggled to haul himself upright in his seat. 'Where did you learn to drive?' Jean-Alice's cell-phone was bleeping maniacally. He put it to his ear, 'Yes?'

It was Miriam.

Hunter ran out of his White House office. The passage was a stampede of late working staffers wondering what in hell was happening. He ran to Vorspuy's room. The General was on the phone.

'Miriam just called. Spellman and Elaine have found

Jack. They're bringing him to the Treasury entrance right now. I'm going to meet him,' Hunter gasped out.

The General stared at the phone. He was in shock. 'That was the Pentagon. The President has called in the FBI. The Bureau is taking over. They're onto us.'

'Spellman's bringing the President in,' Hunter repeated urgently. 'Miriam's on her way here with Phelps to administer the oath. Come on. We've got to get Jack upstairs to the residence. Caro can vouch for him there.'

Heedless of their dignity, the two most powerful men in the government, after the President, sprinted down the corridor, charging through the ranks of their amazed staffers. Down the stairs they ran into the basement. The through tunnel echoed cavernously to their pounding feet.

Jean-Alice had lost her bearings in the government section. 'Which way?' she screamed as she gunned the Blazer up the street. There was a yelp from the rear. Elaine had been thrown against a door pillar. Jack Meade was peering out the windshield trying to figure where they were. 'That's the State Department, take a right here.'

'It's running us back to the park!' Jean-Alice yelled as they rocked around.

'Take a left then.'

Jean-Alice obeyed. Instantly they were engulfed in hammering car horns. 'Not this one!' the President gasped. The Blazer bounced jarringly as Jean-Alice swerved to avoid the oncoming traffic, hit the sidewalk and rebounded into the roadway again. 'Right! Right!' Jack shouted at the intersection, praying as they shot the junction without stopping. Mercifully they hit nothing. They saw lights and greenery up ahead and there was the South Lawn with the White House on their left.

'Turn left. Not here, the next one. This is Pershing

Square. Treasury Building is the big place coming up now.'

'Lights behind us,' Elaine called urgently from the rear. 'We're being chased.'

No kidding, Jean-Alice thought viciously, the way we've been driving. 'This is it,' she shouted. She hit the brakes and they slewed to a juddering halt. Still shaking from the mad drive, she leapt down, grabbing for the rear door. 'Quick, we must get the President inside,' she called to Elaine. Just then two men appeared out of the building, plunging down the steps to join them.

'I'm Hunter, Chief of Staff,' one of them gasped from running. 'Mr President, sir,' he held out his hand, 'Jack.'

The President drew himself up. A great weariness seemed to drop from him. His face broke into a smile. 'Well, Hunt,' he grinned, gripping him by the arm, 'what kept you?'

The other man with Hunter was pumping the President's hand. Spellman recognized him as Vorspuy, the National Security Adviser. A second car screeched up from the other direction. Miriam Sheen sprang out. She rushed up to the President and embraced him.

'Miriam,' the President hugged her back.

'Sir, I have Justice Aaron Phelps here.' She indicated the Judge. Phelps had extracted himself from the car and was staring open-mouthed at the scene on the sidewalk. 'He will swear you in.'

'Sir,' General Vorspuy interrupted urgently before Jack could answer, 'we have to get you inside the mansion.'

'He's right, sir, we've no time to lose,' Hunter said, beginning to hustle him up the steps. 'They've called in the FBI.'

'Who has? My double?'

'Yes, he knows you're alive. And that we know the truth about him. He's got Judge Watson on his side and some of the military people.'

'What about the Secret Service?'

'Blacker's with us. But he's gone missing. We think he's been arrested.'

They were hastening up the steps as they spoke, Miriam calling to Phelps to follow. 'We'll take the tunnel,' Hunter was saying to the President. 'We can't risk going through the wings.'

The President nodded. 'I must get to my wife,' he said.

SAC Pierce's pocket bleeper emitted a discreet sound and displayed a five-digit code. Time to move. From the drawers of the filing cabinet his FBI men pulled guns, gas masks and grenades they had smuggled through the metal detectors. Signing to the team to follow, Pierce went out into the lobby. Across the way was the armored door of the Secret Service control room. Pierce rapped on it. An agent's face appeared at the bulletproof window, scowling. Pierce held up his badge.

The agent pressed the release switch for the electronic bolt and opened the door. 'What you want?' The words choked in his throat as Pierce's 10mm automatic jammed up under his chin. With a heave, Pierce pushed him back into the room. The rest of the team stormed inside, guns out. There were six Secret Service in the control room, three men and three women, two at the communications desk, the others watching the monitors for the closed circuit TV cameras that surveyed house and grounds. Before any could react, each had a gun to their head. In seconds they were disarmed, handcuffed, gagged and rolled to the floor.

'Lock the door.' Pierce snapped his fingers. Three of his men took stations at the communications desk. All radio traffic for the White House detail passed through this room. Now it was under Bureau control. One of the men passed Pierce a phone. 'Headquarters.'

The line was patched through directly to the Director's office. Pierce took it. 'Happy Hour,' he said smiling. 'We have control, no problems.'

There was a pause, then the Director's unmistakable hoarse tone came down the line. 'Proceed with Operation Resurrection.'

'Yes, sir.' Pierce handed back the receiver. He checked his watch. 'Three minutes,' he said. The six Secret Service glared at him venomously from the floor.

Four of the team went back out down the passage. To the rear of the annex second floor was what had once been the old command post before the detail was enlarged following the Kennedy assassination. Now it was a squad room for resting agents. At any one time there would be a dozen or more men and women here waiting to go on duty. The door was part open, desultory chat filtering from inside. The two agents drew on their gas masks over their faces. One took out a cylindrical canister, black with yellow markings. He pulled the pin, counted slowly to four, threw it through the half-open door and pulled the door shut.

Inside the room the grenade bounced once and burst with a devastating crack. Instantly a thick white smoke filled the room. CS gas is a powerful irritant that attacks the eyes and throat. In a confined space the effects are immediate and incapacitating. There were thirteen men and women present in the room. None were masked or anticipating attack. Within two seconds all were fighting helplessly for breath, incapable of resistance.

The detonation drew three more agents running from their offices. Two froze under the drawn pistols of the FBI. A third drew his own weapon, then thought better of it. Two agents paused to secure them while a third tossed another gas grenade into the toilet area. The lead agent straightened up. 'Get Lomax,' he said.

In her room next to Blacker's, Mavis heard the cracks of the explosions and the muffled cries of agents going down. She didn't know what was happening but she knew what she had to do. She slammed her door shut and locked it. Then she ran through to Blacker's and did the same. Now the suite was secure. There were thuds at the far door as the FBI slammed their shoulders against it. Let them try, Mavis thought grimly. All doors in the command post were steel reinforced.

In the corner of Blacker's office stood his safe. Mavis was the only other person who knew the combination. She dialed the numbers and opened it. Inside, clipped to the door, was a matt black Ingram machine pistol with a full magazine. Mavis was not a qualified agent but she knew how to work the gun. Blacker had shown her.

The thudding on the doors increased. She took the Ingram out, cocked it and set it on the desk. Then she pressed the red alarm button.

Where the Treasury tunnel met the White House sub-basement in the East Wing there was a gate and a Secret Service control post with alarms. Due to the heightened security commensurate with the raising of Defcon, two additional plainclothes agents had been dispatched to join the regular detail of four uniformed guards. A half-dozen more agents patrolled the basement passage to the rear which served as a walkway between the two White House wings.

At the sounding of the alarms, with conflicting messages coming over the radio net, the guards reacted uncertainly. 'Should we close the gate?' they asked the agent in charge.

The agent in charge hesitated. The tunnel itself was protected by two gates: a simple steel security grille and a second very much more massive bomb-proof door operated electrically. The heavier door was slow to shut and rarely used. But the tunnel was an officially designated evacuation route and secondary shelter. To close it off might impede escape. He tried to ring through to Control but could get no response. As a compromise he deployed his back-up agents across the tunnel mouth, weapons drawn.

Then a uniformed man stationed in the tunnel mouth came running back. 'Bunch of guys heading this way. Looks like trouble!'

'Close the grille,' the agent in charge shouted.

At that moment Hunter came into view, sprinting for his life. 'Hold the gate,' he gasped. If the barrier were closed against them and the Army came up behind they'd have led the President into a trap.

At the sight of him the guards lowered the guns. They recognized the Chief of Staff. 'Sir, what's going on, can you tell us?' the agent in charge asked him. Hunter was panting too much to be able to speak coherently. He waved behind him. 'There,' he gasped. The agent looked over his shoulder. Running up the tunnel were General Vorspuy and Miriam Sheen. With them were two women, neither of whom he recognized, and a man. The agent's eyes popped – the man was the President!

Automatically he turned to check the digital location monitor. His heart skipped two beats and his chest squeezed under a surge of panic. Here was the President unmistakably tearing toward him up the tunnel – and at the identical instant the screen clearly indicated POTUS as being upstairs in the second-floor residence.

Rex didn't bother with the Hummers. He and the Lieutenant double-timed the infantrymen the half-mile across the Ellipse back to the Treasury. The Lieutenant set a cracking pace. Rex thanked his stars he'd kept in shape. There was a slew of cars outside the building entrance. Clinging to the open door of one was an elderly man in carpet slippers. Rex focused on him and did a double-take as he recognized Justice Phelps.

'What the devil . . . ?' he gasped. 'What's going on, Judge?'

The old man quivered with outraged dignity. 'They abandoned me,' he spluttered furiously. 'Me. They dragged me from my house saying I was needed to administer the oath and now they leave me standing in the roadway. They . . .'

'Who, goddammit?' Rex demanded, ignoring his protests. 'Who did this? Who brought you here?'

'That woman, Sheen. Outrageous! Me, a Supreme Court Justice . . .'

'Who else? Who else was with them, sir?' Rex clenched his fists in exasperation.

Phelps tottered back a step in alarm. 'It . . . it was the President,' he stuttered feebly. 'They're bringing in the President.' He stretched a trembling hand toward the building. 'That way. They went through the tunnel.'

The tunnel. Gritting his teeth, Rex leapt up the steps. The Secret Service on the doors gaped helplessly as the troops doubled past them at the run and down into the basement.

'Detail one squad to hold this entrance,' Rex instructed the Lieutenant. 'No one in or out except military or FBI. The rest of you, follow me.'

He set off on the last lap up the tunnel. Pain jabbed at his side. He ignored it. Up ahead he could hear voices shouting.

At the West Gate entrance, Sergeant Soccu of the White House detail of the Metropolitan Police Force stepped out of his guardpost to inspect the credentials of three cars with FBI plates that had drawn up. FBI agents had regular business at the mansion and all the occupants had agent's badges, so he waved to his partner in the fortified blockhouse to lower the hydraulic steel barrier.

The two leading vehicles drove through and off up toward the mansion. The third car pulled up inside the gate. Two agents dismounted and approached the gatehouse. 'Okay we come inside? We need to ask you people a few questions.' Again they showed their badges.

The guards in the bunker shrugged. They couldn't imagine what business the FBI could have with them.

Unless maybe some kind of security check. But after all they were FBI.

Outside on the driveway, Sergeant Soccu could hear sirens approaching up Penn Avenue. Nothing special in that. This was Washington. The driver of the Bureau car left his vehicle and strolled down to join him. Looking out the gate they could make out a convoy of flashing lights approaching. The FBI main strike force had just transited Pennsylvania Avenue in a thirty-strong convoy of vehicles. 'What d'you suppose that is?' Soccu asked.

The agent shook his head. 'Beats me,' he said.

'Looks like they're coming this way,' Soccu said, surprised.

The sirens cut off abruptly as the lead van turned off the avenue. It too bore FBI markings. It stopped at the barrier and the man beside the driver leaned down to show his badge. 'Okay, bud, let us through.'

'Hold it a moment.' From where he stood under the lights Soccu could see the van was filled with heavily armed men. 'I guess I have to check—' He broke off. Something hard was pressing into his side. It was a gun. He swallowed.

'Take it easy,' the agent from the car advised. He turned and waved up at the guardhouse.

Inside the post, one of the two agents holding the guards at gunpoint leaned across them to reach the switch operating the barrier. 'Y'all relax now an' nobody gets hurt,' he advised as the convoy rolled through and on down toward the mansion.

The two advance cars had proceeded to the West Wing. The TV cameras, which would have signaled a warning of the invasion, were all neutralized, taken out with the control room. At the basement entrance, the agents strode up to the Secret Service on duty at the desk. They exchanged professional greetings. 'Say, do we have to check in our guns?' one of the FBI men inquired.

'If you're coming in here you do,' the Secret Service told them. 'Who are you going to see?'

'We're supposed to receive instructions from the President's secretary, Miss Lipscombe.'

'She isn't here. Went out a half-hour ago. Lemme check the lists.'

Outside there was a noise of many car doors slamming. Then all at once without warning alarm bells began to peal an earsplitting alert.

'What in hell? . . . Oh shit!' the guard said as he found himself staring straight into the muzzle of a 10mm. His colleague looked on with frozen horror as the Bureau men ran round behind the desk. He fumbled for the panic button by his knee. A barrel ground in his ear. 'I wouldn't do that, friend,' a harsh voice grated. 'I truly wouldn't.'

The alarm had gone up early but it was too late to call off the assault. The invading teams bailed out on East Executive Avenue and raced for their pre-planned objectives. Speed now was the essence. Task Force South with fifty agents doubled round to the diplomatic Entrance. Task Force West led by the crack Hostage Recovery Team stormed the executive offices. Past the hapless guards at the entry, the heavily armed troopers sprinted up the stairs to the main corridor and fanned out through the offices. All but a handful of staffers had departed hours ago. Those remaining were herded down into the mess and held at gunpoint. Covering one another with their sub-machine guns as they advanced, the HRT worked their way up toward the residence elevators.

Jay Leeder was working late. He seldom left the West Wing before midnight. He heard the alarms and ignored them. The Secret Service were always calling alerts.

The door opened. Two men in civilian clothes entered. They carried guns. Jay's mouth fell open. The guns were pointed at him.

'Mr Leeder?' said one of the men. He held up a badge. 'FBI. Mr Leeder, you are under arrest.'

Jay tried to answer but his mouth had dried up. He felt as if he was going to vomit. His vision pulsed in and out. He struggled for speech. 'What . . . what charge?' he managed to croak.

'Treason.'

Upstairs in the west hall of the second-floor residence, the Presidential Protection Unit slowly raised their hands. In the doorway crouched helmeted storm-troopers of the FBI's Hostage Rescue Team with machine guns. The Agent in Charge felt the sweat running rivers down his back beneath his shirt. The machine guns were matt-black. Four at least he counted centered on his chest. The same with the rest of the unit. A single false movement and they would all be diced meat. Suddenly death seemed terrifyingly near.

The ranks of the troopers parted to admit a man in civilian clothes into the ring.

The Agent in Charge swiveled his head. His heartbeat was running 140, his breath was coming in short gasps. All he could think was this man held the power of life and death over him. 'Secret Service,' the man said, 'we are FBI. You and your men will lay down your arms.'

In the command post, Pierce swore vilely as lights and sirens erupted around him. His men were desperately throwing switches and punching reset buttons, trying to cancel the alarms. The communication desk lit up with frantic guards and agents calling in – 'What's happening? Are we under attack? Where is the alarm?'

'Christsakes,' Pierce yelled, 'stop that damn noise!' Finally someone managed to pull the master switch to cut the relays. The alarms fell silent. The radio was still jammed with agent calls. 'I'll have it sorted in a minute,' the Bureau man on the desk grunted, fiddling with wires and crocodile clips.

Two floors below in the basement of the East Wing, the Secret Service SWAT team grabbed their weapons off the racks at the first whoop of the alarms and struggled into flak jackets. 'Where's the action?' the team leader screamed into his radio. The primary channel was overlaid with static. He switched to Charlie channel, the Secret Service reserved frequency. That too was blocked. He raced for the stairs, only to jerk to a stop at the corner. Blocking the passage entirely was an enormous steel wardrobe safe. The executive mansion's only heavy weapons unit had been rendered helpless.

In the command post, Pierce's deputy had linked up the transmitter outlets to a military short-wave jamming module he had brought in with them. He cut the jammer in to block further information appeals and flashed his boss a high sign. So far the take-over was running to plan.

The second assault group had forced its way in through the South Entrance. The advance team here was equally successful in neutralizing the door guards. Inside the mansion the force seized control of the lower ground floor area, arresting the guards and cutting off the mansion proper from reinforcement via the wings. One section took up position in the Library and Vermeil Room ready to act as a blocking force. A second section advanced to join up with their comrades in the West Wing. The third group, the largest, poured up the marble staircase to the state floor.

'Goddammit, don't you recognize the President when you see him?' Hunter stormed.

The guards were staring about them wildly, desperately looking for a superior officer to take charge. None of this was in the script. Their ears rang with radio static. Communications were down, the lights on their control

481

panel flashing insanely. They knew Hunter, knew the General, and the man with the pair sure looked like the President. But he wasn't dressed like POTUS and the position monitor was indicating all over the place. The mansion was under armed assault by God knew whom. The FBI was coming in. Standing orders laid down . . . Christ, there wasn't anything in the book for this situation. They had their weapons out, but which was the enemy? Who were they supposed to defend?

From down the tunnel came the sound of thudding boots. The Army being rushed up. Shouts and orders. Thank God, Hunter had just seen Lomax pushing his way through behind the agents. He had run downstairs from the East Wing command post and gripped the situation. 'Let 'em through. Let 'em through,' he ordered. The agents, recognizing him and thankful to have someone take the responsibility off their hands, obeyed. Miriam and the President with Elaine and Jean-Alice in tow surged through the mob around the gate.

Lomax took charge. 'Close up,' he ordered, drawing his gun. Shouldering the others aside, the agents surrounded the President, shielding him with their bodies in a protective screen.

Hunter made a grab for Lomax's arm. 'To the residence,' he bawled. 'Get him to the First Lady.'

Lomax gestured to show he understood. 'You, you and you.' He snapped his fingers at the uniformed guards. 'Hold this gate shut. No one comes through.' Without waiting for an answer he turned. 'Go!' he shouted. The phalanx of agents round the President lowered their heads and charged off up the basement into the mansion. Hunter and the others raced after them.

In the mouth of the tunnel a posse of soldiers appeared, racing for the gate, M-16s at the ready, bayonets fixed. The three uniformed Secret Service left on guard did not flinch. Crouching into the double-handed firing position, they pointed their weapons down the tunnel. 'Secret

Service! Halt where you are or we shoot!' they shouted in unison.

The soldiers skidded to a stop, boots slithering. They were dismayed. Their orders had not included firing on government agents. Or any fellow Americans, come to that. They eased up, breathing hard, and ported their rifles. 'Cool now,' said a two-striper. 'We ain't come to fight you guys.'

'Yeah, we're supposed to be protecting this tunnel,' panted another.

The nervous agents continued to point their guns, bracing themselves to cover the thickening ranks of the infantrymen. 'Stay back! Stay back!' they warned. One of them reached round the wall pillar for the gate controls. He pulled down a lever. With a hiss of hydraulics a heavy bomb-proof door began to rumble across the tunnel entrance.

A clamor of angry shouts arose from the Army. An officer, a lieutenant, began trying to reason with the agents. He had orders, he shouted. The agents waved their guns in his face, holding him off. Then Rex appeared behind him, disheveled and muddied, furiously waving his pass. 'Let me through, damn you!' Seizing a rifle from one of the men, he jammed it in the narrowing doorway, attempting to wedge it open. The steel door ground inexorably on, crushing the high-impact plastic butt into pieces. With a reverberating thud it slammed shut. Locks clunked. The basement was abruptly silent. The agents heaved sighs of relief.

'Can they open that thing their side?' asked one.

'Not without the code.'

'Let's hope to hell they don't have it.'

22

Blacker caught the noise of static jamming interspersed with frantic calls for assistance on his personal radio as he and Karen neared the North-East gate. His first thought was that a terrorist alert was underway. Then he saw the Bureau vehicles lined nose to tail on East Executive Avenue and he knew the truth. That megalomaniac Judge Watson had parlayed his hold over the President into a full-scale take-over of the White House.

'What's happening?' he heard Karen say beside him.

'It's the President, he must have found out the Troika were about to move against him. He's beaten them to it and called in the FBI.'

'What are we going to do?'

'You're going to sit here and keep your head down. I've got to stop this thing before someone gets killed.'

She opened her door, 'I'm coming with you. I have to see the President.'

They left the car and walked up to the gate. Two men stood in the driveway. Blacker ripped his useless earphone out and pulled his Secret Service identification pin from his lapel. As they drew level with the men he flashed his badge at them, keeping his thumb over the Treasury insignia so they would take him for a Bureau agent. 'SAC Douglas, SIOC,' he told them, gambling that the FBI's permanently manned Strategic Information Operations Center wouldn't be involved in tonight's venture. 'This lady is the President's executive secretary. I'm escorting her into the mansion.'

'Let's see some ID, please, lady.'

Karen displayed her pass. One of the agents held it

under the light to check. 'Right you are, ma'am,' he handed it back. 'Okay, sir. SAC Pierce is in command up at the East Wing entrance. Best you check with him before proceeding.'

'That was clever,' Karen muttered as they walked on. 'What do we do now?'

'We have to find the First Lady. There's no telling what the impostor may do to her now.'

Pierce was livid. The alarms had gone off again, filling the mansion with sirens' whoops and pealing bells. Every time his agents tried to reconnect the phone circuits, the alert exploded into life. 'It's that damn woman in Blacker's office,' one of the technicians said. 'She keeps punching the button in there.'

'Then take the bitch out,' Pierce snarled. 'Shoot the door in if you have to, but do it.'

It wasn't that easy, as the agents soon found. The door was reinforced with 5mm steel sheet and the cramped annex corridor gave no room to swing an axe. One of the agents drew his gun, 'Stand clear inside,' he shouted. 'We're going to shoot your lock off.'

Inside, Mavis crouched behind the desk and waited. There was a loud report from the passage and a thunderous crash shook the door but the lock held. Mavis pressed her lips tight together. So they wanted to play rough, did they? Well, she could go one better. Taking a firm grip on the Ingram, she aimed for the wall above the door and pulled the trigger.

A deafening chain-saw hammering filled the room as the little machinegun jerked in her hands and a row of holes chewed through the plaster top left of the door-frame into the ceiling. Through her ringing ears Mavis could just catch the sounds of panic in the passage. She grinned savagely. The concrete blockwork had absorbed the impact of the bullets but the attackers had got the message. This was going to be no walk-over.

*

485

If they had taken the elevators Jean-Alice thought they would have been caught. That was where Lomax saved them. The Secret Service man didn't hesitate. At a run he led them along the basement passage and up the stairs to the ground floor by the China Room. Even as they turned the corner they could hear the FBI troopers bursting into the Diplomatic Reception Room ahead of them. Two steps at a time Jean-Alice leapt up the next flight, half-carrying Elaine, till they reached the state floor. There was a brief glimpse into the North Entrance Hall and the Cross Hall behind, empty and magnificent, then they were pounding on upward again. The alarm bells cut out, then re-started. There seemed to be a lot of shouting but to Jean-Alice's relief no sounds of pursuit. They rounded another flight. The stairs seemed never ending.

The occupation was complete. Resistance had ceased. The Secret Service who could be found had been disarmed and herded into the basement passage. FBI agents had replaced the uniformed branch at doors and guard posts. A black limousine swept up from Pennsylvania Avenue: Judge Watson arriving to take possession of his new fiefdom. The press of vehicles outside the East Wing was so intense his driver was forced to continue on to West Executive Drive. Escorted by a phalanx of Hostage Rescue troopers in flak jackets and helmets, the Judge entered the mansion. Pierce was at the entrance to meet him.

'There are still Secret Service holding out in the East Wing. There's been some shooting but no casualties either side.'

'Good. The media will eat us alive if there's bloodshed. What about the impostor and the rest of the traitors?'

'We have Leeder under arrest. We're still searching for the others. It seems they may have been warned and escaped before we came in.'

The Judge grunted. He snapped his fingers. 'Put me through to the residence.'

An aide dialed an extension and handed him the phone. 'Mr President? I am proud to report the mansion is secure in our hands. The Bureau has done its duty.'

'You fool!' was the savage response, screeched down the line. 'Your men bungled the job. They let the impostor get away. He's up here now!'

Before Pierce could answer there was a warning shout. A plainclothes FBI agent came running from the Cross Hall. 'Sir, we've had a call over the radio net. Chief of Staff Hunter and the President's Counsel are up at the residence. They've a bunch of armed Secret Service and the President's double is with them!'

Under the lights, East Executive Avenue was a mass of jammed vehicles and milling Bureau personnel. The Judge's plan called for plainclothes agents to replace the SWAT teams as soon as the mansion was secure. These were being ferried in by bus and car but the result was temporary chaos. Keeping to the shadows, Blacker and Karen skirted around the security annex. When they reached the edge of the Jacqueline Kennedy Garden, Blacker halted.

'Where are we going?' Karen whispered.

'The french doors opening into the gardens from the east colonnade.'

'Won't they be locked?'

'I have a swipe card and code that will open the lock. If we can reach it. Come on.'

Ducking behind the low hedges, they crept toward the mansion. 'Lucky there's so much damn noise going on,' Blacker whispered. 'The grounds are swept by infrared detectors and there are pressure sensors under the paths. I'm hoping the Judge's men won't have figured out the system enough to tell which alarm is which.'

They gained the wall of the colonnade and peered

cautiously through the glass. Karen's heart sank. Clearly visible was an FBI agent on patrol in the corridor. 'Don't worry,' Blacker murmured. 'Just follow me and act confident.'

He stood up and walked briskly up to the doors, swipe card in hand. Karen trailed behind him, wondering what would happen. The FBI agent saw them through the glass. He put his hand inside his jacket for his gun as Blacker calmly unlocked the door and stepped inside.

'Hold it. No entry through here.'

Blacker went into the routine as before. 'This lady is the President's secretary. She has to go up to the residence. I'm escorting her.'

The agent regarded them stonily. 'You wait right there while I have someone come and check you out.'

'My orders are to proceed directly to the residence.'

'Yeah? And my orders are no one comes down this way without SAC Pierce's okay.'

Blacker sighed, 'You want to check my authorization? Here,' he brought out his White House pass.

'All passes are suspended . . .' the agent replied, then he froze. The muzzle of Blacker's automatic was pointing at his stomach. Before he could recover, Blacker was hustling him through the door behind into the staff lavatories. He used the man's handcuffs to fasten him to a downpipe in one of the cubicles and stuffed his mouth with toilet roll. He pinned the agent's FBI badge onto his own coat and rejoined Karen. Together they ran along the corridor to the service elevator.

Up in the East Wing control post, a buzzer sounded urgently and a light glowed on a CCTV monitor indicating a breach of the mansion's security. The FBI agent in charge in Pierce's absence recognized Blacker and called an alarm. But communications were patchy. The Secret Service radio net was down, the Bureau's own system not yet in place; they were being forced to rely on the house phones. By the time the nearest back-up unit reached the scene, Blacker and the girl were nowhere to be seen.

At the top of the stairs the way was barred by tall mahogany doors. Lomax burst through, the others following. Jean-Alice found herself in the middle of a long, high hall, soft-lit by chandeliers and furnished as a lounge with armchairs and occasional tables, oil paintings, shaded lamps. At either end were arched doorways to yet further halls. A frightened maid peeped around a door, then vanished.

The Hostage Rescue unit detailed to guard the residence was depleted. Several of its number had been told to escort the captured Secret Service down to the basement. As a consequence only half a dozen troopers remained on the floor. Two were in the Yellow Oval Room, guarding the door to the President's room; the others were in the West Sitting Hall by the elevators. The ringing of the bells swamped any sounds from the stairs and they were taken by surprise as the east hall doors flew open and Lomax's group swarmed in.

The four troopers in the hall reacted instantly, whipping their assault rifles to their shoulders. 'FBI. Halt or we shoot!'

'Secret Service!' Lomax brandished his badge. His gun was drawn; so were his men's. 'We have the President here. Put up your weapons.'

The troopers did not flinch. They had been briefed to expect this. 'Back off!' they shouted. 'Drop to your knees, all of you. Do it now!' The Secret Service were directing their weapons at their opponents. Jean-Alice felt a stark terror.

Then a door to the hall opened and the First Lady stepped through.

There was no warning and it was a shock to Jean-Alice to see her so suddenly, close to. Caro Meade was even better than her TV image and the photos in the media. So much more delicate and ethereal with the cloud of dark, dark hair and the bruised lips against the translucent pallor of her skin. She wore a robe of plum-colored silk with the collar up, framing her face.

'Who on earth?' she exclaimed softly, coming into the room. A look of annoyance came into her face as she recognized Hunter. 'Hunt, did you bring all these people up here?' And then before the unfortunate Chief of Staff could answer she saw Elaine and her expression froze. 'What is the meaning of this?' she demanded in her famous husky whisper. 'All this noise has been keeping me awake. Does the President know what's going on?'

'I'm here,' Jack Meade answered.

Caro Meade stared, a slightly puzzled frown creasing the skin between her eyes. At the same moment the impostor burst into the hallway from his own bedroom, a pair of troopers and the Air Force bagman at his back. For what seemed an eternal moment the two men gazed at one another. Neither spoke. There was total silence. Jack Meade took a halting pace to Caro's side. He gripped her hand. She turned stiffly to glance at him, looking at him for an instant as if he were a stranger, then swung back to stare at the impostor in the doorway of the bedroom. Her mouth opened but no sounds came and slowly a look of anguish came into her eyes.

Still no one said anything.

The impostor took a sudden step toward Caro Meade. There was a dreadful intensity in his expression as if he was consumed by inner hunger. Only a few paces separated the two men now. Between them Caro stood, the blood slowly draining from her face. Seeing them together now, Jean-Alice was struck by how appallingly alike and yet dissimilar the two were. The likenesses, the resemblances, were too many to list: hair, eye color, the lines of the face, the set of the jaw. The President, as she thought of him, wore a blue suit, stained and grimed from his flight through the tunnel; the man who had come in the other door was in gray. In all other respects they were mirror images. She half expected the President to reach out a finger as if to touch his reflection.

And yet there was a difference. Subtle, somehow internal. A matter of attitude, of projection more than anything. She could see they were not identical but she could not say which was which. The worst of all possible nightmares. And instinctively along with every other person present she knew Caro Meade was thinking the same.

Caro's hand was in Jack Meade's. Gripping it so fiercely the nails were sinking into the knuckles. A trickle of blood welled up around her fingers. Jack seemed oblivious. His whole being was concentrated on the figure of the man opposing him. A look so intense it was almost tangible. But this was a look not of pain but of fury. A confrontation as primitive and physical as must ever have taken place. Jean-Alice knew too that all their talk of commissions and judicial process, of forensic evidence and witnesses, counted for nothing beside this. It was Caro who would decide. She and no one else. It was her word, her choice. Everything had come down to this single moment.

The impostor reached out a hand, his left. 'Caro,' he pleaded. 'Come to me. Don't look at him. Come to me.' His words seemed to fill the room.

Caro took a tottering half-step in the direction of the doorway. 'Caro,' the impostor said softly again. She loosed her hand from Jack's and brought it up in front of her as if reaching for his. The nails, the tips of the fingers, were stained with blood. She seemed to become aware of this for the first time. All at once a look of fear showed in her face. 'What is this?' she whispered. 'Who are you?' She twisted back toward Jack. 'Who are you both?' she shrieked.

*

The service elevator seemed agonizingly slow. Karen and Blacker felt their nerves twisting as it creaked upward. Surely they must be there soon. And what would they find then?

The service elevator, she remembered, opened onto a small landing behind a concealed door in the West Sitting Hall opposite the President's bedroom. From the same landing, stairs ascended to the third floor where her own room and the solarium were located.

With a final wheeze, the car reached the second floor. Karen tensed.

The First Lady stared at the blood spots on her fingers and at the two men. 'No!' she cried. 'No!' Whether it was this that pushed her over the edge or whether she would have come to her own decision no one could ever say. She looked at Jack. She looked at the President. 'No!' she shrieked again helplessly, and tottered backward.

'Caro!' The impostor sprang after her. Jack Meade awoke from his trance. Seizing his wife from behind, he swung her toward him, out of harm's way. There was no one between the two men now. Bitterness and despair flashed into the visage of the impostor. His hand dived beneath his jacket. While the rest of the room stood too shocked to move a muscle, he whipped out the pistol and leveled it at his rival.

It seemed to Caro Meade the room was frozen in time. As if in slow motion she was aware of Lomax's hand bringing up his own gun. Of the nearest trooper leaning forward, beginning to run. Of the other guards starting from their places by the doors, everyone converging on the man at the center whose hand was reaching out, leveling the gun, his finger curling on the trigger. And somehow the bonds that had turned them all to stone fell away from her. As the hammer on the gun descended she launched herself between the two men.

The shot was louder than anything Jean-Alice could

possibly have imagined. In a moment of frozen horror she took in the impostor's furious, violent expression turning to hatred as Caro Meade pitched herself between him and his victim. Saw the jerk of the gun as it was knocked aside and Elaine slam backward under the impact of the bullet. Heard the scream arising from her own throat and the throats of the others.

Lomax hurled the President to the ground. Behind them the troopers and Secret Service were still paralysed by inaction. Even with a gun in his hand and murder on his face, the aura of his resemblance to Jack Meade still protected the impostor like a cloak of invulnerability. Caro Meade's frantic action had sent her stumbling against him. Seizing her savagely by the hair, he ground the gun into her neck. 'Get back!' he shouted. 'Get back, all of you or she dies!'

At his words, the guards seemed to awake from the spell. As one man they jerked toward him, then froze again in horror. The impostor's finger was on the trigger and there was madness in his eyes. Letting go of Caro's hair, he reached out and snatched the black leather case from the unresisting fingers of the Air Force aide. Then, before anyone could stop him, he forced his victim across the hall to the door opposite.

Blacker had his gun out as the car doors hissed back. He sprang through into the lobby, Karen at his back. In the same moment the door to the hall crashed inward, propelling two figures violently through. One was the First Lady in her gown, the other was the President.

Blacker had braced himself to recognize his charge as President no longer. The instant he laid eyes on him now it was as if a film had been removed from his vision. Just as a trick when once you had seen through it seemed hollow fakery, so the impostor stood revealed as a shabby parody of the real Jack Meade. It seemed

493

astonishing to Blacker that he could ever have been taken in.

The fraction of a second that it took for this to race through his mind was too long. With the speed of a snake, the impostor jerked the gun from Caro's white neck and squeezed off a shot. The bullet missed Blacker's right arm and scored through the muscles overlying his ribcage, the impact tossing him backward into the elevator.

Karen screamed. The impostor bared his teeth in a grotesque snarl. Loosing the First Lady for a second, he reached around to slam the security grille across the door behind him, blocking off the hall. He grabbed Caro again and, forcing Karen in front of him, hustled the two women up the stairs to the third floor.

Blacker picked himself up out of the elevator. His head was ringing where he had struck it on the door and his chest felt on fire but he seemed able to use his arm. Secret Service agents on protection duty routinely wear kevlar vests but he had not been expecting to face bullets tonight.

The guards were battering on the other side of the door. The grille seemed to have jammed it. Retrieving his pistol, Blacker lurched up the stairs in pursuit.

The layout of the third floor was similar to the second. A long central corridor with rooms off either side. As he came out of the stairs, the door to the solarium opposite was open. Another shot boomed through the building. 'Jesus, no!' he prayed and charged in.

To his relief there was no body. On the far side of the solarium a glass door flapped drunkenly in the breeze. The impostor had dragged them out onto the roof.

He ran out onto the parapet and looked right and left. The glow of the floodlights reached this high only faintly, leaving deep patches of shadow. No sign of them in either direction. He hesitated a brief second and set off westward. The guy was crazy enough to hurl himself and the women to their deaths.

At the end of the roof the parapet ran left, northward. Still nothing. He was on the point of turning back to try and intercept them the other side when he heard a scream. He looked again, straining to see in the half-light. His heart skipped a beat. Halfway along the parapet on this side, an iron ladder climbed to the flagpole atop the upper roof. Just short of this, by the edge of the balustrade, he glimpsed something fluttering in the wind. A woman's skirt.

He gave a shout but with the breeze whipping across the roof he might as well not have bothered. He ran as he had never run before in his life.

And then he stopped dead.

The impostor was crouched against the wall of the parapet, the two women huddled terrified in front of him. He was covering them with the gun while at the same time he fumbled with an object at his feet. With sick dismay Blacker recognized the bagman's case.

From the impostor's mouth there came a deadly laughter. 'That's far enough, Blacker. Throw the gun over the side or your precious First Lady gets her pretty head blown off.'

Blacker froze. The appalling choice confronting him momentarily numbed his brain. There was a spurt of flame from the impostor's weapon and a hammer blow struck him in the right side of the chest. His own gun spun from his grasp and was swallowed in the swirling darkness. An icy cold sensation spread through his upper body and he slid forward onto the snow covering the roof.

Dazed, he struggled to keep a hold on consciousness. A roaring noise in his ears drowned out the cries from Karen and the First Lady and his upper torso seemed numb. He put his fingers to his chest. They came away sticky with blood. His breathing seemed okay still: the bullet must have missed the lung. With a huge effort he managed to rise to his knees. The impostor had the bag open now and was tapping at some kind of keyboard device inside. He inserted his authentication card and there was a bleep in response. 'Here it comes.' The impostor grinned wolfishly. 'Watch and weep, Blacker.' His tongue between his teeth, he concentrated, tapping in a series of keystrokes. The device bleeped again twice.

Feet thudded on the roof at Blacker's rear. Someone crouched at his side. It was the President, gasping and frantic. He tensed as he saw his wife cringing by the parapet with the gun on her, the impostor stooped over the bag.

The impostor saw him and jeered. 'Too late!' He closed the bag up again. 'Too late. The order has gone through and there's no way of recall. As we speak an Ohio class submarine on patrol in the White Sea will be coming to action stations. The signal instructs her commander to launch three Trident Two missiles with multiple nuclear warheads at a pre-selected group of targets. I chose Moscow, Leningrad and Gorki. Three cities obliterated at a stroke. It's a God-like feeling, I can tell you. I got a real buzz too out of selecting the ship. SSBN–750, the USS *Pocahontas*, skippered by your old Annapolis room-mate, Andy Lizard. I figured you'd appreciate that, Jack.'

The President's face was a mask of horror. 'For God's sake!' he cried hoarsely. 'The Russians still have a missile force of their own. If you destroy those cities they'll shoot back. You'll trigger a nuclear holocaust!'

The impostor's response was a cackle of savage glee more chilling even than the snow gusts sweeping across the roof. 'Did you really imagine I would go quietly? Armageddon will make a fine epitaph.'

'We can talk this out. There's no need to sacrifice innocent lives . . .' the President pleaded.

'Oh, but there is, Jack,' Callaghan shot back spitefully.

'There is. Because I am someone, you see, and this is going to prove it. I had hoped to be president. I would have been too if only you hadn't come back from the dead. How did you manage that, by the way? I suppose the shock of falling into the ocean brought you back to consciousness. I should have finished you off while I had the chance. My one mistake. But now at least I'll be remembered as long as the human race lasts.'

Madman's logic, Blacker thought, fighting down the pain in his chest. Bring down the world in ruins before you admit failure. Slowly unclenching the numbed fingers of his good hand, he gathered himself for a last effort of strength. If he could just grab that bag away for a second there might be a chance of stopping the device inside or of sending out a recall signal somehow . . .

A figure appeared round the other end of the roof. Lomax working his way up from the north side. He too halted at the sight of the cornered man and the two women. Blacker braced himself. A shrill sound from the bag made everyone start. It was repeated, then settled to a steady high-pitched whine.

Callaghan grinned again. 'You know what that was, Jack? That was the confirmation. The system automatically verifies the dispatch and checks back. It's a kind of fail-safe mechanism in case the President gets second thoughts and wants to call it off. Now Captain Lizard knows he has a genuine order. Will he do his duty, d'you reckon, Jack? I think he will.'

With a sweep of his arm he hoisted the bag and swung it over the parapet into the garden below. Before any of the others could react, he wrenched his two hostages to their feet and began forcing them up in the direction of the ladder behind.

Clutching at the balustrade for support, Blacker struggled after them with the President at his side. Wind-borne snow stung their faces, whitening their clothes.

Disoriented and half dazed, with blood streaming

down her face from blows with the gun, Karen Lipscombe struggled and fought as she was dragged along the parapet. By the ladder the impostor stopped. Lomax was coming up behind him, his own weapon at the ready. Seeing he could retreat no further, the impostor suddenly seized Caro Meade around the waist and, with a terrific heave, hoisted her bodily over the side ready to let her drop. Caro screamed and locked her arms frantically around the balustrade. The impostor swore and clubbed at her hands to loosen her hold. In a desperate attempt to stop him Karen launched herself at him, scratching at his eyes with her fingers. The impostor twisted round and smashed the barrel of the gun into Karen's face, shattering the glass in the Elvis, blinding her. She felt him grip her by the waist, give a heave and knew that he was levering them both out over the balustrade. He was going to throw himself off, taking her with him. She flailed in panic with her fists, trying to free herself but his arm had slid up around her neck and clamped there like a vice. Her fingers scrabbled at the balustrade but could not catch a grip. She heard his insane chuckle ringing in her ears and felt herself slipping outward into the void . . .

As Blacker tottered up, the two locked figures were swaying together on the top of the balustrade. The First Lady had dragged herself back across the parapet and was lying slumped on the roof. The impostor's demented face was distorted in a savage rictus. He leaned outward, clutching Karen by the neck. Then suddenly the top of her head seemed to come away. With a hideous yell, the impostor toppled backward into space, still holding in his grasp the ruined remains of the Elvis headset.

Karen slithered forward. She was falling. With a frantic lunge Blacker threw himself at her, his good arm just managing to catch hers and drag her back. When he looked down, he could see the broken form of the impostor spreadeagled on the roof of the East Wing.

*

'A phone! Get me a phone!' The President burst back into the residence. In the Yellow Oval Room General Vorspuy was already on the line to the Pentagon, frantically trying to countermand the impostor's instructions. The President snatched the receiver from him. 'Who is this?' he demanded.

'General Taylor. Who are you?'

'This is the President speaking.' He spoke with quiet emphasis, the unmistakable manner of a man who did not have to give orders twice. 'Listen to me carefully. I want you to put the senior naval officer on duty on the line now.'

There was a wait of some thirty seconds. To Hunter and Miriam it seemed endless. Then the President spoke again. 'Admiral Spatz?' He snapped his fingers at Vorspuy, indicating that he listen in on another receiver. 'Admiral, this is the President speaking from the White House. You are aware the football has been used to transmit a missile launch order? Yes, that order was unauthorized. I repeat unauthorized. The launch must be stopped.'

He listened a moment. Vorspuy shook his head to the others. Recall was impossible.

'Admiral, that order was transmitted to the USS *Pocahontas*, SSBN–750, in the White Sea. Her captain, Andy Lizard, is an old friend of mine. I want you to patch me through to him.' The President cupped a hand over the receiver. 'Can we put this thing on a loudspeaker, I need the rest of you to hear in case we need suggestions.'

Someone flipped a button and the clipped tones of the Admiral filled the hushed room: '. . . standing orders instruct the vessel to ignore any countermand instructions'.

The President cut him short. 'I know Andy Lizard. He won't kill a million people if he has the slightest doubt of the legitimacy of his orders. Put me through.'

'Sir, I am not permitted to do that in the circumstances. You would be risking the safety of the vessel.'

'Admiral, I decide what is or is not permitted. Patch me through to Captain Lizard. Now. That's an order.'

There was a choking sound from the phone. The Admiral came on again. 'Sir, I have to ask you to verify your status.'

'How do you mean?'

'Please read over the code from your National Command Authority authentication card, sir.'

Jean-Alice felt a chill of fear fall on the room like a shroud. Miriam's face was taut with strain. The President's voice hardened. 'The card and the football have been forcibly seized and used to transmit an illegal launch order. Quit wasting time, Admiral, and have that signal rescinded before you blow up the goddam world.'

'Sir, with respect, we are unable to verify your identity at this time without the authorization code.'

'Dammit, Admiral,' the President snapped. 'I have General Vorspuy here in the room with me in addition to Captain Miller, my Air Force aide. Goddammit, we're not at war. What kind of maniacs are you up there at the Pentagon?'

Another phone shrilled in the room. Vorspuy answered it. His face went white. He turned to the President.

'Sir, launch authority has been confirmed by NORAD. The Joint Chiefs are asking for clearance for a total strike before the Russians can retaliate.'

Jean-Alice and the other civilians felt their stomachs tighten. Events were spiraling out of control.

The President took a deep breath. When he spoke into the phone again his voice was low and dangerous. 'Admiral, you had better be able to recall that order because if those missiles launch and a single death results in any of those cities, I will personally see to it that you are charged with murder. And that goes for everyone else up and down the chain of command.'

'Sir, I am only doing my duty!' the officer protested, dismayed.

'Superior orders are no defense to an illegal act, Admiral,' the President responded grimly. 'We hanged men at Nuremberg on that very count.'

'Sir, I honestly think—'

'Don't think. Act. Patch me through to that boat and do it now!'

This time the delay was longer. The wait felt interminable. Jean-Alice watched the minute hand creep around the clock. How long did it take to arm and prepare a missile for launch? Two minutes? Twenty? She had no idea. All any of them could do was pray.

The President was questioning Vorspuy. 'The sub has to come to periscope depth to receive, isn't that right?'

'Yes, the signal from the football first triggers an ELF transmission to the vessel's underwater antennae, which cues the submarine to break surface with her communications mast ready for a satellite transmission.'

The Admiral came back on. 'Sir, we are transmitting on *Pocahontas*' frequency. There is no response.'

'Can they hear me if I speak?'

'They should be able to, unless they have switched off their equipment.'

'Andy wouldn't do that,' the President muttered. 'He would want to be sure.'

A low throbbing sound came from the loudspeaker, interspersed with bursts of static. 'You're clear to go ahead, Mr President. Please remember this is not a secure line.'

'To hell with that,' grunted Hunter.

The President motioned him to be silent. He cleared his throat. 'Andy? Andy, are you out there? This is the President, Jack Meade speaking. Answer me, please.'

The hiss of empty static seemed to grow louder. 'He won't answer,' said the General. 'He's been trained for this.'

'And I know Andy Lizard,' said the President. 'He's no tunnel-vision missileteer. Andy has humanity. Right now he'll be praying for someone to stop him having to press those latches.'

'Mr President, we are getting no response.'

'Is the channel open? Does he hear us?'

'We think so, sir, yes.'

The President tried again. 'Andy, this is me, Jack. If you don't trust my voice, test me any way you like. Ask me any question. The missiles you are preparing are targeted on major Russian population centers. Millions of innocent people are about to die. Millions more fellow Americans if the Russians retaliate as they certainly will. All those people, don't they have a right to demand you check before committing the world to war? You owe them that much surely.'

There was another long pause. Then more static. Then the Admiral's excited voice. 'We're getting a response!'

'We can't hear anything.' The President's expression was agonized.

'No, sir, he's using burst code. He hears you but he's taking no chances. He's encrypting his reply. I'm just getting the plain text now. He asks . . . he asks "What were your first words?" Does that make any sense to you, Mr President?'

The President shut his eyes tight and pinched the bridge of his nose in concentration. The rest of the room held their breath. Abruptly he opened his eyes again and gave a short sigh. 'Oh shit!' he said loudly.

'How's that again, sir?'

'I said "*Oh shit!*" Andy, you left your gunny bag in the doorway of our room at Annapolis and I fell over it. "*Oh shit*" – those were my very first words to you.'

The hissing on the line worsened. Through it a man's voice was barely audible. 'Jesus, Jack, is that you? Tell me this thing isn't for real?'

The President wiped his brow. 'Thank God for that

502

gunny bag, Andy,' he answered. 'Now come on home and bring your rockets with you.'

'I do solemnly swear that I will faithfully execute the office of President of the United States and will to the best of my ability preserve, protect and defend the Constitution of the United States.'

With the ending of hostilities in the mansion, it was Sewall, the Chief Usher, who had stepped in to take charge. Sewall, who located Phelps still wandering in the tunnel and brought him upstairs, bewildered and complaining, to the residence. Sewall, who set his staff to cleanse the Oval Room of its bloody evidence and selected the Monroe Room for the brief but vital ceremony. Finally Sewall it was who ordered Gina, the First Lady's maid, to find fresh clothes for her mistress.

Caro Meade had insisted on being present for the swearing-in. Pale and bruised from near-death on the roof, she held the bible for her husband, kissing and holding him tightly when the oath was said.

The President had already made his decisions. No word, he decreed, of what had taken place was to be breathed outside of those who now knew. For, said the President, if it were to become known in the world outside then both the office of the President and the authority of the United States would be forever damaged. 'At whatever risk to ourselves, for the sake of the country we honor and love, all traces of tonight must be concealed and removed. And I bind every one of you to silence with me in perpetuity. This is a secret we shall carry to our graves.'

It is hard to keep a secret in a building occupied by close on 2,000 people. Especially when over a hundred of them are guards. Harder still when you consider the cameras in every public room, in the corridors, stairwells and elevators, monitoring every door and window, even the gardens and grounds. To say nothing of the thousands of Secret Service and FBI agents and Army personnel involved or the White House press corps, besides passersby on Pennsylvania Avenue and E Street.

Hard but not impossible. So they did it. There was simply too much at stake to fail. They turned off the cameras and disabled the tapes, the alarms. Every exit had been sealed when the FBI assault triggered the alert. That was standard procedure, nobody in or out. The ground floors were in near panic but the shooting had been confined to the family quarters and they could be isolated.

It was an exercise, the public were informed, to test the capacity to reinforce White House defenses in the event of a major terrorist attack. Weaknesses had been uncovered; that was anticipated. That had been the purpose of the exercise. They would now be addressed. Protection of the First Family remained, as laid down by Congress, the responsibility of the US Secret Service. There had been casualties, that much was admitted: a man described only as a federal employee had fallen off the roof and a former secretary to the President fatally injured by the accidental discharge of a weapon. Investigations had been opened into both circumstances.

In private the President let it be known that there would be no recriminations. It had been, he said, an impossible situation. One which no one could have foreseen and which would never recur. We must put it behind us and concentrate on the future, was his message. He for one would seek no vendetta. In the final analysis all had behaved creditably. The only real tragedy was Elaine's death. For that he took personal blame.

Karen Lipscombe offered her resignation. The President refused to accept it. 'But I betrayed you,' she cried, racked with guilt.

'You saved my wife's life on that roof,' he told her.

'Caro and I owe you a debt we can never repay. Don't make it harder for us by deserting now.'

Jean-Alice and Miriam Sheen together negotiated a satisfactory settlement for Troy and Cal. The President had insisted the two be compensated for their lost scoop. Following their discussions, Miriam offered Jean-Alice a job on the White House staff and Jean-Alice surprised herself by accepting.

If the fallout touched anyone it was Judge Watson. His handling of the emergency had almost precipitated disaster. He had over-reached himself in his bid for power. His resignation 'for personal health reasons' was welcomed on all sides as a new start for the Bureau.

Two days later Lomax accompanied Callaghan's sister to a military hospital outside the capital. She had flown in at government expense from Albuquerque. Together in the morgue they viewed the corpse taken from the grounds of the White House and identified only by a number. She shook her head. No, she declared, the dead man, though battered by his fall, was definitely not her brother Prescott.

Lomax rolled the drawer shut and escorted her back up the stairs. Later the same day he saw Blacker in hospital. Blacker's luck had held that fateful night. The Secret Service badge inside the breast pocket of his jacket had deflected the impostor's second bullet. Surgeons recovered the remains of the spent slug from the wall of his chest. He heard Lomax out. It was as they both suspected.

'I don't think we're ever going to know,' Lomax said. 'Either about Callaghan or the impostor.'

'Maybe it's better that way,' Blacker told him. 'We'll keep looking till word comes to stop. It won't be long; the President wants a line drawn under the whole business.'

Sure enough, later in the week Lomax was the only

mourner at a private cremation performed at an unrecorded facility. The deceased's name was not given and afterward Lomax waited on till the remains had been completely consumed by the flames. On the way back to Washington, he halted the car on a bridge and emptied the contents of the urn into the fast-flowing water below. With the ashes went the last traces of the man who on the steps of the Capitol had taken oath as President of the United States.

Blacker was on duty again the following day. Karen Lipscombe begged time off to fetch him from the hospital.

'I didn't know this was part of your duties,' Blacker growled as she helped him with his sling.

'It is now,' she grinned.

Brad Sewall knew for certain the healing process had begun for the First Couple when Tom, the valet, went to call the President one morning after the attack and, finding his bed empty and unslept in, tiptoed to the room next door and shook the President awake very gently so as not to disturb his sleeping wife.